PORN STAR BROTHERS

PORN STAR BROTHERS

THE NOVEL

L.J. DIVA

★ ROYAL STAR PUBLISHING ★

Chances is an imprint of Royal Star Publishing
www.royalstarpublishing.com.au

Carlos, Pedro, Tomas, and Retribution paperbacks previously released in 2018
This Deluxe Edition paperback novel published in 2018
All Rights Reserved, Copyright ©L.J. Diva 2018

Deluxe Edition Trade Paperback ISBN: 978-1-925683-67-7
Deluxe Edition Dust Jacket Hardcover ISBN: 978-1-922307-31-6
Boxed Set Edition E-book ISBN: 978-1-925683-66-0
Carlos Trade Paperback ISBN: 978-1-925683-40-0
Pedro Trade Paperback ISBN: 978-1-925683-43-1
Tomas Trade Paperback ISBN: 978-1-925683-46-2
Retribution Trade Paperback ISBN: 978-1-925683-49-3
A catalogue record for this book is available from the National Library of
Australia.

Cover design: Royal Star Publishing and Odyssey Books
Cover photos: ASinc/Shutterstock.com
Typesetting in Minion Pro by Royal Star Publishing

 Dedications

In 2014 a vague idea to write a book about a porn star came to me. In 2015 the idea brewed and grew and when my idol, Jackie Collins, passed away, the idea flourished with a vengeance.

Jackie Collins is the only inspiration in my life when it comes to writing. She had the passion, the brains, the ballsy rollicking attitude, and the kind of life that made me want to *be* her.

Without her, these books would not exist, for I would not have had the inspiration to follow in the same 'write whatever you want' league. Without her, I will continue trying to write the kind of books she wrote. Real, ballsy, and bonkbustingly good.

Jackie,

the Porn Star Brothers book series is dedicated to you as so many of my other books are. I thank you for the inspiration you have given me and hope you continue giving me, to go on and write more. I hope that you are well and having a good laugh wherever you are. I miss you and will continue doing so. Sometimes I think I feel you egging me on with my writing. Maybe that's true, and maybe it's just my rampant imagination; the same imagination that has given me the books I have written so far in my life. And sometimes, I really wished I could be you. You will forever be my idol and inspiration and I thank you.

RIP, Miss Jackie C.

And to the three Stefanovic brothers, Carlos, Pedro, and Tomas, without whom I would not have had names for my porn stars.

JUNE 1977

CARLOS

"Ohhh, Carlos, you're such a stud…ugh…ugh…ugh." The blonde Australian girl groaned as she lay underneath the five-foot-ten frame of the man fucking her. She was losing her mind. No man had ever made her orgasm this way before. In fact, no man had ever made her orgasm; period.

Carlos Stephanopoulos made one final thrust into the young girl beneath him and casually rolled off, running his hand through his silken shoulder length golden-brown hair that was as thick as any stud's hair should be. Sweat trickled from his brow as he leant back against the pile of pillows behind him, and he grabbed a bottle of beer from the bedside table and took a swig.

"Oh, Carlos." The blonde snuggled up to him, stroking his manly golden chest. "That was *so* good." She pulled his arm around her but he pulled it back.

After flinging the sheet back from the bed, he grabbed his shorts from the floor and pulled them on. "Glad you think so." His accent was a healthy mix of Greek and Australian, having been born and raised in the land down under.

His father, Spiros, had immigrated to Australia in 1950 where he met Jenny, the young Australian girl he would later propose to and marry. They had Carlos nine months after the wedding with his brothers soon following, and they led a very Australian life in a small town inland from the coast of New South Wales.

When Carlos was fourteen, his father packed them up and moved them all to Greece because *his* father had died, leaving Spiros Stephanopoulos the family business.

At first, Carlos and his brothers hated being wrenched away from the only home they'd known, but while the hankering for Australia stayed with them, they had grown to love Greece, especially the islands of Mykonos and Santorini where they spent their summers, with Carlos getting it on with every bit of skirt he could get his hands on. Oh, yes, their Greek island home was certainly providing a bountiful plethora of young, tanned and incredibly gullible beauties.

Carlos slid on his tank top with the resort's logo on the left breast. He worked at the biggest resort on Mykonos as a summer fill-in and fill in he did. He filled all the girls he could and enjoyed himself immensely. No commitment, no worries. Just summers filled with hot blaring sun and hot horny women.

Of course, *sometimes* he dipped into the pool of older female tourists and, of course, they *insisted* on paying him for his time and energy. The first time that had happened he'd been shocked that a woman was offering him money for services rendered. But after hearing the other workers at the resort say the older ladies liked to pay for extra services, he had dipped his cock more frequently, and now older women were a regular thing and it paid well. The young ones… well, they were just a bit of fluff on the side.

Ah, the Greek islands…so full of beautiful, wealthy women. It was a great place to live!

"Carlos," purred the girl who was young, lithe and full of bounce. "Let's do that again." She knelt on the bed behind him and wrapped her arms around his waist, sliding her hand into his shorts.

He grabbed her hand, removed it, and gave it back to her. "That's enough. I need to get back to work." He stepped into his sandals and headed for the door to the holiday apartment she shared with her friends.

They were on holiday from Australia and Carlos had liked chatting with them to get word from back home, hearing how things had changed since he'd been there. But sometimes, younger girls could be clingy, and this one was being clingy right now.

"Carlos…"

He stopped and turned in the doorway.

She stood naked at the end of the bed. "Don't you want more of this?" Her left forefinger was on her lips while her right hand slid into the bushy thatch between her legs.

The sight of her doing that turned him off. "Nah, I'm done."

Why do so many girls try so hard? he thought as he strode down the cobbled walkways of Mykonos. *They come off so desperately needy, yet the older women always have so much more confidence.* Not necessarily as much stamina, but far more confidence than he'd ever seen in any of the young girls he bedded.

He made it back to the resort just as his lunch break was over and took his position at the spray booth. He always had long lines of beautiful women waiting to be sprayed down with coconut oil before baking to a crisp in the sun. At two dollars a pop, he kept half of what he earned, and it was a thriving business all on its own. Like now, there had been no one waiting at the tent when he'd walked up, but now people, mainly gorgeous women and a few gay men he recognised, were swarming into a line that weaved down the beach waiting for his magic hands to do their work.

"Who's up for a spray?" he called out and received cheers in return. "Well, hello lovely lady, step right over here and turn around slowly." He led his first customer to the left of the tent where everyone stood on a round mat on the sand. He sprayed her down as she turned and accepted her two dollars with a kiss on the hand when they were done.

"Thank you so much, Carlos," the pale redhead from England said and sighed. "Will you be giving massages later?" She eyed off his golden tanned Adonis body, licking her lips, or at least trying to, in a seductive way. All it did was make her look like the child she was.

"I'll be in the massage cabana tonight." He led her out of the tent. "Next."

"Oh, Carlos." A voluptuous Colombian woman known as Connie stepped onto the mat. "Will you save a special massage for me later?"

She stood straight with her shoulders back so her large breasts were front and centre.

And they were quite delightful breasts as Carlos had found out two nights ago when she'd come for a massage and showed him exactly where and how he should massage her. And he'd massaged her all the way to an orgasm for which she'd paid extra.

"Connie, my Luv." His Aussie accent was strong this year as his grandparents had come over for a month. It was winter back in Australia and they'd wanted to see their grandchildren. Desperate for anything from back home, they'd spent so much time with each other that their old Australian speech pattern was in full force. Not that they'd ever completely picked up Greek, but it had influenced the way he and his brothers spoke. His bright blue eyes twinkled. "Do you want me to take you to heaven tonight?" He sprayed her down as she turned.

"Oh, yes, Carlos." Her Colombian accent came thick and fast as black tendrils of hair gently hung down from the riot of curls captured on top of her head. "I want you to *come* and massage me tonight. I pay well." She handed over her money. "For golden stud like you, I pay very well." She wandered off leaving him blushing furiously.

Not that a man should be blushing, but when you're twenty-four and have the world at your feet, having older women hit on you was quite a learning curve. Especially since it was older women who'd taught him most of what he knew.

He'd sprayed down three more women and accepted their money when the dirty old perve, Leon Spenter, stepped onto the mat.

"Hello, Carlos," Leon purred.

Carlos looked at the sixty-something man in his tiny leopard swim briefs, wrinkled and sagging over-tanned skin, and grey thinning hair. "Leon, how are you today?" he asked as he sprayed, keeping his facial expression neutral.

"Oh...delightful." Leon licked his wrinkled burnt lips. "All the more for seeing you, my Greek Adonis."

"Only half Greek," Carlos reminded him, holding out his hand for the money.

Leon pretended to hand it over, but snatched his hand back. "Half Greek or not you're still an Adonis, Carlos." He eyed the hard, muscled, tanned body of Carlos Stephanopoulos; his long, swept-back golden-brown hair, bright blue eyes, kissable lips, and a light sprinkling of chest hair underneath his tank top. "Carlos." He licked his lips again. "You're spraying oil on people and yet here you are wearing clothes. Shouldn't you be shirtless too?"

Carlos sighed. The fags could be the worst, especially when they thought he swung both ways even though he told them he didn't. However, they kept insisting he should and didn't like paying for anything until they got what they wanted out of him. Which they didn't. So they always left disappointed. "Pay up, Leon, or don't come back," he snapped. "You're holding up the line."

Leon saw the Greek temper flare and reluctantly handed over the money. "Just having a little bit of fun, my dear, is all."

"Go have your fun somewhere else," Carlos said, waving the next person into the tent. "I have a business to run." He turned his back on Leon and kept working. *God, what is it with some of these people?* he thought and went into robot mode. He saw, he sprayed, he collected money, but now he didn't care for what he was doing and couldn't wait for the afternoon to be over. Sure his reputation for being a stud had gotten all over the island, and sure he enjoyed most of it, especially the getting paid well part, but the rest of it could be so mundane.

At five o'clock he closed the tent flaps and put up the closed sign, much to the disappointment and murmurs of the line that was still going strong with a few repeat customers. But it was knock off time. He turned off his sprayer and shut up for the night then proceeded to count the day's takings. Two thousand two hundred dollars; not bad for an afternoon's work. He slipped one thousand into a bag for the resort manager, one thousand into a bag for him to take to the bank, and slipped the two hundred into his pocket. He always kept the leftovers, and there were plenty of them, but he never told the boss about them. They were the little extras he kept for himself.

It was a great life, working and living in Greece. He worked in his father's meat shop late fall through winter and into early spring, and lived it up on the beach for the rest of the time. Six months in the shop slicing up raw meat, and six months of sunbathing and hot women wanting hot sex. It was a great life all right, and a great job. Bartending in the morning, spraying in the afternoon, and massaging all night. It was a career he'd had for the last six years since his eighteenth birthday, and it paid so well, much better than his father's shop, that he'd saved up plenty from all the extracurricular activities.

And, of course, what the tax man didn't know wouldn't hurt him. After all, what would he put on his tax form? Sex worker? Prostitute? Lover? Fighter? Resort worker and butcher shop assistant were all he put. The tax man didn't need to know anything else.

Carlos made it home by five-thirty for a shower and a change of clothes. Pedro and Tomas, his brothers, were already there doing the same thing, and all were waiting for their father to get home from the shop.

"Hey, Mama." After kissing his mother on the cheek, he popped a cherry tomato from the salad on the kitchen counter into his mouth. "Grandma." Bending down to kiss her at the table, he asked, "So, what did you guys do today?" before sitting down himself.

Pedro came into the kitchen in his usual white pants and tank, having slept all day after working all night. He was four years younger than Carlos and had the best of both heritages; sharp blue eyes from their mother, and jet-black hair from their father. A lethal combination on a well-muscled young stud and all the girls knew it. So did Pedro.

"Is dinner nearly ready?" Pedro asked high-fiving Carlos and then kissing his mother and grandmother.

"Just waiting for your father," Jenny replied, checking the lamb in the oven.

Pedro grabbed a bottle of beer from the fridge. "Carlos, want one?"

Carlos looked in his brother's direction. "Yeah."

Pedro got out two and handed one over before sitting down next to him on their side of the table. Whenever there were guests, the boys all sat on one side of the table while the guests had the other.

Tomas strolled in from his shower and joined them. The middle son, he looked just like their father; tall, lean, but well-muscled, with jet-black hair, piercing black eyes, and a spread of jet-black hair across his well-toned chest that trailed down to his navel. He was also the quiet one in the family.

"My, how you all look so much like your parents," their grandmother, Sarah, said.

At that moment Spiros Stephanopoulos walked through the door carrying half a frozen lamb on his shoulder. "Is there room in the freezer?" he asked Jenny before walking down the hall into the laundry slash extra kitchen where they had a small walk-in freezer. He'd installed it when he took over the family business and they'd moved into his parents' house. He dumped the lamb on a shelf and walked back into the kitchen. Everyone looked at him in disdain. "What?" He looked down and saw his apron and clothes were meat- and blood-soaked.

"There is no way you're sitting down to dinner like that." Jenny pushed him toward the bedroom. "Go take a shower, dinner's nearly ready."

With a cheeky flick of his wife's behind and a wink to his three manly sons, Spiros went to shower. He was still a fine-looking man at the age of fifty-two, and at fifty-two he still couldn't believe how lucky he was to have met such an amazing woman in Jenny. And still he couldn't believe she'd taken a chance on him; the immigrant Greek boy who'd sailed the seas in 1950 to a little country on the other side of the world known as Australia.

He'd landed in Sydney by himself, being the only one in his family to make the trip to a new promised land, and had met her within minutes as she was one of the helpers at the dock directing strangers to the places they needed to go. And it had been easy to direct him as the distant relatives he was staying with lived right next door to her.

Over the next year, she had taught him English and fallen in love with him, accepted his marriage proposal, and married him after he'd set himself up in a butcher's shop. Meat was all he knew; having grown up in his father's butcher shop, and so he quickly took over this new one, becoming the manager within a year which was good because Jenny gave birth to Carlos and the extra money was helpful.

He was also eternally grateful that she had agreed to move halfway around the world when his father died. It meant he needed to take over the family business and Jenny had urged him to go. Now, here they were ten years after moving back, and she still stuck it out with him, and he made it up to her every year by inviting her family members to stay for the summer. It also helped the boys keep in touch with their Australian roots.

Spiros quickly dried off and dressed, making it to the table just as the lamb came out of the oven. "Smells good." He watched Jenny place the pan in front of him and carved it up. "Let's eat."

They ate in silence for a few minutes before getting into a review of the day.

"You boys have a good day at work?" Jenny asked.

Carlos and Pedro exchanged wicked grins, but Tomas just sat quietly.

"Absolutely," Carlos said. "This resort thing is paying well."

"Better than the shop?" Spiros asked, spearing a piece of lamb with his fork.

All three boys glanced at him. This routine was nothing new. He asked every time their mother did, and they answered the same way every time.

"Yes, Papa, it pays better," Carlos replied.

"Much better," Pedro added. He was becoming a bit of a stud in his own right, and was earning as much money DJing four nights a week on Santorini as he figured Carlos did at the resort.

"Well, I hope you're saving that money for your own home one day," Spiros went on. "And not wasting it on frivolous things like women." He knew his sons had his Greek blood in them, and the stories that made it back to him made his hair curlier than it already was. Especially the stories about Carlos. Although, he was secretly proud of having a stud for a son, the things he heard he could sometimes do without hearing.

"Yes, Papa." Carlos and Pedro knew not to wind him up as he had a temper when the need arose.

"Good. You'll be able to look after your parents when they're old then." Spiros grinned wickedly, the same grin his sons had.

The boys rolled their eyes.

"In your dreams," Pedro said. "I've got my life to live and the rest of it to pay for. I need all the money I can get. Carlos can look after you, he's the oldest."

"Geez, thanks," Carlos drawled and finished off his beer.

They chatted their way through dessert and then the boys left for their night shifts. All three worked hard. While Pedro did only night shifts, it was still a gruelling eight to twelve hours long. Carlos and Tomas worked all day and then worked a night shift until midnight.

Mykonos was great that way. People swam and sunbaked all day while the sun was up, but when the sun went down all they wanted to do was party. Money flowed, beer flowed, drugs flowed, sex flowed, and Carlos was off to the resort to be masseur for the night and make sure the sex and money kept on flowing.

He strolled into the cabana to find Gary, the hot young Australian, finishing off for the day.

"Glad ya made it, mate," he said with a flick of his blond locks. "I'm pooped, gonna have a drink and hit the sack."

"With a woman?" Carlos got a pile of towels ready.

"Or a man." Gary winked and strode off into the night, all six foot five and tanned and ready for anything.

"Oh, Carlos," Connie sang through the curtain.

"I'm not open yet, Connie, you'll have to wait a few minutes." He laid out the new sheet on the bed.

"Well, *I am* open Carlos and ready to be massaged by your long, strong…fingers…"

Carlos frowned and grinned at the same time. As much as he loved getting paid for his job, and loved bedding women each and every night, sometimes it was a bit overbearing.

"You'll just have to wait, Connie." He spread rose petals on the bed, lit candles, and made sure the thick curtains were closed. He couldn't have people catching him in the act of servicing all of these women or he'd be out on his rear.

Checking his watch he let Connie in, marking her off the booking sheet. Every massage had to be booked in so they knew how long for each, and so customers weren't just waiting at the curtain ready to come in. That's why the cabana was in a private area of the resort, only frequented by guests when they were let in. Few staff came and went, so Carlos had not been caught.

Yet.

He closed the curtains after checking to see if anyone was around and found Connie naked on the bed. "Connie," he admonished. "You know we start off slow and build up to the crescendo."

"Oh, I know." She bent her knees and spread her legs. "But I've been waiting for you all day."

He stood between her legs and closed them. "On your stomach first."

She groaned. "Do I have to?" The Colombian woman was full in every sense, from her voluptuous bosoms to her voluptuous thatch, curved hips, strong thighs, and an even stronger vagina.

Clearly, she did her Kegels every day.

"On yer stomach," Carlos said and crossed his arms. "Time's money and you're wasting precious moments."

Connie quickly rolled over, and Carlos mounted the table, sitting on her ass to massage her shoulders.

"Oh…Carlos…" She groaned, gripping the sides of the table.

He slowly ran his fingers up her spine and across her shoulders to loosen the muscles, doing this for several minutes before making his way down her legs until he was standing at the end of the table, massaging her calves, her ankles, her feet, hitting the pressure spots of pleasure.

"Oh, God, Carlos, take me, fuck me."

Carlos knew she was ready, and so was he. Pushing down his shorts, he set his erection free and allowed it solace in the one spot it awaited. Snapping on a condom, he grabbed Connie by the ankles, yanked her down the table until her lower half was barely hanging off the bed, and proceeded to fill her aching soul.

"Oh, Carlos, oh, God yes," she groaned, burying her head in the bed and grasping the sides of it until her knuckles went white.

His hands continued their massage, his penis joined in. Up her spine his fingers went while he matched the movement inside her. Down his fingers came to her backside as he withdrew. Up her spine again, and down her spine again. Over and over.

"Oh, God, Carlos, now, now oh, God now," Connie panted.

His thrusts became fast and furious, grunting into her until he was done and she was screaming his name.

They collapsed on the table, still entwined, but Carlos soon pulled out and cleaned up. Sweat trickled down his face and he pushed his hair back.

"Oh, Carlos…"

He turned to see Connie sitting on the end of the bed.

"Come, my darling." Her arms were outstretched and her bosoms inviting. Carlos was enveloped into her embrace as she pushed his tank top over his head and let it fall to the floor. His shorts followed. She pulled him close and rubbed herself over him. The feel of his hot Adonis body against her no longer youthful one felt refreshing. Her breasts remained hardened against his chest, and his hard-on came back. "Carlos, oh, Carlos," she whispered. "Take me, take me again."

He took her on the edge of the table, with hard grunting thrusts until he was done and she was on her back, remaining inside as she grabbed his hands and placed them on her breasts.

"Squeeze." He squeezed. So did she and he hardened again. "Squeeze."

They played the game until they both came and both stopped squeezing.

"No more." Carlos stumbled back, panting. He was done, and she was only his first customer. Checking his watch, he saw her time was up and quickly dressed, saying, "Time to go, Connie," before brushing his hair back.

"Go, Carlos? Oh, no, I'm not going anywhere. I've booked you out for the whole night. Come to me, Carlos, let's see if you have the stamina to please Constance DeLuca all night. If you can, there is big money in it for you."

Looking at her open arms and open legs he cocked a brow. "Big money?"

"*Very* big money."

He stripped off. "All right then."

*****

Carlos could barely walk the next morning when he turned up for bartending duties.

"Whoa, dude," Antonio said when he spied Carlos. "What happened to you?" He finished making the drink and handed it over to the sexy young thing at the bar.

She winked and waved her fingers at Antonio and then saw Carlos. Her eyes went wide and she stopped sipping her drink which was just as well since she wasn't looking where she was going due to her attention being diverted to the hot bartender that had just arrived. She tripped, her face went into shock, and she fell face first into the sand.

"Oops." Antonio raced around the bar to help her to her feet. "Are you all right, miss?" Antonio picked up the glass once she was standing.

"Oh," she cried in a British accent. "I feel so stupid."

"No, no," Antonio soothed. "Women lose their mind when they see Carlos. I'll get you another drink." He helped her to a bar stool and quickly made another margarita. Taking it back to her, he saw her eyeing Carlos off who was serving another customer. "Here you go… ma'am."

She finally noticed he was there and blushed. "Oh, I'm sorry. I didn't see you…" Accepting the drink her eyes travelled up and down his muscular frame.

"Most women don't," Antonio replied dryly.

"How much?" she asked.

"For what? Carlos?"

She blushed harder. "The drink."

"Oh." Now it was Antonio's turn to blush. "It's on the house. Since you had an accident and all."

"Oh." The redness deepened and her eyes became hooded. "Thank you."

"Welcome."

"I'll just…" She moved and pointed to her friends who all stood wide-eyed and giggling.

"Right." Antonio smiled and waved at her friends whose eyes grew wider and they all blushed.

"Um, thanks."

"No problems."

"Um, bye."

"Bye."

"I'll just…" She backed away from him only to nearly trip again.

"Whoa, careful." Antonio grabbed her before she could fall.

"Oh, um, thanks…" Gazing up at him knowing she was beet red, she felt dizzy. Dizzy over this manly man touching her.

"That's okay. Don't forget sunscreen."

"What?"

"You're red." He waved a finger at her wavy hair. "You don't want to burn in this hot, heady Greek sun." If he played his cards right, he might score with this girl by the end of the day. It's not like Carlos should have all the fun. Right?

"Um, thanks, I'll put it on." She reluctantly turned, and with a wave walked over to her friends who all started teasing her about the hot bartender helping her.

Antonio waved to all of them and got back to work. It was not as if he wasn't good-looking. He was the son of Spanish and Colombian parents, so was full of brooding dark good looks and hot and spicy personality. He'd had no complaints in the bed department either, but when Carlos was around, he got fewer women perving at him and more women asking for Carlos's phone number. He felt like a dud next to the Greek god even though he, Antonio Stephano DeLuca, had been the stud in his high school and college. Growing up half Spanish, half Colombian and being raised in Spain, he'd been celebrated for being his father's son and for being so damned gorgeous. Now, here, he seemed to be a nobody. Even though his father was big time bullfighter Stephano DeLuca, name dropping got him nowhere. Especially on the Greek islands every summer where he came to work while his mother played it up.

Yes, he knew his parents had an open marriage, but that didn't mean he had to like it. After all, they were both in their fifties, but sick of each other and of having sex with the same partner all the time. That's why they had lovers on the side. It was a fact Antonio tried to forget.

He made it back to the bar. "Did you see that little hottie? I think she's into me." He picked up a towel and wiped down the bar, gazing in the direction of the girls who he noticed occasionally looked back.

"Could be, man." Carlos served up two beers and three margaritas. "She certainly noticed you *after* she fell over."

Antonio smirked. "Are you saying she didn't notice me before that?"

Carlos grinned back. "You did see her looking at me, right?"

"Nah, man. She wasn't looking at you at all," Antonio joked. There was an edge to his voice because quite frankly, he was sick of not getting any attention when Carlos was around. It's as if he was suddenly invisible and the only man on the planet was Carlos. "So, what's with the weird walk this morning? Hard night was it?"

Carlos thought back. Connie had worked him hard all night and paid him handsomely for it. Ten thousand dollars for four hours work. All cash under the table. She'd told him he was worth it; he'd grinned and hidden the money in his private stash when he'd gotten home. "Yeah, man, I was hard all night. Got worked real hard." He cracked open a bottle of champagne and poured five glasses.

"By some hot young thing?" Antonio didn't particularly care for Carlos's exploits, but a part of him always wanted to know the gritty details just to see whether he was missing out on any pussy that was in town.

"Nah, man, your mother!" Carlos joked and pulled out more glasses from under the counter.

Antonio blinked. "You screwed my mother?"

Carlos glanced over at him and saw his expression. "Joke, dude!"

Antonio blinked again. "Oh, right. Coz you know, my mother actually *is* in town."

Carlos stopped what he was doing. *"Your mother's in town?"*

"Yeah." Antonio served up a wine. "Constance Philomena Stephanova Constinopolous DeLuca. I'd be surprised if you haven't met her already."

"Connie?" Carlos stopped dead. *"Connie's your mother?"*

*****

"Oh, darling, I have found the perfect stud. He is pleasing all of my needs and does it to me almost every night." Connie DeLuca spoke down the line to her friend Harriet DeVille in L.A.

Harriet was the wife of bigwig porno producer Harry DeVille, and everyone always joked about them being Harry and Harriet. "How big is he?" she asked.

"Big enough to fill me ten times over," Connie replied.

"But how…*big…is he*?"

"Oh, you mean cock size? About ten inches."

Harriet drew a breath. "And what does the rest of him look like?"

"Five-foot-ten, long golden-brown hair, blue eyes, golden-brown tan, muscles from here to there…"

"Would he be good enough for us?"

"Oh, darling, he'd be good enough for everyone."

"Well, maybe I should fly out there and take a look?"

Connie bristled. No one was taking her man while she was in town. "No, no, darling, he is much too busy. You stay and deal with your business, but if he's ever out your way, I'll recommend you."

There was silence.

"Are you trying to keep him all to yourself, Connie?"

"He's hardly all mine," Connie replied. "I don't think I'm the only one he services."

"Is he using protection?"

"Of course."

"At least he has the brains to do that."

"And the head!"

They laughed.

*****

Antonio looked at Carlos in surprise. "Yeah, that's what people call her, why?" He didn't like what his gut was telling him.

Carlos tried not to let his panic show. "Uh, there's a Connie that comes for a spray every afternoon…oil spray…average height, black curls piled on her head, accent, big…" He held his hands in front of his chest. "Ah…" His hands lowered.

Antonio raised a brow. "Yeah, that's my mother." He stepped towards Carlos and poked his chest. "And *you* stay away from her."

Carlos put his hands up in defeat and backed away. "I've not gone near her," he lied, which he had gotten quite good at doing after all the years of being a lothario. "Just oil spray man, nothing else." He watched Antonio back away and turned around. Taking a deep breath, he quietly let it out and got back to work. He'd need to be careful from now on.

*****

That night, as he was massaging the back of a thirty-something starlet, Carlos thought back to Connie and Antonio. There was no way he could ever find out, and he'd already warned Connie that afternoon when she'd come for her spray.

"He knows we know each other," he'd said.

"Who knows?" She'd delighted in his presence.

"Antonio, your son. I work with him," Carlos had said angrily in low tones. "I didn't know you two were related and thank God I never mentioned this to anyone."

"You work with Antonio here at the resort?" Her eyes had mischievously twinkled. "I didn't know he worked at this one. I knew he was somewhere on the islands. Well, what do you know? You work

with him every day, and you work me over every night."

"It's not funny," he'd hissed. "If he finds out it could get ugly."

"He won't." Connie winked and walked away.

He'd fumed about it for the rest of the day and now found himself giving massages once again.

"Is something wrong?"

He blinked and refocussed on the blonde woman before him. "What?"

She was now on her side, posing, one leg bent and moving back and forth to show off the Brazilian wax job she'd had done earlier.

He didn't like them clean, maybe that was the Greek in him, but he preferred his women with bush. Somehow it made them seem like women instead of the pre-pubescent girls they were trying to be.

"Am I distracting you?" The Hollywood star, to whom he couldn't put a name, flicked her long blonde tendrils over her right shoulder and rubbed her nipple.

It turned him off. He wasn't sure why. Maybe her lack of thatch, maybe it was just that the same monotonous women all looked the same. Thin, white, blonde, or sometimes red or brunette, or both, or all three. He preferred exotic sexy types that got his blood racing.

She sat up in front of him and slid to her feet. "Because *you're* distracting *me*." She slid her fingers over his broad chest and muscular arms before sliding them into his shorts.

He stopped her short with his hand and his piercing gaze. "That will be extra."

She gazed up into those big blue eyes that penetrated into her soul. Her gut clenched and danced the tango. Her womanhood had been moist since she first laid eyes on him. "How much?"

"One thousand for a quick fuck, two thousand for the hour. All cash, all under the table and off the books."

She glanced at the delicate gold watch on her left wrist. "Just as well I booked two hours; you have an hour and a half left. That's three thousand dollars." She pushed his top up and slid her tongue down his tanned torso. Going to her knees, her mouth went to his erection as she pulled down his pants. She knew how to please a man, had been taught from an early age by her stepdaddy and had every man begging for more. But this one was different. He didn't want her. She sensed that, and that made it all the more of a rush. Controlling a man that didn't want her. She took him inside all the way, what was known as deep-throating him.

He groaned, how could he not. It wasn't often he got sucked and when he did, if it was good; he enjoyed it immensely.

She licked, sucked and swallowed, getting to her feet when she was finished. "You want me now, don't you?"

He picked her up, threw her on the table, hitched her legs over his shoulders and showed her how much.

*****

"Carlos," the blonde bimbo from Australia called across the bar. "When are we going to get together again?"

He barely recognised her as his lunchtime conquest from several days previous and couldn't even come up with a name. "And why would we get together again? Once was more than enough." He handed a jug of beer to a customer.

The blonde went red. *"What do you mean once was enough?"* she yelled. "You don't get to fuck me at lunchtime, and then go back to work and not see me again." She stood with her hands on her hips, her legs spread, and her face was as red as her teeny tiny almost non-existent bright red bikini.

The crowd went silent. Their eyes flitted back and forth from the furious Barbie doll to the tanned Adonis. It was like a tennis match of mass proportions.

"You don't get to fuck me and leave me, Carlos. You don't get to seduce me into your bed and then leave me like a piece of…of…" She looked around for a word to use.

"Crap?" someone offered.

"Yeah, crap," she said.

Carlos sighed. This wasn't the first time he'd dealt with an airhead like her; he'd dealt with several since summer started and wondered why he kept getting involved with the same type. He had to play it cool and polite, so put down the glass he was wiping. "I'm sorry," he said, leaning on the bar. "I'm sorry if I gave you the wrong impression. I live and work here, *you're* a tourist. I told you it wasn't anything other than a quick fuck and you said okay. And now you're saying *I've* done *you* wrong. Well, I'm sorry you see it that way when I was never anything other than truthful."

"Of course, you told me that." She reddened, well aware of the crowd staring at her. And it was getting to her. "But I thought it would be different. *You* would be different."

"If he told you the truth you didn't have the right to expect anything more," an older woman in a black one-piece said. Her face was hidden by her large sunhat and even larger black sunglasses. "And now you're here attacking him in front of everyone when *you* are the one in the wrong. He told you how it was; you were the one dumb enough to expect more. You don't get it both ways, sweetheart." The woman walked up to the bar. "Vodka martini, two olives, dry."

But Barbie kept fuming. "And *who are you* to tell me I'm wrong and dumb?" She marched over to the woman and ripped her hat off.

Luscious brunette waves tumbled down her back and the woman oh so casually turned to the girl and removed her glasses.

Everyone gasped, and the little blonde bimbo stammered, "Oh, my, oh, I'm so sorry, Ms Villiers."

Vivian Villiers was one of the hottest supermodels in the world, and even at forty she still knocked them dead with her killer body and even deadlier smile. Her hair swayed against her ripe, firm ass, and her breasts were still natural, high, and well-rounded. She hadn't had any children, so her body was kept in shape by two hours a day of Pilates, yoga, and swimming. Plus, she drank more than she ate. Food that is. Whereas she ate men for breakfast, lunch *and* dinner.

"My hat?" Vivian held out her hand. "And *I* am a woman, a *real* woman, who knows an immature, insecure little brat who doesn't get her own way when I see one."

Barbie went deep red and handed over the hat.

"Thank you. *Now,* he told you the truth but you refused to accept it. *Grow up and move on.* I'm sure he's not the only one who's been dipping into that pool." She waved her off. "Run along, little girl."

The blonde finally moved, moved into a run, and then a sprint as she tried to get as far away from the humiliation as possible. The laughter behind her echoed in her ear until she ran all the way back to her small apartment she shared with her friends. She threw herself on the bed and then just as quickly jumped off. That was where they'd fucked, and where he'd left her, never to return. Oh no, Carlos Spiros Stephanopoulos was not going to do this to her. Not to Barbara Weston, the girl he'd so unceremoniously dumped in high school and then ignored. He was *not* going to fuck her and leave her. Oh no, he was going to be taught a lesson. And teach him, she would.

*****

Vivian Villiers wound her hair up into a bun and covered it with her hat. Replacing her sunglasses, she took her seat at the bar and waved off the admirers that had gathered round. "Please, please, I'm here incognito, and you wouldn't even know it was me if that girl hadn't ripped my hat off. Please, let me have my privacy to drink my martini." She turned her back and sat facing the bar, facing the extremely popular Carlos Stephanopoulos whom she'd heard about from her friend, Harriet DeVille. She'd been on Santorini for the last month, but after hearing about the stud at the resort had booked a room and made her way over by ferry. She crossed her long creamy legs and sipped her drink, watching Carlos as Carlos watched her.

He was serving the other guests, but kept glancing at the supermodel at his bar. The gorgeous Viv as she was known, the one he'd had wet dreams about since he was fourteen-years-old, was sitting at *his* bar sipping *his* martini. He was flushed. Flushed with adrenaline at the woman of his dreams sitting there, eyeing him off. He hardened and was excited that she might be one of his conquests.

"Hey, Carlos, time for lunch, my man." Antonio came over and Carlos took off. He didn't know where he was going, just that he needed to get out of there to relieve his hard-on. Having made his way to the massage cabana that was free for a couple of hours at lunchtime, he pulled out his erection to let it run free.

A hand grabbed it from behind.

A female hand.

Carlos turned to see Vivian Villiers behind him.

"Let me," she rasped and stepped out of her black one-piece in one fluid motion.

He grabbed a condom and had her on the table in seconds, entering her before she had time to wrap her legs around him.

"Oh, ugh, God," she groaned at every hard thrust. She locked her fingers into his golden locks and locked her legs together to keep him in.

Hard motions sent *him* forward and *her* over the edge. Coming to a stop he collapsed on top of her, resting his head in his hand, looking down at the dewy complexion made moist by his thrusting, the shy smile made soft by his coming, and the lips so ripe for the kissing. His fingers gently rubbed her face, his hand taking it within his grasp. He kissed her, soft and slow with just a little bit of tongue.

But she wanted so much more and took his tongue fiercely into her mouth. The kiss was as passionate as the sex and barely came to a stop.

"Oh, Carlos," she sighed. "You're as good as they say."

That intrigued him. "As who say?"

"Harriet DeVille."

"Who's she?"

"A friend of Constance DeLuca. Connie told Harriet, Harriet told me."

"Wait." He sat up. "You only wanted me because you've heard about my exploits?" He wasn't sure how he felt about being talked about by a bunch of horny old women.

Viv sat up beside him. "Oh, I've heard." She stroked his penis, making it harden. "You're a very attractive young man, Carlos, and have a lot to offer a woman in that department."

He gazed into her emerald cat-shaped eyes. They were the most striking thing about her. "Yeah, well, you got a freebie." He started to get off the massage table, but her hand on his arm stopped him.

"And that's why I booked you all night for a massage."

He gazed at the beauty before him. Somehow having her pay him made him feel dirty. "Normally I charge two thousand an hour for extracurricular activities, but tonight I'll meet you in your room instead."

"In my room?" She stroked his lips with her tongue, thinking how tasty they were.

"Your room," he said, stroking back. "Because I've dreamt about you since I was fourteen and there's no way I'm going to use my fantasy to fuck you like an animal. Tonight, I'm going to make love to you, all night, and make both of our dreams come true."

*****

"Carlos Spiros Stephanopoulos get back here right now."

Carlos heard his father's yell as he ran into his room. He'd been held back at work and arrived home with only half an hour till his next shift. A shift he couldn't wait to get to. He dumped his bag and ran back to the lounge room. "Papa, I've got half an hour, I need a shower."

"Work can wait. Sit down," his father ordered.

"But Pa—"

"Sit!" Spiros raged.

Carlos knew better than to push it once fire spat from his father's eyes, because all three boys knew not to interrupt their parents when a brother was being chastised. He sat on the sofa. "What? What now?"

Jenny sat beside her husband. "A young girl came to us today Carlos and told us a story. A story about what you did to her."

Uh oh, he thought, *better play it cool.* "What girl?"

"A young girl by the name of Barbara Weston came to me today and told me, in tears mind you, how you had taken advantage of her."

Carlos raised a brow. "Believe me; I *do not* take advantage of anyone."

"What she told us disgusted us, Carlos, so listen," Spiros said. He sat steely-eyed and determined. No son of his was going to take advantage of a young girl. He had raised them better.

Carlos sighed. "Who's Barbara Weston?"

"Carlos," his mother admonished. "Don't you remember the young Australian girl you slept with over a month ago and then discarded like an old shoe? Do you *really* not remember her?"

He shook his head. "Name doesn't ring a bell. Describe her."

"Young, about your age, long blonde hair, big blue eyes, slim, very pretty."

He frowned at the description. "She *sounds* familiar, but only because I saw her *two days* ago, *not* a month ago. And I certainly didn't take advantage of her, or anyone else for that matter." He stood. "Is that it? Some girl makes up a story because she's outsmarted by a supermodel and now she's blabbing that story to my parents? I'm outta here."

"Sit down," Spiros roared. "You do not get away with shirking your responsibilities. Now, I don't know what you're talking about, but you will do the right thing by this young girl and your baby."

Baby!

"Baby? What baby?" Carlos slumped to his seat. "How can she be pregnant in two days? I used protection."

"What do you mean in two days?" Jenny asked. "You were with her over a month ago." She couldn't keep up with her sons anymore.

"Mama, Papa, I only slept with this girl *two days ago.*" Carlos was on his feet again. "I *used* a condom. She *can't* be pregnant by me, ah-uh, no way." He waved his hand. "And if she is, it *ain't* mine. She came to the bar this morning and bitched about me in front of everyone. I told her I had been up front about sleeping with her and didn't want anything else out of it. *She* apparently did, and tried to confront me about it. She only got stopped when Vivian Villiers, *the supermodel,* told her to grow up and get over it. That she was acting like an immature brat. She got embarrassed and ran away. *That's it.* If she's pregnant, *it ain't mine.* Now," he looked at his watch, "I'm gonna be late for my shift and I gotta shower." He left his parents speechless, unsure of who was telling the truth.

"Vivian Villiers," Jenny muttered. "She's here? She's gorgeous."

"And probably embarrassed the poor girl," Spiros replied. "Do you think it may be some revenge thing?"

"What?" Jenny said. "Carlos sleeps with her once and she gets told off by a supermodel and then plans revenge on him? No, I think that would be a bit too much for her to handle."

"Ah, never underestimate a woman scorned," Spiros said, nodding in agreement with himself.

*****

Carlos raced to the cabana and arrived at the same time as Vivian. "Ah," he gasped. "Made it."

"But look at you," she purred. "You're all hot...and sweaty..." She pulled at his tank top.

"And you're all naked under that robe, aren't you," he said, his chest heaving from more than exertion.

"Yes." The wicked grin slid into place.

"Well, we'd better get to it then. I suggest we go to your place." Carlos grabbed her hand. "I know a private entrance. What room are you in?"

"I don't want to go back up." She pulled him to her. "I came down here for some privacy and alone time."

"You may have," Carlos said. "But there's no way I'm making love to you on a massage table, so your bedroom it is." He pulled her to the back entrance of the hotel and they made their way up the private stairs that all of the celebrities used to stay away from the paps, making it to her room without being seen. She locked the door, he yanked off her robe, and she ripped his clothes off.

They stood before the bed facing each other and each admiring the other's body. He grabbed her head, entangling his hand in her hair. She did the same. He bent her head back and kissed her roughly, his other arm holding her tight. After moments of passionate tongue sex, he lifted her and she wrapped her legs around him before they fell onto the bed as one.

After hours of vigorous, seductive and languid lovemaking they lay spent in each other's arms.

Carlos held her tight. He didn't want to let his dream woman go. He relished the tendrils of hair that lay across his naked body and twirled them around his finger. They had been a silken cascade that she flung around her in a frenzy during sex, allowing it to tease him, torment him. Now, he held her against him.

Viv sighed, contented. She hadn't had a man like that in a long time, let alone one nearly half her age. Some would see him still a boy, but he'd just proved he was definitely all man. A young, very virile, man. She ran her fingers down his chest. "You *are* good," she purred. "Probably the best I've ever had."

"Only probably?" he murmured into her hair.

The tropical island breeze floated through the open balcony doors. Three empty bottles of champagne lay strewn across the floor. They had made use of every part of the room. The chairs, desk, bathroom, bed, the floor...

She twirled her fingers around. "Well...I'd say...*definitely.*"

"That's more like it."

Her fingers trailed their way down to his manhood and gently massaged it.

"Ugh...yeah...that's..." He arched his back and sighed.

"I know how to please a man, you know," she said, sitting on top of him.

"Ugh." He grabbed her hips and kept her there, gazing up into her fiery eyes. She came, throwing her head back at the peak, and he sat, making it more explosive. He buried his mouth in her hair, his tongue seeking nipple. His hands moved up to claim them and found them, making them his own.

She sighed and fell beside him. "You really are everything they say you are. You should do it for a living."

"Do what?"

"Have sex."

"I already do."

"But I mean on the big screen." She sat up so they were nose to nose. "Imagine it. Your gorgeous body, that ten inch cock." She stroked it. "All on the big screen. All for everyone to see. The world will want you, just like I do," she said against his lips.

"You mean movies?"

"More than movies."

"What could be more than movies?"

"Pornos, darling. Let the world see what a massive dick you've got."

Carlos laughed and pushed her off him. "Pornos?" Getting out of bed he checked his watch. He was now off the clock. Grabbing his clothes, he said, "Me? In pornos? Movies yeah, but pornos?"

"Have you ever thought about it?" Viv asked, yanking his clothes from his grasp. She knelt on the bed in front of him. "Look at you." He stood before her in the raw. "You're beautiful. The dream guy every girl wants. Sure, you could go to Hollywood and *try* and get into movies. I could help you if you wanted. But for a man with a cock that long and that wide and that…" She groped it, kneaded it, massaged it until he came in her hand and groaned. "Pleasurable," she added. "You need to show it off. Besides, you can earn big bucks on the big screen just for having a big dick." She slid her hand between her legs, feeling the warm juice over her. "Think about it. I can help you."

*****

Consuela Maria Da Vica was preparing for her wedding. She was a young thing, barely twenty-five years old and already considered past her prime, age-wise. But she was still young enough to bear big strong children. She was preparing to marry an older man, as old as her grandfather, purely as breeding stock. Her parents had wanted her out of their home, crying poor when he came along.

He had taken a shine to her and asked for her hand in marriage, paying her parents handsomely. They had packed up her meagre belongings and sent her on her way with her new husband-to-be. She had objected at first. She didn't know him, he needed to court her. But between him and her parents, she was out of her small Peruvian town in no time.

Now, here she was in the beautiful Greek city of Athens, ensconced in her husband-to-be's palatial home. She knew no one, knew nothing, and felt like a prisoner half the time. She wasn't allowed to go anywhere without a bodyguard and servant, a young maid who was the daughter of the cook, and who she was sure was being eyed off by her husband-to-be. And she also had a feeling that he'd given it to the cook over the years.

Consuela spoke broken English, but now had to learn Greek. Not that it mattered, as she was sure she would never be out in public with her husband. She knew she was just for breeding. And here it was, one week before the wedding, three weeks since she'd been brought there, and all that had to be done was get a dress. From a catalogue, she had chosen a simple design which they were having shipped in from the company.

She wandered over to the large balcony doors and stared out at the city. "Oh, what will become of me? Besides a breeder. Will I ever work or play or have fun again?" She'd had so much fun in her small town. Her best friend was married off with children. But she hadn't wanted to be married off herself. She'd wanted to see the world and go to places she'd only ever heard of. Now she was. She was seeing Athens and new and exciting things. Even though it was only because she was being married off.

Her maid came into the room. "Madame." Her broken English was hesitant. "What do you want to do today?" She hovered behind her new mistress. *She's such a young thing*, she thought. *Barely older than me. I wonder if she knows she's marrying my father? I'll kill her…*flew through her mind before she smoothed her apron.

"I do not know," Consuela managed. "I am not allowed out of this house. I cannot do anything."

The maid, whose name was Marta Effidopolous, had already concocted a plan. "I know," she said. Glancing behind her she moved to Consuela's side. "We will go to Mykonos."

"What's Mykonos?" Consuela asked.

Marta's eyes widened at the girl's stupidity. "It is in Greek islands. We can take ferry there. We can go get some sun, have fun. I can dress you in maid's outfit, no one will ever know. We will be gone and back."

Consuela fretted. "It sounds good, but how and when?" The thought of getting out into the air thrilled her, even if it was dangerous.

"Leave it to me," Marta said. "Boss man is leaving Friday for business and not coming back until Monday. We can leave straight after."

The more Consuela thought about it, the more excited she became. "Okay, let's do it." Little did she know what she was in for.

*****

The next few days flew by, with Carlos bedding Vivian more often than not, pleading innocent to his parents, and demanding the Aussie bimbo get a pregnancy test, plus staying away from Connie, his second most voracious customer. When finding out he was servicing Viv, Connie more than offered to join in. He declined. She was annoyed.

*****

The time flew by for Consuela as well. Marta had given her a uniform to wear, and they packed small bags to take with them. Marta let Gustoff, Consuela's bodyguard, in on her plan, making him promise not to say anything to their boss. He agreed. Marta thanked him and told Consuela she could trust him to not say anything, but they needed him to get them to the wharf so they could travel.

Consuela baulked. "Why would you tell him? It must be secret."

"He is my fiancé," Marta lied. "He will help us. Don't worry."

Consuela was so ecstatic about going and so naïve and young, she didn't even know it was a lie.

*****

On Friday morning, after Consuela's husband-to-be had left, Marta,

Gustoff, and Consuela made their way to the car. Consuela was in one of Marta's uniforms and had her hair under the cap. They made it past the guard and out to the ferry with no problem. Four hours later they arrived on Mykonos.

Consuela was astounded. "It is so beautiful," she said.

"Come." Marta pulled her along. "I have booked hotel rooms for us."

They made their way to their hotel, checked in, and found the two bedroom suite to be to their liking. It had views of the beach, was a quick ride to town, and had a private cabana for massages.

*****

Carlos finished up at the bar for the day and made his way to Vivian's room. He'd become addicted to her, no doubt about it, and had stopped seeing other women since being with her. Even Connie. And Barbara had disappeared after being threatened with a lawsuit by his father. If she couldn't prove she was having his grandchild, she could go back to where she'd come from.

Viv opened the door then opened her legs. They barely made it to the bed before joining. When they were done, they drank from the same bottle of champagne and ate oysters and caviar, then made love before he had to leave.

"Are you coming tonight?" she asked as he dressed to leave.

A cocky grin covered his face. "I come every night."

"And then some," she added, sucking on the bottle of champagne to show how far she could deep-throat it.

It turned him on, and it showed as he turned for her to take him into her mouth and do the same to him. "Ugh… Can't… Tonight… Working…ugh…" Giddiness washed over him, and he felt limp.

"Just massages?" she inquired, wiping him off her lips.

"Just…massages…" he replied, shoving it back in his pants.

*****

Marta took Consuela on a trip around Mykonos; the town, the beaches, the windmills.

Consuela revelled in the freedom, sitting on the beach at sundown, letting the sun warm her face. She breathed deeply. The salty air of the islands was exactly what she needed, and she thanked God for Marta, although, she wasn't sure about Gustoff and whether she could trust him. He did, after all, work for her future husband.

Marta found her on the beach. "I have us booked in for massages. I am at seven, you are eight. I will go first."

"Massages?" Consuela panicked. "I have never had massage. What happens? What do I do? What do *they* do?"

Marta laughed. "It is nothing to worry about. You lie on bed and get muscles massaged. You will feel nice and loose when done. It is for eight o'clock in cabana at back of hotel. Be there." She wandered off and made her way to the cabana for her own massage. *Silly little bitch,* she thought, *she has no idea.* Marta found him waiting for her when she got there and was startled. "You are gorgeous," she murmured at the Greek Adonis before her.

"So I've been told," he quipped. "Why don't you lie face down on the bed?" He motioned to the white sheet and rose petal covered table, and she disrobed down to her bikini.

She hardly wore one back in Athens so rarely got to show off her body. It wasn't bad, as she was in good shape and worked regularly on her tan. Her breasts were medium-sized and still sat high. Her bottom was a little too big, but apparently, some men liked big-assed girls. She lay face down on the table, and Carlos got to work. Within minutes he had her groaning. "Oh, God, that is good…good…oh, God."

He pushed his fingers into her back muscles, working them, kneading them up and down her spine. "You're very stiff," he said. "Do you do a lot of bending?"

She thought of all the times she'd bent to service a man. "Yes."

"It shows." Carlos moved onto her shoulders. "Same here."

"Yes, yes, oh, yes," she cried and cried until her hour was done.

"There you go, you can put your robe on. I need to get ready for the next client."

Marta replaced her robe and thanked him. "You are very good."

"So I've been told." He grinned.

She stepped outside and saw Consuela approach, quickly whispering instructions to her.

Consuela nodded and walked into the cabana.

Carlos noticed the exotic creature and immediately hardened. "Well, hello," he murmured. "Take your robe off and lie on the table." He held a towel in front of him after replacing the sheet and rose petals.

She removed her robe and gracefully mounted the table, sitting on the end, swinging her legs. "How do you want me?"

"Oh, hard and fast and slow and long," Carlos muttered, eyeing off the delicate long legs and high, perfect breasts.

Her eyes widened. "What?" She had never heard of such a term, and coming from such a gorgeous man, she did not know what to think.

"Do you…ah…" He licked his lips. "Know what happens in here?" Standing in front of her all wet and slick, he desperately wanted the young thing sitting on the table.

Her eyes stayed wide. "Massages…" she managed. The man was gorgeous and making her heart pound. She'd never seen any man look like this, and definitely not her husband-to-be, or the boys back in her village. But he was different. He was exotic. Not white, not Greek, an exotic mixture of both.

His fingers travelled up her leg to her inner thigh. "I can do more than massage."

Those fingers made her feel things she had never felt before. Her stomach wrenched, her nipples hardened, and she felt wet between her legs. She swallowed and did as she was told.

Carlos's fingers slid into her bikini bottom and pulled them down as she lifted herself. He slid his shorts down, and she saw his erection moving toward her. It was something she had never seen before, a naked man, a penis, nor experienced in any way, shape, or form. Why would she have? She was just a young girl from a small Peruvian village. He lifted her up and onto him.

"Argh," she cried, having never been taken by a man before. Wrapping her arms around him, clinging to him as he gently slid back and forth, she cried out again. The pain from the first time was mixed with the pleasure he gave her.

His tongue invaded her mouth as his manhood invaded her insides. His fingers and hands explored her, as they held her and she exploded into a million pieces she didn't know was called an orgasm.

"Consuela, you dirty little whore," Marta yelled. "What will your husband-to-be say?"

Carlos spun around; still attached to the girl, to see the woman he'd just given a massage to and a big brute of a guy holding a gun on him. "What the…?"

"But, Marta, you told me to," Consuela cried as Gustoff levelled the gun. "Gustoff, what are you doing?"

Carlos dumped her on the bed and turned as the shot rang out. He dived for his clothes and ran like hell hearing the words…

"Is she dead…?"

"…Yes."

*****

Connie heard the ruckus and what sounded like a gunshot. Sticking her head out of her private ground floor room, she saw Carlos speed up to her.

"Quick, I need to hide."

She ushered him into her room and locked the door while he dressed. "Was that a gunshot I heard?"

"Yep," Carlos panted. "Some crazy guy pointed a gun at me while I was um…" He shrugged. There was no time for politeness. "Fucking a client and shot at us. I ran, but I think he got her. I think she's dead. I gotta get outta here."

"Wait just a minute, you should go now. I'll get you to the ferry."

"No, I have to go home." He pushed his hair back as he moved for the door. "I have to get my bags, my money, my passport. I need to go home."

"You need to leave the island," Connie said and came up with a plan. "You go and get your things then find me at the wharf. I'll get you to Athens and the airport. Go, go get your things."

With a nod, he sped off home, barging through the door ten minutes later. He collected his suitcase and bag, changed his clothes, strapped his money belt under his shirt and left a letter for his family, who luckily were out because he could not answer any questions right now. He legged it down to the wharf, careful not to be seen, and hid in the shadows looking for Connie. She turned up with two trunks and a large bag.

"I need the ferry to Athens. I'm going shopping tomorrow," she said.

"Of course." The purser rang up her ticket and helped her carry the trunks over to the waiting area near Carlos. It was in the shadows, and he managed to sneak over to her without being seen.

She spied him and quickly unlocked the trunks. They were empty. "Get in. You can hide until the airport."

Carlos frowned. "I have to hide in your trunk?"

"Do you want people to find you?" she fiercely whispered. "It was all over the hotel by the time I left. The cops have been called and are on their way to your house."

He frowned deeper. They'd find the letter.

"I saw the big brute of a guy and that girl. She was screaming bloody murder that you had tried to rape her and were raping her friend when they came upon you. They said you shot the girl."

"What!" Carlos exploded, but quickly quietened down, slinking back into the shadows. "*I did no such thing.* She was my client. I thought she was there for sex."

"Apparently, she shouldn't have been there at all. She's set to marry some Greek bigwig, but had sneaked out just a week before the wedding while he was out of town."

"Look, I know nothing about that, but some thug tried to shoot me so I need to get out of here." He eyed the trunk. "Even if this is the only way."

They heard footsteps and saw Vivian Villiers approaching.

"Darling, what have you gotten yourself into?" She held her arms open for him.

Carlos embraced her. "I have no idea, Viv, but I need to get the hell out of town."

"Well, isn't it a good thing I decided to come along. I know the perfect way to get you out," she said, eyeing their surroundings for anything suspicious.

"How?"

"Just get in the trunk, darling."

Carlos frowned again, but resigned his fate to an expensive Louis Vuitton trunk. He managed to fold his frame into the trunk and use his bag as a pillow.

"I'll put your case in the other trunk," Connie said and quickly packed it *and* Carlos up as the ferry approached.

Vivian went off to score herself a ticket, and within half an hour they were aboard the ferry to Athens where they arrived within the hour.

The ride was rough for Carlos; he'd never been sea sick but was feeling it now. And the pursers dumping him on the boat hadn't helped. Being dropped a few times made him want to vomit, but Viv and Connie had been able to open the trunk a crack on the way over to give him air until they were on the dock and he was being off-loaded again.

Ugh, this is worse than being shot at. What the hell was that all about? Who was that guy? Why was that woman I'd just massaged standing beside him? And what did it have to do with the girl I was inside of? Jesus, Jesus, Jesus, he silently cursed. *What the hell is going on?*

The trunk was lifted and dropped.

"Careful," Connie cried out. "That is a very expensive Louis Vuitton, and if you damage it, you pay for another one."

There were some more mumblings he couldn't hear and then they were moving. He checked his glow-in-the-dark watch. Ten after ten. He felt every bump and lump as they made their way to the airport, at least he hoped that's where they were going, and checked his watch again when they stopped. Ten-thirty.

The trunk was hefted down and carried up. Where he didn't know. They made a right turn, walked, made a left turn, and he was put down. The voices receded then there was another thud beside him, and more voices receded. He heard Connie and Viv come into the room and they opened the trunk.

"Bucket," was the first word out of his mouth and Viv managed to grab a champagne bucket just as he vomited.

"Ugh." She grimaced.

Carlos looked up. "You try getting around in a trunk and see if you can keep it all down." She gave him a towel to wipe his mouth. "Where are we?"

"On a private jet owned by a very good friend of mine." Viv sat on the bed and watched Carlos stumble out of the trunk. He hefted his bag out with him. "We don't need to show our passports, we can just go."

"You managed that?" Connie asked. "I was going to put him on a public plane."

Viv smiled mischievously. "Private is better, and the friend owed me a favour. No one knows we're on here. But I will have to let the pilot know. Let's take a seat." She went to tell the pilot, and he filed the flight plan. Ten minutes later they were winging their way to Hollywood.

"What am I going to do?" Carlos paced back and forth down the aisle. "I have no idea who those people were, what they wanted, or who they were after. Were they after me or the girl?"

"Nobody really knows," Viv told him. "All I heard was a bunch of screaming as I walked through the lobby. The girl was screaming that you had raped her and were attacking her friend. And her fiancé had tried to save them both."

"That's basically what I heard," Connie said.

"I've never raped anyone in my life," Carlos spat angrily. With the week he'd had he was pissed off big time. He ran a hand through his hair. "What am I gonna do?" Slumping into his seat, he repeated, "What am I gonna do?"

Viv and Connie sat side by side, dressed to the nines in their finery, having left half of their belongings on the island. But hotel staff would send them later. They looked at each other, a plan formulating in their minds.

"Well, darling, it looks like you'll have to go on the run. Change your name, live in another country."

"Away from my parents, my brothers, my job?" He didn't like saying it, let alone thinking it.

"I don't think you'll have that anymore, darling," Connie said. "You're wanted for rape and murder. You wouldn't keep your job."

Carlos sighed. "My life has just gone to shit."

"Not necessarily. Have you thought about pursuing that career I talked to you about?" Viv asked.

His brain was so fogged he didn't comprehend what she was saying. "What career?"

The women shared a glance. "Your porn star career."

Carlos tilted his head. "You expect me to take on a public career knowing full well someone's just tried to kill me and has accused me of rape? I'm an escapee!" he reminded them. "They get one look at me in a movie and they'll know exactly where I am and come and get me."

"Not necessarily," Connie said. "We change your name, maybe your hair…"

He frowned. "How much am I supposed to change in order to stay out of the fuzz's way? How long am I supposed to keep running?"

"Well," Viv replied. "Maybe you don't have to." She exchanged another glance with Connie. "A certain producer we know happens to be good friends with certain people in certain places. If you make money for him, he will make things disappear."

"Things?"

"Problems."

"Like murder and rape charges?" Carlos raised a brow. "He can't be that good."

"Oh, he's very good," Connie said.

"You'd be amazed at what he can do," Viv added.

Carlos shook his head. "I don't think anyone can save me. Hell, I don't even know what the hell is going on." He was tired. All of his energy had been sucked out of him in the last ten hours, and now he was spent.

"Why don't you go and lie down in one of the bedrooms," Viv said. "We could all do with a rest."

"Mmm." His eyes were already half closed. "Okay." He slowly made his way back to the bedroom where Connie's trunks were, grabbed a pillow, and was out like a light.

PEDRO

Thumping music reverberated through Santorini's biggest and most popular dance club and into the night. The crowd was high on life and bouncing up and down with an energy seen only in addicts. The floor shook with the momentum of their fervent dancing and was slick with five hours of sweat and lust.

Club owner, Andros Poulos, looked on from his private enclosed balcony above the dance floor. Night after night the place was packed to the rafters with frenzied club hoppers and party goers. Night after night they bought his drinks, his women, his blow. And it was all because of one man.

Pedro Stephanopoulos.

The hot twenty-year-old stud had become a DJ sensation the year before on Mykonos and Andros had been able to get him this summer. Because word had gotten around, all the tourists from all the islands came to Santorini every night. And it was only the first month of summer.

He gazed across the electric scene before him; Pedro dancing on stage throwing the beats together, women gyrating and thrusting down the front trying to get his attention. So were some of the men. The rest of the crowd was an eclectic mix of men, women, locals, tourists, gays and straights, all blending like an exotic cocktail of spice, lust and sex.

Andros watched Pedro. The hot stud had everything going for

him. Six feet of rock-hard body and jet-black hair with locks hanging over his bright blue eyes. His toned chest glistened with sweat under the lights, and his white shirt hung open, plastered to his body. White pants were slung low, allowing everyone to dream of what he held there. Waving his arms in the air, he encouraged the crowd to yell and scream.

Yes, Pedro Stephanopoulos was a very good investment indeed.

"Papa." Angelina, Andros's daughter, came up beside him.

He was so proud of his baby girl. At eighteen she had finished high school with top honours and had a scholarship to Juilliard in New York. It was not that he couldn't afford to send her, as he was one of the wealthiest men on the island, but she had earned her seat all on her own. Now she was spending the summer with him before leaving in the fall. "Angelina, how do you like the place?" It was her first visit to the club and he wanted to make an impression.

"Noisy," she said, tucking a strand of hair behind her ear. "The bright lights are giving me a headache." The petite girl with her long black hair, big brown eyes, and perfect complexion stood beside her father shielding her eyes.

"Come, come." He ushered her into his office and closed the door. The noise dropped away and the air was almost silent.

"Ah, that's better." She sat on the sofa. "Too noisy for me."

"And yet you're moving to New York, a city that never sleeps," her father argued. "*And* attending a music school. And yet this…" He waved an arm toward the club. "This is too noisy for you?"

She smiled. "Papa, it won't be so noisy at the school, and I'll be staying in a quiet part of the city, so I'll get plenty of peace and quiet."

"Do you have to go?" Andros sat beside her and placed a hand over hers. "Do I have to lose my little girl?"

"Papa." She patted his hand. "You're not losing me. I'm going to further my education."

"Of course I'm losing you." He kissed her hand. "It's not as if you're going to the mainland to school. You're going half way around the world for God's sake. I won't be able to see you unless I fly there."

"And what's wrong with that?"

He sighed. "Nothing. Not if it means my little girl is getting the best education she can." Andros paused and then leant toward her. "Are you *sure* you want to go?"

Angelina laughed. "Of course, Papa. I'm going, and *that's final.*"

He got up and wandered over to the balcony door. "Well, if there's nothing more I can say," he said lightly, half joking. "Then you should go. There's nothing here for you, only too much noise, too much light."

She smiled at his attempted joke. "Okay, Papa. I still have another month before I go. I'll see you tomorrow." She kissed him on the cheek and left. Stopping at the bottom of the stairs she gazed toward the stage where Pedro was, admiring the tall, bare-chested stud. He barely glanced in her direction, but she still felt the thrill of that glance go down to her soul. He wouldn't be the first man she'd bedded, but he was definitely going to be the one before she left for college.

Pedro waved his arm in the air, drawing cheers from the crowd. It was a hot night. A steamy 100 degrees created a lot of sweat and a lot of drinking. He slowed things down with another track and took a few moments to down a bottle of water. "Ladies and gentlemen, I wanna see you get your groove thang on, slow it down now." He danced behind his console, gave his headphones a wipe and downed another bottle of water that Mikos, the bartender, had brought him.

Mikos hovered by the side of the stage. "You need anything else, Peds?" he yelled.

"How 'bout a bottle of juice and something to eat?" Pedro yelled back. "I need to keep my energy up and I'm sweating out the water."

Mikos nodded and hurried away. Part of his job that summer was to make sure Pedro had everything he needed to do the job he had to do. It was his first job and he wanted to make an impression on the boss. At eighteen, and fresh out of school, he needed the job and the money, *and* he got paid extra for taking care of Pedro. So why would he mind? He minded because Pedro got all the girls. Not that he was overly interested in them, but Mikos knew that by hanging around Pedro that maybe he'd get a few girls coming his way.

He grabbed a large jug of juice and poured it into a glass bottle, added a basket of mini burgers and fries to the tray and took them back to the stage, leaving them on the small table behind the DJ booth.

Pedro noticed and waved before turning his attention to the girls down the front. His fingers did a little wave and he winked, sending them into a screaming frenzy, waving their hands back at him. One even bared her breasts.

God, life was good as a DJ!

That girl was still there three hours later when he finished, and she cornered him outside as he was taking a breather.

"Oh, Pedro, you're so hot." She sidled up to him and ran her fingers across his chest. "I want you."

A part of him was surprised even though the rest of him wasn't. It was something he'd been getting for the last month. Women wanting him, men wanting him, it was turning into a summer frenzy of sex, love and holiday romance.

"That's nice," he said, finishing off his juice and trying to be polite. "Glad you enjoyed yourself. I'm off home." He left the bottle at the back door and took off for the beach. After the night he'd had he needed a swim to cool off, and peeling off the sweat soaked shirt that was plastered to his body, he dropped it on the sand. His pants were stiff and dry against his skin from hours of sweaty dancing, so he dropped those as well and stood in his bare flesh.

Summer time on the islands, middle of the night, no one was going to care that he was naked.

He ran for the water and dived in, relishing the coolness on his hot flesh. He did a few strokes to the left, a few strokes to the right, and floated on his back looking up at the sky. It was as if he was part of it, floating in blackness surrounded by stars. He felt himself drift off but pulled himself back. Not a good place to fall asleep. Swimming for the shore he saw a white figure on the sand where his clothes were, and stepping out of the water he noted the figure was a woman.

"Pedro," she sing-songed.

He walked over to her and saw the woman from the club, stark naked and voluptuously curvy. He stirred. "You followed me?"

She noticed the stirring. "Yes. I want you." She threw herself at his chest, and he caught her by the arms. "Take me, I want you, I'm yours." She flattened her body against him and her hot flesh melded with his.

He stirred more, hardening between her open thighs.

Her lips hovered below his, and her hand reached down to guide him, pulling him down to the sand and inside of her, groaning as he entered, cocooned in her warmth. She arched into him, and his mouth inhaled her breast, sucking, licking, biting, teasing it into submission. She came, and he kept thrusting.

"You need to put your clothes back on."

Her eyes opened, and she saw him doing his pants up. "What?" She was confused. *Wasn't he just inside of me making love to me?* "What are you doing?"

"Getting dressed. I just took a swim and now I'm going home. You need to put your clothes on." He nodded at her dress on the sand. "I'm flattered, but not interested." He picked up his shirt, shoes and bag and headed for the dock. He was taking the ferry home to Mykonos for some good food and good sleep.

"What do you mean you're not interested?" she screamed and ran after him. "I'm offering you my body." She jumped in front of him and grabbed her breasts. "I'm offering you these, *this*, on a platter and *you're turning me down*? What?" She cocked her top lip. "Don't like pussy? What are you, a fag?"

Pedro gave her a dirty look. "No, I'm not. I'm just not interested in *you*." He continued on his way, but she attacked him.

"How dare you," she screamed and pushed him down from behind. He fell to the sand and she pounced, planting herself on him, rolling him over and ripping at his zip. "How dare you refuse me?" He grabbed at her hands, but she'd already pulled his cock out and was trying to sit on it. "How dare you."

He got her by the arms and threw her off, sending her rolling across the sand. Getting to his feet, he grabbed his things and ran, pulling up his zip along the way. Making it to the ferry as it pulled in, he reported the woman to the ferry master, who called over a wharf officer.

"What happened?" the officer asked.

"She attacked me because I wouldn't have sex with her." Pedro put his shoes on and examined the red marks on his torso and arms. "I'm a DJ at SantorPoulos, the club owned by Andros Poulos. She was there all night and followed me down to the beach. Then she attacked me when I told her I wasn't interested. She followed me. She's crazy, crazy man." He saw they weren't taking him all that seriously, although, at the mention of his boss, they had perked up. "I seriously doubt *my boss* is going to like the fact his patrons are attacking his staff."

"Of course, of course," the officer said. While he didn't know Andros Poulos personally, his chief did. "Tell me, a description of her."

"Average height, a mop of brown hair, curvy figure." Pedro shrugged. "That's about it. Don't know her name. She wasn't Greek, so probably a tourist."

The officer took notes. "Of course. So many tourists on this island. It will be hard to find her. We will keep a lookout for a woman matching that description and see if she attacks other men." He nodded. "Mr Stephanopoulos."

Pedro sighed. He knew he wasn't going to get any help from the police whatsoever, so he jumped on board the ferry and headed home, watching the sun rise over the horizon, sending the sky into a rainbow of colours. After a nice hot shower and an equally hot breakfast, he was going to sleep all day.

He got off the boat and walked home, arriving to find his house in an uproar. "Mama, Papa, what's wrong?" He saw Tomas sitting on the sofa next to his grandparents, stunned into silence.

"Wrong?" Spiros yelled. "Wrong! What's wrong is your brother has gone and shot someone and raped two women."

Pedro turned Tomas. "Tomas, how could—"

"Not him," Spiros roared. "Carlos." He paced back and forth across their small lounge room.

Pedro stared at his parents. "What? Wait, are you saying that Carlos...no...he wouldn't."

"And now he has disappeared and no one knows where he's gone,"

Jenny said, tears sliding silently down her face. "The police were here last night. They ripped the place apart looking for him. I've only just finished tidying everything." Her eyes went around the room.

Pedro shook his head. "No...I can't...no...he wouldn't." He looked at his brother. "Tomas?"

Tomas finally looked up, a desolate expression on his face. "What?"

"Do *you* know what happened? You work at the same resort."

Tomas inhaled slowly then exhaled, his head moving from side to side. "I have no idea. I was on the other side of the resort. I heard there had been gunshots and that the masseur was involved. Nothing else." His mind wandered off again.

Pedro ran a hand through his hair and felt the sand and grit in it.

His mother saw him. "You go," she said. "Go and have a shower and I'll make you some breakfast." She waved him toward the boys' private quarters. "Go freshen up and I'll make your favourite. Go." Looking around at nothing, she finally moved from her spot in the middle of the room.

Pedro saw the scene around him and took off, seeking refuge under the spray of cold then hot water. He alternated between the two as he soaped himself down and washed off the dry sweat and salty grit. He thought about Carlos.

What in the hell had he gotten himself into? Were the cops *really* after him for rape and a shooting? It was well known that Carlos loved women and was paid to please them; he didn't need to force a woman into sex. And shooting? Carlos had never held a gun in his life. None of them had. Not even back in Australia when they were kids. Their parents had wanted nothing to do with guns, so they'd never learned how to shoot.

He turned off the taps and stepped out. Wrapping the towel around his waist, he wondered what this meant now. *Are the cops hunting him down? Where is he? What really happened? Is he still on the island? What if they catch him? Who were the women? Why was there a shooting? And most importantly, who got shot?*

He quickly dressed in the shorts and tank he slept in and started feeling the effects of needing sleep, barely making it into the dining room just as breakfast was ready.

"Eat up." Jenny placed a plate of eggs, bacon and sausages in front of him and lovingly slid her hand over his hair. "You're still a growing boy, you need your strength." She planted a kiss on his forehead.

Tomas sat down morosely and picked at his toast.

"What's wrong with you?" Pedro wasn't sure he could down so much food just yet, so poured himself a tall glass of juice.

Tomas gazed at him. "Huh?"

"Jesus, you're out of it." Pedro finished his drink and dug into his food.

Tomas shrugged a shoulder and went back to picking at his toast.

Spiros finally made it to the table. "Our son may have ruined his life, but he will *not* ruin ours. We will try to stick to our normal routine. Breakfast, lunch and dinner. Meat shop, home. He will *not* ruin our lives too."

"Do we actually *know* what happened?" Pedro asked as his mother and grandparents sat down with their own food.

"He raped and shot, enough said," Spiros spat.

"Except, Carlos *wouldn't do that, none of us* would. You raised us better than that," Pedro argued. "He *wouldn't* do that."

"Well, he did." Spiros slammed a hand down on the table. "He did, end of story. Eat your breakfast."

"Well, *I* don't believe it," Pedro replied, defying his father. "We know Carlos, you raised him, he wouldn't rape a woman any more than me or Tomas would. And why would he shoot anyone? Who did he supposedly shoot and why should we believe anything the cops say? They're just as corrupt here as on the mainland."

"Because he ran away like a gutless coward after he did it. That is not a son I raised." Spiros's face was as black as thunder. "That is no son of mine."

"How do we know he ran away?" Pedro demanded. "He could be hiding out until he can tell his side of the story."

"Because he left us a letter," Jenny said quietly.

Pedro zeroed in on her. "What?"

She looked up. "He left a letter on the table. I found it before the police got here."

"What does it say?" Pedro asked eagerly. "Read it."

She slipped it out of her dress pocket and handed it to him. He read it out loud. "If you're reading this then I've gone. I've been planning to leave for some time, using my twenty-fifth birthday as the date I travel overseas to a new land. But if I'm not twenty-five then something has happened to make me leave. I've left some money toward expenses and hope all is safe and well with all of you as it may not be with me. Don't worry, it'll be fine, love Carlos."

"Sounds like he already had that prepared," Tomas finally piped up.

"Sounds like he has no idea what's going on," Pedro replied. "No mention of the current problem. Look…" He gazed at his parents. "Something is clearly wrong and we need to find out what actually happened."

"No." Spiros banged the table as he stood. "No more talk of him. No more." He shoved back his chair and stormed out of the house.

"But, Mama—" Pedro started.

"Stop," she said sadly, patting her son on the hand. "Just finish your breakfast and get some rest. You have work again tonight, don't you?"

"Yes, Mama."

"Then finish up and rest." She went back to eating her own food.

Pedro exhaled loudly and returned to his food, finishing what he could before hitting the bed in his room. He was physically tired, but his brain was racing. He needed sleep and needed to calm down. *Breathe in slowly, and out slowly.* He thought about being attacked and how it must have gone down with Carlos. *Breathe in slowly, and out slowly.* He thought about his parents and wondered what the hell was with Tomas. *Breathe in slowly…breathe out slowly…*

CARLOS

The private plane landed in L.A. on a warm sunny Saturday, fifteen hours after it's mysterious departure from Athens.

Connie woke Carlos. "Time to leave, darling," she said.

He yawned. "Where are we?"

"We're in L.A.," Viv said, coming into the room. "I've made some calls, and our passports will be checked on board, but we should be free to go after that."

"Our passports? But they'll know where I'm from." Carlos felt panic start to rise, but squelched it down.

"That's what one of my calls was about," Viv said, collecting her things. "The person doing the checking is a big fan of mine and will see to it personally we are let through. And as far as I know, nothing has hit the newspapers over here yet, so it's probably been contained on Mykonos."

Carlos thought about his family. *What the hell must they be thinking? Had they read the letter? Or had the cops gotten to them?*

"Don't worry; we'll lie low at my place for a few days while we get some things sorted out. Then we'll help you start your future," Connie said.

"Will it be a future where I'm not arrested and charged with murder and rape?" Carlos asked.

The women shrugged. "Who knows?"

"Great. So you can't even guarantee it."

"Hello, Miss Vivian, it is Marco," a voice called out.

They stopped.

How much had he heard?

Vivian left the room to greet him. "Of course, Marco, how are you darling?"

"Oh, very good, Miss Vivian, I am here to look at your passports."

"Of course. Here's mine, the others are just getting theirs."

Connie and Carlos retrieved theirs and walked into the aisle.

"Ah, oh, my God." Marco's eyes lingered upon Carlos, and Carlos panicked. "You are gorgeous," Marco went on, so clearly gay. "And what is *your* name?" He held out his hand.

"Carlos," he said simply and handed over his papers.

Next, Marco checked Connie's and handed them back. "And you are here in L.A. for?"

"Work," Viv said. "Boring!"

"Play," Connie said smugly.

Carlos said nothing.

"Well, everything is in order," Marco said, handing back passports. "Enjoy your stay ladies." He eyed the gorgeous Adonis before him. "Carlos," he purred and turned on his heel.

Once he was gone, Viv laughed. "You certainly got off to a good gay start. One fan down, five million to go."

"Yes, and speaking of going, is the limo ready?" Connie asked, peering through a window.

"Ready and waiting," Viv said.

"Good, let's go."

They carried out bags and trunks and settled into the back of the limo. The ride took half an hour to wind their way through Laurel Canyon and pull up at the high metal gates which buzzed open. The chauffeur drove them up to the front door.

Climbing out, Carlos saw a huge one level home spreading left and right with thick greenery, bushes and trees, large windows, and a high brick wall.

Connie showed Carlos to a bedroom with a view of the pool out back. "This is for you, darling. The whole wing is yours. I'm at the other end."

Carlos cocked a brow. "You mean you don't want me staying with you?"

Connie's wicked laugh echoed around the room. "I wish. But you're not on the job while you're here, you're my guest, so I will leave you alone. Come outside when you've freshened up."

Carlos opened his suitcase and pulled out his clothes. T-shirts, jeans, basic necessities and nothing fancy. In his bag was a small variety of clothes and personal effects. They had been packed in there for over a year now. His getaway plan for when he left Mykonos. Except that would have been on his twenty-fifth birthday with a one-way ticket to somewhere. Now he was in Hollywood at twenty-four with a one-way ticket and the prospect of never seeing his family again. He put his things in the huge walk-in closet and took a shower in the large tiled bathroom. Dressed in the clothes he'd left out, he met Connie, who'd also changed, and Viv by the pool.

Huge serving platters of food were on the table and jugs filled with juice, coffee and water sat next to them.

"Help yourself, darling, you must be famished." Connie shoved a forkful of omelette into her mouth.

He wasn't, but the smell made his stomach grumble, and he piled a plate high with food.

Viv got off the phone as he put the first spoonful into his mouth. "I just spoke to Harry about your problem. At first, he didn't want to help sight unseen, but Connie and I convinced him you're worth it, so he's helping you. He's getting his private investigators to Mykonos today to find out what's going on and to track down those two people. We're going to find out who they are and what they're up to."

Carlos swallowed and took a gulp of juice. "Is it wise to tell people?"

"Harry runs a porn studio; privacy is his middle name. If the secrets about his actors got out he'd be in deep financial trouble, so keeping secrets and personal issues out of the press is his speciality."

"So, if I work for Harry, he'll cover up my past?"

"As much as he can," Viv said. "Well, he covered up *my* porn movies."

Carlos looked up in surprise. "*You? You* were in pornos?"

"When I was a wee lass," Viv said, blushing in embarrassment. "I hated the fact I'd done them and regretted it badly, but I needed the money and didn't do any more. Harry covered them up."

"Wait, *you* did porn movies, and hate that you did, but you want to push *me* into doing them instead?" Carlos was confused by the weird contradiction.

Viv shrugged. "It wasn't for me. But it is for you and I think with your talent…" She squeezed his hand. "You'll go a long way and be a big, big star. Big…huge!" She held her hands about two feet apart.

"I'm not that big." Despite his love of sex, it was still embarrassing for him to hear women talk like that.

"It's true," Viv replied. "And Harry wants to meet you tomorrow."

"That soon?"

"That soon."

He nodded. "Okay. Is it safe for me to get around? How will I get there and where am I going?"

"For a start, Connie and I will be taking you in her limo, so you don't need to worry about getting there or being seen. And second, we'll be going to their house so it will be a private setting."

"And what will I need to do? Do I need to perform?" He raised a brow jauntily. "With one of you?"

Connie tittered.

"Oh, you've already performed." Viv blushed. "Probably not, no, you will need to show him your goods, so wear something you can slip out of easily."

"So, like every other day of my life then," Carlos joked despite the seriousness of the situation.

"Pretty much," Connie said.

"And then what?"

"Then you have a career as an actor," Viv replied. "You'll be famous."

He pulled a face. "Great."

"You just relax for the rest of today and catch up on your beauty sleep. You still look tired. I'll be back tomorrow," Viv said, getting up.

Carlos rose and hugged her. "Thank you, for everything." They kissed.

"Anything for you, darling." She wiped his mouth free from her lipstick. "See you tomorrow. Connie." She waved and disappeared into the house.

Carlos spent the afternoon relaxing by the pool, catching up on the news, and reading the magazines Connie had by the bucket load around the house. He caught up on local celebrities, his favourite bands, and who was supposedly doing whom in Hollywood circles. He watched programs he'd never seen before on TV and wondered in amazement at all the things he'd missed out on living in Mykonos.

He followed up a delicious late dinner with a swim in the pool, and floating on his back, he looked up into the night sky at the millions of stars and thought how they looked so different when viewed from the other side of the globe. He wondered about his family, how they were coping and if they were in trouble. He hoped not, but then considering what had happened he couldn't be sure. After taking one last swim, he headed inside for bed.

PEDRO

Pedro's alarm went off at six p.m., and his eyes flew open. "Oh." He took a deep breath, jumped out of bed and changed. Walking into the lounge room, he found his mother wringing her hands.

"Don't worry, Mama, it will all work out. Carlos will come home. This will be sorted. We'll all be together again."

She smiled, but it didn't reach her eyes.

He kissed her cheek and left for the ferry, sailing across the water and making it to Santorini by seven-thirty.

"Mikos," Pedro greeted. "I'm going to need a bodyguard tonight, as well as lots of food and drink."

"What's this about a bodyguard?" Andros questioned as he patted Pedro on the shoulder. "Does my resident DJ need protection?" He took the seat beside Pedro at the bar.

"I'll say," Pedro said. "Some crazy woman from last night followed me down to the beach and was standing naked for me when I got out after my swim. Then she started screaming when I told her I wasn't interested and ran after me, pushed me down and scratched me." He showed the red marks on his skin. "Then she pulled my cock out of my pants and tried to sit on it. I pushed her away and ran for the wharf to tell the officer what had happened. Unless I see her again and point her out they probably won't catch her."

Mikos shook his head. "Dude, that was some wild cat. She was buck naked waiting for you?" He could only guess what Pedro Stephanopoulos looked like in the downstairs department, but if his brother Carlos was any indication of the family genes, then Pedro was packing heat as well. Not that he'd intentionally set out to see Carlos naked, he'd just happened to be sneaking around the masseur's cabana and heard a woman screaming out 'more, more' and had been curious enough to take a peek. There was Carlos in all his Greek Australian glory of ten inches of thick, strong muscle. Mikos had watched him enter the woman over and over, pleasing, pleasuring, making her groan and writhe on the massage table. It had turned him on so much he had to relieve himself in the bushes before leaving. It was not as though he had a girlfriend to take it out on, so the bushes and his hand had to do. He wondered if Pedro did the same things.

"Well, my boy, we'll just have to hire a guard to walk you to the ferry and back. Can't have any more women attacking my star attraction," Andros said. "The club opens in a few minutes; why don't you go and get ready?"

Pedro took his water bottle and clambered up on stage. He already had his set list ready, as he planned them a week ahead, so he gathered the records together ready to play. He hadn't mentioned anything about Carlos, and didn't even know if the news had travelled, but Greek islands were like Greek villages; news got around pretty damn fast.

He set up the first record, an extended 12 inch that was going to play for a good twenty minutes. He always started with something simple as the doors opened at eight, but the place wasn't really going until eight-thirty when his gig started, so they played music while people settled in and got warmed up.

The doors opened and he set the needle on it.

This time also gave him a few minutes to eat and psyche himself up. And tonight he needed psyching. He loved music and desperately wanted to be a world-renowned DJ, but whatever the hell was going on with Carlos had got him out of sync.

Finishing his food, he swallowed the last of his juice and stood to get himself limber. After shaking his shoulders and stretching his arms above his head to stretch his back out, he swung his arms around in circles and jumped on the spot, loosening up every muscle he had for the onslaught of his performance. He needed to get all thought of everything, and everyone, out of his brain, preferring to start each show with a clear mind and body.

Last night popped into his head. What in God's name had possessed that woman to follow him, get naked and expect sex, then attack him and try and sit on his cock? What the hell was in her head that she wanted to sit on him and was going to assault him for it? He shook his head. He didn't know, but he didn't like it, and he hoped she didn't turn up tonight. He peered through the curtain and saw her front and centre.

"Shit!" He thought for a moment. "Hey, Mikos," he yelled and waved the bartender over. "Tell Poulos that crazy woman from last night is here again and ask if I can get one of the bouncers to keep an eye on her."

"Sure thing." Mikos walked off, and ten minutes later, just before Pedro was set to go on stage, one of the bouncers came behind the curtain.

"Mr P said to guard you against some crazy woman?"

"She's crazy all right." Pedro pointed her out to the bouncer. "Keep an eye on her for me." He took to the stage and grabbed the mic. "Ladies and gentlemen. Welcome to Club SantorPoulos. I am Pedro Stephanopoulos your DJ, are you ready to rock tonight?" He waved his arm in the air. A chorus of screaming came back at him. "Then let's get down to the funky beats of The Trammps and *Disco Inferno.*"

The night went from there, and he finished up ten hours later with a resounding rendition of Thelma Houston's *Don't Leave Me This Way* that had the whole club singing at the top of their lungs and wildly, drunkenly, waving their arms in the air.

Pedro set up the system to play a 12 inch to take them out for the rest of the morning until the club shut, then left the stage.

"Here." Mikos handed him a burger and bottle of juice. "Rehydrate."

Pedro took the bottle and swallowed half the juice before taking a breath. "God I am so hot," he whooped. "Everybody loves me." He waved his arms in the air and did a little dance. "Everybody loves me, yeah, yeah," he sang. "Everybody loves me, yeah, yeah."

Andros came backstage. "They certainly do. The club is full every night that you're here. Are you sure I can't convince you to work seven nights a week?" He straightened his suit and eyed the stallion before him. Thank God Angelina didn't come to the club.

Pedro shook his head. "Nah, man. I need time off to party and have some fun. Four nights is enough for me."

"Yes. I'm sure it is. Especially now."

Pedro stopped dancing. "What? Why now?"

"Well, with your brother and everything…" Andros gave a slight shrug. "Do you need time off?"

Pedro licked his lips. "What do you mean? What about my brother?"

Andros checked his watch. "Well, it's just that…" He waved a hand. "It's gotten out that Carlos assaulted two women and shot one."

Pedro's temper flared and he grabbed Poulos by the collar. "Don't you dare talk rubbish about my brother like that, he did no such thing. He would never hurt a woman like that. We were raised better than that."

Andros's bodyguard pulled Pedro off his boss and twisted his arm up behind his back.

"Ow, get off me."

"It's all right, Magnus, let him go. Clearly the whole deal about his brother has him upset," Andros said and waved his bodyguard off. "Clearly Mr Stephanopoulos is close to his family and very upset by the current events, but if he ever," he stepped close to Pedro, "touches me that way again, with violence in his mind," his eyes flashed, "then he will need a lesson in etiquette. Has he got that clear?" The threat in his voice made it very clear.

Pedro glared darkly at him and brushed down his shirt. "Yeah, things are *very* clear now." Grabbing his bag, he stormed out the back door and down to the beach for a swim.

Stripping off, he waded into the cool calming water and swam out to the platform that was for tourists to lie on. He climbed up and spread out, flat on his back, looking up at the sky. Yeah, he got Andros's message loud and clear. He didn't mind using you but if you crossed him, look out.

After a few more minutes in which he formulated a plan, Pedro swam back, collected his things, and headed for the ferry.

CARLOS

Sunday morning, Viv arrived with some news. "Harry's investigators are in Mykonos and have contacted your family. They're okay and not in any trouble."

Carlos sighed and leant back in his seat, breakfast forgotten. "That's good."

Viv looked at her watch. "We'd better get going. Harry and Harriet are dying to meet you."

They quickly finished breakfast and made their way to the limo for the ride to Harry DeVille's private residence. The drive took them twenty minutes, and they entered a gated driveway with a long winding drive that wound its way up to an impressively sprawling two-storey house.

"Wow." Carlos stared as he looked up at the place.

"The house that porn built," Viv told him.

"How many has he done?" Carlos asked, turning around to gaze at the expansive lawns and gardens.

"One thousand, two hundred and forty-three," Connie said. "But who's counting?"

"And how many built this house?"

"One hundred and two," Viv said.

They walked up the huge stone steps and were greeted by the butler. "Mr and Mrs DeVille will see you in the office," he said.

"Thank you, Deveers," Viv said warmly and led the way down the hall on their right into a maze of rooms full of bedroom, office, and street scenes with cameras, lighting, and screens. They walked into the office and came face to face with Harry and Harriet who were ready and waiting for them.

"So, what do we have here?" Harry DeVille said, getting up from behind his desk and walking over to stand in front of them. "Let's see the goods."

Carlos pulled his t-shirt over his head and stepped out of his pants.

Harry DeVille's eyes lit up at the golden tanned Adonis with the ten inch cock before him. "My, you are perfect."

Harriet licked her lips and fingered the pearls around her neck. "I want to try him out."

Harry arched a brow. "Me first."

PEDRO

Pedro had three days off, so he went in search of Carlos. He went to the resort and spoke to all of his co-workers.

Antonio had no idea where he was, but had noted that his mother had disappeared without a word at the same time. She had since called to let him know she was back in Los Angeles dealing with some things.

He spoke to some of the maids who were working that night and all reported hearing the same thing. A scream, a gunshot, another scream, and then some big hubbub followed. And no one had seen Carlos since. Many speculated about what had happened, what he'd done, *if* he'd done it, and who the person was who'd been shot, but no one could categorically come up with a definite timeline, or had any proof to show for that night.

Pedro scoured the streets, the paths, the windmills, even took the ferry to all of the islands to see if Carlos was hiding out, it was all to no avail, so he went to the last place he wanted to go.

The police station.

"I'd like to talk to the detective in charge of the shooting at the Mykonos Desert Resort."

The officer eyed him up and down. "And what is your interest?"

Pedro sighed. "You're investigating my brother for the crime."

The officer, a tall, thin man with a thin moustache, stopped leaning on the counter and stood straight. "*You* are the brother?"

"Yes. Just get the officer in charge, please," Pedro snapped.

"*I* am the officer in charge."

Pedro turned to see a fat man of Greek descent, maybe mid-fifties, with a fat face and sweaty complexion. "Good. I want to talk to you about the charges you have against my brother from the Mykonos Desert Resort."

"And why do you need to know? Besides being his brother."

"Because I want to know what you know." Pedro got impatient. "What charges are you bringing against him, and what are you doing to prove his innocence and solve the case?"

"What we are doing, Mr Stephanopoulos is of no concern to you, regardless of the fact it's your brother we are investigating."

"I have a right to know," Pedro stated.

"No, Mr Stephanopoulos, you do not. Now leave my station or I will have you for obstruction."

"Obstruction?" Pedro laughed. "How am I obstructing anything? Are you kidding?"

"No, Mr Stephanopoulos. I am not. Now leave." The cop's hand went to his belt.

Pedro finally noticed the other officers had gathered and frowned. "Mmm," he mumbled. Something was definitely going on here. "I'll leave," he said. "But I don't like the fact no one will tell us what's happened to Carlos." He left and headed home.

The officer ushered his co-workers away and went back to his office where he dialled a number and waited for the call to connect. "We have the young one sniffing around…yes…yes…all right. I will." He hung up and told one of his constables to tail Pedro Stephanopoulos.

*****

Pedro was back at work Wednesday night, fuming over a wasted three days. There was no sign of Carlos, no one knew anything or saw anything. The cops weren't co-operating, and a wall of silence had gone up.

And now he had Andros to deal with.

"I want you to work more nights," he told Pedro before work.

"I told you no. My contract's for four nights, and that's it." Pedro sorted through the records and put them in order of play.

Mikos brought in a burger and juice for Pedro's preshow meal and was waved away by Andros.

"You mean *this* contract?" There was tearing sound.

Pedro looked up to see Poulos holding two pieces of ripped paper.

"You don't have a contract," Andros said. "So, now you work the whole week."

Pedro got angry and stood up. "If I don't have a contract then I don't work *any* night of the week. Guess I shouldn't be here now." He stepped off stage, but Andros stopped him with a hand on his chest.

"I was just joking."

Pedro glanced from his hand to him. "Were you?"

Andros removed his hand. "Of course. I was just testing you." There was a slight nervousness in his voice. "I really want you here every night, Pedro. I'd even give you a raise to be here."

Pedro picked up the burger. "I told you. I need time off to have a life. Four nights is enough." He went back to sorting the records, his back to Andros.

Andros seethed under his tightly starched collar. *No one does this to Andros Poulos. Oh, no, not without consequences.* He pulled a small vial out of his pocket and quickly tipped the powder it contained into the bottle of juice. "Well, that's a pity." He pocketed the vial. "We could have made lots of money."

Pedro turned around. "Don't you already?"

Andros smiled his Cheshire cat grin. "Of course, but we could always make more." His fingers played with the vial in his pocket. "I'll let you get on with it." He left the backstage area and walked through the club, shaking hands with the first patrons through the doors, and made his way up to his office to watch the show. And what a show it would be.

Pedro started the night's festivities. "Ladies and gentlemen, welcome to SantorPoulos, here on Santorini. It's hot out there, it's hot in here, so let's see how much hotter we can make it. Let's party."

The crowd screamed. The place was packed as it was every night he was there, and he saw the woman who had attacked him front and centre.

He played for half an hour then sculled back the juice, not realising the special ingredient. The room spun as fast as the disco balls. The lights flashed before his eyes. He was euphoric. Higher than he'd ever felt before. Like he could fly.

He closed his eyes and danced freely behind his console. The hours passed in moments and he was even more lost in the beat. He laid down a 12-inch track, removed his headphones and jumped into the crowd to dance.

All the women screamed and gathered around him, bumping and grinding with him, *against* him. The brunette woman pulled his shirt off so he was bare, and all the women reached out to lay a hand on him.

They gyrated as one, waving their hands in the air, whooping and hollering to the music. He was high on life, free as a bird, and had never felt this way in his life. He didn't know where it came from, or what it was, but he knew he wanted more.

He took to the stage for more beats and ended the night before jumping off stage to knock back the water Mikos had left for him. "Woohoo," he yelled. *"That was awesome!"*

Mikos came back in. "Here's some food. You burnt a lot of energy up there."

"Woohoo." Pedro danced around. "That was freaking awesome. Oh, God, I felt so free." He grabbed the burger and all but inhaled it.

Mikos shook his head. "I don't know how you do it, man. You eat burgers all night and still look like that."

"It's because of the en.a.gee," Pedro stated. "I burn it all off under those lights. Whoo. I'm gonna go for a swim. You wanna come?" He grabbed his bag and headed out the back door.

"No. I gotta finish up here." Mikos's voice trailed off. "Don't wait for me…" He had another couple of hours to go anyway.

Pedro raced down to the water, stripped off, and dived in. It felt good on his hot skin, and a few laps wore him out. "Man, I gotta get home and get me some sleep."

He headed for the wharf and took the ferry home where he found the place quiet and dark, and after a shower fell asleep in bed.

*****

Angelina Poulos had her eye on the DJ at her father's club. He didn't know who she was yet as they hadn't met, but she planned on changing that very soon. She pulled the skimpy crocheted dress she planned on wearing when she introduced herself to Pedro from her wardrobe. He would take one look at her and not want anyone else. She slipped it over her head and pulled it down over her bottom. Flesh in all the right places. Holes for her nipples to poke through, if the need called for it because she was not wearing anything under it. Stepping into high strappy red heels, she fluffed out her hair and eyed herself in the full-length mirror.

Sex on legs with dangerous curves in all the right places.

*****

The alarm blared in Pedro's ear at 6 p.m.

"Ugh." He half woke, groggy, dizzy, tired. "Ugh." He knew he had to get up for work, but the pounding headache made him want to stay in bed.

The alarm went on and on, and his mother came in. "Pedro?" She saw him half awake and leaning up on his elbow. "You don't look good." Moving to her son's side, she felt his forehead and cheeks. "You're not burning up." She looked into his dull blue eyes. "Maybe you're coming down with something?"

"I don't feel good," he mumbled. "But I gotta get up for work." He sat on the side of the bed and put his head in his hands. "Ugh."

"I'll get you something." Jenny left and came back with aspirin and juice. "Take these, they'll help."

He downed four and freshened up. "Ugh. I gotta go. Love you,

Mama." He kissed her on the cheek and headed for the ferry.

Two hours later he opened the show, and half an hour later, he was downing the bottle of juice that Mikos had left and that Andros had left the special ingredient in.

Half an hour later, he was high as a kite and feeling so good he got down into the crowd again. The women loved him and adored him and gyrated against him. He floated back up on stage and danced to the music in his head before downing another bottle of juice.

That's when he saw her.

Standing backstage, a hot sexy number in a hot sexy red dress. Hair down to her sexy ass, and sexy tits that had sexy nipples poking through the holes in the dress.

He eyed her, laid down a 12-inch track, and danced off stage into the side room to her. "Well, hello." He kept moving as she moved with him.

"Hello, yourself," she purred, thrusting her breasts forward so her nipples were prominent through the material.

He spied them, and the fact she wasn't wearing anything under such a see-through dress made him hard.

She slid the dress up little by little as she danced against him.

The erotic closeness made his heart pound and his cock ache, more so when she unzipped his pants.

He towered over her by half a head and the heat of intimacy at the moment was multiplied by a million.

She pulled him out and massaged him.

He breathed hard.

She pulled her dress up to her hips to show her offering.

He breathed harder.

She rolled a condom on him.

He breathed, turned her, and had her against the table, gripping it as he took her from behind. In time with the pounding beats of the music, he thrust, and she met those thrusts, grinding, grating against him, her breath coming in short gasps.

He had her by the hips, but she moved his left hand up to her breast. Her nipple seized the moment and surged through the hole in the dress and into his waiting hand. She made him squeeze it and grunted some more.

The song came to its crescendo, and so did they.

Pedro gasped and grabbed the bottle of water from the table. He knocked it back while still inside of her, waiting until he drank the last drop before exiting. He stumbled back. "Ugh," he puffed. "Oh, God."

Angelina flicked her hair over her shoulder, slid her dress down, turned around and zipped him up. "Time for you to get back on stage."

He shook his head and took a deep breath, having no grasp on what or how or who had just happened, but he liked it. Getting back on stage, he stumbled behind his console. He was woozy, light headed, but still managed to get the next record on.

Andros noticed from his office. "Magnus, get another bottle of juice down to Mr Stephanopoulos. It looks like he needs some refreshment."

Magnus nodded and left the room.

Andros watched him walk across the club, get the juice from Mikos, and take it backstage. A few moments later he walked back out. Andros watched Pedro's behaviour for the rest of the night.

*****

Pedro didn't see the girl again until Saturday night after he finished work and was heading to the beach for his nightly swim. "Hey, it's you." He saw her waiting at the sand. "From last night."

"Hello, Pedro," Angelina murmured seductively, moving her scarcely bikini clad, very curvy, very sensual body.

He greedily eyed her figure. "I didn't see you after that, uh…"

"Fuck session."

His brows went up. "If that's what you want to call it."

She seductively moved over to him and trailed her finger up his sweat soaked chest. "That's what it was, and that's what I want again."

He hardened. "Where do you want it?"

She looked around. "How about here. I can't wait."

"On the beach?" He glanced around. "We'll be seen."

"How about out on the platform? I'll race you." She ran for the water and dived in. He chased her, dropping his bag and clothes before slicing through the cooling water to the platform out on the ocean. He made it as she climbed out and saw her quickly untie her bikini straps to reveal her luscious naked body. She lay down, arched her breasts, put her arms over her head, and held her legs together.

He knelt above her and spread her legs which she willingly moved.

"Don't forget protection." She handed him a condom, and he rolled it on before sliding into and onto her. Her body felt so right against his as he smoothly and assuredly moved inside of her as he feasted upon her body.

She led him, guided him, showed him what to do. "Oh, God Pedro, oh, God," she cried into the night as he sped up. Her legs wrapped around him, her nails dug into his back.

"Ugh." He grunted and delved his tongue into her willing mouth.

"Ugh," they groaned together until he was done.

He collapsed on top of her, and she held him tight until he leant up on one elbow, his head in his hand. He stroked her hair, her face, her lips. "Who are you, you wicked woman?"

She smiled as seductively as she moved. Everything was seductive about her, and he was captured and enraptured by it. "I'm a woman who knows what she wants."

"And a woman who clearly *gets* what she wants," Pedro said. His watch beeped. "Fuck, I gotta go or I'll miss the ferry." He slid out of her and picked up her bikini. "Last one back." He dived into the water and was halfway back before she even got off the platform.

He was zipping up his pants when she emerged like a goddess from the water and casually walked over to him.

She took her bikini and tied it up.

"I gotta go." He picked up his bag. "Will I see you again?"

"Of course." She ran her tongue over his torso. "You don't think I'd walk away from this do you?"

He grinned, relieved by her words. "Good. I gotta go." He was in the shower an hour later when Tomas walked into the bathroom.

"Hurry up, little brother, I need the shower."

Pedro turned off the tap and stepped out, grabbing the towel Tomas handed him. "Doesn't anyone get any privacy anymore?" He picked up his electric razor and started shaving.

"Whoa!" Tomas's wide eyes were looking at his brother's back. "What have you been up to, or should I say, *who* have you been up?"

Pedro glanced at him. "What do you mean?" He saw his brother's gaze on his back and turned around to look in the mirror. Red nail marks were on his back. "Fuck!" he muttered. "Didn't know they were there."

"Who is she?" Tomas started brushing his teeth.

Pedro sighed. "Don't know."

Tomas raised a brow. "You had sex with a woman and you don't know who she is or what her name is? What does she look like? How long have you known her? Where does she come from?"

Pedro sighed again. "Yes, petite, curvy, long black hair and gorgeous, two days, and don't know."

"Jesus, Pedro." Tomas paused his brushing. "You met a girl two days ago and don't know her name. Do you know if she's even legal?"

Pedro stopped with wide eyes. "Uh, no. I *think* she is. She definitely knows what she's doing."

"Just because she knows what she's doing doesn't mean she's old enough to be doing it. Jesus, Pedro," Tomas repeated. "You finished? Get out." He shoved his brother out the door.

*****

Andros Poulos sat behind his desk. His plan was working, but it needed time and needed co-operation. With his daughter moving to New York in a couple of weeks, he needed Pedro to work seven days a week to bring in the money. Not that his side businesses of sex and drugs didn't, but he wanted more. *Needed* more. Everyone wanted drugs. Everyone *needed* drugs. And Pedro was going to help him with that even if he never knew it.

*****

The brunette woman who had attacked Pedro sat in her room at Santorini's Bellisima Hotel. It was far from the best accommodation, but she didn't need the best, just the cheapest. She rifled through the photos of Pedro that she'd taken. Him at the club, on the beach, in Mykonos, at home. Yes, she knew where he lived, knew he had two brothers, knew one was now missing, and knew he was the man she wanted for a husband and as the father of her children.

Yes, she would get Pedro Stephanopoulos in her bed if it was the last thing she did. She looked at the letter she'd received from a lawyer, threatening her with a lawsuit if she didn't stop stalking some guy she'd fucked. Screwing up the paper she threw it into the rubbish bin where it landed next to the empty box of brown hair dye.

*****

After three days off with a pounding headache, Pedro couldn't wait to get back to the club to lay down his tracks. It lifted him, in ways he didn't think other people could imagine, especially lately. Getting lost in the sounds, the bass, the melodies, had helped him deal with the situation with Carlos and now he needed a fix.

Having knocked back his regular burger and bottle of juice, he proceeded to get the crowd high on life. He spied Angelina backstage during the last set, but she had disappeared by the time his stint was over. Grabbing his bag, he headed off to the beach hoping she was there. And she was.

"Hey." He ran the last few metres to her and swept her off her feet. His tongue delved and her legs wrapped around him. They barely made it a few paces before falling onto the sand where he plunged into her and had his way.

"Ugh, God, Pedro," she groaned as he rode her. "Oh, God."

It was over, and he was picking her up and taking her out to the platform where they rested. "Oh, God, that was good." He sighed.

She sat on top of him. "Was it good because it was sex with me or because you're high on drugs?"

His grin faltered. "What? I don't do drugs."

"Well…you do. Magnus put it in your drink."

He pushed her aside and sat up. "What?" he demanded angrily. "He put drugs in my drink? What the fuck!" He ran a hand through his hair. "What the fuck would he do that for?"

"My father's orders." She shrugged.

"Your father?" Pedro looked at her. "Who's your father?"

"Andros Poulos," she said simply.

Pedro stared. "What?" exploded out of him. "Andros Poulos is your father? Fucking hell. Why didn't you tell me? Fuck! I've been fucking my boss's daughter."

"I do have a mind and body of my own you know. I can do what I want."

"Are you even *old* enough to do what you want?"

"I'm eighteen." She tossed her hair over her shoulder. "And you're twenty, so it's only two years' difference."

"But you're my boss's daughter," he stressed. "Fuck."

"And Daddy's got his henchmen putting drugs in your drink. I saw him when I was there."

"Did he see you?"

"Nope. I hid behind the curtain."

"Fuck." Pedro rested his elbow on his bent knee and his head in his hand. "Fuck."

"Yes, we did, and you're very good at it."

He looked at her. "And we shouldn't be doing it. What if your father found out? He'd kill me."

"He probably would."

"He's already threatened to force me to work seven days. He pretended to rip my contract up the other day."

"You do know what my father does, right?" she asked curiously.

"Runs clubs."

"And guns and prostitutes and drugs."

Pedro frowned. "And now he's putting drugs in my drink. That's not on. Not on at all." He rubbed his forehead. "No wonder I've had headaches every day. I thought I was coming down with something."

"Nope. Just coming down from a drug-fuelled high."

"Do you know what an arsehole your father is?"

"Yep. He doesn't want me going to Juilliard in the fall."

Pedro's brows flew up. "You're a musician?"

"Classic piano and violin," she said. "I won my way in I was that good."

"And you're going to New York?" An idea formed in his mind.

"Yep. I'm going next month so I have a month to settle in before school. I wanted to get my fill of Greek island life before I went."

"I heard there was a new club opening there…"

"You should go. You're very good, and with your looks, everyone would want you."

"Think so?"

"Know so!"

Pedro agreed. "Definitely an idea. It's not as though Carlos is here anymore."

"I heard about that. I'm sorry."

He sighed. "Yeah, so am I. I can't find anything out. The cops wouldn't tell me. No one knows where he is."

"You'll find him."

"I hope so." He looked at his watch. "I gotta go." They swam back to the beach and got their belongings. "Will you be here tomorrow?" he asked, slipping on his shirt.

"I'll be waiting right here."

"See you then." He kissed her and wandered off.

She had watched them, hiding behind a stone pillar. The whore and Pedro. *Who the fuck does she think she is messing with my man?* She'd seen them fuck on the sand. Had only been a few paces from them, and had wanted to rip the whore's hair out. Had watched Pedro thrust into her with the magnificence of a stallion and then watched as he carried her to the water to swim to the platform where they'd talked. This was the second time she'd seen them together. The first was the other night after the club when she'd followed Pedro down to the beach and saw them fuck on the platform. She watched the girl walk down the cobblestone path and followed her all the way home where she climbed up the vines to a balcony and slid open French doors.

She took a few photos and vowed to find out who lived there.

*****

The next night, Pedro took a bag full of bottled water and juice from home. He substituted every bottle that Mikos or Magnus brought him and dumped it down the small sink backstage. They thought he was drinking it, but he was drinking his own. He felt good. Not high like previous nights, but as good as he had been. His headache was gone, he was feeling fit, and he partied until it was time to go home with Andros none the wiser.

He met Angelina at the beach, and they swam out to the platform where they made love. "Ah." Pedro rolled off her and she snuggled into his chest. "I'm not high, and that was even better."

"And how did you manage that?"

"Took my own from home and tipped theirs down the sink."

"Good for you. Outsmarting my father."

"I don't know how long it will last, though," he said. "How long can I keep it up before someone finds out?"

"As long as you need to." She leant up on her elbow. "Is New York still a plan?"

He smiled. "It's getting more serious every day. I got money saved up, my passport, a bag already packed."

"You *are* serious!"

"Yeah." He thought about it. "I packed it last week just in case."

"In case of what?"

"In case I found Carlos, or in case your father thinks ripping up my contract will make me work seven days a week."

Angelina sighed. "He can be forceful at times. He locked me in my room when I was sixteen. I had been sneaking out, and he found out, so he locked me in. It didn't last long. I got out and he realised I was too much like him to contain, so he let me set my own limits.

"How'd that work out?"

"I won a scholarship to Juilliard. How do you think it worked out?"

"Well, apparently." He kissed her, and she laid her head on his chest. "I should go soon. Gotta get home, and I bet you do too."

"Not yet," she said, leaving kisses down his stomach. She enveloped his member whole and delighted him with her prowess.

"Wow." He sighed. "Clearly I'm not your first."

"Clearly, I'm not yours, either," she replied.

"Nope."

"I think I should name it. Do you have a name for it?" She sucked some more.

"A name for what? My penis?" Pedro laughed.

"Yes."

"You're kidding, right?" His watch beeped, and he grabbed her and rolled off the platform into the water. They came up for air. "Time to go." They slowly swam for the shore and dressed. "See you tomorrow?"

"Same time, same place," she said, kissing him and watching him walk away. Once he was out of her line of vision, she headed for home and was on her way down a quiet road when she heard footsteps behind her. She slowed for a few moments then turned to fake out the stalker behind her, running smack bang into a woman with dark hair. "Oh, sorry. I didn't realise you were so close."

The woman stumbled back in shock.

"Here, let me help you." Angelina held out her hand.

The woman snarled. "Don't offer your hand to me, whore." She swung at Angelina with a clenched fist, but Angelina blocked her attempt with a quick spin kick. The woman was down and clutching her stomach.

"You whore," she rasped from the ground.

"I have no idea who you are or why you're calling me a whore, but if you come near me again, I will do worse than that." Angelina flicked her hair over her shoulder and went on her way.

"You whore," the woman screamed. "Stay away from him, he's mine. Stay away from him." She groaned in pain. "The baby…the baby…"

JULY 1977

PEDRO

Pedro kept an eye out on Saturday night. Andros had come down to talk to him before the show asking how he was, how he was feeling.

"Great," he'd said. "Better than ever."

"Fantastic," Andros had replied. "Mikos, keep the juice flowing all night."

And that was it. Pedro made sure that every bottle of juice went down the small sink in his backstage area, or down the toilet when he pretended to be peeing.

He danced around the stage, imagining himself in New York, in a club with a different crowd. A crowd full of rich men and richer women. Women who wanted him and him alone. Screaming for him, reaching for him, ripping his clothes off and taking him into their mouths.

Oh, how he wanted that.

He decided there and then if he lasted the summer in Santorini he'd be ready for the bright lights of New York City come September. He finished off the night and thanked everyone for coming. Backstage he towelled down and grabbed his bag.

"Pedro." Andros came through the door. "Great show my boy, how do you feel?"

Not this again!

"Fine, Mr Poulos." He high-fived the part-time DJ who took care of the beats in the wee hours and shut everything down and packed it away for him. "Why do you keep asking?"

"Just wondering," Andros said. "I'm having a big party here next week. A going away party for my daughter and her friends. I was wondering if you would DJ. I'll pay you your going rate, of course. It will be Wednesday night. I know you don't normally work that night."

"I'll let you know tomorrow." Pedro hefted his bag onto his shoulder. "I'll have to check to see if I have anything else on. Is that all?"

"Yes, yes, of course," Andros said. "Have a good night. And have a good sleep. You'll be doing this all again tomorrow night."

"I will. Bye." Pedro was out the door and heading for the beach. He met Angelina there and all but dragged her out to the platform. "Did you know your father's throwing you a going away party at the club next Wednesday? He asked me to DJ for it. Oh, God, what are you doing…?"

Her head lifted from his groin. "Getting your microphone warmed up."

"My what?" He laughed. "My microphone? Is that what you're calling it?"

"For now." She grinned. "I'm coming up with different names to see what suits it most. Figured I'd go for a musical theme for a name. Are you warmed up yet?"

"For what?" he teased.

"This," she replied and mounted him.

"Oh, God." He threw his arms out and lay back on the platform as she worked her way up and down. The slick wetness, the warmth, the sweet, sweet motherlode.

"So, are you going to do it?"

"Ugh, huh?" He came to. "Do what?"

"DJ at my party."

His eyes slowly opened and he focussed on her face. "You want me to? What if he realises we know each other?"

"How could he? I don't go to the club, so it's not as if I would have met you anywhere else." She slid up and down.

"And how will we keep our hands off each other?" He slid his hands up her thighs to her hips and onto her breasts, and she held them there as she moved.

"Who said we have to?" She clenched, and he groaned. "I'm sure I could slip backstage and you could slip inside during a break. It will be over in a flash, and I'll be back at the party before Daddy even sees I'm gone."

"And what if he does see that you're gone, and I'm gone, and we're gone together?" He thrust up into her.

"Ahhhh." She sucked in air. "Then I'll say," she mumbled. "I was thanking you for being the DJ at my party." She sighed. "That was good."

He breathed deeply as she collapsed onto him. "Yes, it was."

She stroked his arm slowly, her head on his chest, her ear above his heart. The stars overhead blanketed them, and she heard the beating of solitude. Stretching, she clenched around him and relaxed fully.

"So, what do we do?"

"Nothing. Pretend we've just met and I'm thanking you for playing my party, nothing more." She looked up into his eyes. "Don't worry."

"Easy for you to say," he said.

*****

Wednesday night the party started at seven.

Pedro was behind his deck, Angelina and all of her friends on the dance floor, and Andros on stage embarrassing his daughter.

"We are here tonight to say farewell to my little girl, Angelina."

Her friends cheered, and Pedro saw her go red. As red as the hot lace dress she had on. The same dress he'd first fucked her in, except this time she had a slip under it.

"She has worked her little Greek butt off to get into one of the most prestigious music colleges of all time, and now she is flying off to New York, on the other side of the world. Away from her papa, her friends, her family. So tonight we say goodbye to my little Angelina." Her friends cheered once more and closed around her.

Andros waved at Pedro who started the music and got the crowds moving for the next eight hours.

At three in the morning things slowed down. Pedro was out the back in the alley taking a break, and Angelina managed to sneak out to see him. She flew into his arms, and he spun her around.

"We have to be careful. What if your father sees us, or Magnus, or Mikos, or anyone else?"

She smothered him in kisses. "I don't care. I am *so* happy. That was so good." She kissed him. "Fuck me."

Shock flew over his face. "What? Here? Someone will see." There was a sound at the back door and Pedro saw movement. "Someone *did* see. You'd better go."

"No. I don't care," she said defiantly.

He put her down. "Go. I don't need trouble from your father. Go."

"Pedro," she said. "He *won't* find out."

"Pedro!" bellowed through the back of the club and out the door.

"He already did. Go, go," he whispered, and she ran down the alley.

Andros burst out the door. "Where is my daughter? What are you doing with my daughter?"

"Your daughter?" Pedro frowned. "Your daughter's not here." He put his hands out and looked around. "I'm just having a break."

"My daughter *was* here." He barged over to Pedro, got him by the shirt, and hauled him up against the wall. "I know my daughter was here and that the two of you were kissing."

"I wasn't doing any such thing." Pedro put his hands up. "I haven't touched your daughter."

"Magnus saw you, heard you, heard her ask you to fuck her," he spat, and droplets flew onto Pedro who frowned and turned away. "If you lay one hand on my daughter I will kill you."

"I haven't touched your daughter," Pedro muttered through clenched teeth. Andros's face was in his, and he was feeling the panic rise.

Angelina was hiding behind some trash cans and had seen and heard everything her father said and did, and she didn't like it one bit. Gripping a lid, she sneaked along the wall, came up behind her father, and smacked him hard on the back of the head.

Andros Poulos dropped like a lead balloon.

Pedro stood plastered against the wall, gasping for air as Angelina stood in the middle of the alley holding the can lid.

"What the fuck did you do?" Pedro whispered loudly.

Angelina had a big grin on her face. "Oh, something I've wanted to do for a very long time," she gushed.

The door burst open and Magnus came barging out. "Mr Poulos, Angelina." He flew to Angelina's side. "What did this man do to you?" He started toward Pedro, but Angelina cracked him on the back of the head with the lid. Magnus fell like a tonne of bricks onto his boss.

"This is crazy," Pedro cried hoarsely. "What are you doing?" He looked down at the two men at his feet. "You're crazy if you think you can get away with it. What the fuck are you doing?"

"Giving us a head start." She dropped the lid onto the men. "Get your stuff, and let's go."

"Go where?" He looked at her in a daze.

"To my place. Come on, get your bag." But when Pedro just stood there staring at her, she ran inside, snatched his bag from backstage, ran back out, and grabbed him by the hand. "Let's go."

They took off through the winding streets of Santorini until they reached her house. She climbed the trellis and went into her room, hauling two suitcases onto the balcony. "Here, catch." She dropped one at a time down to Pedro and then went in for two small bags which went the same way over the balcony. She put her carry-on bag and handbag over her head and grabbed her violin case. After climbing back down, she adjusted her bags. "Let's get to the wharf. We can take a plane to Mykonos for your stuff and then fly to Athens for the airport."

"What?" Pedro was still in shock. "This is crazy."

"Come on." She ushered him down to the wharf where the family seaplane was and got the pilot to kick start it into life. "Mykonos and step on it." She crammed her bags and cases into the small plane, and fifteen minutes later they landed in Mykonos. She hurried Pedro to his home, and he quietly went in and got his case and bag. Leaving a quick note for his parents on his mother's bedside table, he kissed her on the cheek and left as quietly as he'd come.

They raced back to the wharf and added his luggage to Angelina's.

"Athens, and step on it," she told the pilot.

A half hour later they landed at the dock and loaded a taxi. "Thank you," she told the pilot. "Spend the night in Athens on me." She shoved money into the man's hand. "Go and have a drink or three."

He nodded his thanks and grabbed the next taxi.

"What was that for?" Pedro whispered in the back of their cab.

"If he's out of action my father can't find him, or us," she whispered back.

They got to the airport and Angelina paid the driver handsomely. "Take the night off," she said, and he doffed his cap.

Gathering their bags and cases, they rolled in to buy some tickets. There was a wait of thirty minutes on the plane to New York, and they quickly sent their luggage off and went to wait at the boarding gate.

"This is crazy." Pedro pulled her to a quiet place. "They're probably awake by now and calling the cops if they didn't half an hour ago."

Angelina looked at her watch. "Father was probably out for most of the time, and then he would have sent his goons looking for me and you in Santorini first. He would have asked my friends if they'd seen me or knew where I was. He'd be sending someone to check your parents' place, and he probably would have found out that our seaplane has gone. But he won't think we have completely gone unless he realises my luggage is."

"And then he'll know we're here and we have another," he checked his watch, "twenty minutes to go."

"He won't know until it's too late." She dug around in her bag and pulled out a scarf which she wrapped around her hair, completely covering it in a bun. She slid a sleeveless lightweight kimono jacket over her dress and tied it up. "There, that's me." She looked at Pedro. "Change your top and put a cap on."

With a shake of his head, he dug into his carry-on and changed his shirt, much to the delight of the women in the area, and pulled on an old baseball cap.

"Flight 333 from Athens to New York City is now boarding. Flight

333 from Athens to New York City is now boarding."

"That's us, let's go," she said, and dragged him through the boarding gate and onto the plane.

The next fifteen minutes for final boarding and then the ten minutes on the tarmac were hell for Pedro, whose stomach remained clenched the whole time. It wasn't until he was in the air that he relaxed. He was headed for New York City and a crack at international stardom.

TOMAS

The pounding on the door woke Tomas Stephanopoulos from a deep slumber. He heard his father stumble through the house to answer it, only to hear a man burst in demanding to know where Pedro was.

Sliding out of bed, he pulled a t-shirt on and went into the lounge room. "What's going on?" He eyed the big brute of a man standing in their home.

Spiros sighed. "Can you see if Pedro is in his room, Tomas?"

After examining his father's expression for a moment, he turned and walked into Pedro's room. Empty. He went back to his father. "Not here." His eyes moved to their large windmill-shaped wall clock. "But then it's probably too early for him to be here. Why are you looking?"

The man, Magnus, was guarded. "He left a gig early. Mr Poulos wondered if he'd come back here and was okay."

"You couldn't have called?" Tomas asked, intrigued by what was happening.

Magnus nodded. "Forgive my intrusion." He backed out the door, and Spiros shut, locked, and bolted it behind him.

"That was strange." Tomas crossed his arms. "Very strange."

"Not really." Jenny emerged from the bedroom. "Especially since…" Her hand flew to her mouth and she sobbed.

Tomas saw the letter in her hand and took it when she held it out. "Dear Mama and Papa, something bad has happened and I must leave. I'm okay and will call when I can. I love you both, Pedro."

"What?" Spiros thundered. "Another son has left us. What *is it* with these two boys? The eldest and the youngest have both gotten themselves into trouble and left instead of staying and sorting it out. What did I raise? Criminals? They should be ashamed of themselves." He slumped onto the couch. "They should be ashamed."

Tomas looked from his father to his mother, who sat beside her husband, to the letter. It wasn't possible. Just not possible. First Carlos, then Pedro. What the hell was happening for his brothers to be leaving so suddenly? Why hadn't they heard him come home? Why hadn't he woken them and said something? He wondered what the man at the door was telling his boss. That Pedro wasn't there? Why had he left work early? He never leaves early. Wasn't it a birthday party for the boss's daughter? So what happened for Pedro to take off before the job was done? He re-read the note. *Something bad has happened.* What could that be? What could it mean? With both Carlos and Pedro in trouble, it was time someone found out.

*****

Tomas went to work later that morning at the Mykonos Desert Resort, the same resort Carlos had worked. He was the personal trainer in the hotel gym and started at nine every morning, much to the women's delight, as many were also clients of Carlos.

"Oh, my dear." Bette Olander held out her bejewelled seventy-year-old hands to him. "I have heard the terrible news that your other brother has left."

Jesus, news travelled fast on the Greek grapevine.

"How did you hear that, my dear Bette?" Tomas took her hands and air-kissed both cheeks. "*We* only just found out early this morning."

"Well…" She glanced around to see if anyone else was watching. "I heard it from Bertha, who heard it from Willow, who swears she overheard two police officers talking about a seaplane that had disappeared without booking a flight plan, and that the DJ from

Santorini had disappeared with the boss's daughter. Well…" She stepped closer to him. "I remember you telling me about your brothers and what they do, and I put two and two together. Especially since Carlos had already gone. I'm so sorry."

Tomas breathed in. "So am I. Now, do you want your workout session?"

She looked surprised. "You don't want to talk about it?"

Shaking his head, he said, "Not today, Bette. Let's get you onto the bike." He guided her over to the exercise bike and started her off. "Five minutes and then we move on. Gotta get you warmed up."

She mounted the bike in her deluxe velvet workout tracksuit, with the bejewelled collar to match her bejewelled hands, ears and wrists. Bette Olander never did anything half-assed. Why would she when she had millions to her name and clothed herself in the best those millions could buy? Jewels adorned her at all times. Her feet were swathed in jewelled kitten heels, and anything she wore had some sort of shiny, sparkly ornament on it.

At seventy, she'd had her share of rich husbands who provided her with rich homes and anything else their money could buy. Now, in her twilight years, she was spending it how she liked, when she liked, and on whom she liked, and she liked Tomas Stephanopoulos very much.

Although, she thought he leant more to the male side of things, she wasn't in it for sex. She'd given up on *that* back in her fifties. No, she liked Tomas because he made her feel special, wanted, and like a young girl again. Besides, she'd already had one closeted gay husband and wasn't after another one. No, Tomas was simply a young man who made her feel alive. And she recommended him to all of her friends, telling all of those rich snobby Miami women who either had no husbands or no sex lives with their husbands to come down to Mykonos and spend the summer with Tomas. He would get them into the best shape of their lives.

She studied him as she cycled. Five eleven-ish, jet-black hair, dark brown eyes, in the best condition a man could be in. Abs that you could eat food off, arms that could carry you, and legs that could wrap around you. Yes, he was a fine specimen of a man, regardless of which way he turned.

Bertha finally made it through the door dressed from top to bottom in white spandex that showed off the figure she'd worked so hard for. "So sorry I'm late, dear Tomas, I was having a massage from that new man they've hired to replace your brother. He's okay, but not as good-looking." At fifty-nine, Bertha St John was twice widowed and twice engaged. This time it was to a twenty-five-year-old stud she'd picked up in Miami the year before. With the plastic surgery she'd had to look younger, she looked forty, and he'd been the trainer she'd gone to when she wanted to lose weight and tighten up. And she tightened up all right. He tightened her up in ways she'd never known and promptly suggested they get married. Now she was waiting until her sixtieth to do so.

"That's okay, Bertha." Tomas air kissed her. "You can warm up on the bike. Bette, time to change." He escorted Bette to the stretching machine, and Bertha took her place.

"How are you, dear, with your brother being gone?" Bertha asked, patting her dyed brown bun into place.

Tomas sighed. It had been this way when Carlos had left, and now they were reliving it with Pedro. "We're fine. Obviously, they thought it was time for them to leave for bigger pastures than the Greek Islands. They have their things." He shrugged. "Whatever they need to do, they're doing it."

"I'm finally here." Willow Bertran floated through the door. "Oh, Tomas." She came over to him. "I am *so* sorry about your brother. The police are involved, and now that nightclub owner wants to press charges against poor Pedro." Her blue-green bejewelled kaftan settled around her. "I'm so sorry."

Tomas frowned. "What do you mean, the police are involved? What charges?"

"Oh, my dear." She took his hand. "Do you not know?" She looked over at Bette and Bertha. "Have none of you heard?" They shook their heads and stopped exercising. "Well…" Willow settled in for a long chat. "It seems that Pedro was DJing at the going away party Andros

Poulos was having for his daughter, Angelina. She's going to Juilliard in New York, you know." She fluttered her lashes. "Oh, I love New York, it's so lovely, especially in the fall."

"Get on with it, Willow," Bertha told her.

"Oh." Willow fluttered. "Well, it seems that sometime during the party Pedro and Angelina were caught in the alley and Poulos demanded they stop but Pedro hit him over the head and then hit the bodyguard over the head, and they have both left the island for the mainland." She gasped for breath.

"They're in Athens?" Tomas muttered, thinking about the new information.

"Doesn't mean they're *still* in Athens," Willow said. "But at least you know they're not here anymore."

Tomas sighed; a deep guttural sigh that filled him as he breathed in and then left him on the exhale. "At least we know something. But what are the charges?"

"Assault on Poulos and the bodyguard, rape and kidnap," Willow said.

Tomas's frown deepened. "Rape and kidnap? Who'd he rape and kidnap? The daughter? Angelina? How old is she anyway?"

Willow touched a finger to her lip. "Eighteen, I think."

"Well, that's hardly rape and he..." His voice trailed off as he remembered the red marks on his brother's back that morning in the bathroom. He'd asked if she was legal. Pedro had said he'd hoped so. Shit! "Do they know for a fact Pedro kidnapped her?"

"Well..." Willow's gaze wandered off so she was looking at the ceiling. "Not really."

"What do you mean, *not really*?" he asked.

"Well," she repeated. "They're taking Poulos's story as gospel."

"So, he could be lying to get my brother into trouble?" Tomas sighed once more and scratched his head. "What is it with my brothers getting into trouble? What is with these people wanting to blame my brothers..." He wandered over to the floor-to-ceiling windows and gazed out over the ocean. "What the hell is going on?"

"Tomas, darling," Willow called. "Are we getting on with our session?"

He heaved another sigh and turned around to see other guests had come in for their morning workout. "Of course, of course, let's get to work."

*****

Tomas hit up the resort's beach bar at lunchtime. "Hey, Antonio."

"Hey, man, haven't seen you for a while." Antonio was shaking a martini for a guest. "Here you go, ma'am." He slid it toward her then glanced at Tomas. "What can I get you?"

"A juice, and news on my family."

Antonio stopped what he was doing to stare at Tomas. "Yeah, I heard about Pedro. Disappeared like Carlos, huh?"

Tomas raised his brows and knocked back the drink Antonio gave him. "Seems so. What have you heard?"

Antonio threw a smile at a guest and took another order. "That he got into it with a club owner on Santorini, attacked him, and now there are charges."

Tomas sighed. He'd been doing a lot of that lately. "Yeah." He watched Antonio flirt with the girl. "That's what I heard. But what I don't get is this only happened in the early hours of this morning, yet everyone knows more than the family does. And besides which…" He stopped while Antonio served another customer. "How come the cops haven't knocked on our door yet?" He eyed off the good-looking, lightly tanned, dark-haired guy a few paces away. They guy eyed him back and smiled. Tomas blanched and looked away.

"You don't know they haven't. They could be at your place right now."

Tomas thought about it. "Yeah. Jesus, I won't know anything more until I get home."

Antonio handed a margarita to a customer. "Any news on Carlos?"

Tomas shook his head. "Nothing. We've been told the charges have been dropped, but no letter, no call, nothing." He glanced over at the hot stud that was still standing nearby. Teeny tiny red swim briefs held a huge package together. A soft gathering of chest hair spread across lean, tanned muscles and down into the briefs. He saw the man looking with a cocked brow and even cockier grin and reddened. "I gotta go. Let me know if you hear anything," he told Antonio and walked toward the hotel.

*****

When Tomas arrived home at five-thirty, he found his mother crying over the hot meal she was making. "Mama." He moved to her side and held her in his arms. "Mama."

"Oh, Tomas, what are we going to do?" she sobbed.

"About what? Tell me what's happened." He stroked her hair as he gently swivelled his body left to right in a semicircle, like rocking a baby to soothe and calm.

"The police," Jenny cried into his chest. "They were here today asking about Pedro. But I didn't tell them anything. What *could* I tell them? That my son had disappeared?" She sniffled.

"Did they hurt you?" He pulled back to look into his mother's eyes. "Did they touch you, or hurt you, or even," he looked around, "wreck the place looking for him?"

She shook her head. "No. They checked his room, looked in the others, asked me a bunch of questions. But no, they didn't touch me, or hit me."

"Who? Who didn't touch you, or hit you?" Spiros walked into the kitchen. "Who?"

"The police were here asking about Pedro," Tomas told him, seeing a mirror image of himself.

Spiros sighed and ran a hand through his thick black hair. "They were at the shop today too. Asked a bunch of questions. Stupid bloody cops." He saw his wife's tear-stained face and gently pulled her into his arms. "There, there, we'll get through this. I don't know how, but we will." He looked at Tomas. "Have *you* got any idea what your idiot brothers have done, or are up to?"

"Why would I?" Tomas shook his head. "But it seems the whole island has heard more than we have."

"How could they do this?" Spiros hissed. "To their mother. We did not raise them that way."

"This may not have anything to do with what they did," Tomas said. "*We know* they'd never hurt women, *we know* they'd never shoot anyone, or assault anyone. So maybe they were just in the wrong place at the wrong time."

"Rubbish," Spiros said. "My boys have gotten themselves into something *they* can get themselves out of."

PEDRO

Just two days later, on a sunny New York Friday, Pedro stepped out of the brownstone in Gramercy and stood on the street. He breathed deeply; still not believing he was in New York. Life had been a whirlwind since leaving Greece, and they'd hidden with Maggie, a friend of Angelina's, who was going to Juilliard as well.

Her parents were away for the rest of the summer, and she had the place to herself. They had gone there straight from the airport, and with one look at Pedro, Maggie was saying yes to everything. Yes, to them hiding out there. Yes, to not telling Angelina's father she had seen them. Yes, to anything Pedro asked for, and he'd asked for a map of the city and raided the phone book for a list of all the clubs. He wanted to get started job hunting right away, but Angelina had other ideas.

"Shouldn't we lie low for a while?" Angelina had purred in his ear the night before. "My father will be after us."

"You've changed your tune from two days ago," he'd said. "But no. I'm here. I want to work, it's what I love."

"Well, you're what I love," she'd murmured and slid her mouth around him.

Now he was ready to hit the streets for a job. Having heard about a hot new club that would be opening soon, he decided to start there and set out for 254 West and 54th Streets, finding the building work still going on outside. He stopped a worker and asked where he could find the owner or manager and was directed inside. Pedro walked into a spacious club with disco dance floor, stage and DJ booth, tables, and groups of people running around testing everything.

"I want the lights to go there, there and there," a man was yelling.

"Excuse me, I want to audition for the DJ position," Pedro said to him.

"It's already taken." The man glanced at him and did a double take. He eagerly eyed the hot-looking guy in front of him, but the clothes turned him off. "Position's already filled, kid." He turned away.

Pedro scoured the room, saw some people looking at him, and did what he did best. He dropped his bag and ripped his shirt off. "How 'bout now?"

The man looked back and didn't stop looking at the beautiful Greek god before him. The jet-black hair and bright blue eyes would be an attraction and so would that body. "What job did you say you wanted?"

"DJ. I've been DJing in the Greek Islands for two years."

The man eagerly nodded. "It looks like it. Get up on stage and show us what you got." He nodded to the DJ booth.

Pedro smiled his charming smile. "Give me a minute to pick something out." He walked past his admirers, dropped his bag and shirt beside the booth, picked a couple of records and donned the headphones. Within seconds he was mixing the tracks, scratching the sounds, and making sweet music to the crowd of onlookers. He danced, he sang, he moved to the music and went on until the songs were done. He removed the headphones. "I get the job?" he called down to the guy.

"Yep, kid." The man broke into applause, and the rest of the room followed. "You get the job."

Pedro collected his things, went over to the man and shook his hand. "Knew you couldn't resist me."

The man raised a brow. "With a body like that *no one* will be able to resist you. Go and see Stew about the payroll and get yourself signed up. You'll get a thousand a week."

"A bit of a downgrade from my last job, but I'll cope with it," Pedro joked.

"What were you earning on your last job?" The man wondered if he fucked women for money. Or men. *Wouldn't mind trying that out myself,* he thought.

"A thousand a night."

The man eyed the smooth, creamy skin and hair-free chest. "You're definitely worth a thousand a night." *Oh yes,* he thought, *I'd pay that for five minutes with you.* "Stew," he yelled, and a man came scurrying over. "Get this kid on the payroll for a thousand a night. He's our new DJ."

Stew eyed Pedro. "Sure, come with me."

Pedro shook the man's hand. "I didn't catch your name," he said.

"Eddie. Eddie Monteif."

"Well, thanks for the opportunity, Eddie, I won't let you down."

"Oh, I know you won't, kid. I know you won't."

Pedro started following Stew, but stopped and turned around. "What's the name of the place going to be so I know where to tell my friends to go?"

"Studio 69, kid. *Studio 69."*

TOMAS

On Saturday, Tomas spent the weekend on Santorini to see if he could find out what was going on. He walked the island by day and went to SantorPoulos at night. Striding into the club, he saw a new DJ on stage, but the place was only half full. Most of the crowd was standing around drinking or talking. Making his way over to the bar he ordered a beer. "I thought this place was jumping? A friend of mine told me it was the place to be on Santorini."

Mikos, the bartender, grimaced. "It used to be, but the reason the tourists came here left."

"What do you mean?" Tomas frowned. "Was there food poisoning or something?"

Mikos laughed. "Nah, man. The DJ flipped his lid and assaulted the boss out back in the alley." He flicked his head in the direction. "Took off with the boss's daughter, apparently. No one knows where they've gone." He went to serve another customer.

Tomas looked around as he sipped his beer. The place was a tourist haven for skimpily clad women and hot men in shirts and shorts. The DJ was good, but not his brother.

"You want anything to eat?"

Tomas turned around to see Mikos. "No, thanks. This is fine for now." He lifted his beer slightly. "So, what's this new DJ like then?"

"He's all right." Mikos poured a beer. "Not as good-looking as the last one, not as hot as the last one, and not as good on the decks as the last one.”

“He was that good, huh.” Tomas hid a grin.

“Yeah,” Mikos said. “He was *that* good *and* better.”

Tomas stayed for another beer. The club, and club scenes in general, were not his thing, but Pedro’s, so the loud music was getting to him. Seeing no one he knew, he left and waited outside for a while, surprised to see Andros Poulos leaving by a side exit.

“I want Athens searched,” he was saying as he buttoned up his blazer. “Clearly they were taken to the mainland, and clearly they were going for the long haul with the amount of luggage there was. In the meantime, I’m going to get a private investigator to check into flights out of the country to see if they took off overseas. I want you to get the information I want. Regardless of how you get it.” He stepped into the back seat of his car.

“Yes, Mr Poulos.” The burly bodyguard shut the door and walked around to the front, getting behind the wheel.

So, that’s *Andros Poulos,* Thomas thought, trying to see through the dark night and club lights, but he couldn’t get a good look. He wandered over to the exit to see the car heading straight down the road and up the hill. “How am I going to get any information about what’s going on?” he muttered.

“Had enough already?”

Tomas spun around. “Huh?”

Mikos lit a cigarette. “Of the club? Had enough of the club already?”

Tomas gave a small laugh. “Yeah, clubs aren’t really my sort of thing.” He shrugged and tried to get more information. “My friend insisted I come to see the DJ, but he’s not here so, not much point me staying. I think my friend will be disappointed that he’s gone. She really talked him up and said how packed the place was.”

“Yeah.” Mikos took a long drag. “It was, but he bolted Thursday morning, and when everyone finds out he’s not working, they leave.”

“Thursday? You mean two days ago?” Tomas asked innocently.

“Yeah man,” Mikos said. “Two freakin’ days. He’s gone for two freakin’ days and the tourists are down by half. Mr Poulos ain’t happy.”

“No. I guess he wouldn’t be,” Tomas agreed. “This DJ must have been something for you to lose half your patronage in two days."

"Yeah," Mikos said, drawing back. "He was something. Pedro Stephanopoulos. Hot stud. Drew the women and men in every night he was here. The place was packed to the rafters, and more were lined up outside to get in, but never could because no one ever left the club until he left the stage. Ten hours he was on stage. The women loved him."

"Wow. Pity I missed him," Tomas said, leaning against a stone wall. In actual fact, he had seen Pedro the year before work a crowd for the same amount of time and marvelled at his stamina and extreme talent. He was proud of him for achieving his dreams of being a DJ and being in the music industry. He went in harder. "So, if he's taken off with the boss's daughter like all the rumours are saying, that must make things awkward."

Mikos shrugged nonchalantly. "The boss is like a bear with a sore paw, yelling at everyone. Fired two kitchen staff yesterday, but his assistant had to hire two more just to keep the food going. Poulos doesn't care; he's got bigger things to worry about than his club."

"Must have cared about being assaulted by the guy that took off with his daughter? Was she underage; is that why he's pissed?"

Mikos flicked his cigarette to the ground where he stepped on it and shook his head. "She's eighteen, old enough to go off with a guy if she wanted. She was going to some big school overseas, so he had no problem with that."

"Was the assault bad?" Tomas asked. "He seemed okay when he left just now."

"Not too bad." Mikos opened the side door. "Took a trash can lid to the back of the head. So did the bodyguard. No one knew they were out there for about two hours. But not my business. You coming back in?" He held the door open.

Tomas put up a hand. "No, thanks. I think I'll get going. Let my friend know he's not here anymore."

"Suit yourself." Mikos let the door close on its own.

Well, that's interesting, Tomas thought. *But if Pedro* did *assault him, one, why did he do it, and two, why has he left the country?* He took the path back along the beach wondering what Andros was up to. *What in the hell is going on? Two brothers within weeks of each other and now I'm here on my own. What about me? What do I do now? What about mama? Did they care what she thought, or did they think our parents would be better off without them and their troubles sticking around? And papa? He was all but ready to give up and disinherit them. How could he? He raised us better than what he thinks they've done. It's as if he doesn't care if they've even done it. The cops on our doorstep are enough to make him believe they have, and that isn't fair.*

He reached his hotel and went up to his room. Opening the balcony doors, he stood staring at the distant lights of the islands and the way they mingled with the millions of stars in the sky that enveloped them *and him* with their sheer power. It was an awesome sight you couldn't get anywhere else.

He sighed. "Carlos, Pedro, where are you? Where the *hell* are you?"

*****

Sunday morning, Tomas walked around Santorini asking people about Andros and whether they knew anything about the assault on Thursday morning. No one did so he headed home, tired, dejected, and annoyed.

Maybe I should just let them go? Whatever has happened they're now off living their own lives. At least I hope they are... "Oh, sorry." He reached out to the person he'd bumped into. "Hey..."

"Hey..."

"I...sorry...I...did you drop anything." Tomas became flustered as he looked around.

"No, got everything," the man said and stepped out of the way as passengers from the ferry jostled them aside.

Tomas moved with him. "I, uh, saw you the other day, didn't I?"

"At the beach bar." The man nodded.

Tomas felt the flutter; the weird, unusual flutter in his stomach. "Yeah." He stared at the six foot hunk before him. "Yeah."

The hunk smiled. "Do you work at the resort?"

"Yeah," Tomas said for the third time. "I'm the personal trainer in the gym."

"Oh." The man cocked an interested brow. "I've been wondering if I should get into the gym while on holiday."

"Are you staying at the resort?" Tomas took a step closer.

"I am." The man took a step closer.

"Maybe you should come in for a session."

"Maybe I should."

Tomas stared.

The man stared.

"I uh." Tomas took another step. "I'm back at work tomorrow."

"Do you do private sessions?" The man removed his sunglasses.

Tomas drowned in aqua blue eyes such as he'd never seen. Bluer and more aqua than the ocean surrounding them. He breathed in. "Um, yeah, I do, at night."

"I'll have to book you in then." He took a step closer and ended up toe to toe with Tomas.

Tomas swallowed, his throat clenched, his stomach clenched and it was freaking him out. "Please do," he finally managed.

*****

"Tomas, darling," Bette said Monday morning. "Have you thought of leaving the nest?" She was straddling the bike in the resort gym.

"Have never thought about it." He helped Bertha with her weight exercises.

"Now that Carlos and Pedro are gone, what will you do?" she continued.

Tomas moved on to Willow who was standing on the vibrating belt machine.

Willow was groaning in pleasure, hanging onto the machine head as if it was a man's as he pleasured her with his tongue. "Oh, God, this is good. Oh, God."

"Don't overdo it," Tomas told her before answering Bette. "I don't know what I'll do. Even though this is my home, so is Australia. Maybe I'll have to reconsider my options now."

"You're still young," Bertha added to the conversation. "You could travel and see the world before settling down with a young lady."

"Or an older one." Willow sighed as she stepped off the machine. "Oh, God that was so good."

"Or if you aren't interested in *those* things," Bette slyly said. "Someone *else* to settle down with."

Tomas flashed her a look. "And what do you mean by that?"

Bette, for all her years, didn't back down. "Tomas, darling, *we know*."

"Know what?" He glanced around the gym to see who was watching or listening.

"That you are of the opposite persuasion," she said, getting off the bike and going to his side. "It's okay dear, that's what we love about you; that you're not interested in getting us into bed, or trying to charm us to get our money. You're the kind of young man every older woman wants in her life."

"And what would that be?" He stared down at her, his heart pounding in his chest. He'd never discussed his sexual orientation with anyone. He'd never needed to. He just wasn't interested in dating. The opposite sex or otherwise. He didn't feel sexual toward anyone, so had remained single. He was only twenty-two after all.

"Gay, darling."

Bertha and Willow crowded around him, much to the annoyance of the other women in the gym who wanted some time with him.

"We know you prefer men," Willow whispered. "And that's okay with us."

"Better than okay," Bertha said. "We can be open and honest and not worry about you trying anything."

Tomas became angry, but kept his cool, and removed their hands from his arms. "Thank you for your concern ladies, but my sexuality is no one's business. Please go back to your stations, or move on to the next." He left them and moved onto to another client.

"That went down like a lead balloon," Willow said.

"Maybe he hasn't realised it yet," Bette said. "He *is* still young. He may not have figured it out."

"But the rest of us have?" Bertha asked.

"I had a gay husband," Bette said. "So I saw firsthand what he couldn't quite figure out for himself. He's young, he'll get there."

*****

Tomas took his lunch break in the private gardens of the resort. It backed onto the beach, and staff members were allowed to use it. He sat and contemplated what the ladies had said. He'd never questioned his sexuality, never had reason to as he'd never been attracted to anyone. He just wasn't interested. As his mother said, he'd know when the right person came along. Yet clearly the right person had never come along, not that it mattered, he *was* only twenty-two. Neither Carlos nor Pedro had girlfriends. Carlos did whatever he wanted, but had no one serious, and Pedro had only recently found himself a girl, even if she was the boss's daughter. So why did *he* need to worry?

He thought about the guy he'd run into, twice, and sighed. The revelation worried him. *I'm sitting here thinking about a man and not a woman. Am I gay?*

He stopped thinking, breathing, being.

Am I gay?

Just because you have the tingles for a man doesn't make you gay, he argued with himself.

Yeah, but it's not like I've had the tingles for a woman.

True.

Suddenly the world seemed a heavy burden on his shoulders, and the weight of it on his chest made it want to collapse. Another sigh came from the pit of his stomach. Sighing was something he'd done a lot of since Carlos left. Standing, he breathed deeply and realised there was only one thing to do. Stop worrying about his brothers and start worrying about himself and his own future.

Whatever the hell that was.

*****

"Any word from Carlos or Pedro?" Tomas asked his mother when he got home.

She looked up, teary-eyed, and put the wooden spoon down. She'd been making lamb stew, but didn't have the heart to put into it. "No."

"Oh, Mama. I'm so sorry." He hugged her.

"What for? You haven't done anything." She patted his arm.

Silence.

"No," he finally said. "But I may be about to…"

She looked up with worry and surprise on her face. "What do you mean? What have you done or what are you about to do? Tell me, Tomas!"

"Mama, it's okay," he reassured her. "I haven't done anything. It's just…" He sighed yet again and leant against the kitchen counter. "With Carlos and Pedro gone, where does that leave me?" He shrugged a shoulder. "What do *I* do now?"

"You have your job, don't you love that?" She moved over to her son, sensing he was in crisis.

"I love my job at the resort, but that's just the tourist months. What about when that's over?" He shook his head and lowered his voice. "I don't want to go back to working in papa's shop over the winter. I just don't. I hate it." Tears sprang to his eyes at the thought of betraying his father by not wanting to work in the shop. "What do I do now my brothers have gone? What kind of life do I get to have?"

Jenny felt her son's pain and took him into her arms. "Oh, Tomas, my poor baby." She always knew he was different to his brothers. They were outgoing, he was not. They were boisterous, he was quiet, preferring to go about his business on his own. She had wondered when they would find nice girls and settle down, but each had preferred their lives as they were, deciding that marriage and children could wait. Now two were gone, and Tomas remained.

She stepped back. "Whatever you decide will be up to you. You don't owe your father or me anything. If you don't want to work in the shop anymore, that's fine. If you want to go and live or work somewhere else to pursue your dreams, then go. Don't feel guilty." She stroked his cheek, and he smiled. "If everything that's happened has made you question your part in life then please, *please* do whatever will make you happy."

"Even if that's leaving home?"

She put on a brave face. "Even if that means leaving home. And believe me, I know all about leaving home. I did it for your father, so I can hardly stop my boys from doing it too."

"Didn't you feel guilty when you left Grandma and Grandpa? We certainly didn't get a say in it."

Jenny frowned. "*Of course* I felt guilty leaving my family and taking you boys away from your home, and school, and friends. And for years I fretted that I had made the wrong decision, but you all loved it here so much I never thought any of you would leave." She saddened. "Guess I was wrong."

"Oh, Mama." Tomas hugged her. "We're not boys anymore. For whatever reason Carlos and Pedro left it was clearly necessary. If I leave, it will be my choice."

"Are you thinking of leaving?" Spiros asked from the doorway, having heard snippets of conversation as he'd come in.

Tomas and Jenny looked up in surprise, and Tomas shrugged. "My brothers are gone, so what's keeping me here? Maybe I should go and see the world. Maybe go home to Australia and see my aunts and uncles and cousins." He shrugged again. "I don't know. What I do know is that maybe my time for leaving is coming."

"And what about the shop?"

"What about it?" Tomas asked. "You just hire other people."

Spiros felt his anger rise. "*But it's your legacy.* You're the only one left to work there."

"*No,* Spiros," Jenny told him. "It's *your* legacy. Your father was the reason I packed up my life and my children and moved half way around the world. He left the shop to *you, not* the boys. It's not their legacy, it's *yours* and don't tell them otherwise." She gave him the evil eye that always made him back down. "It's *your* shop, and I won't let you force them into working there if they don't want to. Are we clear?"

He knew better than to argue with his wife; the strong Aussie woman who had left everything behind and sacrificed so much for him. He backed down. He didn't like it, but knew he had to for the sake of his family. What was left of it anyway.

Jenny looked at Tomas. "If you want to go, go. We won't stop you."

Tomas looked from his father's sheepish expression to his mother's determined one and kissed her hand. "But you'll cry a lot won't you?"

"Of course I will. My babies have nearly all left me."

*****

Over the next few days, Tomas did a lot of thinking. Where would he go? What would he do? He hadn't planned to leave, but had a healthy bank balance from all the years of working, doing extra training on the side and under the table. He knew Carlos had made a tonne of money doing extra work and was heading for being a millionaire thanks to all those rich women he screwed for fun. But he wasn't like that. Nope, he wanted to make it without using people to do it. He'd been training, and not much else, and decided to ask the ladies what they thought.

"Oh, I think it's a brilliant idea," Bertha said Thursday morning. "You could come to Miami and train all of the women I know. They'd pay handsomely to be told what to do by someone as gorgeous as you."

"I hadn't considered Miami," Tomas said, helping Bette with her stretches. "Lean a little more to the left," he told her as she bent. "I haven't even picked a place to go. I just know that with my brothers gone it's time to spread my wings."

"If you want somewhere that's similar to the islands then it's really only Miami or L.A. with their beaches and rich people—"

"In need of one on one attention from a hot stud like you," Bertha interrupted.

"And tropical atmosphere," Bette continued. "They might feel like home compared to anywhere else."

"I do have my native Australia to go back to. I have a lot of family there. And bend right," he told Bette.

She bent right. "But Australia is such a tiny little place when America is bursting at the seams with rich women who need to get in shape and want to pay a man to do it for them."

"What about San Francisco?" Willow asked from the floor. She was in the cobra yoga pose and went into downward dog.

"Why San Francisco?" Tomas asked.

"Well, that's where your people are." She bent into upward dog.

Tomas cocked a brow. "*My* people?"

"Don't listen to her," Bette said with a wave of her hand. "She's not all there."

"You know…gays." Willow slid into child's pose.

"As I said," Bette went on. "Don't listen to her. Come to Miami."

Tomas was frowning. "My sexuality, whatever it may be, is no one's concern."

"Of course not, dear," Bertha said. "Shut up, Willow. Come to Miami. Between the three of us, we can give you a place to stay, get you clients, and get you up and running in no time."

"That's right." Bette bent forward from the waist and touched the floor. "Between the three of us, we can get you a few hundred clients right away. And I have a huge ballroom that's not being used if you want to hold classes." She rolled into a standing position. "We could buy equipment if you need it, and when you're able to move into your own space, we'll help you set up your own gym. What do you say?"

Bertha and Willow gathered by her side.

"Oh, yes," Bertha said. "Maybe Luiz could help you out. He's a trainer."

Tomas put his hands up to stop them. "Ladies, this is all very nice and kind of you, but I haven't even decided what I'm doing, or where I'm going."

"Doesn't matter," Bette said. "The choice will be Miami. Even if we have to pack you up and take you home with us."

"Absolutely," Bertha and Willow agreed.

Tomas laughed. It had been a while since he'd done that. Laugh. "Thank you for your kindness and generosity. I will definitely think about it. Now, let's get you back to exercising."

*****

That night, Tomas had his first client of the evening. The guest had booked a two hour session of exercise and sauna. He was organising the towels and water bottles when his client walked in.

"Am I late?"

Tomas looked up to see the man from the bar and ferry. The aqua eyes were bright across the room. The tanned torso strained through the tight tank top, and his manhood strained to be released from his incredibly snug and tight exercise shorts.

The man closed and locked the door. "Don't want anyone disturbing us." He walked over to Tomas. "Hey…"

Tomas smiled despite himself and the butterflies wreaking havoc in his stomach. "Hey."

Silence.

"You booked a session…" Tomas finally said.

"Yeah. It was the only time I could get in. I have you for two hours."

Tomas blinked. "Me…" he breathed. "You have me…?" He swallowed.

"Yeah," the man breathed back. "I have you." He watched Tomas trying to get a hold of himself. "Have you even *been* with a man?" he asked softly.

Tomas breathed…and shuddered. Was a man who he wanted to be with? "No…"

"Well, I can do without the workout, so how about we get straight to the sauna?" He reached out, his fingers entwining with Tomas's as he led him to the steam room.

"I…ah…" Tomas backed up against the door. "Wait, what…?"

"Shh," the man said, putting a light finger to Tomas's lips. "We'll go slowly." He poured water on the rocks and steam filled the black tiled room.

Sweat dripped from Tomas's forehead as he watched the man slowly remove his top…up his body…over his head…onto the floor…oh, God, how he wanted the masculine…manly…male…flesh before him.

Fingers hooked into those teeny tiny shorts, and he sensually pushed them down revealing a manhood that matched the size of his own. The shorts slid to the floor. "Come." He held out a hand to Tomas, who had no control over his brain, taking his hand and guiding him to the wall near the rock box. His hands went under Tomas's tank to slide it over his head. It fell beside his own. His hands slid into his shorts and lowered them slowly, his fingers caressing Tomas's thigh muscles. The shorts fell.

"Wait...I..." Tomas breathed and grabbed the stud's hands. His insides started to freak out. What the hell was he doing? "I...I... don't..."

"You've never been with a man."

Tomas blushed, embarrassed, what for, he didn't know. "I've never been with anyone," he gasped, lightheaded and dizzy with the first stages of lust. "I just haven't found...anyone."

"There's a first time for everything," the man said. "I'll go slowly. Nothing heavy, no expectations, let me teach you. Let me *show* you..." He moved closer, nuzzling Tomas's cheek. His tongue darted out to taste him, to lick his earlobe, taste his neck. His lips moved seductively in the hollow at the back of the jaw under the ear, and Tomas groaned.

The man slid his fingers up Tomas's arms and across his broad chest. His lips made their way down his neck to his collarbone and drank the sweat that pooled there.

Tomas felt his body weaken and sag against the wall. God, he had never felt these things before, for man or woman, so why now, why with this one, why did it feel so damn good...why was he turned on? Why was he falling? Oh, God...how he was falling...

His cock was hard, the bare naked feelings catapulting themselves around his insides were new, and exciting, and daring, and he wanted all of them. He swallowed as the man's tongue, and lips and fingers made their way down to his right nipple, sucking and tasting and teasing. "Oh, God," barely came out of his mouth mixing with the whirling steam, making him light-headed in such an enclosed space.

The man greedily sucked on the nipple, his mouth moving across the hair smattered across Tomas's chest. The sweat clung, nourishing him to go on. His mouth and hands and lips moved down. Hands settled on hips, tongue settled in his navel, mouth settled in the V of his lower body. Kneeling between Tomas's legs, his fingers went into his underpants, pulled them over his erection, and down to his ankles.

"Oh," Tomas breathed in the steam. "Oh." His head went back against the wall, and he felt the man take him whole. "Oh, God…oh, God." All breath left him, and he bowed, his head falling forward to see the man between his legs capturing all of him.

The man's hands moved their way up his inner thighs, massaging, manipulating until they found what they were looking for; the precious globes either side of Tomas's manhood that had disappeared into his mouth.

Tomas slid his hands through the stud's hair and hung on. Guiding him, holding him, keeping him there, and knowing what to do without having ever done it before. It was natural and rhythmic and right. His head went back, his body arched, and he fed the man exactly what he wanted to give him.

Himself.

The man did exactly as he wanted.

Sucked.

And Tomas let him.

The twelve inches that were Tomas Giorgio Stephanopoulos was long, strong and gloriously hard and, oh, so fucking ripe for the picking.

Or sucking.

Tomas's testicles were a handful, matching the size of the penis in every way. The man held them, handled them, squeezed them to make him orgasm. He sucked more, taking it, swallowing it, making Tomas Stephanopoulos his for the taking.

Tomas arched against the wall as he came in the man's mouth. Screwing up his face at the pleasurable explosion, screwing up his hands in the man's hair to hang on and not let him go…he allowed himself a release he'd never experienced before.

He collapsed against the wall, breathing hard as the man left a trail of kisses up his penis to his torso to his neck to his lips. They kissed. Tomas had never felt the pleasure of a tongue in his mouth, let alone a man's, and he liked it. The kissing was urgent, passionate, and the man's tongue invaded, taking all of him.

The steam rose, swirled, surrounded them as they touched. The man guided Tomas's hands to him, wrapped them around him, guided him to explore. He placed his forehead against Tomas's, and they both looked down between them. Their hands greedily held and rubbed and felt. He rubbed his own against his lover's and two cocks entwined, two balls became four, and two men rubbed against each other.

Tomas had never held a man, never touched what was the same as his. The hardness, the roughness, the feel and weight of another man in his hands was exhilarating, arousing, and dangerously tempting. Dangerously tempting him to do things he had never thought of doing before. Yet he wanted to do them again and keep on doing them.

The steam rose, swirled, surrounded them as the man moved away, added more water to the rocks, and led Tomas to the bench. He laid him down and lay next to him. They kissed, explored and touched every inch of each other until the man gently rolled Tomas onto his back and rolled on top of him.

Tomas responded. Opening himself, wrapping his legs around the man. He hitched his legs up and around his waist, and without a second thought, the man entered. Tomas cringed for a moment. "Ah."

"Relax," the man soothed. "Just relax."

Tomas relaxed and felt the man rock back and forth. The rhythm, the steam, the headiness was all too much. "Oh, God," he groaned.

The man's mouth covered his, his tongue did as much damage as his penis on Tomas's nerves, sending him over the edge as the man's hand dipped down between them to take hold of the man beneath him.

They both climaxed.

They both relaxed.

The man stroked Tomas's side. He was leaning up on his elbow, his face beside his lover's. "You're gorgeous," he said. "Manly, beautiful, amazing." His fingers blazed up and down Tomas's side. "Muscular, sculptured…perfect."

Tomas felt alive. Here he was lying underneath a man, and he'd never felt so calm, so at peace. A soft smile spread across his lips. "It's genetics."

"And genetics gave you a twelve inch cock?" The man's fingers lightly swept over it, and it moved.

"More than likely." Tomas moved his fingers over his lover's. They joined. "You have a fairly healthy percentage yourself."

The man grinned. "So I've been told."

Tomas took a deep breath and slowly let it out. What a place for his first time to be in. A steam room of all places, in the resort gym. "Shit! What time is it?" He tried to check his watch, but it was fogged over. "Your two hours are probably up."

"Relax. If the next customer complains just tell them you had a guest who needed special attention." He pulled Tomas back and kissed him.

Tomas responded and got lost once again in his new lover. Finally, though, he pulled away. "We really need to go. I have other clients." Reluctantly he sat up and grabbed a towel, wrapping it around his waist. "We'd better go." Picking up his clothes as the man grabbed his own towel, he unlocked the door. Walking into the hallway, he saw the clock read ten-ten. "Shit! Ten minutes late for my next client and I need a shower."

He heard a jangle of keys in the gym door and froze, and within seconds the manager walked in.

"I'm sure there is a reasonable explanation for him running late." He looked up and saw Tomas wrapped in a towel. "Ah, there you are, you're running late." He saw the man come out beside him wrapped in a towel as well. "I see you were in the sauna so obviously lost track of time. Try not to next time."

The man spoke up. "Sorry I kept him. I had a strenuous workout, and he helped my muscles recover in the steam room. We didn't realise what the time was. Do we have time for a shower?"

"I know that voice." Bertha stuck her head around the door. "Luiz, there you are. I've been looking everywhere for you. You should have told me you were coming for a workout, I would have joined you."

Tomas stood horrified. Not only was his manager, his boss, standing before him, but he and his new lover were standing in nothing but towels, dripping wet and holding their clothes. And now Bertha had stuck her head around the door.

"Luiz?" he asked, uncertainly, gazing at the muscle man beside him that he'd just given himself to.

"Yes. Hello, Tomas darling. Remember I mentioned my fitness trainer fiancé? Well, it's Luiz. Luiz, I see you've met Tomas, what a hunk, huh? Isn't he everything I said he was?"

The pit of Tomas's stomach fell to the floor.

"Yes," Luiz purred, laying a hand on Tomas's shoulder. "*Everything* and then some."

All Tomas wanted to do as he looked from Bertha's blank expression to Luiz's smirk was vomit.

*****

Tomas called in sick Friday morning and spent the day in bed. He was absolutely gutted that the man he had been with was his client's fiancé. How he'd managed to get through the rest of the night was still a blur, with two more clients before midnight, and he vaguely remembered stumbling home and crawling into bed where he now lay wanting to vomit.

His stomach muscles were clenched, his arms were wrapped around him, his legs curled up under him. He was in the foetal position.

"Tomas." Jenny knocked on the door. "Are you all right, sweetie?"

God, the shame. He buried his face into his pillow and tried not to sob. His first encounter with anyone had turned into his worst nightmare.

Jenny opened the door and saw him curled up which made her worry even more. Closing the door, she sat beside him. "I know something is wrong." She laid her hand on his arm. "You've never had a day off in your life."

He couldn't hold it in any longer. A sob escaped from his throat, and the floodgates opened. His body shuddered with shame, regret and pain.

"Oh, my baby." Jenny lay beside him stroking his hair, holding him close. "What is it? What's happened? Oh, my baby boy." She held him until he was finished. "Tell me what's wrong."

After a few moments, he shifted his head. His face had been buried the whole time, and now he peered out with one eye. "I can't."

"Why not?" She stroked his hair.

Silence.

"Because I'm too ashamed." He closed his eye and turned his head back to the pillow.

"Whatever it is it can't be that bad."

"It is."

"Please tell me."

With a heavy sigh, he turned his face enough to say, "I had sex last night."

Jenny's brows rose. It wasn't the first time she'd had to deal with sons having sex, but it was the first time for Tomas. "Were you safe?"

Another sigh. "I think so."

Her brows rose higher. "What *do you mean, you think so*? Did you *not* wear protection?"

"*I* didn't."

"So, you left it up to her? Women can't wear…oh…" She softened. "Tomas."

He sobbed. "I'm sorry."

"For what?"

"Being a disappointment."

Her heart broke. "Aw, sweetie, you're not a disappointment. You're only twenty-two, you're still discovering who you are and what you want to be and do." She hugged him tightly. "I always wondered why you were so quiet compared to your brothers, and then I realised you're exactly like your father. He keeps a lot of stuff in too, but it's not a *bad* thing." She kissed his cheek. "Neither is being different to others…if it's not women you're into…"

"Mama." He shifted uncomfortably.

"No, Tomas. There's nothing to be ashamed of. If you have feelings for a boy or man, then you should try to understand why. Besides, would you rather talk to your father about this?"

His head shot around to look at her. "God, no."

She smiled softly and lay back against the headboard. "I can't say I'm not disappointed, but…" Her head moved up and down as she thought, "I will support you if you want to explore…things…" She blushed. "Your sexuality with men."

His legs uncramped themselves and he spread out as he turned to her. "Really?"

Her smile widened. "Really."

His eyes closed for a moment. "Even if I stuff up royally?"

"What happened?"

He sighed and stared at the corner of the ceiling. "I saw…a man… on the beach the other day and then again coming off the ferry on Sunday. He's…" He softened. "Gorgeous. Aqua eyes I drown in…" His lips turned up at the corners. "He came into the gym last night. He'd booked a two hour session just to see me, and he took me into the sauna…" He blushed. "It was my first experience."

"And…"

The shame came back. "And when our time was up I was running late, and the manager unlocked the door and came in."

"Were you dressed?" Jenny prayed that he had been.

"Ah…" Tomas blushed deeper. "We had towels around us."

"Well, at least that's something."

"Yes, but…" Tomas made a face. "Then Bertha, one of my clients, popped her head through the doorway and that's when it all hit the fan."

"What did?"

"Bertha recognised the man I'd just been with as her fiancé Luiz," rushed out of his mouth. "Oh, God, I'm so stupid." He swung his legs around and sat on the side of the bed then shifted, as the ache of newly used muscles made him a tad uncomfortable. "The first time I'm with someone, and I don't bother getting his name or even finding out if he's attached."

"And why not? We raised the three of you better than that."

"And yet Pedro did the same thing, and Carlos beds women by the truckload without getting their names," Tomas scoffed. "I'm not the only one making stupid mistakes."

"No, you're not. But I thought *you'd* be more sensible."

His head dropped into his hands. "Ugh, so did I."

"So, what do you do now?" They had raised their sons to think for themselves, to find their own way out of the problems that were going to arise in their life. She prayed that Carlos and Pedro were doing that right now.

"I don't know," he moaned. "I had sex with an engaged man. As if having sex with a man isn't bad enough, he's engaged."

"Don't feel ashamed about the fact he's a guy. The problem is he's attached, and you didn't find out beforehand. You should talk to him, but that's your choice. You need to think long and hard about what you want with the person you want to be with. Regardless of *who* it is. If this was a mistake, admit it, own it, and move on. If you have real feelings for him, admit them, own them, and deal with the consequences. The choice is yours. I can't tell you what to do."

With another sigh, he straightened. "No. Only I can. Thanks, Mama." He leant over and kissed her on the cheek.

"Why don't you have a shower and I'll get you something to eat." Jenny squeezed his arm and went to cook up a hot breakfast, albeit a late one, and Tomas spent the rest of the day on the balcony thinking about his future.

PEDRO

Pedro was laying down the tracks on Friday night, the opening night of *Studio 69*. He was dancing behind the deck wearing nothing but short shorts, which didn't worry him after wearing not much more growing up on Mykonos and DJing in next to nothing. He did a double spin and waved his arms in the air getting cheers and whoops from the crowd.

While the atmosphere was the same, the essence was different. This was stylish, upper class and rich. It *was* New York after all. Rich women paraded past him on the floor, and so did the men. He saw celebrities from his favourite TV shows and movies, singers, musicians and bands. They were the high social elite of the city and they all stopped to look at him, the hot new DJ in the hot new club.

There had been no word from Andros, not that that meant anything. He could be waiting to make a move, but Pedro would deal with it when it came.

Angelina was down in the crowd thrusting her hips left, right and centre. She was with Maggie and a few other friends.

Waiters in short shorts roller-skated around dealing out drinks and anything else people wanted. It was electric. The atmosphere was filled with heat and sweat and lust and sex. It was so electrifying that Pedro was glad to be a part of it.

Ten hours later he finished up as the doors closed in the early hours of the morning. Angelina and Maggie had gone home, stragglers had lingered, and now the club was being cleaned up.

"Hey, kid," Eddie called out. "Great job tonight. Worth every cent you are." He was puffing on a cigar and sitting with a group of men Pedro didn't know.

"Thanks, Mr Monteif." Pedro pulled a t-shirt on to a loud round of boos. "Not the first time I've had that happen." He laughed and went to the staff room and changed out of his shorts.

Mike Gatos, one of the bartenders, came in. "You were great up there. How long have you been DJing?" He threw a t-shirt over his head.

"Two years," Pedro replied. "The summers are big on Mykonos and Santorini."

"Yeah, I've heard." Mike stepped out of his shorts. "You wanna go play some more? I find that I can't wind down for a couple of hours." He pulled a pair of jeans on. "Takes me a while to get to sleep."

"No, thanks." Pedro stood and threw his bag over his shoulder. "Got a girl waiting."

"Lucky you. That hot little number in the red dress?"

"Yep."

"Lucky bastard." Mike threw a rolled up towel at him.

Pedro laughed and ducked. "That's what everyone says. Night."

"Night."

Pedro walked outside and hailed a cab. Getting back to Gramercy in half an hour, he was showered and by Angelina's side.

*****

The woman walked back to her flimsy hotel room and cranked the air con. It was hot, stuffy, and she was too damn sweaty. How the hell did Pedro put up with it? Pulling the latest pack of developed pictures from her bag, she eagerly pored through them and picked out the best three, pinning them to the large corkboard on the desk, alongside all the other pictures of Pedro and a few of Carlos that she'd managed to take before he shot through. She stroked Pedro's face in her favourite photo. He was standing on the beach naked and on full display. Her tongue peeked out to lick her lips. She'd always tried to do it seductively, practising in the mirror for hours, but it never came across that way. She just looked like a girl licking her lips.

Her finger headed down from his face to his manhood. Oh, how she loved his appendage and would love to measure it, feel it in her hand again, feel it inside of her. She nearly had once, but he'd pushed her away. He had been scared, she understood that. They'd never made love before, and she had come off as a bit pushy. But he'd soon see how wonderful she could be. More womanly, more adult, more than that whore he was sleeping with. Who the fuck did that little tramp think she was to be taking her man. And doing her karate shit…the bitch had kicked her in the stomach.

"The baby, my baby, our baby," she murmured at the picture of Pedro. "Our baby." She stroked his penis and saw it grow, saw it rise. It was bigger than Carlos's, he was only ten inches, while Pedro packed an extra inch, and oh how that extra inch would come in handy. Oh, how it would fill her so. Fill her to every inch of her body and make her come with such pleasure. So much more than Carlos. He was good, but Pedro was better. And he would soon be hers.

She collected the photos of Pedro and Angelina together in New York and on Santorini, fucking each other. She put them in an envelope and sealed it tight. It was already addressed to Andros Poulos care of SantorPoulos in Santorini. "Oh yes, whore, I will get rid of you. Daddy's going to know exactly where you are and who you're with." Screwing up the excess photos, she threw them into the rubbish bin where they landed next to the empty box of red hair dye.

TOMAS

Saturday morning, Tomas took a boat to a small island off Mykonos which had a tiny little cove that faced the endless ocean away from everyone else. After pulling the boat up on the sand, he grabbed his bag and towel and set about sunbaking for the rest of the day.

He was lying back on his towel, eyes closed and covered in shades, when he heard a motor. Lifting his head, he saw a small motorboat come into the cove and beach itself.

Luiz stepped onto the sand, waving an arm excitedly.

Tomas's heart beat faster. So did his erection.

Luiz ran to him, a broad smile on his face. "I found you."

"Why did you follow me?" Tomas sat, knees up, arms on his knees to hide his acknowledgement.

"Because I wanted to be with you." Luiz knelt in front of him. "You didn't come to work yesterday. I followed you today. I want you, Tomas. I want to be with you."

Tomas frowned at the tanned god before him. The tanned god that was making him melt in the Greek summer sun. He'd come there to think and be alone, to decide on the course of his life and not to see the man who'd so forcefully made it explode. *So not helping matters.* "Please leave. I need to spend some time alone."

"No." Luiz stood and removed his shorts, revealing his own engorged member, before kneeling again in front of Tomas, pushing his legs apart, moving between them. He took Tomas's face in his hands.

"Luiz." Tomas pulled back. "I don't want to do this. You're engaged to Bertha for Christ's sake." He pushed the hands away, leaning back to do so, and that gave Luiz the moment he needed to push Tomas onto his back, whip his shorts off, and lie on top of him.

"Luiz, what are you doing?" Tomas demanded but gave up the fight when Luiz's tongue delved into his mouth. His hands grabbed, his legs entwined, his tongue greedily attacked back.

Luiz made his way down Tomas's neck.

"Luiz, no, we can't," Tomas gasped as Luiz moved down his chest. "It's not right...you're engaged...you're...oh, God...Luiz..." He felt the warmth around him. The wet, slick mouth and its dastardly tongue. "Oh, God," he groaned and grabbed Luiz by the hair.

Luiz stayed there until Tomas came before making his way back up to cover him wholly. "Let me love you," he whispered, rubbing himself against his young lover. "I want you, Tomas."

"Oh, Luiz...I want you, too..." Tomas whispered, before being consumed with passion and desire he'd never felt before.

They stayed conjoined in the sun for hours with the tropical breeze caressing their hot, naked sun-drenched bodies until they came up for air.

"Oh, God," Tomas gasped as Luiz rolled off to lie beside him. "Oh, God."

"Oh, God indeed." Luiz stroked Tomas's stomach. "You are amazing, Tomas Stephanopoulos."

Tomas glowed in the sun. "You're pretty amazing yourself for a man who's engaged to a woman."

Luiz sighed and gazed over the ocean. "Bertha is..." He waved his hand trying to think of the word.

"Your fiancée," Tomas finished the sentence.

"A means to an end." Luiz sighed. "I know, I know, it sounds bad," he said to Tomas's shocked expression. "But Bertha came along at a time when I didn't have a lot of clients and business wasn't going too well. So I gave her what she wanted."

"Do you do that to all rich old women?" Tomas sat up in disgust.

"No, no." Luiz sat up beside him. "Look, I..." He sighed again and scratched his head. "I've known for a few years now that I was into men. That doesn't mean I haven't been with women. I have."

"So, you're a whore," Tomas spat. "And now you've made me one."

"No," Luiz said firmly. "I'm not, and neither are you. I've been with three women and five men. You're the fifth. I first had sex with a girl at eighteen and didn't really like it. I experimented with a couple of guys, but that's all it was then, experimenting, coz we were young and naïve and had no idea how to have sex with a man. I tried again with women. But again, women didn't interest me. I met a guy, and it lasted six months, another guy lasted two years, and then there was Bertha, and now there's you. I'm crazy about you Tomas." He shook his head. "I'm crazy about you. You're gorgeous and perfect. More than any other man I've ever met or been with."

"Little comfort." Tomas snorted. "You're using a perfectly lovely woman for your own needs. Financial needs."

"And she probably knows it," Luiz said. "I've been with her a year. We don't have sex a lot, but it is companionship."

"So, what the hell is this?" Tomas spat, getting up and stalking down to the water's edge. He put his hands on his hips and stood looking out over the ocean. *How could I be so stupid?* he thought. *The first time I feel anything for anyone and it had to be the fiancé of a client. Jesus, how stupid can I be? And now I've gone and done it again.* He rubbed his face. "God how could I be so stupid." Hands slid around his waist. "Don't," he commanded.

Luiz's hands stopped at Tomas's navel. "Tomas, I didn't plan for this to happen. I didn't plan to meet someone." Lips kissed Tomas's shoulder lightly, leaving kisses along his neck. "I'm crazy about you." His right hand slid downward. "We don't have to tell anyone. We're here, in this private cove." A tongue flicked out to touch his ear. "With no one around." His fingers found what they were looking for and received a groan in return. "Tomas," he whispered. "This will be our little secret. No one will ever have to know." His hand curled around Tomas as he hardened. "Let us have today." His tongue travelled along Tomas's neck as his head fell onto Luiz's shoulder.

Tomas groaned. The man that lit a fire in him had him in the palm of his hand. The fingers worked their magic, stroking, kneading, plying up and down. The left hand stroked his stomach, lazily moving back and forth across his abdomen, dipping into his navel, stroking down to join the other hand, both of them massaging everything he was as a man. His knees were so weak he couldn't stand up any longer, and he slid into the water, Luiz right behind him, supporting his weight as he couldn't support himself.

Luiz knew he needed him; knew he had to keep him. And if this was the way to do it, by seducing him with sex, then he would. He knew how to please a man, and Tomas was the man he wanted to please. The thought of being inside of him, of having him inside took him to breaking point. And here on the deserted tropical island with no one around, he would have him.

He lowered Tomas to the sand, the water gently lapping at his thighs, and took him whole into his mouth. Tomas groaned his acceptance, and Luiz sucked harder. He rolled it around in his mouth, savouring its flavour, its length, its width. Tomas Stephanopoulos was the man he wanted in his mouth. The man he wanted his mouth around. He plied the testicles with forceful fingers until Tomas arched and groaned and he took him for all he had. Oh, yes, Tomas Stephanopoulos would never want anyone else.

*****

Tomas hadn't planned on spending the night on the island, but that's what had happened, and now it was a rush to get back home late in the afternoon. After spending all Sunday frolicking and making love, Tomas and Luiz took their boats back to Mykonos, with Tomas feeling guilty all the way.

"Weren't you supposed to be back yesterday?" Jenny asked as he came barrelling through the door all suntanned and guilty.

"What? Um, yeah." He stopped. "Um…I ended up staying, took the time to sort some stuff out." He inched his way toward the bedrooms.

"Go and have a shower," Jenny told him, knowing something had happened. "Dinner will be ready soon."

Tomas raced for his room, got his bag ready for the next day and hit the shower, strolling out just as his mother served dinner.

"So…what did you decide?" Jenny asked, handing a bowl of salad to him.

Tomas looked from her to his father before taking some salad and passing the bowl on. "About what?"

"About staying here or travelling?" Jenny laughed. "What did you think I meant?" She saw his guilty look. "Oh, you do have other things on your mind."

"Like what?" Spiros asked, picking up a lamb chop. "What's going on in my son's mind?"

Tomas gulped. This wasn't going to be easy. "Well…" He wiped his sweaty palms on his shorts. "If my plan goes through, I thought of travelling to America. Seeing the sights."

"That would be nice. Anywhere in particular?" Jenny popped a cherry tomato into her mouth.

"Miami," Tomas said. "The ladies at the gym have gone on and on about it, with its beaches and sun. It sounds like a great place to go."

"If it's beaches and sun you want, we have that here." Spiros waved his fork. "We live on an island for God's sake."

"But it's not America," Tomas said, shrugging a shoulder. "I want to visit other countries and cultures."

"Mmm," Spiros mumbled, jamming lettuce into his mouth. "Pah, other cultures."

"*Yes*, other cultures. They *are* half Australian remember." Jenny eyed him. "So don't 'pah other cultures'." She imitated his gesture.

"Mmm." Spiros finished up. "I'm going to Mikado's for a drink." He left them to it.

Jenny sighed, hating that Spiros went off for a drink every Sunday night instead of spending it with his family. But he had insisted on doing it, and no woman was going to stop him. He'd received an evil eye for that one, but she had allowed him to do it since he was home every other night. Once the door was shut she moved in. "What else happened this weekend? Did you see him?"

Tomas reddened.

"Tomas." She frowned. "He's engaged."

"I know, I know," he wailed. "I couldn't help it." Looking plaintively at the ceiling he continued. "I was there on my own, and then he turns up and says he followed me and one touch and a kiss later I'm putty in his hands." He closed his eyes in embarrassment. "Literally."

"Aw, sweetie." She reached over and patted his hand. "What are you going to do? Do you love him, or is it just some kind of first-time attraction?"

"Love?" Tomas's eyes flew open. "No…I…" He shook his head slowly, trying to decipher his emotions. "Not…love…just…"

"Pure unadulterated lust," Jenny finished with a raised brow.

His blush deepened. "Yes."

"So, what are you going to do?"

His deep sigh came out slowly. "Confess to my crime."

*****

Monday morning, after a guilt-filled gym session, Tomas pulled Bertha aside. "My dear Bertha, there is something I need to confess and apologise for."

"Oh, darling, what do you have to apologise for?"

Bette and Willow gathered round.

Tomas glowed red with shame. "I've done something that is unforgivable, and I'm sorry."

"For what? What could you have possibly have done?" Bertha asked.

"I met a man," Tomas said softly.

"Oh, how wonderful," Bette cried. "Tell us all about it."

"But why would you need to apologise to me for that?" Bertha asked, confused.

The shame was too much of Tomas. "I first saw him at the beach bar last week and then on the ferry. I didn't know who he was, but he tracked me down to the gym and seduced me." He stared, shamefaced,

123

at the floor. "He made me feel things I've never felt before, and I let things happen, and I shouldn't have, and, dear Bertha, I need you to forgive me. It will never happen again." He took her hands, his eyes pleading.

"But why do I need to forgive you, Tomas?" Bertha asked, her silky kaftan wafting around her ankles. "I don't understand any of this and what I have to do with you meeting a man."

"Because I did not know the man's name until you said it, dear Bertha. Said it in the gym Thursday night." He swallowed, his face crumpling up with the pain of guilt he was feeling. "I'm so, so sorry."

"Thursday night?" Bertha asked slowly, completely bewildered. "What happened Thursday…oh…you mean when I found you with Luiz…oh…oh, dear Tomas."

"I am so sorry, Bertha," he sobbed at her changing expression. "I didn't know he was Luiz, your Luiz. He never told me his name and I stupidly never asked. Please forgive me for I have done very bad things. Please, please forgive me." Tears flowed down his face, burning his flesh with shame and guilt.

Bertha's heart went out to the poor boy. She knew about Luiz's sexual past and knew it would possibly happen again. "Do you feel you've been taken advantage of?"

He swallowed the big fat lump of guilt in his throat. "Yes. Especially over the weekend when he followed me out to one of the islands and had his way with me," he choked. "I told him I'd never been with anyone and…" He closed his eyes in shame. "I let him do that to me anyway. I couldn't stop him, even if I wanted to. I am so sorry, Bertha. Please, please forgive me. I'm begging you."

Bette and Willow stared from Tomas to each other to Bertha. They had never seen a man cry over being gay and taking a lover, but clearly, Tomas was a sensitive young soul still learning about the ways of life, love, and gay sex.

"Oh, Tomas," Bertha said, patting his hand. "It's perfectly okay. If he was going to screw anyone, at least it was you."

Tomas looked up under swollen hooded eyes. "But I—"

She shook her head. "I knew he was gay, he told me and was very honest about it from the beginning. He'd had sex with men *and* women, but he was hot, and I was lonely, and he's very good at what he does, isn't he?"

Tomas blushed at the memories.

"Don't worry about it. At least he has good taste." She laughed. "We both do."

"But I—"

"I know," she said. "You had sex with an engaged man." She gave a woeful nod. "A *gay* engaged man, but I knew what I was in for and probably knew when I brought him here that *someone* would come along. Of course, someone *would*, the place is full of beautiful young bodies. But that's not going to stop me from making you come to Miami. Now, we've been thinking—"

"But, Bertha." Tomas shook his head in confusion at the sudden change of subject. "I slept with your fiancé. That is unforgivable. What I did was so wrong." His guilt and shame was eating him up inside, and he felt himself withering away as he was being eaten.

"Tomas, there is nothing to forgive," she said, trying to make him understand. "End of discussion. I don't hate you, I don't want you dead." She watched his expression rise and fall. "Stop feeling ashamed for finding love or some form of it. If being with him made you happy then so be it. Maybe we can share him, or, maybe it's time for me to get a younger fiancé." She laughed. "But back to you. We want you to come to Miami. We want to help you out and introduce you to our friends. Say you'll come."

Bette laid a bejewelled hand on his arm. "Please say you'll come."

"But I have not been very kind to you," he told Bertha. "I'm sick just thinking about what I have done."

"Then stop feeling sick," Bertha demanded. "It's done, it's over, because what's done cannot be undone, and anyway…I was just with him for companionship. Sex was only in the beginning and ended quite quickly. I'm not really into that sort of thing anymore, so I paid him to stick around. He wines me and dines me, travels with me, and I show him off to my friends. Tomas…" She touched his cheek. "I really don't care if he slept with someone. But I *am* glad he picked you. Now, stop looking confused and be done with the infidelity. It means nothing and is no big deal. *We* have been talking and want you to come to Miami with us."

Tomas swallowed and the lump in his throat shrunk. "And Luiz?"

"Well," Bertha said. "We either keep him or get rid of him. I'm not fussed either way, but if you want a fresh start without guilt…say you'll come to Miami."

"Yes, say you'll come," Bette and Willow echoed.

AUGUST 1977

TOMAS

On the first of August, Tomas stepped off the private plane of Bette Olander onto the tarmac at Miami Airport.

It was a beautiful bright day with not a cloud in the turquoise blue sky as the sun shone down, layering the world in a warm, soft glow.

Tomas turned his face up toward that sun, feeling its warmth radiate on his face. He breathed the salty air drifting across on the gentle coast winds.

"Does it feel different?" Bette asked

"To what?" He looked at her in her bejewelled kaftan and kitten heels.

"To Mykonos, darling," Bette said, taking her handkerchief from her clutch and dabbing at her face. "It's still very warm."

"Well, it is still summer," Bertha said from beside her as their luggage was transferred from the plane to Bette's limo. "Of course it's going to be hot."

The driver held the back door open and they piled in, with Tomas taking the window seat.

"You're going to love it here," Willow told him, adjusting her own bejewelled kaftan. They were all the rage that summer and all of her friends wore them as well, so she didn't care that Bette and Bertha had them on. Everyone else had them on too. "It's just like Mykonos only more glamorous."

"The night life is amazing," Bertha added, sitting in her own kaftan and bejewelled headpiece. She glanced at Bette and Willow. The three of them were like queens of the ocean in their frothy creations.

Driving down the coast to Coral Gables they rolled through extravagantly wealthy neighbourhoods with magnificent mansions behind iron gates. They came to a stop in front of one of them.

Tomas's eyes widened as they stopped at the front door. "This is your house, Bette? It's beautiful." He gazed across the expansive white home with its four round pillars, balcony, and white railings. Lush green lawns spread across the plantation-style grounds.

"Thank you, darling. Now come, I want you to see the ballroom. It faces the back, so it has an amazing view of the backyard and gardens with French doors that open all the way." She led him through the front door. "Thank you, Webster," she told the butler who'd opened the door and taken her things. She conducted everyone through the large entrance hall and opened a door on their right. A huge ballroom extended through the whole side of the house from front to back with French doors that folded back against the walls. "Webster, grab the door for me." Bette opened them and slid one side back while Webster opened the other.

They all stood looking across the terrace onto the gardens with their waterfalls and ponds, and onto the emerald lawn beyond.

"What do you think?" Bette turned around and moved to the centre of the room, waving her hands as she spoke. "We could get some equipment in and place it over that side near the front and leave this part for working out and stretching. We could do aerobics and yoga here." She spun around, clasping her hands to her chest. "Don't you just love it?"

"Oh, absolutely." Willow walked over. "It's perfect, and the cool breeze will keep us cool for the rest of summer."

"It's the perfect room," Bertha said. "Lots of space for everyone. That's if we even end up exercising. We may all just want to look at Tomas."

He heard her and blushed, and was glad he was still gazing out over the beautiful gardens so they couldn't see the glint of shame that flew over his face. It still made him uncomfortable, being around Bertha.

Cheating with her fiancé made him feel guilt so huge it would probably never subside. They had both decided to say goodbye to Luiz. Tomas made that choice on the grounds he was a mistake. He wanted to start fresh in a new town. Bertha had finally decided she wanted a man that wasn't gay.

Luiz had cried, getting down on his knees, begging to be forgiven and taken back. "Tomas, please, I love you, please, don't let me go. You're the only one I want. I can fix it with Bertha so we can be together. You and me, just us, just here. We can live together here on Mykonos," Luiz had pleaded as he knelt before Tomas that past Saturday when he had been told it was over. "Take me back. Don't let this stop us from being together. Don't let my past with Bertha stop us from being together. I love you, Tomas. For me, you are the one. The only one. *The one I want to spend the rest of my life with. I have chosen who I want, and it is you, Tomas."*

It tore Tomas apart inside, killing off each little blood vessel that filled his heart. His first experience at love had to end in mind-numbing heartbreak.

Luiz had pleaded with both of them.

Both of them had said no; one more efficiently than the other.

They needed a clean break and what happened in Mykonos stayed in Mykonos. Luiz had been told to find his own way home and that his things would be packed and waiting for him when he returned.

"Thinking about our gigolo?" Bertha laughed daintily, noticing Tomas's faraway gaze as she floated over to him. "Don't worry, it's a fresh start for both of us, and don't you know, Miami is the new spot to be for men hooking up with men. So we'll have to get you out and about." She laid a gentle hand on his arm.

Tomas's blush deepened, and he took Bertha's hand in his and gave it a soft squeeze.

"Oh, yes," Bette said. "With all of the people we know you'll be hooked up in no time."

"I don't know." Tomas shook his head. "With the mess I've just gotten myself out of I'm not sure I want to get into another one."

"Nonsense," Bertha said. "We'll help you find a nice boy to be with.

Now, let's figure out what we need here so we can get started."

With Tomas to guide them, they spent the next hour figuring out what equipment they would need and where they could put it. One phone call and five minutes later they had bought that equipment from a store and it was being delivered that afternoon.

"What's next?" Bette asked. "Ah yes, new workout clothes for you. We'll have to take you shopping tomorrow."

He shook his head in disbelief. "I…this is too much. You have done so much for me, I can't even begin to repay you or thank you. I don't know how I'll *ever* pay you back."

Bette waved a hand. "With all the women that will want to come, I'll charge them per hour, and we'll make our money back in no time."

"Oh yes," Bertha said. "I've already called Marina to tell everyone. They're all on board."

"And I've called Sandra to let her know, so the grapevine is in full swing. You're going to be busy all day, every day," Willow added.

Tomas's brows rose. "*All* day, every day? Seven days a week?"

Bette laughed. "Well, not seven days a week, but some of the ladies like to be early morning and some late evening. We can set up a schedule once you've met them and find out what their needs are. In the meantime, we'll show you the sights and get you settled."

Half an hour later, Tomas was in the guest room overlooking the back garden and wondering how the hell he'd managed to get there. His family had fallen apart, and now all he had left was a group of three wise ladies to guide him. He unpacked his suitcase and carry-on bag, hanging his few clothes in the closet. *I'll have to get some more of those now I'm here. Especially since it's still summer and I'm in need of new clothes,* he thought.

That afternoon, they were waiting when the workout equipment arrived and spent an hour putting it in place and setting it up.

Finally, at four-thirty, they collapsed in the garden chairs on the back terrace while Webster served iced tea.

Bette held hers up. "To Tomas, to new ventures, to new *adventures*, and a new life."

"To Tomas."

That evening, they cruised through the city and dined at *Flair et Saveur*, an expensive restaurant where only the rich dined, feasting on lobster and caviar, washing it down with Cristal champagne. After dinner, they went to *Sexe et Faveurs*, a mature club that catered for people over forty; *wealthy* people over forty who wanted pretty, *very* young things to play with. In *every* sexual manner.

The club was low key, with dimmed lights, a cool and casual but tasteful décor of oriental carpet and red walls, and lustfully decadent desserts of all kinds.

Tomas wandered after the ladies and saw young blonde things chatting up older men, and young men chatting up older ladies. There were even a few same on same meetings going on, with young hot boys kissing and groping older men, and older women getting it on with young girls.

"We're very discreet here," Bertha told him as they took their seats. "No tales ever walk out that door, and no one breathes a word about it. What do you think?"

"Mmm." Tomas looked around. "It's not really my thing. But clubs of any kind don't really interest me."

"How do you expect to meet anyone?" Willow asked, adjusting her sparkling diamond bracelet.

"I don't," Tomas replied, catching the eye of the young thing on an old man's knee across the room.

"Don't what?" she asked.

"Don't expect to meet anyone," he told her, glancing away from the couple across the room. "After Mykonos and everything that happened, I'm going to take my time, get a feel for the place and my new job, and then we'll see if I want to meet anyone."

"You need to get back on the horse darling." Bette patted his hand. "We'll make sure to introduce you to a lot of young men we know and let all the girls know to rally their troops as well."

Tomas laughed lightly, but then noticed someone walking toward him and stopped in a heartbeat. His life fell before his eyes. "Go away." His voice broke. "We told you goodbye."

Luiz came to their table. "Tomas," he pleaded and nodded to the others. "Bertha."

"Luiz," she said stiffly.

"Tomas please, I must talk to you." He knelt beside his ex-lover, his fingers sliding over his hand. "I love you, please, I want to see you, and I *need* to be with you."

Tomas pulled his hand away. "Please leave. I don't want to see you." His discomfort was felt and seen by everyone at the table, *and* in the club. All eyes were on them, and it was embarrassing.

"Tomas," Luiz pleaded once more.

"You heard him, Luiz," Bertha cut him off. "Leave." She clicked her fingers at someone, and two burly men in suits came to their table and stood on either side of Luiz. Taking his arms, they hauled him to his feet.

"Please, Tomas, I love you. I want to be with you. We need to talk," he yelled as he was carried away. "I want you back."

"Jesus," Tomas muttered. "I didn't think he'd follow me again." He glanced around at the other patrons, staring in distaste or curiosity. "Can we leave? That was embarrassing."

"Of course. Let's go to *The Joy Stick*. It will be much better than this," Bertha said, ushering the others out of the booth.

They made their way outside and waited while the driver got their limo. Fifteen minutes later, they walked into the club to blaring music, flashing lights, and people of all races, colours and creeds.

"Oh, I love this place. You can be so free here," Willow squealed and excitedly clapped her hands before wafting away in her gold lamé kaftan. She twirled around in circles in the middle of the dance floor, the lights reflecting off the lamé making her a human disco ball. The people around her cheered.

Tomas felt someone grab his hand and turned to see Bertha intent on leading him up a small flight of stairs to a seating area. They joined a small group of women all dressed to the nines and middle-aged or older.

"Violet, Marie, Beatrice, this is Tomas, from Mykonos. The personal trainer we were telling you about." Bertha swung him around and he fell onto the couch next to Violet.

"Hello," he said, straightening himself.

"Hello," the three women said together, all eagerly eyeing off the hot new thing in their lives.

"Are you ladies friends of Bette and Bertha?" He eyed the hungry women laden with the riches of their wealth and status.

"Yes, we are," Violet said, smoothing her salt and pepper hair. The bun was surrounded in crystals that matched the choker at her throat and the bracelet on her wrist. At sixty-four she was in desperate need of a healthy young man and had demanded that the girls bring their new acquisition home from Mykonos. When they'd called to say they were, she couldn't stand the wait.

Tomas felt like a piece of meat. They were salivating, licking their lips while eyeing him hungrily, and he was the sacrificial lamb.

"So, you're going to be our personal trainer?" Beatrice sipped her champagne. At forty-five she was the youngest of their group of friends and was on to husband number three. But now she had the Greek god before her she was wondering if she should make him husband number four. Or just take him on as a lover. She crossed her legs slowly, hoping to show him she wore no underwear, and maintained eye contact. He didn't flinch and kept his eyes on hers, nowhere else.

"Why don't you go and mingle," Bette said over the music. "Relax, have fun, go fly a kite with Willow."

Tomas smiled. "I think I might." He knew he was being offered a way out and gladly took it. Walking back to the dance floor, he took the circuitous route. He wasn't quite dressed for the place; his black suit and unbuttoned matching shirt were a touch too formal for the crowd, but he looked hot, and the crowd noticed.

Men and women eyed the hot hunk of Greek man meat that casually strolled around them, hands in pockets, eyes on the lookout. Tomas felt the vibrations through the soles of his shoes. Felt them reverberate through to his bones. Clubs weren't his thing, but this one...this one was different.

He watched the people. They had no inhibitions; they just let themselves be free. Free to dance the way they wanted, dress the way they wanted, express themselves the way they wanted.

He walked past a couple of men in leather chaps and not much else, kissing against a wall. Not far from them were two women, and not far from them were two people fucking. *Clearly, anything goes in this place*, he thought as he completed the circuit.

He stood watching Willow swirl around and made his way through the crowd that seemed to part just for him. Eyes stared, hands reached out to touch, and he found his way to Willow's side.

"Tomas, darling," she panted. "Don't you just love it here? You can be so free." She twirled. "I love it, I love it, I love it."

He closed his eyes and let his body relax, getting into the rhythm of the music. Pedro had the natural beat in the family, but he could feel what Pedro used to go on about for hours. If you just relax and let it take you away, you can dance.

He swayed, he rocked, he grooved and let the music take him away.

"You didn't tell me he could dance," Violet told Bertha. "He's got rhythm besides gorgeous looks."

"I didn't know," Bertha said. "I've never seen him dance. I've seen his brother Pedro though; he's a gorgeous boy. And the eldest, Carlos; my, how he knows how to pleasure a woman. I just didn't know about Tomas's dancing."

"So, rhythm runs in the family," Violet said, sipping her champagne.

"It definitely seems to," Bertha said, watching Tomas sway his way around the dance floor. The crowd parted for him and Willow as they sashayed to the music.

"He's hot. What does he do besides personal training?" Marie asked. She was head of an all-female law firm that dealt with the wealthy women of Florida. At fifty-nine she was one of the richest women in the state and had acquired her wealth without the help of a husband.

"Besides men you mean?" Bette mischievously winked.

"Oh." Marie's face fell. "He's a fag? What a waste."

"True," Bette agreed. "But that means you get attention and not just a man wanting to get in your pants for your money. Besides, he's a very good trainer. Just you wait and see."

"When do we start?" Beatrice asked.

"Next week," Bette replied and knocked back her fifth glass of champagne.

Violet had been thinking after Bette's reply. "He's into men…?"

"Yes," Bertha said.

"Has he ever done movies?"

"Not that I know of." Bertha eyed her friend. "What are you thinking?"

"You know Marcus is into making movies, and, of course, it's big business, especially, same on same."

"I still can't believe you're in business with your ex," Beatrice said. "Most of us can't stand our exes, or to be around them once they're gone."

"When you're in business and making a motza you want to *stay* in business," Violet replied. "It's become big in the gay scene to have same-sex movies. And if he's into men…"

"Are you going to ask him?" Marie asked.

"Who, Marcus?" Violet asked.

"No, Tomas," Marie replied.

"Oh." Violet blushed. "Yes, I guess I should ask if he'd be interested."

Tomas twirled Willow around and spied a hot looking guy over her shoulder. He looked away, not interested in getting involved again, but quickly looked back anyway. The man was standing at the edge of the crowd watching with everyone else. His dark hair was slicked back, his black shirt opened to the waist revealing a light covering of hair. He had a three-piece white suit on, á la Tony Manero from *Saturday Night Fever*, and dark eyes that couldn't take themselves off Tomas.

Tomas turned, swinging Willow in another direction, so he didn't feel the connection from those eyes. *Not again. Please God, not again,* he thought. *One attraction to a man is enough. I don't need to get involved with another so soon.*

"How gay is he?" Violet asked the girls.

"What?" Bertha choked on her drink and patted herself down.

"How gay is he?" Violet repeated, her eyes not leaving Tomas on the dance floor. "A little gay, a lot gay?"

"Well, I…" Bertha shook her head as the others looked on in amusement. "Didn't think you *could be* a little or a lot gay. Gay is gay."

"What I meant was, is he just *realising* he's gay, so inexperienced in the field of gayness and gay sex, or has he been fucking his own kind for years?"

"Oh," Bertha said. "That's what you meant. He's only had the one experience and that was with my ex-fiancé."

"What!" Three stunned faces swivelled in her direction.

She sighed and revealed all. "I knew Luiz had been with men, I knew he would possibly pick up while on holiday. I just didn't know it was going to be with my personal trainer. The poor boy was so upset about it when he realised who Luiz was that he apologised profusely. What can I do?" She shrugged a shoulder. "It is what it is, and we have ditched Luiz for good."

"So, he's only had the one experience," Violet murmured. "Fresh meat."

"He's only *been* with one man. I don't know how many experiences," Bertha said and turned her head to watch Tomas. "It's such a pity." She sighed.

"He would be new to the whole thing. We could work on that angle. Have him play a poor boy that is taken advantage of. Do the whole, first time thing," Violet said. "Yes, yes, that would be a very good angle."

Tomas turned, straight into the path of the man in the Tony Manero suit. Their eyes met, the fire ignited, and a stunned Tomas turned again, this time heading for the bar. He wasn't a big drinker, but he needed a beer and knocked one back in five seconds flat then ordered a second.

"You're a great dancer. Do you take lessons?" the voice beside him said.

Tomas turned to see the Tony Manero lookalike.

Tony Manero grabbed a beer and leant on the bar.

"What?" Tomas said, dazed.

"Have you been taking lessons?" Tony lookalike repeated, his lips turning into a small smile.

Those lips turned Tomas on. "Uh," he muttered, looking down at the bar. "No."

"Well, you're great. Hey, have you ever been on *American Band Stand,* or one of those shows as a dancer in the background? You'd be great."

"Um." Tomas shook his head. "No. Never been on a show." *Be cool, just be cool,* he told himself. *Don't make a fool of yourself, just be cool. No expectations. Nothing. Just be cool.*

"How about movies? You ever been in a music clip?" Tony went on.

"Ah, no. No music clips either."

"Mmm, well if you need a job, I could get you into the scene. A buddy of mine is a music producer and does music clips. He could always use extras."

"That…ah…" Tomas knocked back another beer. "Sounds good."

"I'm Roger."

"What?" Tomas finally turned to look at the tall hunk of man beside him.

"I'm Roger. Roger Dencott." The Tony lookalike was holding out his hand.

Tomas stared from the hand to the deep dark eyes that he started drowning in. *Play it cool, Stephanopoulos. Play it cool.* He started backstroking. "Tomas." Shaking hands, he felt tingles go roaring up his arm.

"Nice to meet you…Tomas," Roger said, hanging on a few moments more, feeling the tingle race up his arm and across his body. "Let me give you a card." He reluctantly let go to dig a business card out from his pocket. "This is my friend, get yourself along to a recording and you'll be in a film clip."

Tomas took the card, never once taking his eyes off Roger.

"Well, look at that." Violet held her glass up in the direction of the bar. "Our young ingénue has met my other star."

The women turned to look and watched Tomas and Roger talk.

"That's good isn't it?" Marie asked. "If he gets to know them away from work he may not be so uncomfortable *at* work."

"Yes, very good idea, Marie," Violet said. "But I certainly didn't plan this. Looks like Tomas caught Roger's eye all on his own."

"So, what do you do?" Roger asked, leaning an elbow on the bar and taking in the full length of the dark, brooding man before him; a dark, brooding man who had taken his fancy and turned him on.

"Personal trainer." Tomas was feeling relaxed now, and he should after three beers. He casually glanced at the man beside him, and those tingles kept going, and going and going on down to his groin, stirring him.

Roger studied his face. "You're not from here, though."

"No, Mykonos. I've just come over. Landed today actually."

"Ah, then you'll need a chaperone to get you around Miami." Roger took a swig of beer, wanting it to be Tomas sliding down his throat instead of the amber fluid.

"Ah." Tomas laughed lightly. "I have three of those. What about you? What do you do?" He finished off his beer and turned around to lean on the bar so he faced the crowd.

"I'm an actor. I also help out with the setup and production of the movie. Lights, cameras, etc."

"Cool." Tomas nodded. "Anything I would have seen you in?"

Roger grimaced. He wasn't sure if the hot-looking stud was even gay considering he'd turned up with three older women. He could just be a gigolo. "Well, unless you've seen *Hunk on Hunk, Hot Balls,* or *Big Dick* then probably not."

The titles bounced around in Tomas's brain. "Oh, my God." His eyes closed and he bowed his head. "Are they…gay…movies?"

"Porn, yes."

Tomas kept his eyes closed, scared to even open them. "You're a gay porn star?"

"Yes."

Ah, Jesus!

*****

"So, we saw you talking to a young man in the club last night," Bette said Tuesday morning.

They had been working out for an hour after taking an hour to warm up and get their act together. There were fifty women in Bette's ballroom, each paying ten dollars an hour to have a session with their latest Greek stud acquisition. Tomas had given each woman special attention, and now they were sorting out a schedule with Bertha.

"I was," he replied, wiping himself with a towel. "This is an amazing turnout. Thank you so much for this. If it weren't for you ladies, I wouldn't have a head start on a business."

"Don't worry about it." Bette laid a hand on his arm. "With this turnout, the equipment will be paid for at the end of the week, and then you'll start getting your share." That's the agreement they had come up with. The equipment would be paid for before they got a wage. Tomas had insisted on buying his own clothes and car, having saved a lot from his years at the resort, and insisted on paying board while he lived there so Bette would keep a portion of the income until he was set up in his own home and business.

"So…who was that young man at the bar? You were talking quite closely."

"Not really." He stepped away to grab a glass of juice from the refreshment table.

She followed. "Were you not interested?"

"Nope."

"Not interested because you're not ready for another relationship?"

"Just not interested."

"And what does he do?"

"He's an actor."

"In movies?"

"In gay porn." Tomas handed her a glass of juice. "He's a porn star."

Bette's brows rose. "Well, *it is* a well-known gay club so it was obvious that anyone you spoke to besides us, would be gay."

"I don't have a problem with talking to gay people. But he's in porn."

"Have you seen a porn movie?" Violet asked from beside them. She had come over just seconds before and heard the conversation.

Tomas sighed. "No."

"Do you know the industry is huge? *Especially* gay porn."

"No."

"Maybe you should come by the studio sometime." She fished a business card from her purse. "My ex and I run a very lucrative gay movie business, very tasteful, very classy, none of this hot horny fucking stuff. The actors in our movies make sweet love, and they are *massive* sellers. You should come along and have a look. Maybe you'll like something you see…or *someone.*" She touched Bette on the arm. "I have to go. I'll see you both tomorrow. Bye Tomas."

"Violet." He looked down at the card. *Seralift Productions. Movies for All Kinds. Marcus and Violet Seralift.*

The other ladies wandered over to say goodbye and to thank Tomas for their workout. He kissed their hands and thanked them for coming, leaving them giggling like schoolgirls reliving some fantasy.

Once they were gone, Bette broached the subject again. "And what was wrong with the young man you talked to?"

"Nothing." Tomas busied himself wiping down the equipment.

"It wouldn't hurt for you to get out and about on your own. Meet people, see new places, make friends."

"I know." He dumped the towels into the laundry basket for Webster. "I'm just…" He sighed and rubbed his forehead. "Not ready to get involved."

"Who said anything about getting involved?" Bette asked. "Go out and make friends. Go and see Violet and watch a movie being made. It might make you feel more comfortable with your sexuality."

He flashed a glare at her. *What is it with other people going on about my sexuality? Why can't they just leave it to me to figure out?* "I'll think about it," he finally said.

*****

The week was full of sessions. Tomas took individual clients in the morning, and small groups of five in the afternoons. He started at eight and finished at six. He saw Violet and Bette talking on Friday morning after the workout and got a wave from Violet as she left. "What was that about?" he asked.

"She's invited us to watch a movie being made tonight at the studio. Would you like to go? See what it's all about?"

"I don't know." Tomas backed up. "It's not something I'm into."

"Oh, come on, you're in a new place to have new experiences," she cajoled. "You might learn something new about yourself."

*****

At seven that night, they drove up to the large iron gates of *Seralift Productions* and were escorted through winding roads to the studio. There was a huge sound stage with several scenarios set up in several rooms with the current one being played out in a steam room.

The moment Tomas saw the set he backed up. "No, no, I don't need to relive that moment."

Bette grabbed his arm. "Get over it, Tomas. What happened, happened. Deal with it. Now let's stay and watch."

They stood at the back of the studio watching as steam was pumped into the room and crew ran around adjusting lights and cameras.

Bette spied Violet and went off to see her, leaving Tomas alone and against the back wall.

One of the crew walked past, but stopped and turned. "Hey. I thought it was you. What are you doing here?" He saw Tomas's terrified look and began to worry. "It's Roger," he reminded him, "from the club last week. Are you okay?"

Tomas stared at the ordinary-looking guy before him. He had on jeans and a t-shirt with unstyled dark brown hair that curled around his ears and brushed his jawline. He didn't look like the actor he'd claimed to be. And he certainly didn't look like Tony Manero anymore. "I thought you said you…"

"I am." Roger smiled. "But I'm not in every movie, so I help out on others. I'm fixing lights today. How come you're here?" He couldn't stop the slow burning stirrings in his pants and hoped it wasn't too obvious. This one seemed young and inexperienced. He needed smooth, calm nudging in the right direction. And that would be *his* direction if he had any say in the matter.

Tomas blinked and relaxed, unwinding his arms from around himself. "I came with Bette, a friend of Violet's." He nodded in their direction. "She invited us."

Roger glanced over his shoulder briefly. "Cool. You'll get to see how a movie's made."

"Yeah." Tomas let out a gush of air. "I'm not into this sort of thing."

"You don't have to be into the content, but it's fun to see a movie being made." Roger wanted to ask what was wrong, why he was so tense and wound up, but knew Tomas would need to reveal that in his own time. And he had a feeling that big secret was what was stopping the Greek stud from letting himself go.

"Yeah, whatever," Tomas muttered, hearing steam being pumped onto the set. The panic rose. "I need some air." He turned and bolted, not knowing where he was going and not actually caring, as long as it was away from the scene that reminded him of the biggest mistake of his life.

Roger followed, bouncing along lightly like Pepé Le Pew stalking his prey.

Tomas made it to the other end of the studio into an empty bedroom scene. Seeing no one around, he collapsed onto the bed and gasped for air.

"Are you okay?" Roger came up to stand beside the bed. "Does this *really* make you sick? Is it being *gay* that makes you sick?" He stared down at the very confused and anguished face before him.

Tomas gulped air, and a sob came out. "I don't know."

Roger let out a deep breath and sat beside the forlorn figure on the bed. "*Are* you gay?"

Tomas moved his head back and forth. "I...I...don't really know."

"So, it's all new to you, then?"

Tomas nodded. "Yeah."

"Okay, that's...that's okay. Coming out is hard. Figuring out you're gay is harder. It took me five years."

Tomas finally looked at him. "For what?"

Roger shrugged a shoulder. "Everything. Figuring out I wasn't interested in girls. Thinking that meant I was interested in boys. Trying to sort out my *emotional* feelings on top of sorting out my *sexual* feelings. And when I finally let go of everyone else's expectations I realised I was actually gay. How long's it been for you?"

Tomas hugged himself tighter and sighed. "Just…last month."

"Wow, you *are* new to this. No wonder you seem confused."

"It's not just that."

"Wasn't a good experience?"

"No."

"Yeah." Roger nodded. "Had those." He inspected Tomas's profile. "How old are you?"

"Twenty-two."

"Jesus, still so young. I remember being twenty-two; wasn't all that good for me either."

"It's not that it wasn't good." Tomas shifted uncomfortably. "It's just…he was the right guy at the wrong time and…" He broke off.

"It was your first?"

Tomas nodded. His throat was now too clenched to speak.

"Did he take advantage of you?"

Tomas remained silent, his frown deepening.

"Did he rape you?" Roger's blood boiled. How dare anyone take advantage of such a sweet young kid!

Tomas looked up in alarm, and his throat unclenched. "What? No, no, it was nothing like that. No, nothing like that at all."

"Then why are you so cut up about it?" Roger was confused. If he hadn't been forced, then it was consensual, but something was going on inside the man he wanted to get to know.

"Long story short." Tomas sighed. "I bumped into him twice at the resort I worked at, and he seduced me in the steam room, and then I found out he was the fiancé of one of my clients. A *female* client."

"Ouch!" Roger felt like laughing and crying at the same time.

"Yep."

"And now we're making a steam room movie."

"Yep."

"Brings back memories."

"Oh, yeah." Tomas nodded. "Good *and* bad."

"So, your first experience was in a steam room. How do you feel about sex with men?" Roger's insides went tight at the thought of being in a steam room with Tomas. It was definitely something he would change for the better. Give him new and improved memories of it.

Tomas looked at him strangely.

"It makes you gay," Roger said.

Tomas looked away. "I've never been attracted to girls. Never wanted to kiss one, have sex with one. But I never felt anything for boys either. I just felt…nothing," he barely whispered. "And all of a sudden I fall head over heels for a guy I didn't know, and I let him… do those things that felt so good…" His eyes closed and his voice drifted away. "It was *so* good."

"It is with the right person."

"He *wasn't* the right person. He was taken, and now it's over, and our lives could have been wrecked. It was my fault. *My* fault for not asking his name. *My* fault for being with a man I didn't know." His head dropped into his hands. "I still feel so guilty about it."

"Everyone does stupid shit they feel guilty about." Roger slapped him on the back. "You ain't no different."

Tomas heard it. He lifted his head and looked at Roger. "Did I just detect a hint of Australian accent?"

Roger's eyes widened in surprise. "How did you…?"

"I was born there." Tomas grinned. "My mother's Australian, my father's Greek. He immigrated in 1950, met mama, and then had my brothers and me. We moved to Mykonos ten years ago when I was twelve."

Roger was charmed by the Australian boy beside him. "Yeah, where were you born?"

"Armidale," Tomas said, now fully relaxed. "We grew up there until we moved back."

"How come you moved from Aus to some Greek island?" Roger

was intrigued. Being Aussie born made him one step closer to being with him. Tomas was growing on him by the second. He'd never felt so much for someone so fast, and it was dizzying. And exhilarating.

"My grandfather died. Papa took over the family business. What about you?"

"Wollongong, born and bred. Came out here a couple of years ago to get into the big movies and fell into the other kind instead."

"How'd you do that?" Tomas was warming to the Aussie man beside him. They had something in common and could maybe be friends.

Roger shrugged and gave a small laugh. "Still not sure. I was auditioning for big movies, little independents as you do, and met Marcus. He asked if I had a problem getting my gear off. I said no. I built up to the gay porn. At first, I was an extra, and then had the starring role in straight movies. When Marcus found out I was gay, he asked if I'd be interested in switching. I gave it a go and liked it."

"How do you…?" Tomas blushed and glanced away.

"I like a man who blushes," Roger teased.

The red glow deepened. "How do you not get involved when you're doing it?"

"You block yourself off. You're just an actor in a movie seducing your partner."

"Is it hard?"

"Well…I always am."

"Oh." Tomas briefly closed his eyes.

"Why don't you come and watch. It's not so bad."

"It's a steam room. It will be."

Roger laughed and slapped him on the back again. "Come on."

They made it back to the stage as the actors took their places.

Roger attended to his light, and Tomas walked over to stand beside Violet and Bette.

"All right, everyone, places," Marcus yelled as he barged over to his chair. "In five, four, three, two, one, and…action."

During the movie, Roger occasionally glanced over at Tomas. Most of the time he was looking at the ground, but when he wasn't, there was unadulterated pleasure on his face. The memories of that time were obviously coming back in a rush over and over, but then he'd look ashamed and glance away before looking back and remembering.

He's sweet, Roger thought. *Still young, unaffected. Gorgeous, beautiful, young, sweet.* He found himself smiling as the movie action rolled to a stop.

"And cut," Marcus yelled. "Print, we're done. See you all Monday." He noticed Violet with Bette and a hot young stud. "And who do we have here?" He stalked over to them. "Bette, Violet, and who are you?" He eyed Tomas up and down. "Fresh meat?"

Tomas frowned, clearly uncomfortable with the attention. "Definitely not!"

"And why not?" Marcus bellowed. "You're gorgeous. Look at you. Strong, athletic, dark and exotic. What are you…Italian?"

"Half Greek," Tomas replied quietly.

"How do you be half Greek?" Marcus inquired.

Tomas took a step back at the attention. "I'm also half Australian."

"Australia." The light dawned. "Hey, Dencott, get over here." He waited while Roger walked over. "Aren't you Australian?"

"I am." Roger raised a mischievous brow at Tomas, making him blush.

"You know hot stuff here is half Australian." Marcus waved a cigar at Tomas.

Roger smiled at a blushing Tomas. "So I've heard."

"Well, what are the odds of that?" Marcus asked, puffing on his cigar. "Two Aussies in one movie."

"Oh, no, I don't," Tomas protested.

"Nonsense," Marcus bellowed. "An Aussie twosome."

"No, really, I—" Tomas cut in.

"Marcus," Roger spoke firmly. "Tomas isn't interested." He stared Marcus down. "Leave him alone and stop badgering him."

Marcus's gaze moved from Roger to Tomas and back to Roger. "Okay," he finally said. "I'll back off." He looked at the half Greek stud. "But I'm keeping my eye on you kid. I want you for my movies, and I'm gonna have you."

"Back off, Marcus." Roger laid a hand on his arm. "It's time we all got going home. Ladies, why don't I walk you to your cars?" He held an arm out for Bette and Violet and escorted them and Tomas out to their cars. "Pushy isn't he," he muttered to Tomas.

"Ah, yeah," Tomas replied. "Very." He opened the car door.

"Hey, um, what are you doing this weekend?" Roger asked.

Butterflies fluttered around Tomas's stomach. "Ah, nothing, at this stage."

Roger shrugged. "How about hanging out? I can show you the sights, introduce you to some friends. Show you some of the places that are safe to hang out."

"Ah." Tomas breathed and backed up to the car. "I don't…"

"He'd love to," Bette called through the door. "Come to my place tomorrow. 2715 Orchid Way, Coral Gables. About ten."

"Uh, Bette," Tomas muttered.

"Oh, for heaven's sake, you need to make friends, so deal with it. Now say goodbye and get in."

Tomas blushed, embarrassed by the motherly tone. "Ah, bye." He slid into the car.

Roger smiled. "Bye."

*****

Promptly, at ten the next morning, Roger turned up in shorts and a tank. It was a hundred out, and he was already hot. Not because of the weather, but because he was spending the day with Tomas Stephanopoulos.

The door opened, and there he stood dressed in the same outfit; shorts and a tank. All tanned, toned and terrific.

"Hey." Roger felt his heart swell along with a few other things.

"Hey, uh, just give me a minute." Tomas popped back inside, and Roger turned to look at the front garden, lush and green and buzzing with God's creatures. *Breathe Roger, breathe.*

"Hey, I'm ready." Tomas closed the door behind him and saw the Mustang convertible. "Cool ride. You got sunscreen?"

"Yeah, in the glove box."

Tomas grinned. "Still call it a glove box?" He jumped into the passenger side. "Cool."

"Of course." Roger got in beside him. "I've only been here two years; it's still bonnet, boot, and glove box. But getting used to Fahrenheit instead of Celsius and driving on the other side of the car *and* road, that's just plain weird."

Tomas laughed, and Roger gunned the engine and drove out of the driveway both so lost in each other they didn't even notice the car tailing them.

"So, where are you taking me?" Tomas asked as the warm Miami breeze whipped his black locks back and forth.

"I thought I'd take you to the beach. Have you checked that out yet?"

"Not yet."

"We could have lunch at a little place owned by a friend of mine, and one that is very gay-friendly. You won't be harassed there. We can spend the afternoon strolling Miami Beach, then I can drop you off to freshen up, and I'll take you to *Love Stick*. It's fast becoming the place to be here in Miami."

"Sounds great. I haven't been out much since we got here. I've spent weeks training the ladies, and haven't had much time for anything else."

"I think it will help if you have a fellow Aussie show you around and we can talk about home if you want to."

"God, I miss the place sometimes. My grandparents were out a couple of months ago. Papa brings them over for mama so she still gets to see them."

"That's nice of him." Roger took a right-hand turn.

"Yeah, means a lot to us too."

"How many of you are there?"

"Just me and my two brothers. I'm the middle child."

"Ah." Roger grinned. "The dastardly middle child."

"The quiet, non-boisterous middle child."

"Ah, well, that explains everything."

"What do you mean by that?"

"Your whole demeanour is quiet, reserved, introverted." Roger pulled to a stop at Miami Beach.

"Yeah," Tomas said. "I guess I am."

"So, what do you think?" Roger sat up on the back of his seat. "Is our beach as good as Mykonos or Australia?"

Tomas joined him and took in the sweeping beach with its glorious yellow sand and aqua blue water. "It's great," he said enthusiastically. "Not as good as Mykonos mind you, but still great."

After a fun-filled day that made Tomas relax, Roger dropped him off to change and picked him up an hour later. They spent a couple of hours at *Love Stick*, the restaurant bar that was the current popular spot for gay men. Roger introduced Tomas to some of his friends, and they relaxed over drinks and music. Arriving at Bette's just after one in the morning, Roger escorted Tomas to the front door.

"What are you doing?" Tomas smiled.

"Escorting my date to the front door," Roger replied.

Tomas stopped short. "Date?"

"Well…isn't that what we've been on?" Roger arched a brow.

Tomas's mouth moved, but nothing came out.

"Is being on a date too much for you right now?" Roger asked softly.

"Yes," came out in a rush. The feelings welled in Tomas's throat.

Roger nodded. "Understandable. Just two guys hanging out then. I'll go and leave you to it." He held out his hand. "Good night."

Confused, Tomas took the hand offered. "Night." And held on.

So did Roger.

Tomas blinked and breathed.

So did Roger.

Tomas breathed and reluctantly let go. "Night."

So did Roger. "Night."

From the shadows in the street, Luiz watched the scene play out on the terrace. The anger boiled over and burned his insides. His fists clenched either side of him. *No one touches my Tomas but me. No one. I have no idea who you are or what you want, but it won't be my Tomas.*

*****

Monday morning at eight, Tomas had a one on one with Marie Von Burstenstore. She had been with Violet and Bertha at *The Joy Stick*.

"And go down on your right leg, extend your left leg back, arms up above your head." Tomas held his left hand on her stomach as he slid his right hand down the back of her left leg. "Extend it, straighten the hips." He shifted her hips slightly. "Lengthen the spine, reach back." His hands slid up her spine to her head. "And stretch."

"Oh," she groaned. "That's good."

"Stretching always feels good." Tomas slid his hand down her back, over her hip and down her leg. "Stretch it out."

"Oh." She sighed. "I meant you. You're good."

"So I've been told. Now come back up and do the same to the other side." He stood as she did and walked around her while she positioned herself to stretch.

"Are you gay, Tomas?" Marie slid down, right leg back, left leg steady.

"What's that got to do with anything?" He slid his hand down her leg to strengthen it.

"I want a man. I *need* a man. A healthy, fit, young man. And I'd love it to be you, but if you're gay, then that's obviously not going to happen." She turned her head. "Unless you change your mind or decide you're bi or something. I need a man, Tomas."

"I'm not that man, Marie." He smiled. "Do the child yoga pose for a few moments, and we're done for the morning."

"Maybe I should have snagged that Luiz stud from Bertha. He was hot." Her voice was muffled as her head was on the floor, but he still heard her.

"What about Luiz?" His heart pounded like a hundred horses' hooves in his chest.

"Did you ever meet him? I think she took him to the Greek Islands with her. Young, hot, a Mediterranean style delicacy. Now that's she's dropped him I wonder if he's free." She slowly sat up, knowing full well Tomas had met Luiz, having heard it all from Bertha at the club.

She just wanted to see what Tomas said about it. "She hasn't said what happened. Did you meet him?"

"Uh." Tomas walked over to the side table for a towel. "Briefly." He handed it to her as she stood.

"Hot hunk of horny looking man meat, isn't he." She dabbed her face while watching his. "I'd love to get that into me. What about you?"

Tomas blushed and stayed in control. "I'll see you tomorrow, Marie."

*****

During the week, Tomas was bombarded with personal invitations into the ladies' boudoirs which he politely turned down. Now, with it being Friday night, he wanted some male company.

"Why don't you call him?" Bette checked herself in the hallway mirror. She was going out with the girls and had invited Tomas to come along, but he had declined.

"Call who?" he asked innocently, leaning against the wall next to the mirror.

"Oh, pish," she scoffed. "You know full well who I mean. That young man from the studio. What's his name? Roger?"

"Yeah." Tomas drifted away. "Roger."

"From the look on your face, I'd say you were taken with him, so I suggest you call him. Right," she checked her purse, "I have my money, my powder, my lipstick. I'm off. Have fun and call him," she said as the door closed behind her.

Tomas wandered down the hallway to the French doors that led out to the back terrace, thinking about Roger. He wasn't sure if he should call. What if he was too busy? What if Roger wasn't interested? Was *he* interested? After what happened with Luiz he didn't want to rush into another relationship. Not that this was a relationship, just a summer thing, a friendship even. But still, the guilt lingered. He glanced down the hallway at the phone, wondering if he should call.

The phone rang.

Tomas bolted down the hall and picked it up. "Hello, Bette Olander's residence."

"Tomas? Is that you?"

"Roger?"

"Yeah, hi."

"Hi."

"I, uh, was wondering if you were doing anything tonight. It's been a hectic week, and I thought you might want to get together and do something."

"Uh, yeah, sure, but ah, I don't really feel like going out…maybe you could come over here…have dinner…" He waited while his insides freaked out.

"Sure. I'd love to. See you soon."

The dial tone sounded, and Tomas almost screamed for joy. *Calm down, calm, down.* He dropped the phone into the cradle and went in search of food in the kitchen. He found plenty in the well-stocked fridge.

"Do you need something, sir?" Webster asked, walking through the door.

"No, thanks, Webster. I'm having a guest over, but we'll make something ourselves. You have the night off."

Webster nodded. "Very well, sir."

Fifteen minutes later the doorbell rang, and Tomas ran like an eager puppy to answer it. *Calm down, calm down.* He checked himself in the mirror before opening the door. He saw Roger's smiling face and his stomach did flip flops. "Hi, come in."

"Hey," Roger said. "Busy week?" He stepped into the entrance. "Wow, as impressive as the outside." Between the wide hall, sweeping staircase, chandeliers at ten paces and all of the ornate woodwork, it really was quite impressive.

"You hungry?" Tomas shut the door.

"Ah, yeah." *But not for food,* Roger thought.

"Great. The butler's got the night off, so I thought we'd make something." He led the way into the kitchen that was opposite the ballroom at the back of the house. "I can cook a few things, but I'm not great." He pulled open the fridge door. "See anything you like?"

"Absolutely."

"Great. We can—" Tomas's hand was grabbed, making him stop. He looked into Roger's eyes, so brown that he drowned in them. His heart pounded, and so did the blood causing his penis to become engorged. His breath was hard.

"Can I kiss you?" Roger asked softly. "I've wanted to all week."

Tomas swallowed the lump that had risen to his throat. "Ah...I..." He breathed out. "Yes..." came out in a whisper.

The fridge door forgotten, Roger stepped toward him. He was six three and towered over Tomas by four inches. He moved slowly, not wanting to scare him. His fingers interweaved with Tomas's and everything about his being was on fire. It had been a long time since he'd been with anyone as no one had interested him. But now this beautiful half Greek God was standing before him. His lips moved in and landed on their chosen spot.

It was sweet, gentle, but Tomas wanted more. He kissed back, opening his lips and delving his tongue into Roger's mouth. *Oh, God, he feels so good. It feels so right. Roger feels so right.* His arms slid around Roger's waist as their tongues danced wildly in a synchronised tribal beat. "Oh, God," he gasped in between tongue mating. "I want you. I want this."

Hands slid all over the place, exploring, touching, caressing. Mouths and tongues tasted until Roger finally pulled away and took Tomas's face in his hand. "Is this what you want? You've only been with one person. You're still new to this."

"Yes," Tomas whispered. "Yes." After a kiss, he led Roger upstairs to his room. He had the opposite side of the house to Bette, so it wouldn't disturb her to have a guest over. He locked the door before walking over to the bed and flinging back the covers. He turned to Roger.

"I want you," he whispered and slid his hands under Roger's polo top, moving them up his body to push the top over his head. Greedy hands slid down, up, all around. "Oh, God look at you," he gasped softly. Hands slid into shorts and briefs and slid them down to set

Roger's erect manhood free. With trembling hands, Tomas stroked him. He hardened further, so he massaged him.

A groan escaped from Roger's throat before he grasped Tomas's hands. Undressing him, he marvelled at the tanned Adonis. Dark hair spattered his body in all the right places, especially around his twelve inch cock. "Jesus, Tomas." His hand slid over the package. "That's a hell of a cock you've got."

"Take it," Tomas whispered. "It's yours. Do what you want with it."

Roger's thumbs slid down over the tip getting a sharp gasp, and a head tilt in reaction. He motioned for Tomas to lie on the bed and proceeded to do exactly what he wanted. Burying his head in Tomas's crotch, he took great delight in feeding from the fountain.

Hours after, they slowed down, languishing on piles of pillows as the night-time summer breeze wafted through the open balcony doors.

"Jesus, Tomas." Roger's fingers trailed up and down his abdomen. "And you reckon you've been with only one man and had one experience. That's a hell of a lot of experience for one encounter."

Tomas kissed Roger's chest as he lay curled against it. "It was an encounter, but being with you made it all better. It's relaxing. No concerns, no worries. I'm still learning, and you're a great teacher." His fingers slid around Roger's torso. "You can teach me so much."

"You're definitely open to it. That's for sure." Roger smirked. "Very open."

Tomas slid a leg over Roger's. "Absolutely. I want you to teach me everything you know."

"And what about what you'll teach me?" Roger gently slid a finger across Tomas's face. "What will you teach me, Tomas Stephanopoulos? How to be young again?"

"Aren't you?" Tomas smiled "You can't be much older than me."

"I'm twenty-nine, nearly thirty."

"Well, that's okay." Tomas kissed him. "Means you have more experience at this. More time to learn things, do things." Another kiss, long and lingering. Followed by another and another as Tomas made his way down Roger's smooth bronzed body to the inner sanctum. Tomas had never taken a man before so set about things slowly. He gently kissed Roger's cock all the way along the shaft, making it rise to the occasion. Planting kisses all over it, he gently kissed the end, getting a sharp intake of breath in return. Slowly, gently, he licked and tasted before sliding his mouth over the top.

"Ah!" Roger arched. "Make sure to relax your mouth, no teeth," he gasped, spreading his legs for Tomas to lie between.

Tomas positioned himself and took Roger whole, regaling him with his tongue before sliding off and turning around. He sat with his back to Roger and mounted him as Roger's hands went to his hips to guide him.

"Ah," Tomas groaned, grinding up and down. "Ah, God." He rubbed himself until they both came and he dismounted. Turning around he slid up Roger's body and lay half on half off as Roger enveloped him in his arms.

"You're learning." Roger kissed his forehead. "Definitely learning."

In the shadows on the street, Luiz clicked the light on his watch. Five past two. He eyed the Mustang in the driveway and knew it belonged to that guy he'd seen with Tomas last week. He'd been there since after seven and hadn't left. He glanced around to make sure no one was watching and proceeded to race up the driveway to the car, remove his knife from his pocket, and stab all four tyres. He unscrewed the petrol cap and poured sugar into the tank, then scratched up and down and along the sides, trunk and hood. When he was satisfied, he raced back to the street, and with a smirk slipped into the shadows and disappeared.

They woke in each other's arms, floating out of a deep, peaceful sleep to find themselves enmeshed. It was as if they'd been doing it all of their lives. The warm breeze drifted through the curtains and over their semi-naked bodies. The sheet was a tangled mess and wrapped around their legs.

Roger breathed deeply. His arms were around Tomas as though it was the most natural thing in the world, as was waking together. This was something he wanted to do every single day. He'd never met anyone like him, and for all the partners he'd had, none were like Tomas. Maybe it was his naivety, his newness, his lack of experience with sex in general, let alone gay sex. He stroked his lover's chiselled cheek bone and marvelled at the man beside him and the way he fitted him like a glove, as though they were made for each other.

Tomas breathed in and opened his eyes a fraction. He was in Roger's arms, and it felt like heaven, felt so right. His head was on his chest, and he smiled, sliding his hand up Roger's side. He tilted his head back to look at his lover who was watching back. He blushed and buried his head in Roger's chest. "Morning."

Roger kissed his head. "Morning. How do you feel?"

Tomas smiled. "Happy, alive, free." He moved upward, and Roger rolled onto his side so they were facing each other. Stroking Roger's face, he said, "I'm so happy."

Roger matched his smile with one of his own. "Good." Their fingers entwined between them. "So, what do you want to do today?"

"You." Tomas grinned and kissed him. "All day."

*****

Sunday afternoon, they rolled out of bed and had a late lunch on the back terrace.

"What are you doing this week?" Tomas asked around a strawberry. He bit into the sweet delight. "Anything interesting?"

"I'm filming a couple of movies and helping out on others." Roger took a sip of freshly squeezed juice. "Wanna come watch?"

Tomas's mood blackened. He'd forgotten that Roger was a porn star and now the thought of his man having sex with someone else disgusted him.

Roger noticed the change. "It's just work. Just a job, nothing more. I made the decision a long time ago to never get involved with people I worked with. So I never have. And many of my co-stars also have partners, so there's no involvement. We get in, get out, job done."

Tomas glanced up. "What's it like?"

"What?"

"Having sex with someone in front of people, in front of cameras, people watching you naked and," he made hand gestures, "being connected physically."

Roger set down his glass. "At first it was weird. When I did the two straight porn movies, it was weird on two levels. One, because everyone was watching, and two, because I didn't want to be with women. When I moved to gay porn, it was a bit easier being with another man, and I got used to having Marcus yell out directions. He doesn't always, but sometimes, you just have to forget they're all there. Shut them out and get on with it."

"Have you…" Tomas played with his napkin. "Ever had a partner that disagreed with what you do?"

"No."

Tomas looked into Roger's big brown eyes. "Ever?"

"I've been single the whole time I've been in America, so you're the first. Do you disagree with what I do?"

"I…" Tomas shook his head and shrugged. "I don't know. All of this is new to me and still a bit weird. And I'm uncomfortable with being on display."

"You're not. Unless you want to be," Roger said slyly.

"What do you mean?"

"Well…" Roger raised a brow. "What if *we* did a movie together?"

Tomas blinked. "Us? In a porn movie?"

Roger blinked. "Yes."

Tomas looked everywhere but at Roger. "I…ah…I… Oh, God."

"Would it be so wrong? You, me, you could make a lot of money doing it."

"Money's not the issue."

"Why don't you come and watch me do a movie and see how you feel?"

"Watch you?" Tomas was horrified. He didn't need to see his new lover having sex with anyone else.

"Tomas," Roger said. "It's not that bad. I'd love to do one with you. Why don't you come by tomorrow night and watch?"

Tomas sighed in defeat. "Maybe."

"Meantime." Roger wiped his mouth. "I better get going. Walk me to my car?" His fingers reached for Tomas's and wound around them.

They walked out to his car and stopped in horror. "What...the... fuck..."

"Oh, my God, Roger." Tomas stared, horrified at the damage to the Mustang. The paint had been scratched, the tyres were all flat.

"What the fuck," Roger repeated, circling the car to check the damage. "It's scratched on every surface. Fucking hell!"

"How could this have happened?" Tomas asked, standing on the mansion steps.

"Fucked if I know." Roger ran a hand through his hair. "But it's going to cost me a fucking bundle."

"So, what do we do? Call a garage?" Tomas asked.

"Guess I'm gonna have to. You got a phone book?"

Half an hour later, the tow truck arrived and hitched the Mustang up, towing it away to be repaired. Tomas drove Roger to the auto shop and sixty minutes later found it was worse than they'd first thought. Sugar had also been poured into the gas tank.

"Fuck it!" Roger spat, pacing around the office. "Who the fuck would do this? And at Bette's place. That means someone *came onto* the property and trashed my car in the middle of the night. That's fucked up that is."

Tomas tried to soothe him. "Maybe it was the local hooligans. I don't know. But maybe you should make a police report."

"Oh, hell yeah, I'm making a police report." Roger stood with his hands on his hips. "As soon as I can get another car."

"Is there a rental place around? I'll drive you," Tomas told him.

*****

Eight o'clock Monday night, Tomas reluctantly popped by *Seralift* studios and stood in the background as Roger filmed his love scene with a tall, dark African American man, and regardless of the reservations he'd had, he actually found it quite arousing. He watched the way Roger expertly manipulated the man into doing what he wanted. The way he moved him, bent him, made him do everything right from the beginning. From the kisses to the touches to the thrusting in perfect sync.

Tomas found himself in need of relief; relief he would find only in Roger. For all his doubts, what he'd just witnessed was a hell of a turn on. When it was over, the crew dispersed and only Roger was left.

"So…what did you think?" Roger slipped on a robe.

"Of what?" Tomas smiled coyly.

"Of the movie. What I do." Roger stood in front of him and took his hands. "What did you think?"

Tomas linked his fingers through Roger's. "Ah…" He blushed.

"Yes," Roger quietly cajoled.

Tomas blushed harder. "It was…hot…"

"Good." Roger pulled him into his arms and kissed him. "Would you like to try it out?"

"Try what out?" Tomas stroked Roger's chest.

"Making a movie together," Roger said against his lips.

"Ah." Tomas pulled back. "I know it looked hot, but…"

"Let's give it a go." Roger's fingers slid under Tomas's top and down his shorts. "I can go again. We can film it, and you could be a star, Tomas Stephanopoulos," Roger whispered against his cheek. His fingers circled Tomas's manhood. "You could be a star, Tomas."

Tomas groaned and leant in, resting his head on Roger's cheek. "Oh, God." The pressure from Roger's hand was doing damage to his resolve. The manipulating fingers added to the destruction. "It couldn't hurt to try it. Just once." He touched his lips to Roger's.

Roger grinned. "Let's make a movie." He led Tomas to the steam room set.

"Oh, no, I can't." Tomas baulked.

"No," Roger said. "Time to make new memories so you can get rid of the old ones." He set the video cameras rolling, turned on the lights and the steam machine. "Now, let's make some magic." He dropped his robe and helped Tomas out of his clothes before taking him into the steam room. His fingers slid up Tomas's arm, and he leant in close. He pleasured and pleased and aroused him in all manners using his mouth and tongue, and had Tomas shaking at the knees, weak from the attack on his senses. Weak from the steam.

"Oh," Tomas whispered. "Oh, God," escaped into the steam as Roger went down on him. "Oh, God." He held him in place, pulsating in time to the rhythm of his mouth. "Oh, God."

Roger's tongue lapped it up and kept on going, up Tomas's torso and into his mouth. He rubbed his erection against his lover's and turned him around to face the wall, spreading his legs with his knee.

Tomas looked weakly over his shoulder. "I want you."

Roger kissed him and stood between his legs hard and full and ready for take-off. He rubbed himself back and forth, pushing against the back of Tomas's testicles, pushing up toward the anus. Back and forth he rubbed while his hand slid around to the front to do equal damage. He handled, cajoled, kneaded.

"Oh, God," Tomas cried against the wall, his head falling back. "Oh, God." He came in Roger's hands, and Roger entered, bringing him to the brink again. "Oh, God," Tomas yelled. "Oh, God, oh, God, oh, God." He came a second time and collapsed against the wall. "Oh, God, what you do to me."

"And I want to do it every single minute of every single day." Roger kissed his neck and nuzzled his ear.

Tomas gasped, waiting for his breath to settle. "I want you to do it every single minute of every single day."

Roger's fingers enclosed Tomas's on the wall beside their faces. "I want to come inside of you, make love to you, make you mine."

"I want to be yours," Tomas panted. "I *am* yours. All yours."

Roger kissed his way along Tomas's shoulder, looking out into the studio. Marcus was standing there open-mouthed and staring, with Violet beside him, fanning herself with her handkerchief.

"We're done," Roger whispered and withdrew, quickly collecting his robe and Tomas's clothes. He blocked the view so Tomas could dress. "We have company," he whispered when he was done. "Be cool."

Tomas panicked, but nodded, and let Roger lead him out of the set and over to Marcus and Violet. Having his love life on view was not what he wanted, and having sex with people watching was not on. His stomach tightened in knots.

"Enjoy the show?" Roger asked, keeping a protective step in front of Tomas. "It was a private moment between a couple... But what did you think?"

"Fucking brilliant," Marcus said. "That was the horniest, steamiest, best piece of fucking I've seen in my whole career in the industry. You two," he thrust a finger at them, "have the most explosive fuckable chemistry I've ever seen. You, my boy," he told Tomas, "are now my biggest star, and the two of you," he waved his finger, "are now going to be a couple if you're not already. But I mean in movies. Just the two of you, starring in my movies. They're going to be big, big I tell ya. Welcome to the industry kid. Come on, Violet, let's make some plans." He walked off leaving her standing there.

"Well!" She fluttered her hanky. "Now I know what all of us ladies are missing out on. Whoo, hot in here." She quickly followed her ex-husband.

Roger shut down the cameras and steam pump, leaving the overhead lights on. "I'll just get dressed, and we can go."

While he dressed, Tomas desperately thought through what had just happened. He was being intimate with his lover, but Marcus and Violet had been watching. Could he do that for a living? Could he do that and more in front of other people, a whole sound stage of crew, watching, filming it for the whole world to see?

He wrapped his arms around himself and held on tight. Could he do this in front of people for the world to see? Would being with Roger make it all worthwhile? He watched Roger do up his pants and marvelled at his body, knowing he was in love with the man before him. So desperately in love. For the first time ever. For the first time in his twenty-two years, he was in love. And it was with a man. Could he do it *for* him? Could he do it *with* him? His brow furrowed. He felt the pain of indecision and knew he had to make a choice. Work *with* his lover, or watch him work with other men. Could he do that? Could he seriously stand by while his new lover made love to other men for a living? In that very moment, he didn't know. But it was a decision he was going to have to make.

Once Roger was dressed, they left hand in hand.

In the shadows of the studio, Luiz lurked behind a sound stage. He'd followed Tomas there and watched the first movie, then stayed and watched, in horror, him replicate their time in the steam room at the resort.

"No one does that with my Tomas," he spat viciously. "No one touches him, fucks him, or sucks him the way I do, and that little cock sucker's going to pay for taking Tomas's memory of me. *No one* gets my man but me." He held up his large silver knife, and the light glinted off the cold hard metal.

Oh, no. No one gets my Tomas. Clearly, my first warning was not enough. No, looks like I'll have to step it up a notch.

Leaving the studio he hid in the shadows, watching them walk hand in hand to their car and leave.

No one gets my Tomas. He brandished the knife.

It was August, and Carlos was on the set of his very first porn movie, sitting in a director's chair with his name on the back, reading his script and running through his lines. He glanced around the room, a room in Harry DeVille's home, set up like a studio with lights and cameras and made to look like a cabana.

Talk about art imitating life.

Harry had taken one look at Carlos that fateful day two months ago and knew he was everything he'd heard about from Harriet, who'd heard about it from Connie and Viv. The half Greek Adonis was everything he'd wanted, and Harry knew exactly how to make him a star. He'd use the same concept of what Carlos's life had been. Resorts, cabanas, and private massages.

He'd had his writers get a script together, hired his best actress, and set about turning Carlos Stephanopoulos into Carlo Stefan, the biggest and brightest porn star in his stable.

Of course, the name change was important, even though it didn't take a genius to figure it out. But at least the cops weren't looking for him. No, Harry's PIs had turned up some very interesting information about the crime committed, the people behind it, and how it had affected all involved. He assured Carlos all was okay, and so was he.

"Well, my boy." Harry slapped Carlos on the back. "How are you today?" He sat in the chair beside him.

Carlos smiled. He hadn't minded the name change or the new hair style, but reliving his life on the island was straight out weird. "Good, Harry," he said. "But this is just…" He waved the script in the air. "Reliving my life. It's nothing different, nothing new."

"No, no, Carlos; it's not. But one look at you after the stories I'd heard and I knew that women worldwide would want you to massage them…" he winked, "in every way. It's perfect for you. With your looks, look at you." Harry eyed him up and down. Carlos had kept the tan up while in L.A. and worked out to stay in shape. "Women are going to die over you."

Carlos smiled. "I hope you're right. I'd hate to be a failure and let you down. Especially after everything you've done."

"The only way you've let me down is by not letting me try out the goods."

"I don't swing that way, Harry."

"I know, and I respect that. Doesn't mean I can't be unhappy about it. How are you holding up with everything else going on?"

Carlos nodded. "Good. I talked to my family yesterday. Both of my brothers have left the island, but my parents are still there. They're grateful the whole thing has died down and all but disappeared."

"Yeah." Harry sucked on his cigar. "Even I'm surprised about that one. Some bigwig from Athens is involved somehow and shut it down pretty quick. Didn't want the publicity, apparently."

"Do we know who the bigwig is?" Carlos ran a hand through his now short-ish hair that was the latest style for men.

"That was all kept hush-hush." Harry blew smoke rings. "I'm thinking he paid off the Greek Feds to keep it quiet."

"Am I still wanted for murder and rape?"

"Not that we could see. The charges seem to have disappeared."

"Just like my brothers." Carlos sighed.

"Your parents holding up with all the kids out of the nest?"

Carlos smiled. "Barely. All of Mama's babies have fled the nest within months of each other. Papa…well…he's pissed off about his son's legal issues and that we won't be working in the meat shop this winter."

"Do meat shops do good business in winter?"

Carlos laughed. "With the three of us working there, yeah. Everyone buys from us in the winter, and all the other stores complain they get no customers. *'Your sons are putting us out of business,'* they complain. *'Good,'* Papa says, *'then I'll be the only meat shop on the island'.*"

"Meat shop, huh." An idea formed in Harry's mind. "Meat… shop…"

"Yeah." Carlos saw the faraway look on Harry's face. "What are you thinking?"

"A great idea, kid. A big money-maker involving meat." Harry slapped him on the back and stood up. "And you're the meat." He walked away laughing.

"Okay, we're ready to go," the director yelled. "Carlo, Neesa, take your places. The lighting's ready, camera's ready. Harry!"

Everyone took their positions.

Carlos was standing in the cabana in his white tank and shorts. The curtains billowed softly, fake candles were lit. The massage table was covered in a white sheet and rose petals. He shivered, remembering the last time he'd been in a place like that.

"Ready on set…three…two…one…action…"

Carlos was tidying the towels when an exotic beauty walked in. Creamy chocolate skin, long limbs, short hair, and a mouth as big as it needed to be to take a man into it.

"Well, hello," Carlos greeted. "Lie face down on the table and we'll get started.

"Oh, no, darling." She slid her one-piece straps off her shoulders, down her body, and stepped out of it, much to Carlos's satisfaction. "I prefer face up." She gracefully sat on the bed, swung her long, lithe legs up and lay down. She arched her back slightly to push her large breasts up, and bent her legs, spreading them for all to see. "Come, darling. Massage me from the inside out."

Carlos took his time, even though his cock wanted to get things going now. He massaged her legs up to her inner thighs.

"Ugh, oh," she groaned, arching. "Come, darling, come."

Carlos slipped off his clothes and mounted the table between her legs. Pushing them down, he manoeuvred himself so his knees were outside of hers, her legs now shut.

She arched higher. "Ugh, take me, darling, take me."

His hands did their magic across her abdomen and up over her breasts.

"Ugh, oh, God." She clenched the sheets. "Oh, God, you're good."

A wicked smile spread across Carlos's face, and he shifted position so he was sitting farther up. His penis lay between her breasts as he gently squeezed them together, massaging all three at once.

Her nipples were harder and larger than he'd ever seen, and so was he. He forgot there was a camera crew watching and felt as if he was back home working. Working the exotic beauties he'd had every lunchtime, every night-time. His hands moved up to her shoulders and throat, massaging the muscles to relieve the stiffness.

"Oh, God, come," she rasped. "I'm coming, come, come."

Carlos shifted again. In one motion he knelt, tucked her arms under his legs and sat on her breasts. He lifted her head and led her mouth to his cock that was so ready to be sucked. "Come," he commanded. "Come."

She sucked greedily as he controlled her head, thrusting it back and forth over his shaft. He groaned and his head flung back. "Suck, suck." Faster and faster he thrust her head and she clung to the table, groaning and moaning. And before she knew it she flung her legs up around his shoulders trying to lock her ankles in place. He flung them away, but she pulled her knees up and grabbed his arms, letting the world see it all. She didn't care. He didn't care. They showed the world that they came together.

It was over, and they stopped in the same positions, panting, sweating.

He released her head. She released him. And they relaxed until he slid down her body and off the table. He dressed and offered her a towel.

She lay there. "That was the best massage I've ever had."

"Glad to have pleased you," he said and walked out of the cabana.

"And…cut," the director yelled…finally…

Carlos walked from behind the cabana. "How was I?"

Everyone stared at him, even Neesa, in dead silence, and when he frowned, one by one they started applauding, starting with Harry. He even got a standing ovation.

Carlos reddened, his cheeks burning his face. He'd only ever been applauded by some of the women he'd serviced, not by a room full of men.

Harry came over to him with Harriet not far behind. "My boy." He slapped him on the back. "You've just made us a million dollars."

"Really?" Carlos's eyes widened. "You'll sell that much?"

"Maybe more." Harry walked him over to his chair.

"Oh, if only you'd do that to me, Carlos," Harriet said with Neesa behind her. "I would love for you to do that to me."

"I'd love for you to do that to me *again*," Neesa said. "I don't know how you did it, honey, but you have learned things and know things that I've never seen any man know. There's definitely something about you." She fondled his hair as she stood by his side. "Definitely something about you."

"It's the half Greek thing," Harry said matter-of-factly. "Look at him. Golden body, muscles up to here…" Harry indicated with a hand to his face. "Big blue eyes, golden hair. He's the Golden God."

"I like the sound of that." Harriet fluttered in front of him, pawing at his knee.

Harry nodded. "Yeah, yeah, so do I. From now on you're Carlo Stefan, the Golden God. And we'll do more than just Cabana movies. I've got a few ideas forming. *God-like* ideas."

Harriet gasped. "Oh, I know. Do supernatural movies. He's the God of Greece and he comes down to be serviced by all the different women every night." She rubbed his leg, her hand moving higher which he politely moved away with a gentle squeeze.

"You got it, Harriet. Reading my mind again. David," Harry bellowed, and a young guy in his twenties with short brown hair and glasses came running over with a clipboard. "Take down this idea." Harry led him away as he belted out his thoughts and David tried keeping up with them.

"Is that it for today?" Carlos asked.

"We may need to do another take." Neesa tickled his ear. "Just in case they didn't get it all the first time."

Carlos grinned. "Are you up for it again?"

"Well, if you do *that* again, I'm up for anything."

His grin got bigger. "So am I."

As it turned out, they only needed to do a few checks for lights and sound and that was it, much to Neesa's disappointment.

Carlos's first day on the set was done.

*****

Viv, Connie, and Carlos rocked up to *Troubadour*, one of L.A.'s biggest clubs, that night for a celebration. The whole cast and crew were partying, thanks to Harry, for a job well done and a future to look forward to.

Carlos felt out of his league. Every which way he turned there were celebrities, musicians, and actors. Robert Redford, Michael Jackson, Johnny Carson.

Viv led them to the corner of the club and picked up three glasses of champagne, handing one each to Connie and Carlos.

"Carlos, my boy," Harry yelled out from his prime position in the centre of the space where he was surrounded by beautiful women and gorgeous men, plus staff and crew. "Welcome to the world of sex. Cheers."

"Cheers."

Champagne, wine, beer, all flowed freely. Cocaine, acid and painkillers were snorted, popped or injected even more freely, and Carlos found himself veering away to the centre of the room with its dance floor, loud thumping music, and hypnotic beats. He found himself taken away, just as his nights on Mykonos. He danced up a storm with women wanting to dance with him and men wanting to kill him…except for the guys who wanted to fuck him as badly as the women.

Carlos watched the room and the people in it. His white suit and black shirt brought out the tanned skin and golden locks. His dance moves brought everyone to him, and he found himself dancing with a girl who looked too innocent to be at a club like that.

She stood wide-eyed as he gyrated and thrust at her, not moving, clutching her purse to her chest. The rose-coloured dress with its skinny straps brought rosiness to her cheeks, and her long curly hair was swept back with rose barrettes.

Carlos finally noticed how spooked she looked and stopped dancing. "Are you okay?" He leant in, his hand on her elbow.

"What?" She couldn't hear him.

He waved a hand toward the exit and guided her through the crowd until they made their way outside to the relative peace and quiet. "Whew, that was noisy," Carlos said, leading the girl a few feet away from the crowd waiting to get in. "Now." He turned to face her. "Are you okay?"

"Uh." She gazed up at the gorgeous man she'd allowed to lead her away from her friends. "Why wouldn't I be okay?"

"Because you looked scared and out of place." Carlos took in her features. Big brown eyes, button nose, rose-red lips. She was slim, pretty, and he was stirring.

"I'm...fine..." she said slowly, not sure she should even be standing on the street with a man that looked like a god, let alone outside of the club she'd tried for a whole year to get into.

"Well, you didn't look it." He saw her shivering, took off his blazer, and laid it around her shoulders.

"Oh." She looked everywhere but at him. "Thank you."

"I'm Carlos. What's your name?" He was close enough to smell her scent.

She smelt his and breathed it in. "Rosalee."

Their eyes connected.

Their lips connected.

Their tongues connected.

And before anyone knew it he had her against the wall in the alley next to the club.

"Ah, oh, oh." She arched against the wall, head back, knickers down, leg hooked over his arm and around his waist. He filled her, and she felt every glorious inch of him.

Fear, surprise, passion, desire, all finally ripped through her as he picked her up and she wrapped her other leg around him. "Oh, God," she screamed as he buried himself in her.

Carlos grunted. It was good to have plain old sex again. Picking up some woman and having his way. It wasn't paid for, wasn't booked in, and wasn't a performance. It was pure pleasurable sex, and he hadn't gotten that since Mykonos. Not even Connie or Viv had wanted his services.

He came to a screaming halt and slowly let her slip back to the ground. Releasing himself, he tucked it away as she dazedly pulled up her knickers and smoothed down her dress. "What do you say we go back to my place?" He'd gotten a small apartment at the beach a month ago because he didn't want to live off Connie anymore, and with the money he'd saved from six years of resort work he'd had enough for a hefty down payment.

Rosalee stood staring at him. "Who are you?"

He frowned. "Uh, Carlos."

She blushed. "I know. I meant who *are* you? Are you a celebrity, actor?"

"Yeah…actor."

She turned the same pretty colour as her dress. "Have I seen you in anything?"

"Not yet. I just shot it today."

"Oh, when will it be out?"

"Next month."

"And you have your own place?"

"Yep, wanna go?"

"Yes."

He took her hand and they hailed the limo that had brought him there. After giving the address to the driver, he sat back and they sipped champagne from the mini bar.

"So, it's your first movie?" she asked quietly.

"Yep."

"Will you be doing anymore?"

"I have a whole list of them ready to go."

The alcohol added to the headiness of post sex and they were already locking lips by the time they stumbled into his bedroom and onto his massive animal print covered bed.

"I don't normally do this," she whispered as he slid her underwear down and her dress up before lying naked under his expert hands.

"Do what?" He quickly undressed and lay beside her, pulling a satin sheet over them.

"Have sex with a man I don't know in a cheap alley and then go home with him to fall into bed." She sighed at the touch of his hand.

"Well, there's a first time for everything." His lips followed his fingers and explored her body. She sighed at every touch, every kiss, and he felt like a normal twenty-four year old again. He'd never fallen in love before.

Love!

Where the hell did that come from?

But the feelings he was having lying next to her were vastly different to what he felt while he was fucking every other woman. No, *she* was vastly different. She wasn't out for sex, it had just happened. They had met, been attracted, and it had just happened. Now, he was feeling good about it. And it wasn't bought and paid for.

"Oh, Carlos," she murmured as his fingers found their way between her legs, she arched, instinctively spreading her legs to allow him access. And he obliged, sliding into her as though he had all the time in the world.

Sex was slow, rhythmic, and they rested in between each session, drinking champagne, eating various fruits and berries he kept in the fridge. They talked, they kissed, they made love. They were so enamoured with each other they didn't notice the shadow on the balcony.

The man peered through the half-open curtain. The room was mostly dark except for a few candles, but he could make out Carlos Stephanopoulos and the young brunette he was bedding.

Continuously.

"Doesn't he ever stop," muttered the man who'd managed to climb over the first floor balcony to Carlos's second floor apartment. Feeling highly inadequate, he pulled his straining cock out and relieved himself on the pot plant. He'd seen the little thing she was and had found himself hard at the way her lithe young body moved. Now he was letting his own seed go before making his way back down to the ground. "Ugh," he grunted, getting to his feet. He hurried back down the street to his car, drove to the nearest phone booth, and rang his boss. "Yeah, I found him. I know where he lives. Yeah, with a woman. Young, pretty. Can't keep it in his pants. Yeah, keep following, yeah, okay. Take them both out. Got it."

SEPTEMBER 1977

CARLOS

Carlos stepped out of the limousine to flashbulbs and screaming, standing on the red carpet, savouring the attention, wearing a blue suit and white shirt.

Harry and Harriet stepped out behind him and stood either side. "Well, you've made it, my boy."

"How could I have made it when the movie hasn't even been seen yet?" Carlos waved at fans as they made their way up the carpet.

"Because the trailer that's been playing has everyone so damn hot. So do all of the photos we've released."

Carlos blew kisses to fans as they went inside *The Pussycat Theatre* on Santa Monica Boulevard. The theatre was the place to be to debut all porno movies, and tonight was Carlos's night. It had been a month since he'd filmed it, and he'd made three more since. Now, Harry was setting him up with other ideas.

He shook hands with some of the industry's leaders, and kissed Connie on the cheek before they took their seats inside. Half an hour later, they emerged to explosive clapping and whistling. The movie had gone down well, and they were heading back to Harry's for the after-party.

"So, what next?" Carlos asked from his seat in the back of the limo.

"We release it from tonight and make that million I told you about," Harry said.

"I meant with my career. The movies. What next?"

"Well, we've got that meat shop movie up next, based on your days working there, so that's in pre-production right now. Just have to get the scripts in a couple of days." Harry lit his cigar and puffed.

"Great, so one a week then?"

"One a week."

"Do I get a pay rise?"

"Oh, you definitely get a rise." Harry patted his crotch.

"Harry," Carlos admonished. "Not what I meant."

Harry guffawed. "I know. We'll see how well these Cabana movies go and then talk business."

"And I've been thinking," Carlos said as they rolled up to the house. "I want to be a part of it. A bigger part. I want more control over the way I'm portrayed. I may have made a living from being the resident masseur in the cabana, but I want to be more than that. I want to dictate my future. After all…" He got out of the limo. "My career will be over by the time I'm thirty."

"Not necessarily, my boy." Harry led the way into his house. "If you continue looking that good, you could keep going until your forty or older."

They stepped into the expansive and obscenely decorated living and entertainment room and were enveloped in a sea of staff, crew, celebrities, other porn actors, movie actors, and all manner of people who came to one of Harry DeVille's personal parties.

A glass of champagne was shoved into Carlos's hand, and a stirringly gorgeous brunette led him to two crowded sofas full of hot randy women.

"Carlos," they cooed. "Come join us."

"Or just come," a wickedly delightful African American with cropped hair and large red lips said. She opened her mouth wide. "Oh, yes, do come."

Heat raced over Carlos's face, and he was sure he was beet red. Of course, he was used to horny women hitting on him, but here in Hollywood, it was so blatant. "How about we leave that for another day." He was pulled down onto the couch full of women, finding himself lying across their laps and being fondled. "Hey, ladies." He turned on his back, and the black woman with the big mouth unzipped his pants, pulled out his cock, and started sucking it.

"Whoa, hey, not now. Leave it out. Hey." He was covered in a sea of women as they gathered around to feed on the cock of Adonis.

"Hey." His voice became deep and guttural as they all took him. "Hello, ladies." He grabbed the head of the blonde whose lap he rested his head on and pulled her lips to his. He was sucked and tongued by the women, and at some stage thought he saw a man in the pool, which brought him to his senses. "Whoa, okay, that's enough." He rolled off the women, jumped up, and stumbled over them as he made his way outside while trying to put it back in and zip himself up.

"Oh, come back, Carlos. We want more."

He ran out into the backyard and around the penis-shaped pool to the other side, trying to get some space, and time, to recuperate. He felt used, not that he hadn't enjoyed it, but it wasn't work, and he wasn't getting paid. It was just a bunch of horny women hungrily attacking a horny man. He pushed his hair back. "Jesus!"

"Hello, Carlos."

Spinning around, he came face to face with the Hollywood starlet who'd given him head back in Mykonos. He couldn't think of her name then, and couldn't think of it now. "Hey, you came to my cabana on Mykonos."

"That's right." Her blonde hair was piled on her head with loose curls hanging around her face. She wore a tight, short purple dress with slashes down to her crotch. The back was the same. Purple stilettoes, fiery red lipstick, and some gold jewellery finished off the outfit. She walked seductively up to him. Face to face they stood, while her fingers did their job and her tongue occupied his.

He pushed her away. "I'm off the clock."

"I'll pay." She pulled a wad of hundreds from her gold clutch. "Just like last time…" Casting a glance back at the house she said, "Unlike all of those women that took advantage of you in there."

"How much?" He eyed the money.

"One thousand for a quick fuck wasn't it?" Her lips nuzzled his.

He breathed. "All right."

She pushed him backwards, and they found themselves at the back of the pool house, with her plastered against the wall, her dress around her waist, and her legs around his as he ploughed into her.

"Suck it, suck my tit," she demanded as she was smashed into the wall. She felt the roughness and knew her back would be marked.

His mouth closed around the rubbery nipple and sucked it into a hard lump.

"Harder, suck harder," she cried, gripping his jacket while trying not to break a nail. "Fuck me, fuck me, oh, oh, oh…"

Carlos finished with a final thrust and waited to catch his breath before letting her slide to her feet. He put it away, straightened his clothes, and caught his breath, watching as she put her dress back in place.

"Oh, God," she groaned. "I love it hard and fast. Here." Holding out her hand with the money she snatched it away when he went to take it. She leant against him, pulled his pant waist out and shoved the money down his shorts. "It deserves it," she purred and left him to go back to the party.

He pocketed the cash and waited until she was in the house before carefully making his way to a bench in the garden. Sure it was all about free love, but did he need Harry to know he made some on the side?

Pushing his hair back, he breathed deeply, gazing up into the sky, wondering about his parents. He phoned once a month to be safe, and while they were okay, they hated their sons not being there. And his brothers? Where the hell were they? Pedro was only twenty, Tomas twenty-two. He hoped they weren't getting themselves into anything like he'd done and that they were safe.

"Carlos, my boy, what are you doing out here?" Harry plodded over and sat beside him. At sixty-six he was feeling old, and his body was showing it. His hair was grey and thinning, his skin was over-tanned and sagging. He was no longer the great actor-producer of his time. Well, not in the old way, but he was in the porn way, and he was making a killing.

"Taking a break." Carlos continued staring up at the sky.

"You're one of those now."

"One of what?"

"A star!"

Carlos grinned. "Ya think?"

"I know," Harry said matter-of-factly. "All those women get to ya did they?"

Carlos laughed. "In more ways than one."

"So I saw."

Silence.

"Harry?"

"Mmm?"

"What I said before…I was serious."

"About what?"

"Taking control of my future."

"So, what do you want to do?"

"I want final say on the scripts. There's not much to them, but I want them to be realistic and authentic. To me anyway."

"Okay kid, you can get a look at the scripts."

"I want final say."

"We'll see when they come in."

PEDRO

"Won't your father know you've started classes?" Pedro asked the morning of Angelina's start at Juilliard.

She shrugged. "Probably, if he has someone watching the school, or if he can be bothered making the call. They'll probably just write and tell him." She dressed for her first day in a pretty summer dress and cardigan. It may have been the start of fall, but it was still hitting the high 80s.

"What if he comes here?" Pedro hadn't even been to sleep yet having gotten home from the club as she was getting up at 6:30.

"Then we'll deal with it," she said and grabbed her bag. "Wish me luck." She stuck out her lips for a kiss.

"Good luck." He gave her what she wanted and slept the rest of the day until he strode through the back door of the club at six. He'd been there just over a month, and it still felt amazing. September in New York was beautiful. Angelina was beautiful. Life was beautiful, and Pedro knew he had it all. All he'd ever want to do. DJ in one of the hottest clubs in the world and *Studio 69* was just that. It had become the hottest place to be, to be *seen* in, and he was a part of that.

"Hey, Pedro, what's up, man?" Mike walked into the staff room after him.

"Hey, man, nothing much." Pedro pulled his t-shirt off and unzipped his jeans.

"I hear some bigwig producers are coming in tonight," Mike said.

"Music producers?" Pedro slid into his shorts.

"Nah, man, *movie* producers." Mike pulled up his own shorts; short, gold and tight.

"What sort of movies?" Leon, a roller-skating bartender asked as he came through the door. "Big screen movies?" He fluttered his false eyelashes and did a twirl. "I could be in movies. Don't I have the face for it?" He held his hands under his face to frame it. Leon was a gay black man who talked as flamboyantly as he walked, *and* dressed. Today he was wearing a tight crop top, even tighter leopard print pants, platform boots, and a pink feather boa.

"Hey, Leon." Pedro smiled indulgently, pretending he hadn't heard it all before. "I didn't know you wanted to be in movies. You never said anything."

"Oh, darling," Leon's New York accent came thick and fast as he sat beside Pedro, crossed his legs, and clasped his hands together on his knee. "Let me tell you about the time—"

"Enough already," Mike said. "We've heard it a million times, and we've only been working here for six weeks."

"Well, make it a million and one then," Leon replied before being cut off by Richard, the staff manager.

"Eddie wants you all out on the main floor for a little chat before we open."

"We'll be there in a minute," Pedro told him, and Richard retreated.

"How could that poor man's mother call him Richard," Leon said as he fussed around in his locker.

"What do you mean?" Mike asked.

"Well, their surname is Head, don't ya know," Leon replied. "And his name is Richard. She clearly didn't think about that one."

Mike and Pedro shrugged at each other. They had no idea what Leon was talking about.

"Oh, for heaven's sake." Leon rolled his eyes. "His name is Richard Head. The nickname for Richard is Dick." Leon spread his hands. "His name is Dick Head."

Pedro and Mike snorted. "Get out," Pedro said and grabbed his bag. They walked out to the main floor and waited for Eddie to talk.

"Boys," he called. "We've got some very special people coming tonight. They'll be my guests for the evening, so they are to be treated very well indeed. Whatever they want, whatever they need, we will supply it. You got that?"

"Yes, sir!"

"Good boys," Eddie said. "The other thing is that they are big time movie producers and are on the lookout for new talent."

"Ooohhh, that's me, that's me." Leon waved and twirled around.

Eddie sighed. "It could be any of you, all of you, one of you, none of you. So be on your best behaviour and give them what you've got. Right?"

"Yes, sir!"

"Right, now let's get ready for tonight." He clapped his hands and the staff went their separate ways.

Pedro stepped behind his deck and booted up the system. He always came alive when he got behind his booth and set the needle on the records. It filled him like nothing else ever did.

Not even Angelina.

People started piling into the club and headed straight for him. He had the same fans every night; socialites in their thirties, gay men in their twenties. Every night they were first in the door, they stood in front of his booth all night, and were the last out the door.

He waved to Bev Marie, the high-end fashion model, and threw a cheeky grin at Sara Holdare, the CEO of a hot cosmetics company who became a millionaire by the age of thirty-eight. And that was three years ago. Now she was sitting on *tens* of millions and knew how to flash the cash.

Martine Krevnokov was in the crowd. The wife of a Russian oil baron made her life in New York while her husband lived with his mistress in St Petersburg. Her nickname was Ice Queen for the blondest of blonde hair and bluest of blue eyes. The silver sable fur coat seemed out of place for September considering that summer was hanging on. She was dressed in a skin-tight silver jumpsuit that showed there was no way anything was underneath it, and silver glittered heels so high Pedro wondered how she didn't fall. Or break an ankle.

Stan Kosnov was beside her dancing as though his life depended on it. He was a business man by day, dancer out of the closet by night, and he'd taken a shine to Pedro.

Pedro danced behind his console, waving his hands at the crowd, getting them screaming and singing.

"I told you the kid was good," Eddie told his guests.

"He's gorgeous," a woman said, and the others agreed. "But quite a few of them are good looking." She was Greta Von Burro, American born, and of Swedish descent. Her parents had been refugees after the war. She'd grown up in Chicago, Illinois, but resided full-time in New York.

"I like the bartender," a man in his late thirties said. He was Thomas Derbon, publicity and management. He'd been out of the closet for two years and had no problems telling people that.

"Which one?" Greta asked.

"The brunet with the smattering of hair…Ohhh." He shivered delicately. "I love chest hair…delicious."

"Well, take your pick," Eddie told them. "Whichever one you want."

"Stephanie," Greta said to the brunette woman with her. "What do you think?"

Stephanie Martison was a forty-something director and producer who loved men and loved cocks even more. "Definitely the DJ. Look at him. Tall, dark, handsome, gorgeous, dances, DJs. I wonder if he sings." She sipped her champagne. "I definitely wouldn't mind trying him out."

"*You* would," Greta said. "Carson, what about you?"

"Considering Harry's latest acquisition, we need someone outstanding. Someone who's going to make the girls crazy and make the men want to be him." Carson Trumack was a forty-something star-maker. Everyone he'd picked had been a winner.

"Yes," Greta said, looking in Pedro's direction. "He *is* gorgeous."

The woman entered the club and made her way to the centre of the dance floor. She watched Pedro spinning and dancing on stage and saw all of the people gathered in front of him. The one she didn't see was Angelina. The whore wasn't there to support her man. Why would she be when schooling was more important? *I'll slash the bitch's face,* she thought viciously, but quickly calmed down. She was bumped from behind. "Hey, watch it," she snapped at one of the roller-skating waiters.

"Sorry," Leon called and rolled away.

She went back to watching Pedro.

Down the front, Bev and Sara were trying to carry on a conversation.

"I wonder if he's single." Bev adjusted the bosom of her dress to show more cleavage. "And I mean single single, not single but dating."

"Would it be a problem if he was?" Martine joined in. The ladies knew each other from social engagements, but weren't friends. "Look at my husband, Sergei. I am here, he is with mistress."

"Not everyone willingly cheats on his girlfriend or wife," Sara told her.

"No." Martine slithered up and down. "But many do. And many don't care."

Over on the sidelines, Stephanie was intently watching. "Look at the way he has these women eating out of his hand," she said. "They're almost lining up to be with him, to be picked *by* him."

"I'd love to be picked by him." Thomas sipped his drink.

"He has them lined up against the stage every night," Eddie said. "He's been our most popular staff member."

"How much do you pay him?" Greta asked.

"A thousand a night."

"Oh, he's worth so much more than that," she replied.

Down in the crowd, the woman made her way through it, not taking her eyes off Pedro. She came to a stop behind the three women whoring themselves at the stage and listened while they stared adoringly up at him.

"Does it really matter if he's single?" Bev asked. "I wanna fuck him anyway."

"I wonder how big his penis is," Martine added.

"I'd love to get my tongue in that mouth," Sara said.

"I'd love to get my mouth around his cock," Bev interjected.

"You whores," the woman spat. "You can't keep your legs together or your mouths shut, you always have to go after other women's men. You're all a pack of fucking whores."

"And what the fuck are you?" Martine asked. She was Russian bred all the way. "What business is it of yours what we do?" Eyeing the little red-haired girl with the mousy complexion and plain figure, she said, "Run along little girl, you're not wanted here." She clicked her fingers at a waiter. "Get security, this girl is harassing us."

The waiter rolled away.

"Time to go, little girl," Martine told her.

The commotion that came next was heard through the whole club, and everyone stopped and stared as Martine Krevnokov got the red-haired girl into a headlock after she had tried to claw her eyes out. Bev and Sara stood back laughing as security removed the woman from Martine's Russian Ice Queen grip.

Pedro saw the whole thing go down and kept the beats going as security dragged the woman away. The woman looked vaguely familiar, but he couldn't place her. Half an hour later, while on his break, he was called over to Eddie's table.

"Hey, kid, I want you to meet Greta, Stephanie, Thomas and Carson; they're the producers I told you all about."

Pedro nodded his greetings. "Nice to meet you. Enjoying yourselves?"

All four eyed off Pedro's body. Six feet of rock-hard deliciousness topped off with a chiselled jaw, straight white teeth, and big blue eyes.

"You ever thought of acting, kid?" Eddie asked.

Pedro shrugged. "Who hasn't?"

"We're not talking about *normal* acting, though," Greta said. She leant toward him in her seat. "We're talking movies…porn movies."

Pedro frowned. "Then nope, not interested," he said with a brief shake of his head.

"But look at you, you're gorgeous, and if I may be bold, I bet you've got a big cock," Greta followed up.

Pedro's frown deepened and his hands went to his hips. "Excuse me?"

"Here, take a look at Harry DeVille's latest acquisition." Carson pulled a photo from a folder. "He's gorgeous, but I bet you'll make a million more."

Pedro took the 8x10 photo and looked at the guy in it. Recognition dawned and his brows flew to his hairline. "Oh, my God, Carlos…"

"You know Carlo Stefan?" Four voices asked him.

Pedro looked up in confusion. "Who? Carlo Stefan? No, no, this is Carlos Stephanopoulos, my brother."

"Jesus Fucking Christ," the four of them said at once.

"Carlo is your brother?" Greta asked, barely daring to believe what this could mean.

Pedro huffed. "Ah, yeah!" He looked at his brother standing in a replica of the cabana he worked in. It was all Carlos. "Where was this taken? *When* was it taken?"

"Last week for his upcoming debut in one of the hottest porn movies ever released. It's a publicity shot for the movie," Thomas told him. "Are you *sure* he's your brother? You look nothing alike."

Pedro looked up from the photo. "He's older than me by four years and takes after Mama who's Australian. Our brother Tomas looks exactly like Papa, and I take after both. So yeah, this is definitely Carlos. Where is he, do you know? I haven't seen him since June on Mykonos."

"He's in Hollywood," Greta replied. "Harry DeVille is a huge go-getter in the business and he got your brother. So…" Standing, she walked around him. "How about making yourself *our* latest acquisition?" Staring up into his eyes she was mesmerised. "We could do so much with you, Pedro Stephanopoulos." She melted into the floor.

Pedro glanced from her to the others, seeing them all eagerly waiting for his reply, to the photo in his hand. *Carlos…a porn star?* "I don't know," he finally said, looking at his watch. "My break is nearly over. Can I keep this?" He waved the picture. "I need to think this over."

"Of course," Greta slid her fingers over his hand. "I'll leave our details with Eddie for you to pick up later. I look forward to hearing from you."

"Uh, yeah." Pedro backed away and all but ran for the stage.

"We need him." Thomas stood beside her. "He's the brother of Harry's latest stud. *Can you believe the coup? We need* him. *I* need him." Thomas licked his lips. "God how I need him."

"Keep it in your pants, Tommy boy," Greta told him. "He's reluctant. Didn't you see the look on his face when he realised it was his brother? Something is definitely going on here. He didn't even know where his brother was. I wonder what the story is."

Stephanie moved closer to them. "And did you hear what he said? There's *another brother.* God, if he looks like those two then whoever scores him won't know what hit them."

"I'd like to see all three up close and in person." Carson joined them. "*And* in a movie together. Imagine it!"

In unison they tilted their heads, imagining Pedro, Carlos and the other brother in a porno together.

"We could call it *Porn Star Brothers,*" Thomas murmured, imagining his mouth sliding around cocks so big. "Carlos is ten inches. I wonder what Pedro is."

"Yours if you want him," Eddie yelled from his seat.

They turned and took their seats.

"*Can* we have him?" Greta sat by Eddie and laid her hand on his. *"We want him."*

"Well," Eddie drawled. "He's still mine by night during the week… but what he does during the day and on the weekend is up to him. Think you can work around that?"

"Oh." Greta smiled. "Absolutely."

Pedro finished off for the night and headed for the staff room. He was changing when Mike and Leon walked in.

"Whoo, dude! Did I see you talking to those bigwigs with Eddie?" Mike asked.

Pedro gave a half grin. "Yeah." He pulled his pants on.

"And did they want you to star in their latest movie?" Leon flapped around him. "The Greek God of *Studio 69.*"

Pedro made a face. "Yeah."

Leon and Mike stared.

"They what?" Mike asked.

"They want you for their movie." Leon stared, wide-eyed.

"Yeah." Pedro put his stuff away.

"Oh, my God," Leon squealed. "We've got the next big movie star on our hands." He started dancing.

"Except it's not a normal movie," Pedro said.

Leon stopped. "What do you mean…*not a normal movie?*"

A guttural noise came from Pedro's throat and he looked up at the ceiling. "Ugh, they want me for pornos."

Silence.

"Oh, my God, you're kidding," Leon screamed and jumped up and down. "They want you for pornos. Oh, my God. You have to do it. Look at you." He eyed Pedro up and down. "You have *got* to do it. You'd make a gazillion dollars."

"No." Pedro shook his head. "I don't know if I want to be in a porno. It's bad enough my brother is, and I've only just found out after three months of not knowing where he was or what he was doing."

"Wait…what…?" Leon stopped him. "Your *brother* is in pornos." He exchanged glances with Mike. "You didn't tell *me* you had a brother." He playfully slapped Pedro's arm. "Do you have a picture?"

Pedro dug the 8x10 out of his bag and handed it over. "I just found out tonight that he's in L.A. doing pornos."

Leon took the photo and his eyes grew to the size of saucers. Mike leant over his shoulder. "Oh, child," Leon said. "Mmm, mmm, mmm, mmm, mmm. What a tasty morsel your brother is." He peered closer. "Is that ten inches?"

Pedro snatched it back. "All right, enough, thank you." He glanced at the photo and put it in his bag. "I have no idea what Mama and Papa are going to say when they see this."

"They don't know?" Mike asked, zipping up his bag.

"I don't know," Pedro replied. "I haven't spoken to them since I left in July."

"Time to call your folks and tell them." Leon threw an animal print fur coat around his shoulders and adjusted a matching hat on his head. "I'm off darlings, to get *my* fill of ten inches somewhere else since I can't have your brother." He flounced out the door then stopped. "By the way…if he's ten inches, how big are you?"

"Get out." Pedro pointed at the door.

Eddie walked in after Leon walked out. "Here's Greta's details for you. She said to call her if you're interested."

Pedro took the business card and looked at it. *Greta Von Burro, Adult Movie Producer, 555-6567.* He sighed and threw it into his bag with the photo. "Thanks, Eddie."

"You're not sure about it are you, kid?" Eddie asked.

Pedro sat heavily on the bench in the middle of the room. "I think it was more the shock of finding my brother and seeing what he was doing than being asked if I'd do it too."

"You and your brother close?" Eddie asked, sitting next to him.

"We are…were. He took off in June and we haven't heard anything since."

"And when did you take off?"

"July." Pedro stared at him.

"Told your parents?"

He looked away. "No."

"Then how do you know he hasn't called them?"

Pedro sighed. "I don't."

"Then it's time to call your parents."

With a deep sigh, Pedro left and walked home to Angelina's apartment to find her getting ready for school. "You got a minute?"

"Can you tell me while I get ready?" She ran around their room grabbing her bag and shoes. "You can help me pick out a dress."

Pedro sat on the bed. "We had some big movie producers in last night and they offered me a lead role."

Her eyes lit up. "Wow, really? That's great. How about this one?" She held up a blue floral dress.

"No." Pedro shook his head at the choice.

"That's awesome," she continued. "What movie?"

"A porno."

Silence.

She turned from the closet. "A what-o?"

"A porno."

Walking over, she stood in front of him. "They want you to star in a porno?"

He nodded. "Yep."

Her mouth moved while she thought about what to say. "Ah, what, ah, did you tell them?"

He shrugged. "I said I needed to think about it."

She drew in a breath. "And what did you tell them that for?"

"Because of this." He pulled out the photo of Carlos.

She took it. "Ah, Carlo Stefan." Shaking her head, she went on. "Who's…?" Then she realised from seeing the look on his face.

"Ugh," Pedro muttered. "My brother's doing pornos."

"Ohhh," came out in a sigh. Angelina tucked a strand of hair behind her ear. "And they want you?"

Pedro got up and stood looking out the window of their tiny apartment. "Apparently, he's some bigwig's latest acquisition and they were looking for one for themselves to compete. They had no idea I knew him. When I mentioned it, they got all excited and all but begged me to be their new star." He shook his head. "I was so confused at seeing Carlos that I said I needed to think about it."

"Fair enough," Angelina said. "So, now what?"

"My boss suggested I call my parents since I haven't spoken to them since I left." He shrugged a shoulder. "He may have gotten in contact with them. I don't know."

"Then maybe it's time you did." She glanced at the clock. "Have a chat with your parents first. Don't worry about the porn stuff for now. You obviously need to get the Carlos thing sorted out." She threw on a pink dress and grabbed her bag. "I gotta go, I'll see you later." She kissed him. "I love you."

"I love you, too," he said and watched her leave. Sitting on the bed, biting his lip, he deliberated for twenty minutes before he called his parents.

The phone rang and rang… "Hello."

"Mama."

"Pedro…? Oh, my God, Pedro, my baby. Where are you, are you all right, what are you doing, why haven't you called or written, when are you coming home?"

"Mama, slow down. I'm okay. I'm more than okay. I'm awesome."

"Where are you?"

"I'm in New York."

Silence.

"New York? What are you doing there?"

Silence.

"I followed a friend over and got myself a job in a new club as a DJ. It's great, Mama. Everything I wanted. The club is famous, the people are famous. I get paid the same amount I did in Santorini."

"At Andros Poulos's place?"

Silence.

"Yeah."

"And this friend of yours…" pause, "…is Angelina Poulos…"

Silence.

"Yeah."

"He came to us, Pedro." Her voice rose. "He came to us and told us you had raped his daughter and assaulted him. Then the two of you disappeared. He was going to press charges and have you hunted down like a dog."

Silence.

Pedro frowned at the news. "I'm sorry, Mama, but I did no such thing. Angelina is eighteen and she's going to Juilliard. She's the one that hit him and helped me leave." He sighed. "Look, have you heard from Carlos?"

Silence.

"Yes. He called last month. He's in Hollywood doing okay. He's happy and healthy, and the charges against him have been dropped, apparently."

Pedro let out a whoosh of air. "That's good, oh, that's good to hear."

"Unlike you, Pedro. Have you spoken to him?"

"No. I didn't even know where he was."

"Do you know where Tomas is?"

He frowned again. "He's not there either?"

"No. He left to spread his wings not long after you, but that was his choice, not because he was in trouble. All of my babies have left me, and I didn't know where any of you were."

"Oh, Mama, it's okay. I'm in New York, and Carlos is in Hollywood. Making a name for himself in movies, I think."

"How do you know?"

Silence.

"I saw him in a publicity shot for a movie that's coming out soon."

Silence.

"Oh…he didn't say anything to me. Said he didn't want me to know too much in case someone tried getting information out of us."

Pedro nodded. "Wise move. The less you guys know, the better. What about Tomas? You haven't heard from him?"

"I haven't heard back since he left. I think he was going to America too. Miami, maybe. My babies have left me," she cried.

"Mama, Mama, don't cry," he soothed. "We're okay, we're alive."

"Not if Andros Poulos gets you."

"Well, he hasn't yet, and I'll deal with him if he does. I gotta go. I love you, Mama."

"I love you, Pedro, my baby. Call soon."

"I will. Bye."

*****

Andros Poulos sat behind his desk in his office at the club. He was pissed. Not only had Angelina taken off for New York, but she'd taken off with his stud DJ in tow. The stud DJ who'd been fucking her. He ripped open an envelope. Sales had been down since Pedro had gone, and while he wasn't paying out a thousand a night, he was losing more than that in tourists. No one wanted to come now Pedro was gone. And while the new DJ he'd hired was good, he didn't cut it the way Pedro did.

Pulling photos out of the envelope, he looked at Angelina and Pedro on the streets of New York, in the club, and fucking on the beach. His hand shook with uncontrollable rage, and he screwed the photos into tiny balls. He'd been warned against seeking revenge upon Pedro, but now he would no longer heed that warning.

He knew Angelina was at Juilliard; he had called, but now knew Pedro was with her. He'd kept his distance by having a man watch his daughter, but he'd never seen Pedro with her. If he worked in a club, he'd be out all night and sleeping all day. No wonder he'd not been seen.

Andros now knew where he was and a plan started formulating. He was going to get Pedro Stephanopoulos if it was the last thing he did.

*****

The woman walked into her apartment wondering if Andros Poulos had gotten her mail yet. *What will he do?* She gazed at her corkboard full of photos. *I hope he takes that whore home,* she viciously thought. *Get her out of Pedro's life forever.*

"And then we can be together," she mumbled to the photo. "You and me and the baby." Sliding her hand over her stomach, she marvelled at the bump. She couldn't wait for them to have their baby, it would be such a gorgeous child with her papa's looks and her mama's smarts.

She checked the time. She'd been banned from the club after that fiasco the other week and had simmered for days, but it didn't stop her from standing outside the staff entrance every night waiting for him. To see him, to hear him, to smell him. God, he was beautiful.

Following him home every morning, she then followed that whore to school, coming back here to while away the days as he slept. *Maybe I should stay one day and be with him while she's not there? Yes…a* plan formulated. *Yes…that's what I'll do. I'll follow him upstairs and be with him while he sleeps.*

*****

Andros called his manager into the office. "Markos, you need to take over. I have business to attend to and will be gone for a few weeks." He collected some things from his desk.

"And where will you be in case you are needed?"

"I will call once I'm there. In the meantime..." He grabbed his briefcase. "Tell no one I'm gone. Regardless of *who* it is." He walked toward the door but stopped. "Especially...*him*..."

Markos nodded. "Yes, sir."

*****

Angelina woke Pedro when she got home, stripping off and massaging him until he rose to the occasion. She bounced up and down on him until she was a frenzied wild child, high on a natural drug.

He lay back and let her do her thing, watching as she threw her hair around, grabbed her breasts, screamed the place down, and let all the neighbours know she wanted him to fuck her.

"Ah," she gasped, her body weaving around. She pushed her hair back and flung it over one shoulder. "Oh, I've waited all day for that. To bounce up and down on your disco stick." She grinned and waited for his reaction.

Pedro cocked a brow *and* a lip. His arms were under his head and he was enjoying the start to his night. "Disco stick? Is that what we're calling it today?"

It always went down this way.

He'd come home from work and she'd be going to school. She'd come home from school all horny and wake him up for sex until he went to work and give his dick a new name.

She collapsed on top of him. "Yep. Oh, God, oh, God, oh, God you're so good." Her lips kissed his flesh and landed on his left nipple. "Oh, God, you're so good. How am I ever going to share you?"

His brow furrowed. "What do you mean, *share me?*"

She looked up and rested her chin on his chest. "How am I going to share you with all of the porn chicks you'll be fucking when you make your movie?"

He pushed her off and sat on the side of the bed.

"Hey," she protested. "I wasn't done."

"Then don't bring up pornos."

She spun around so she was sitting on his lap facing him. "What would be so wrong with doing that? It's huge right now."

"It's sex for money and movies." Pedro dropped her on the bed and got up to stand by the window. "It's disgusting. I don't want to do it."

"You do it every day with me."

"That's different." He glanced back at her. "I love you, we're together, we have sex, together, with no one else. I don't pay you for it."

Angelina stretched languidly on the bed. "Have you *seen* a porno?"

"What?"

"Have you *seen* a porno?"

He turned. "No, I haven't."

"Then how do you know how disgusting it is if you've never seen one." She spread her legs.

"I…" He became distracted by the beautiful goddess that was so willingly open in front of him.

"Maybe you should watch a few, or go and see your brother's when it's out and *then* make up your mind."

He sighed, relented, and climbed between her legs. "Maybe I should."

OCTOBER 1977

It was Saturday, the first of October, and Carlos was reading the scripts for the meat shop scenario. "This is awful." He threw his script down on the table. "It's not even what would happen in a real meat shop."

Harry agreed that it wasn't the best. "But it's not a real meat shop. So what do you want to do?"

"Give me a couple of hours to come up with something and I'll show you." Carlos went back to his apartment, drew on previous experience, and wrote a script. He threw it down in front of Harry two and a half hours later. "*This* is real."

Harry read through it, nodding, making faces, making small sounds. He put down the papers. "This is much better than the tripe David presented me with."

"That's because he looks as if he hasn't had any experience doing those things."

"He hasn't," Harry bellowed. "And maybe that's the problem." He got up and paced around his desk. "Carlos, my boy. If you can write that, then lend your hands to a few other ideas and we'll see how things go. Do you think you can give me four more of those?" He waved at the script on his desk.

"Already in the works, Harry." Carlos grinned. "The ideas came to me and I made notes. I'll write them up tonight."

"Good, good." Harry clamped a hand on Carlos's shoulder. "You'll be getting credits for them; hence you'll make more money. Is that a good start to you having more control over your career?"

"It's a start," Carlos agreed.

PEDRO

At the same time his brother was dealing with scripts on the other side of the country, Pedro rocked up to a movie theatre, behind dark glasses, a cap, and clothes, to see his brother's movie debut. Because Angelina wanted to see it, it had to be a weekend screening. And because Mike and Leon wanted to see it, it had to be a day screening, so Saturday it was, and Angelina brought Maggie for support.

They bought their tickets, entered, and sat up the back. Leon and Mike to Pedro's left, the girls to his right.

The theatre filled quickly with men and women. The lights dimmed, a few people cheered, and the movie started.

For Pedro, it was like every day on Mykonos. Carlos worked as a bartender by morning, spray tanner by afternoon, but by night, the masseur came out in him.

And so did his cock.

All ten glorious inches of it emerged onto the screen for all to see, to the delight of everyone, bar Pedro, in the room.

"Whoo," Leon squealed. "Oh, my God, I want that in my mouth." He clapped excitedly.

Pedro just stared, embarrassed by his brother, yet turned on at the scenario.

The sex was fast and hot and all mouths, cock and pussy.

"Oh, my God, do that to me, do that to me." Leon fanned himself.

It faded to black after fifteen minutes, and Pedro let out a gush of air. "Oh, my God." He looked at the boys. Leon was faint in his seat and fanning himself, and Mike was wide-eyed, still staring at the screen.

He glanced at the girls. Maggie was red with embarrassment, her eyes to the floor, and Angelina had her hand between her legs under her skirt. "Hey." He pushed her hand away. "That's my brother."

"And he's fucking hot," she stated. "You didn't tell me your brother was *so fucking hot* because that publicity shot *does not* do him justice."

"You didn't ask." He stood and made his way out of the theatre. The others followed.

"You have to do something like that," Angelina said, taking hold of his hand.

He shook his head. "No, no I don't."

"Oh, my God," Leon sang, coming up to his side. "If your brother can do that imagine what *that* could do." He waved a finger up and down Pedro's body. "We know what you have under there." He glanced at Angelina. "Miss Thing knows what you got in your pants, and *we* know you've got everything else. You need to show it off." He wiped his forehead. "*Who knew* you brother was so goddamn fucking hot. I need to get me some of that."

"Carlos doesn't swing that way and neither do I," Pedro said, removing his hand from Angelina's and taking off down the street. They chased after him with Maggie and Mike trailing behind, chatting about things.

"Sweetie," Angelina cooed, catching up. "Considering what you look like and what you can do with your cock and the fact it's bigger than your brother's..." Pedro went red, and Leon's eyes were the size of saucers, "this is something you could make a lot of money doing."

"It's *not about the money*," Pedro said. "I make a thousand a night, it's not the money."

"Then what is it?" Leon asked. "You get nearly naked every night too; you clearly have no problem doing that."

Pedro thought about that. *He* DJed in shorts in a club full of women and men. *His brother* was now baring his Greek cock in movies. Why couldn't he? They made their way to a pizzeria where he slumped into a booth. "I dunno. Pornos?"

"Why not?"

He sighed. "I can't really think of a why not."

*****

"If my brother can do it, so can I," Pedro told Greta over the phone Monday morning. "When do I start?"

"How about today?" She tried to contain her excitement. "You can come into the office, we can talk about the movie we have lined up, you tell us what you think and show us the merchandise."

That made him feel uneasy, but he had made the decision. "I haven't had much sleep, but I can make it. Where do I go?"

Thirty minutes later he was standing in a luxurious office atop the Chrysler Building on the east side of Manhattan. The studio took up the whole floor, and he was ushered into the office of Greta Von Burro where Thomas, Carson and Stephanie stood around eagerly waiting for him.

"Pedro, do come in," Greta said. "Welcome, welcome. Come in."

He moved into the room and dropped his bag by the door. "I'm still not convinced this is a good thing," he said. "I'm not exactly comfortable with this."

"Oh, but we have the perfect movie for you." Stephanie moved closer to him. "It's perfect." Her eyes greedily moved up and down. "It's about a DJ who does private parties for the elite and ends up giving them so much more. If you know what I mean." She seductively licked her lips.

Now, Pedro was interested. "That's what I wanted to talk about."

"We'll have time for talking later," Greta said, moving to his side. "But right now we need to see if you've got what we want." Her hand wandered over his.

"No." Pedro stopped her hand. "*We talk now,* and I get it in writing before you see anything. I want a say in how this goes. If I'm gonna drop my pants and have sex with women I don't know, then

I'm getting what I want in writing."

Greta saw the determination in his eyes. "And what do you want?"

"I want *this* movie, and any others I do, to be classy, tasteful and completely different to what my brother does. I want *that* in writing. *Before,*" he stressed the word, "I drop my pants."

Greta's eyes roamed up and down. "Martha, come and take a note."

Within the hour Pedro was signing a contract in duplicate.

"Well, now, we'll set everything up for this Saturday. I'm sure Eddie won't have a problem with you working for us once a week," Greta said, handling the contract.

"He did say we could have whatever we wanted," Thomas added, his eyes hungrily moving up and down the hunk of man meat before him.

"Now." Greta stepped back with the others. "Let's see the merchandise."

Pedro sighed inwardly, still unsure about everything that was happening, and pulled his shirt over his head. He let it fall to the floor and gave them a few moments to marvel at his tight abs and smooth tanned skin. His fingers went to his pants, unsnapped the button and slowly pulled down the zip, oh so casually pushing his pants down to his ankles. He stood and heard a noise behind him and saw staff with their hands and faces against the window of Greta's office peering at him. He slid his briefs down to join his pants and received cheers from everyone outside, and wide-eyed looks and even wider mouths from the four before him.

He flashed a cocky grin and put his hands on his hips. "So...think I can outdo my brother?"

*****

The woman had followed Pedro from Angelina's apartment to a midtown building and waited for him there. It was a long wait. A wait that was interrupted by people coming and going, even a security guard. She'd told him she was pregnant and did not feel well, asked if she could just sit and rest. He'd brought her a cup of water and some crackers. But after the first hour, she knew she needed to leave.

I'll have to go somewhere else, she thought, finally leaving when the guard asked if she wanted him to call an ambulance. "No, thank you," she said. "It's just my blood sugar. I feel better now." He nodded and helped her out the door. She took a moment to scan the area and decided to wait just down on the left; since the apartment was in that direction, she had a good chance of seeing him when he passed her. She waited just off an alley for another hour for him to come out. He walked by, and she followed as he went home. It was twelve o'clock, and she knew he wouldn't be leaving until six.

After watching him go inside, she went back to her own crappy apartment, not seeing the man in the car watching Angelina's place *and* her.

CARLOS

Monday morning, Carlos was on the set at Harry's house, and one of the rooms had been set up like a meat shop. He'd had a hand in the layout, explaining that since he was used to his father's store, it would be better and make him feel more comfortable if it was a layout he knew.

The cabinets were in place, filled with fake meat, the lighting was set just so, and Carlos and an exotic-looking woman called Mariska got into their outfits. He was to play the butcher in his white shirt, unbuttoned down to the navel, and white pants that had a spring lock on the front so he could rip them open in an instant. His butcher apron completed the look.

Mariska, herself of Greek lineage, with her long dark glossy black hair that curled down to her waist, big black innocent eyes, and a wide lipped mouth, wore a simple floral dress that flared gently around her knees. She would be the innocent young maiden out to buy some meat, and he was the man to give it to her.

They took their places on set and waited for the director to yell *action*.

Mariska walked through the door followed by a gentle sea breeze which not only ruffled her hair but Carlos's as well.

He did a casual head flick in slow motion and set his blue eyes upon the young girl before him. "Hello, lovely young lady, what can I get for you?" He flexed his chest under the lights so the camera could pick up his golden chest hair.

"Oh," Mariska murmured. "I just came in for some…meat…"

"Then let me show you our selection." He pointed out the different cuts from various animals and waited at the counter while she stood making up her mind.

"I just don't know," she finally said through her big lips and innocent eyes. "Do you have any…sausage…?"

"Sausage! I'll show you sausage!" Carlos ripped his apron off and his pants undone to reveal his big Greek sausage at full attention. "It's ripe and hard and just waiting to put itself in your mouth." He lifted up the counter, stepped toward her, grabbed her waist and slammed her against the curved meat cabinet.

Tearing open her dress, he thrust that Greek sausage into her over and over while her arms flailed above her head.

"Oh, oh, I just came in for some meat." She hitched her legs up, and the camera zoomed in on her bouncing breasts, so big and full and juicy.

"Oh, oh, I love sausage," she groaned as Carlos kept going and going and going. "Oh, God, oh, God, you're so, oh, God, I can't take it anymore, oh, God, oh, God, help me. Oh, God, I'm going to explode, oh!" She convulsed on the orgasm, the likes she'd never felt. "Oh, God," she screamed and slammed her head against the cabinet. "Oh, God." She arched, she bent, she breathed.

And Carlos was done.

He held her while her legs slid down to the floor and leant into her, his hands on her breasts, kneading their voluptuousness. "And that is how you have sausage," he breathed into her neck.

"Oh, God," she groaned. "I love sausage. Give me more."

He slid out of her and helped her stand. "Not now, my little sausage lover. I have other customers to worry about." And with that, he put his sausage away, donned his apron and wrapped up a packet of sausages for her. "Your sausages." He presented her with the parcel.

She quickly did her dress up and took the package. "Thank you, I'll be back tomorrow."

"Yes," Carlos breathed. "*Come*…tomorrow."

She walked out the door, and Carlos went back to cutting meat.

"And…cut, print!" the director yelled. "Good job people. We've got a winner there."

Carlos walked off the stage and collapsed into his seat next to Mariska's. "Are you okay? You seemed to hit your head pretty hard."

She rubbed the back of her head. "I'm okay. It's not the first time I've hit something on a set. But that was the first time I've had an explosive orgasm like that. You're quite the master." Her gaze lowered to his crotch. "You definitely know that sausage can please a woman."

He grinned and leant on the chair arm toward her. "Years of practice and being told what to do by women."

"Well…" She sighed and gazed into his gorgeous eyes. "You definitely have been taught well and taken notice."

"All in here." He tapped his temple. "Catalogued and in order."

"Do you ever just *make love* to a woman?" Mariska asked, sipping an iced tea that the actors' assistant had brought her. "I haven't been able to have boyfriends because they all get the weirds about me having sex for a living. So I end up single."

Carlos thought back to Viv and Rosalee. "I used to. In Mykonos, I'd see different girls during lunchtime. Since then there've only been two ladies I've been with, but that reminds me to call one. I'll see you later." He ran off to change and then called Rosalee. He hadn't seen her in over a week and now felt like having a nice dinner and dancing. He called her home number. "Hey Rosalee, how about dinner and some dancing. I know a great place… Rosalee…"

"Uh-um," she stuttered. "Why don't you come over now? I…I… need you now."

"Um, yeah, sure. I'll see you soon." He raced out the door and drove to her place, wondering why she sounded so strange. *Out of it is more like it,* he thought. *But I didn't think she did drugs.* He parked outside of her small house, bounced up the stairs and knocked on the door. It creaked open. "Rosalee?" His hand pushed it further. "Rosalee?" Stepping inside he closed it behind him. "Rosalee?" Walking past the small kitchen into the small lounge room he looked through the open door to the bedroom. She was lying naked, spread-eagled on her bed.

"Carlos," she lazily called. "I'm waiting." A giggle escaped from her lips. "Fuck me." She bent her legs and motioned him inside her. "Fuck me."

He stepped into the room and frowned. "Rosalee? Are you okay?" He'd never seen her in that state and wondered what she was on.

"Fuck me," she screamed at him, her womanhood on full display between spread legs. "Fuck me, Carlos, fuck me."

"Rosalee, I..."

She got to her knees and grabbed him, pulling him down on the bed, yanking his penis from his pants and sitting on it.

"Rosalee, I—"

"Fuck me, Carlos, woohoo." She waved her arms around. "Ride 'em cowboy." Her breasts bounced up and down, and her hair fell in curly waves. "Fuck me, fuck me," she screamed wildly, and Carlos rolled her over so he was on top and hammered home his seed.

Rosalee was so noisy he didn't hear the footsteps.

He barely felt the pain.

All he saw was black.

Something cold was splashed on his face and he came to. "What? What? What happened? Rosalee?"

"Ohhh, Carlos," she purred.

He blinked to clear his vision and saw Rosalee on the bed with a strange man between her legs. "Rosalee?"

"Carlos," she groaned and bent her legs.

"That's not me, Rosalee," he yelled and struggled, finding himself tied to a chair. "Hey, what's happening? What are you doing? Rosalee, snap out of it."

"She won't."

He looked up at the voice to his right. It belonged to a man whose face was covered in a weird Halloween mask.

"We gave her too much blow for her to snap out of it."

"What the fuck? Rosalee," Carlos yelled. "Rosalee, snap out of it, that's not me. That's not me."

"That's not me," Rosalee sing-songed. "Carlos..." Her legs were wide to give him passage, and he felt good inside of her. The room spun in every shade of every colour imaginable. Carlos sucked her breast, licked her neck and buried himself in her mouth.

"Rosalee, that's not me. You're being raped." He struggled with his bonds, his splitting headache, and the crazy scene before him.

"Rape?" the man beside him asked. "Do you see rape? She thinks it's you. She's making love to her man."

With fear and panic rising in his throat, Carlos struggled to stand, but his head was making him weak, and sick, and unsteady. "Rosalee." What the hell was going on? "Rosalee." He weakened.

The man came with final grunting thrusts and rolled off. "Your turn." He stood up, zipped up, and looked down at Rosalee. "Fucking good."

The other man unzipped and got on, but he was rougher, faster, biting her breasts and neck, making her cry out in pain, or what pain she felt.

"Ow, Carlos, that hurts," she cried, gripping the man's jacket.

"Shut up, you whore. If you can take it from him, you can take it from me."

"Rosalee," Carlos yelled again. "That's not me, hey—"

The second man grabbed his shirt. "You shut your mouth."

Carlos struggled, but the man cracked him on the head. Dizziness came upon him. "Ugh, stop...stop..." In a daze, he watched the man finish up and roll off. After zipping up his pants, he picked up a small black kit from the bedside table and removed an already prepared syringe.

"What...what are you doing?" Carlos slurred through blurry vision.

"Dealing," the man said, and injected it into Rosalee's arm.

"Wait, no," Carlos yelled, but was hit over the head.

All went black...

His eyes slowly blinked open.

He was lying sideways on the floor.

He tried to move his arms. They were no longer tied to the chair, and he sat up. His brain wasn't functioning properly, but he saw enough to know Rosalee was dead, and he was in her house.

The sirens snapped him to attention. "Fuck!" He climbed to his feet and took another look at the woman. Drug paraphernalia, cocaine, needles, mirrors. They were all over the bed. "Oh, Rosalee…"

The sirens got louder.

"I gotta…Rosalee," he muttered. "Ugh, my head." He grabbed it to stop the pounding. "Rosalee," he wailed.

The sirens got louder.

He stumbled out of the room and through the lounge. "What… when…" The house was a mess. Furniture tipped over, magazines and pillows tossed everywhere. Stumbling for the front door, he could hear the sirens coming down the road. "Fuck!" He turned and stumbled out the back glass doors, onto the patio, and into the yard. "Fuck!"

The sirens stopped out front.

"Fuck!" Stumbling off the terrace, he crashed through the side fence into the neighbour's yard. "Fuck!" He held his head.

"Come quickly," a female voice said, and arms pulled him up and half dragged him through a side door, upstairs, and into a bedroom. "Stay there. I'll deal with this." She closed the door and went downstairs to watch the hubbub next door.

Police swarmed the house, the yard, her yard, the street. For an hour she watched them search and stand and talk before they knocked on her door.

"Yes." She stood before two detectives.

"I'm Detective Star, this is Detective Drew. We want to talk to you about what's happened next door," the tall brute of a man with an old scar on the left side of his face running from his ear down his jawline to his chin said.

"And what's happened next door?"

"There's been an overdose and a potential murder."

"Well, then let me describe to you the two men I saw leaving the house by the back door." She gave them a description of the men, their car, and the time they had arrived and left.

"You have a great memory. How'd you remember all that?" Star asked.

"I'm a photographer. I have a very visual memory."

"And your side fence? What happened there?"

"A gardening accident, yesterday."

"Do you know who owns the car out front of next doors?"

"My guest. There were cars in front of my house, so the only place left for him to park was in front of the house next door."

"Then we need to talk to your guest."

"He's not well and is sleeping at the moment."

"Then we'll have to catch up with him later."

"Yes, you will."

The two brown-suited detectives stared at the elegant black woman in a vibrant red dress and large gold hoop earrings, not even figuring that she was lying to them.

She stared back and kept her expression neutral.

Carlos came to an hour later, when something was being dabbed on his forehead. He blinked and grabbed his head. "Ugh. My head."

"I have some aspirin and water," the woman said.

His eyes opened to see her on the edge of the bed, dabbing his forehead with a wet cloth. "Who…what…?" He tried to focus, but the pain in his head was too much.

"Take the aspirin and rest. I'll get you something to eat." She left him alone and went downstairs, catching glimpses of the police next door while she made sandwiches. She took them upstairs and placed the plate on the bedside table. "Now." She took a seat in the chair next to the window. "Let's discuss the situation. Two men pulled up to the back of the house, walked through the back gate, put masks on, and entered the house by the back door. You arrived half an hour later through the front door. There was feminine screaming amidst, I'm sure, acts of lovemaking, and then the two men left, doing everything in reverse. And then you stumbled out as sirens wailed and you stumbled into my garden through the fence. I got you inside as the police turned up. An hour later, two detectives told me a girl is dead, overdose or possible murder. Now…" She glanced from the window to him. "Tell me your side of it."

Carlos sat on the side of the bed and finished off the water. "Who are you and why should I incriminate myself? I should go." He stood up, but the dizziness made him sit back down.

She smiled. "I am Aneeka Ne Masta, world-famous photographer who has a shoot with you, Carlo Stefan, the hottest, newest porn star, on Wednesday. As luck would have it, I have proof that you were not the only one there and I have already given the police a description of the two men and their car. But…" She glanced outside. "They have probably checked your car's licence plates and discovered who you are and that you have been what…dating my next door neighbour."

Carlos swallowed the big fat lump in his throat. "Hadn't thought of that."

"And if there are any other neighbours home, who knows what *they* told the police."

"Fuck!" Carlos spat. "Fuck, fuck, fuck!"

"You could be in it up to your neck," Aneeka said. "So, tell me your side."

Carlos sighed. "I called Rosalee to see if she wanted to go to dinner and dancing, but she said to come over. She didn't sound good, so I raced over and found her door open and her naked on the bed. We had sex and then I was hit over the head." He got up and stretched before going over to stand beside Aneeka to look over the house. "When I came to, I was tied to a chair, and there was a man fucking Rosalee. She thought it was me, and I yelled at her that it wasn't, but… there was another man in a mask and he fucked her after the other man and then he…" He choked and turned away. "He got a needle and stuck it in her arm. Then I was hit over the head. I came to, heard sirens, found myself untied and Rosalee dead. Her place had been turned over. There was drug shit everywhere. I stumbled out the back because the cops were coming in the front. I fell into a fence, I think… was that yours?" He stared down at the amazing-looking woman in the chair. She nodded. "I have a photo shoot with you this week?"

"Yes." She stood up. "I don't suggest using your car, they may have it bugged. Wait until dark and Harry will come and pick you up. I'll call him."

He stopped her at the doorway. "What if I need to prove I didn't do this? If they've already checked my car, they'll know I'm not a guest here, but the man Rosalee fucked occasionally. Can you prove others were there?”

"Of course, Mr Stephanopoulos. I'm a photographer. I took pictures." She left to call Harry who sent his chauffeur in an ordinary sedan to pick Carlos up at nine that night.

PEDRO

Andros Poulos had flown by seaplane to Athens and a private jet to New York. He'd been there a few days, ensconced in a penthouse suite at the Waldorf-Astoria hotel, and had been keeping an eye on the comings and goings in Angelina's apartment. The man he'd hired, Stavros Christopoulos, had been watching the apartment, and Angelina and Pedro, twenty-four hours a day, seven days a week for the last few weeks since he'd known where they were. Now, he was in town and sitting in the car with Stavros.

"Who's that woman? The one with the red hair?" Andros asked.

"Dunno," Stavros said. "But I see her a lot. Follows Pedro around. I don't think he knows she does it."

"And what hours does he work?"

"Comes home about six-thirty in the morning and leaves about six at night."

"And Angelina?"

"Leaves about seven-thirty and comes home about three-thirty."

"Is she in all night?"

"Most nights."

"And when she's not?"

"At the club."

"Yes," Andros stroked his chin. "What is this club?"

"*Studio 69.*"

"Is it good?"

"The place to be. All the celebrities go there."

"Mmm, looks like I must go and see for myself. But not before I deal with Angelina."

"When will that be?"

"Tonight, once he's gone and it's dark."

*****

Angelina came home at three-thirty and bounced away on top of Pedro as per their afternoon interlude.

"Ugh, what time is it?" he groaned.

"Three-thirty-five," she grunted.

"Ugh, Angie, I've only had three hours sleep. I need more." He lay there, and his eyes drifted closed.

"And how come you didn't get any sleep?" She threw her head back.

"Because I called up that producer and went to see her about doing the porno."

Angelina slowed to a stop. "You went to see her about doing the movie? Are you going to do it?"

He sighed. "Considering my position right now, it's not like sex with a stranger will be any different."

"But did you sign up to do it?" She grabbed his nipple and twisted. "Tell me."

"Oooh, you little." He shoved her hand away and bucked up underneath her. "Stop damaging the merchandise."

Laughing, she said, "Is that what they're calling it? I'm calling it the heat seeking missile today." Her hands flung her hair back. "What happened when they saw this delicious merchandise for the first time?" She clenched around him making him groan.

"Oh, honey, they loved it. The *whole staff* loved my heat-seeking missile."

She clenched, he thrust.

"When do you do your first movie?"

He thrust, she clenched.

"This Saturday on Long Island."

"Ugh." She convulsed and subsided. "Can I come?"

"I think you just did."

CARLOS

After turning off the lights, Aneeka ushered Carlos out the back door, through her gate, and into the open door of the sedan, all under the cover of darkness.

Carlos got to Harry's half hour later and spilt the whole story.

"There were TV crews and cops and people gawking," Harry bellowed.

"I know, I saw them."

"And what the hell were you doing there?" Harry stalked around his office.

"I called her to see if she wanted to go to dinner and she insisted I come over and it all went to shit." Carlos paced in the opposite direction so they crossed paths in the middle.

"Fuck, Carlos. You sure as fuck know how to get yourself into trouble, don't you?" Harry sucked his cigar as he walked.

"They'll know that's my car sitting in front and wonder why I haven't gone anywhere."

"You'll have to go and get it yourself."

"But what do I say if the cops ask?"

They stopped pacing in the middle.

"We'll have to think of something. Aneeka lives there, so we'll say you were visiting to talk about the photo shoot."

"But what if someone saw me go into Rosalee's?"

Harry blew smoke in Carlos's face. "We'll say she wasn't home and you went next door to talk."

Carlos nodded and waved the smoke away. "Could be reasonable. But what if someone's watching and I don't go and get it? Or ask why I didn't go next door when they turned up because I had been there and they turn up then they want to know why I didn't care enough to go next door and find out," he rambled. He was as scared as he had been in Greece.

"Well." Harry puffed. "We could say you did drugs together and then wandered next door to Aneeka's, but you passed out on the couch or something."

"Yeah, yeah." Carlos paced again. "And I'll walk out tomorrow and cry and pretend that I've just found out and stare at the house and take off, but I'll have to get back there to make it look believable in case the cops are watching." He shrugged. "Then if they pick me up it will look credible."

Harry nodded. "Then back to Aneeka's you go."

PEDRO

Andros watched Pedro head off to work at six-thirty and waited another two hours until it was dark. He exited the car, walked quickly across the street and entered the building. He knew which apartment was hers. He owned it, so, of course, he had a key. Making sure no one was watching, he slipped the key into the lock and slid inside. The TV was on, but silent, the radio was blaring, and he found Angelina dancing around naked in the bathroom, pinning her hair up.

"Daddy!" she exclaimed and grabbed a bathrobe from behind the door. "What are you doing here? How did you get in?"

Andros peered at the rumpled sheets. "This is what your life is?" He gripped her arms and ripped open her robe, yanking it from her body.

"Daddy!"

He pushed her down onto the bed and climbed on top of her. "This is what you've made of yourself?" he spat, staring into horrified eyes that looked like his own. "This is what you've become? A whore whoring out her body to the first man who'll have her?" He put his arm across her throat to hold her down. "This is what you want to be? A whore fucking any man who'll come between the legs you spread."

"Daddy," she pleaded through her tears as she grabbed at his arm. "Daddy, don't."

"Don't what?" he spat. "Don't call you a whore? Don't say you fuck men? Don't say you give your body to them?" He glanced down the length of her five-five frame and saw the smooth body of an eighteen-year-old girl. He hardened and grabbed her breast, crushing it beneath his hand, squeezing into his palm.

"Daddy, stop it." Angelina frantically tried to push his hand away. "You're hurting me."

"Does *he* hurt you?" Andros asked, shoving his hand between her legs. "Does he hurt you when he does this?"

"Ow, stop it. You're my father, you shouldn't be doing this, you can't do this."

"Well, see, that's where you're wrong, little girl." He shoved his fingers in and out of her womanhood as she screamed. "Your mother was a whore too, just like you. Or should I say, you're just like her, putting it out to any man that will take it. And wouldn't you know, she ended up pregnant. I never did find out if you were really mine…" He crushed his mouth to hers.

*****

The woman had followed Pedro to the club, but since she was banned, had decided to go back to Angelina's. Walking along in the dark, she'd seen a man leave a parked car and go into the building. Under the faint light of the street lamp, she thought she recognised him as Andros Poulos.

"He's here," she whispered excitedly. "He's here. Now he'll tell that whore not to mess with my man." She moved slowly and quietly along the street until she was across the road from the building; looking up, she saw two figures fighting in the bedroom. She knew it was the bedroom because she'd seen Pedro stand there naked and had managed to lie her way into their place one night when neither of them was home. The curtains were drawn, but the flimsy fabric still let shadows through.

Shadows that fought.

Shadows that had one another by the throat.

Shadows that picked up objects.

The smaller shadow picked something up and smashed it over the larger shadow's head.

The light went out.

Stavros was still in the car waiting for his boss. He hadn't taken any notice of the window, but had spied the woman who had followed Pedro earlier, standing down the road opposite the apartment looking up at it. He glanced up and saw the light was out. He sighed. That meant nothing. He went back to watching the woman who stood staring up. "What is she up to?" he muttered.

*****

Angelina stood over the body of her father. He wasn't dead, but she had knocked him out with the lamp. He lay on the floor, and she stood there panting. She was battered and bruised and sore. But she hadn't been raised a Poulos for nothing; using her karate skills on her father didn't faze her.

Taking a deep breath she got to work. Throwing on a dress over underwear, she packed a huge overnight bag with clothes and toiletries, and packed her backpack with school books. She packed Pedro's belongings into his case and quietly left the apartment. She'd have to wheel the stuff down the road and try and flag a taxi. They couldn't go back there, and she'd made sure to grab their passports, her violin, and Pedro's money stash, leaving nothing valuable behind.

After making her way out the front door, she walked down the side alley to the next road over where she hailed a taxi. "Gramercy," she told the driver. She'd try and get a bed at Maggie's and leave their stuff there. But she had to get to the club and warn Pedro, because if he went home and her father was there, he'd be dead.

*****

Now, where's she going? the woman thought, spying Angelina sneak out and down the alley. She followed, watching her struggle with bags and a case. *That looks like Pedro's case. Why would she be sneaking out after dark with that?* She watched as Angelina made it down the alley and hailed a taxi. She hailed her own. "Follow that cab."

*****

Stavros looked up to see the woman wander across the road and down the alley beside the building. *'Bout time she left.* He checked his watch. Nine-thirty. *Boss didn't say how long to give them.* He glanced up and saw the light still out. *Must have moved into another room,* he pondered. *I'll wait until he comes out.*

*****

Angelina knocked on Maggie's door, but her mother answered instead. "Oh, hello Angelina, Maggie's not here…oh, my God, what happened to you?" She saw the luggage. "Did that boy of yours beat you up? Come in, come in." She grabbed the case and helped her inside. "Andrew, call the police."

"No, no, please no," Angelina begged. "It wasn't Pedro, believe me, he's working. I just, we, need a place to stay for the night. We'll find our own place tomorrow, but I didn't know where else to go. Please," she begged. "It wasn't Pedro. We just need a place to stay."

Andrew Boltworth came charging down the hall and saw the bite marks, scratches, blood and bruises on his daughter's friend. "If it wasn't your boyfriend then who was it?"

Angelina looked at both of them. "My father."

*****

The woman told the driver to stop outside of the brownstone and made a note. "We can go now." She gave her address and sat back.

*****

Stavros saw the blue and red flashing lights coming down the road and wondered where they were going. Glancing up at the apartment he saw it was still dark. He watched the police car stop outside of the building, and two officers get out and go inside. *What the hell,* he thought, hoping Andros would come out soon.

The two officers, Devron and Burns, entered the building after getting a call about a domestic.

Devron looked at his notebook. "Third floor, apartment E." They climbed the stairs, found E, banged on the door and called out. "Hello, is anyone in there?"

The door to apartment F opened. "Oh, good," a short, middle-aged woman with a tight bun and stern face said. "You're here. Now tell them they need to stop fighting, or get out of the building."

"Ma'am," Burns said. "Do you know their names?"

"No, I don't, but she's out all day, and he's out all night. Get home at all hours, and when she gets home at three-thirty, there's screaming and groaning."

Burns and Devron exchanged amused glances.

"And do you know how old they are?" Burns asked.

"Young, teenagers, maybe, early twenties. Way too young to be living together out of wedlock. So please do something," she said and slammed the door.

Devron snorted. "A young couple working two different shifts and she wonders what the screaming and groaning's about."

Burns grinned and knocked again. "Hello, anyone home?" There was a sound. "What was that? Hello, can you hear me?" Another groan. "Sounds like someone's in trouble." Burns tried the handle and found the door unlocked. His hand slid in to flick the light on, and they held their pistols up. "Hello," he called, pushing the door open. "NYPD, I'm coming in."

They walked into the entrance and turned right into the lounge. There was nothing out of place, but as they moved into the back hallway, they saw the body on the floor.

Andros had come to and managed to crawl as far as the bedroom doorway.

"Sir, sir, are you all right?" Burns checked his pulse. "Thready, call for the paramedics."

Devron got on the radio while Burns turned on the bedroom light. The place was a mess. The bed was out of place, clothes were falling from hangers in the wardrobe, drawers were open and half empty. The bedside lamp was smashed on the floor, and there was blood on the white sheets.

"Sir, sir, who did this?" Burns bent down. "Can you tell me who did this?" He leant in closer.

"My daughter," Andros whispered. "Where is my daughter?"

"Bloody hell, there's a daughter," Burns said, helping Andros to sit against the wall. "Can you tell me what happened?"

"My daughter, where is my daughter?" Andros rasped.

"Was your daughter with you? Does she live here?"

"Yes, she was here. He did this. Where is my daughter?"

"Who's he, sir? The intruder?"

"No, no," Andros gasped through his busted ribs. "Her boyfriend."

"And what's his name?"

Andros licked his lips in concealed delight. "Pedro Stephanopoulos."

*****

Angelina left her things at the Boltworths' and took a cab to 69 where she managed to get in the back door because Pedro had introduced her to the guards when she'd gone with him. She managed to get Leon to tell him she was waiting backstage and now waited for him to take a break.

Half an hour later, he took his break and came rushing over to her. "Leon said you'd been in a fight. Oh, my God, what's wrong?" He gently held her face in his hands. "Oh, my God, look at you. What happened? Who did this? Are you hurt? Were you raped? Angie, what happened?"

"My father," was all she said.

*****

"Are you sure it was him who attacked you?" Burns asked.

"Yes," Andros said with steely determination. "He attacked me for seeing my daughter and then attacked her."

"And where would he be now?"

"At the club. *Studio 69.*"

"And what does he do there?"

"He's the DJ."

"And how long ago did this happen?"

"A couple of hours."

*****

Pedro was disbelieving. "Your father? He's here? He did this?" He shook his head and set off for the door. "I'm going to kill him."

She lunged after him to stop him. "No, don't, that's what he wants you to do. He'd want you to lash out at him so he can have you for assault."

He stared at her. "But he deserves—"

"I know," she soothed him. "But there's more."

Eddie walked backstage. "I heard there was a problem." He saw Angelina's battered face. "There's clearly a problem."

"Yes," Angelina said. "My father, Andros Poulos, is going to make trouble for Pedro. So you'd better make sure that there are witnesses to him being here all night because my father's on the rampage. If he's even my father." Her face dropped.

"What do you mean?" Pedro gently touched her arm.

"He told me while he was assaulting me that he may not even be my father. That's what gave him the right to try and..." She sobbed.

Pedro frowned. "What did he do to you?" The sick feeling in the pit of his stomach made him want to vomit.

"He sexually assaulted me and tried to rape me." She gulped and gasped trying to keep her emotions in check.

"I'm going to kill him," Pedro roared.

"No, no, no," Eddie said, putting a restraining hand on Pedro's arm. "You're going to do no such thing. Because *this* is what we're going to do."

*****

Stavros waited in the car, watching as an ambulance arrived and the attendants went upstairs. Ten minutes later he saw Andros being carted down on the stretcher.

"Fuck!" He banged the steering wheel. "How long has he been there and I've sat here waiting instead of going up. Fuck, fuck, fuck!"

He watched Andros being loaded into the van and started the car when the paramedics shut the doors and climbed in, waiting until they drove off before following.

*****

Pedro was on stage when the cops came for him. He saw them, kept an eye on them, and watched Eddie walk over to them and escort them backstage where they would talk to Angelina.

"And this is Miss Poulos. I believe she needs to talk to you." Eddie stood off to the side.

"Miss Poulos, we're here to talk about what your boyfriend, Pedro Stephanopoulos, did to you and your father."

Angelina stood up and turned around. "Don't you mean what *my father did to me?*"

They stared at the bruises and marks on her face, arms and neck.

"What about this?" She took her dress off to reveal bite marks, bruises on her thighs and scratches. "Pedro left for work at six-thirty, my father came through my door at eight-thirty and did this to me. Eddie here can vouch for Pedro's whereabouts at eight-thirty as can the incredibly rich women and men who have been in front of the stage since the place opened. Pedro was nowhere near my father when he was in my apartment."

Burns and Devron looked at each other, unsure of what to do. "Are you saying that your father did this to you and not your boyfriend? We need to make that clear because your father wants to press charges."

"That's exactly what I'm saying, and you can add sexual assault and attempted rape to that list." She watched their expressions change. "Oh, yes, apparently, my daddy may not be my daddy after all, and he used that as an excuse to get back at my dead mother, who, apparently, was also a whore."

Devron and Burns stared at Angelina. The red marks, the bruises. The swollen cheek and lip.

"I want to press charges against Andros Poulos for breaking and entering, trespassing, physical assault, sexual assault and attempted rape." Angelina donned her dress.

The officers exchanged a glance, unsure of what to do. "Wait here a moment ma'am." They moved to one side, and Burns used his radio. "This is Officer Burns. We're at *Studio 69* talking to Angelina Poulos, the daughter of Andros Poulos. Mr Poulos has made a claim against his daughter's boyfriend of assault. Problem is, the daughter is also badly beaten and is blaming the father. She wants him charged."

"And the boyfriend?"

"Left for work at six-thirty and the father turned up at eight-thirty says the daughter."

"Well, then we have a problem. Take the daughter's statement. We'll need her to come in and be photographed, so, just bring her in."

"Yes, sir." They turned back to Angelina. "Ma'am, we're going to need you to come to the station and make a statement. But we also need to talk to Mr Stephanopoulos."

"But he—" Angelina started.

Burns put his hand up. "Just to get his side of the story."

"I'll get him to take a break," Eddie said.

A few minutes later, Pedro was backstage and holding Angelina in his arms. "What's all this about," he demanded. "Have you arrested him?"

"Not yet," Devron said. He was a six foot tall black man still in the closet, and at thirty-six, wasn't ready to come out of it, although, with Pedro standing before him, it was hard not to. "We need to ask you a few questions."

"And waste everyone's time," Pedro said.

"Do you know Andros Poulos?" Burns asked.

"Yes."

"How?"

"I was a DJ in his club in Santorini in May, June and part of July."

"Is that how you met his daughter?"

"Yes."

"How did you part? On what terms when you came to New York?" Burns asked.

Pedro glanced down at Angelina, and she nodded. "He found out we had started dating and attacked me in the alley behind his club. He threatened to kill me." He felt a little vulnerable standing in tiny gold shorts and knee-high lace-up gold boots in front of two strapping cops with guns.

"Did you tell the cops?" Devron asked, his suspicions aroused. He exchanged a look with Burns.

"On Santorini?" Pedro scoffed. "The cops are crooked and in the pocket of all the rich business owners."

"What happened then?" Burns asked, making notes.

"I hit him over the head to make him stop," Angelina said, her head on Pedro's chest. "He had Pedro pinned against the wall."

"What then?"

"He fell to the ground and his bodyguard came running out, and I knocked him out too. We ran to my house and got my things, then took a seaplane to Mykonos for Pedro to get his stuff. We flew to Athens and boarded a plane for here. I started at Juilliard in September."

"Had you heard from your father between then and now?" Devron asked, taking his own notes.

"No," Angelina said. "Nothing until tonight."

"And you've been here since…when?" Devron asked Pedro, eyeing the six feet of smooth Greek muscle before him.

"I usually get here about quarter to seven."

"And everyone can vouch for you?"

"Yes."

The officers put their notebooks away. "Okay, we need you to make a statement at the station. Can you come with us now, Miss."

"I want someone to go with me," she said. "I can call Mrs Boltworth."

"We can wait until she gets here," Burns said. "If you feel more comfortable."

"Yes." Angelina blinked. "I will."

Pedro looked down at her. "I should come."

"No, you finish your set," she said. "Then go to the station tomorrow."

"Are you sure?" He held her face. "Are you sure? If you want me there…"

"I'll be fine with Mrs Boltworth. We're staying with them until we can get our own place."

Pedro nodded. "And that will be tomorrow. Better get a car too."

"We'll go shopping tomorrow." She kissed him. "Go back to work."

He kissed her back. "You sure?"

"I'm sure."

"I'll see you tomorrow." He left her in Eddie's capable hands and went back to work.

*****

Stavros walked into the hospital and found his way into Andros's room. "Boss." He leant on the bed rail. "Boss."

Andros opened his eyes and saw him. "Where the hell were you when I needed you?"

Stavros went red. "I am embarrassed to say I thought everything was all right and you didn't need help."

"I didn't think I would," Andros said. "But my daughter has learned her skills and knows how to fight. At least I have put the blame where it belongs."

"And where's that?" Stavros asked.

"On Pedro Stephanopoulos."

"And how did you manage that?"

"By telling the officers that he beat my daughter and me."

"And what if she says he didn't?"

Andros closed his eyes. "Then I will have to find another way."

CARLOS

And at four past four in the morning, with lights off, Carlos sneaked back into Aneeka's house and waited until morning for the performance.

"No, no," he shouted and slammed out the front door, racing down the path and next door to Rosalee's. "No," he wailed as Aneeka came up and comforted him. "No." He collapsed onto the doorstep as the two detectives came up.

"And you're Carlos Stephanopoulos," Detective Star said, flashing his badge. "And you're under arrest."

"For what?" Aneeka questioned. "For being upset that a girl he dated has died? He didn't even know until this morning."

"Yeah." Star gave her the once over. "Strange, that. And you just *happened* to have conveniently seen two other men enter and leave the house."

"I did."

"Like we can take your word for it when you've been harbouring a criminal."

"Hardly a criminal." Aneeka stood. "A client. I am doing a photo shoot with him this week and he came over to discuss it, but passed out. And yes, smartass," she sassed the detective. "I can prove there were two other men there because I have photographs."

That wiped the smirk off Star's face and he exchanged glances with Drew. "Well, oh—"

"Yes," she interrupted. "I know. That's why I developed them yesterday and was going to give them to you at the station today. Now, are you still going to arrest Mr Stephanopoulos and on what grounds?"

Neither man liked being sassed by a woman, let alone a Negro woman. Who the hell did she think she was?

"Actually," Drew jumped in before Star could say anything. "We should get Mr Stephanopoulos's side of the story." He flipped open his notebook. "Mr Stephanopoulos." He looked down at Carlos who sat sobbing on the step. "Were you here yesterday?"

He gulped. "Ye-yes."

"At what time?"

"I don't know. Lunchtime or after."

"And what were you doing here?"

"I had called Rosalee to see if she wanted to go to dinner, but she demanded I come over here."

"She demanded?"

"Yes."

"What did you do?"

"I got in my car and drove over."

"About what time?"

"I don't know."

"What then?"

"The door was open, so I went in and called her name. I found her on the bed, naked. She wanted sex, so we had sex." He shrugged.

"And did you have any drugs?"

He winced. He had never taken drugs in his entire life and wasn't about to start.

"Well?"

"Yes," he lied.

"What?"

"A line of coke."

"That was it?"

"Yes."

"Then what?"

"Then Rosalee passed out, and I stumbled around a bit and went out the back. I found Aneeka's address in my wallet and realised she was next door so I went over and we talked about the photo shoot this week."

"How long for?"

"What?"

"How long did you talk for?"

Carlos shook his head. "Don't remember. I think I passed out."

The detectives turned their attention to Aneeka.

"Yes, he did and didn't wake up until about six this morning. That's when I told him about what he'd missed out on, and he told me his girlfriend lived there."

"Girlfriend?"

"We've dated about a month or so." Carlos wiped his face. He was done. "Can I go now? I need to get to work."

"And what do you do?"

"I'm an actor and writer."

"And drug-head by the look of it," Star said.

Carlos's face flamed with the fury.

"We'll get in touch with both of you if we have any more questions," Drew said. "Now, about those photos."

"Can I go?" Carlos climbed to his feet.

"Yes."

Carlos thanked Aneeka and made it to his car as she led the officers back to her place for the photos. He got in, took a deep breath, glanced at the house, and drove away.

*****

"You're damn lucky Aneeka took photos of those men coming and going. At least they have other suspects to look into so the heat should be off you for a while." Harry paced back and forth in his office. He'd just reamed Carlos out for ten straight minutes. "What *is it* with you and trouble?"

Carlos was deflated. He sat slumped on Harry's couch, having gone straight home from Aneeka's for a shower and shave, and then headed for Harry's.

"What the hell am I going to do with you?" Harry stopped to stare down at him. "Maybe I should keep you under lock and key."

"He could stay here," Harriet suggested from her position next to Carlos.

"Or maybe I can get you a bodyguard," Harry suggested.

Carlos looked up. "A bodyguard? I don't know if—"

"At least until this garbage has died down," Harry argued.

"But—" Carlos started.

"No buts!" Harry was definite.

"He has a nice butt," Harriet piped up.

"*Not now*, Harriet. No buts. You *will* get a bodyguard when you're out and maybe a guard to sit out front of your house at night. And *don't even think* of sneaking out, or seeing a girl, or screwing anyone, because it ain't on!"

"I wish he'd screw me."

"*Harriet, for the love of God*," Harry told his wife.

Carlos stood. The two Harrys made him uncomfortable sometimes, especially the way they leered at him like meat. "I'm gonna go home. When's the photo shoot with Aneeka?"

"Wednesday, and don't miss it. You'll have a bodyguard on your way out."

Carlos nodded wearily. "Right. Will you be there?"

"Of course. I never miss Aneeka's photo shoots."

"Okay, see you then." Carlos walked outside with Harry yelling something about *'follow him, sit outside his apartment, you're his bodyguard now,'* and then a tall, short-shaven guy dressed all in black followed him out to his car. "Ah, you're…"

"Tony Vega, bodyguard."

"Okay. Are you coming with me?"

"Got my own car."

"Right." He drove off with his bodyguard tailing every move, unaware *he* was being tailed by another car.

PEDRO

Tuesday morning after work, Pedro went to the police station to give a formal statement about his knowledge of Andros Poulos and his whereabouts Monday night at eight-thirty. After two hours, he took a cab to the Boltworths' and found Angelina asleep in the spare room.

"I won't let you stay here with her; you'll have to find somewhere else to stay," Mrs Boltworth said as they stood in the doorway.

"That's fine," Pedro replied. "I'll go and get us an apartment and a car, and we'll be out of your hair by tonight."

"That's not what I meant," she said.

"But that's our plan," Pedro told her. He kissed Angelina on the cheek and left to look at apartments.

*****

The police walked into Andros Poulos's hospital room at twelve-thirty.

"Ah, here you are," Andros said. "Have you caught the son of a bitch yet?" He waited while the officers traded looks.

"We've spoken to Mr Stephanopoulos, sir, and we won't be pressing charges against him."

"What?" Andros demanded with what little energy he had. "He did this to me. He assaulted my daughter and me. Where is Angelina? Have you found her? I want to see her."

The officers traded another look.

"We have found your daughter, Mr Poulos," Devron said. Andros quietened. "And she was at the club with Mr Stephanopoulos. We had a chat."

"A chat?" Andros said. "She was at the club with our attacker, and all you had was a chat?"

"We did more than that, sir." Burns' anger grew. He was a thirty year veteran of the force and had seen and heard a lot, but what he'd heard out of Angelina's mouth was just plain sick. "We took your daughter's statement down at the station."

"Good, good," Andros muttered. "Now you can arrest that boy she is with."

"And we took photos of every part of her body. The scratches, the bruises, the cuts and marks."

Andros winced. "What he did to my poor little girl."

"And what your poor little girl told us was quite sick, Mr Poulos."

"Yes, yes it is." Andros waved a hand. "Now go and arrest the bastard."

Burns exchanged an amused glance with Devron. "If you insist."

"Yes, yes, I insist."

"Mr Andros Poulos, we are arresting you on suspicion of breaking and entering, assault and battery, sexual assault and attempted rape. You have the right to remain silent, anything you say or do will be used against you in a court of law. You have the right to an attorney. If you cannot afford an attorney, one will be appointed to you. Do you understand these rights as they have been read to you?" He snapped one side of the cuffs on Andros and the other to the bed rail.

"But-but-but what is this?" Andros raged. "What are you arresting *me* for? *He* is the one who assaulted us. *He* is the one who beat me up and hurt my daughter." He thrashed his arm back and forth. "Take these off me, you bloody idiot. *I am not under arrest. Pedro Stephanopoulos is under arrest.*"

"*No,* Mr Poulos, *you* are," Burns gleefully told him. "Your daughter revealed everything. How you walked in on her, pushed her down on the bed, and then groped her and tried to rape her. You sick son of a bitch," he spat, pointing his solid forefinger into Andros's face. "You're damn lucky it was her fighting back that landed you in here because if I'd caught you, you'd be down in the morgue. You…" he thrust his finger, "are under arrest." The two of them turned and left.

"You cannot do this to me," Andros screamed. "You cannot do this."

*****

With help from Eddie and Greta, whom Eddie had called, Pedro was able to rent a nice furnished apartment with security within a couple of hours. He had a red Corvette an hour later, and some flowers and chocolates for Angelina before picking her up at the Boltworths'.

"We have a nice view of Central Park, we're not far from Juilliard or 69," he told her as he piled their cases and bags into the trunk. Angelina had gone back to the apartment with Mrs Boltworth to get the rest of their things. "It's furnished, it has security, you'll love it." He took her into his arms and kissed her.

She snuggled into his chest. "As long as we're together and safe, I'm happy." He helped her into the car, much to Mrs Boltworth's anger, and Maggie's disappointment, and drove to their new home with underground parking for the new ride. They took the lift up to the seventh floor where he unlocked the door, opened it a crack, and then swept her into his arms.

She laughed as he moved inside. "You're only supposed to carry me over the threshold when we're married."

"Well…" Pedro grinned cheekily. "I hope one day we will be."

That stunned her, for they had never discussed anything serious, let alone marriage. She was busy at school, he at 69, and they were still too young to be legally attached.

He set her down in front of the expansive window. "Look at that view."

She shook the thought out of her mind. "Oh, wow." They looked over the greenery of Central Park. "It's beautiful."

"And ours to look at every day." He ran back to bring the luggage in and locked the door. "Come, come and have a look." After flying over to her and grabbing her hand, he led her into the bedroom. "We have views here too and a nice bathroom. It's only a one-bedder, but that will do for now, won't it?" He slid his arms around her tiny waist.

"Yeah, it will do nicely," she agreed.

*****

Andros spoke to an attorney. "*What do you mean* they're not pressing charges against Pedro? *He attacked me.*"

"Mr Poulos," Miles Frankmore said. "Your daughter has pressed charges against *you, you…*" He emphasised with a finger pointed at Andros's chest. "They are not charging Mr Stephanopoulos because he was at work, and *your daughter* has named *you* as her attacker." In all these years he'd never come across someone as narcissistically delusional as Andros Poulos.

"But that is absurd."

"But that is the law."

"Then the law is an ass."

"Then get another lawyer."

"Fine, I will. You're fired."

"Good. Good day, Mr Poulos. Here's some free advice. Your daughter has taken out a TRO against you. You have to stay away from her or you'll be arrested. Do you understand?"

Andros waved him away. "You are not my lawyer. I do not have to listen to you."

Miles sighed. "No, but then I have a feeling you won't listen to anyone."

When he left, Andros called Stavros. "Get over here, I have a plan." Twenty minutes later Andros was spelling out plan B. "Shoot him."

Stavros raised a brow. "You want me to shoot him?" He looked around. "Where, when, how?"

Andros rolled his eyes. "Must I tell you how to do *everything*? When he is alone. When no one else is around. Preferably at night and with a gun.”

“You want me to just go up to him and shoot him, or do it in a drive by?”

“I don’t care. I want him dead. Leave me now.” He had to make arrangements for getting out of the hospital. He wanted to go back to his hotel, but had been told he was no longer welcome, so needed an apartment.

*****

There was no sex for Pedro and Angelina. She hadn’t wanted to, and he insisted they didn’t. She needed to heal, and he had no problem giving her time, so they slept holding each other.

She kept waking, which was no surprise, and he barely slept because he wasn’t used to sleeping at night. So he stood guard for any little sound, any little bumps in the nights. And when she woke from frightful dreams he soothed her back to sleep.

CARLOS

On Wednesday, Carlos showed up bright and early for his first photo shoot. He'd been in the business a few months, but had never had his photo professionally taken, and was looking forward to Aneeka taking them. Checking up on her previous work, he'd loved what she'd done. Everything from celebrities to porn stars, to landscapes; there were no bounds to her creativity.

His outfits were already waiting for him which made it easy to deal with. So he dressed and got hair and make-up done.

Aneeka turned up with her posse and set to work telling the crew where things needed to go and where she wanted Carlos to pose. After an hour she called everyone to attention. "All right, everyone, let's get to work. Carlos, get yourself into your cabana." She placed him where she wanted him. "And you are holding up well?" she asked quietly while she tucked his hair behind his ears and adjusted his top to show more flesh.

"As well as can be expected. You know Harry's given me a bodyguard?"

"So I heard." She tweaked his nipples so they protruded through his skin-tight tank top. He raised a brow. "We need you on display," she said smoothly. "You can do the rest." She nodded at his crotch. "Hard and penetrating. Okay, everyone, let's get to work."

For the next half hour, she directed Carlos in the cabana, from seducing the camera, to removing his clothes, to displaying his manhood with a towel hanging from it. She called time, and they moved on to the next set.

Carlos posed holding meat, in his uniform, out of his uniform, and only in his apron. They broke for lunch and Aneeka pulled him aside. "I gave the photos to the police. They were still quite surprised that I had taken them. I told them it's not often that strange men break into people's yards and enter the back door then leave hours later. Besides, my studio faces that way and I saw everything. I even sneaked out for a picture of their car while they were inside." She sipped a vodka and lemon.

"That could have been dangerous." Carlos knocked back a shot of tequila.

"Yes." She smiled. "But I have done more dangerous things than taking a photo of a car. Besides, all I had to do was step out of my own gate. Have you heard from the police again?"

"Not yet." He glanced across the crowd of movie and photo crew. "And hopefully, I won't. But knowing *my* luck with women and strange men, it will keep happening. I think I'm cursed."

"Cursed?" She arched a brow.

Carlos grinned. "Let's hope it doesn't happen a third time."

"Let's," Aneeka agreed. "Okay, everyone, back to work."

They spent the afternoon doing casual shots of Carlos in and by the pool, making sure to get him wet for full effect. Lounging and listening to music, drinking at the bar came next, and then they finished off for the day with sunset shots to take advantage of the smouldering rays as they lit up his tan and gorgeous blue eyes.

As they packed up after the shoot, the police turned up to speak to Carlos. They glanced around Harry DeVille's palatial home as they were led into the lounge.

"Detectives, we meet again," Aneeka said as she laid her camera in her bag. She always packed her own equipment to make sure no one damaged or dropped it.

"Ms Ne Masta." Detective Star nodded. "What a coincidence that you should be here when we want to talk with Mr Stephanopoulos again."

"It's not a coincidence, Detective," she replied smoothly. "You knew full well we were having a photo shoot. We told you on Monday."

Star moved uncomfortably at having been called out. "Yeah, well, it's a good thing you're here too; it will save us the trouble."

"Trouble with what, Detective?" she asked.

"Coming out to see you, Ms Ne Masta."

"And why would you need to see me again?" She zipped up her bag.

"Because we've spoken to some more witnesses…"

"And what witnesses would they be?" Aneeka asked. "Are they any better than me? Did they supply you with descriptions and photos and a car license plate?" She watched their uneasy expressions. "Well?"

"No," Detective Drew replied. "But they gave us other details like what time Stephanopoulos arrived and how long he was gone."

"As I told you—" Carlos started.

"Yeah, we get it, big boy," Star interrupted. "You fucked, snorted, and stumbled next door, but what we find funny is…" He stepped over to Carlos and poked his pen in his chest. "Is that *no one* saw you stumble over to Ms Ne Masta's." He aimed his pen at her. "Or do you want to tell us what really happened to that side fence of yours?"

"As I said—"

"Yeah, yeah, gardening accident." Star paced back and forth between them. "See, I get the feeling that the two of you are hiding something from me, from us." He waved his pen between him and Drew. "Now." He stopped. "Tell me I'm wrong."

"Detective." Aneeka stood straight and tall. "We have told you everything there is to tell. I gave you a description of the men and provided you with photographs. We have told you that Carlos was at my place because we were discussing *this* photo shoot." She waved an arm toward the gear still remaining. "That you can clearly see we have finished. Ask anyone here. We've been shooting all day. Now, I am going home to develop my photos. You know where I live if you want to continue harassing me." She nodded. "Detectives, Carlos." She gathered her bags and left with her staff, passing Harry on her way out.

"What in fucking hell are you doing in my house?" he bellowed as he walked down the steps into the lounge room. "I said—"

"We heard what you said." Detective Star put up his hand. "We came to talk to Mr Stephanopoulos."

"Not without a lawyer you don't," Harry snapped. "Now get out of my home."

Star went to open his mouth.

"Out." Harry pointed to the door. "Now."

With a disgruntled last glance at Carlos, they left.

"Now you." Harry pointed at Carlos. "Get home and stay there until shooting next week, your bodyguard's going to be there twenty-four hours a day, seven days a week, to stop these fuckers from getting to you. Now go."

Carlos reluctantly left and drove straight home, his bodyguard following.

So did the man in the dark sedan. He stopped at the phone booth to call his boss and was told to wait to see if Carlos was in for the night and if so, then to go to the photographer's house and do his job. He got in the car and drove to Carlos's and waited until ten p.m. He didn't get out of his car; he didn't want to be noticed by the bodyguard sitting in his own car outside. Once it was obvious Carlos wasn't going out, he drove to Aneeka's house and waited until everyone's lights went out then quietly alighted from his car and made his way to the back yard.

PEDRO

Wednesday morning, Pedro drove Angelina to school; even though it wasn't far, he wanted to make sure she made it safe and sound into Maggie's waiting arms. And she had insisted on going back, not wanting to let the assault stop her from getting on with her life.

"I'll be here to pick you up at three-thirty," Pedro called out the car window.

"Okay, see you then." She waved and walked off with Maggie.

Pedro went home and slept until three, and was back to pick her up. They went home and ate, and caught an extra two hours sleep before he had to go to work.

"Don't leave me here," she cried out, clinging to his hand when he went to leave.

He stopped. "Babe? What's wrong?"

"I'm scared," she said, tucking a strand of hair behind her ear. "I don't want to be alone."

"You have locks and bolts and security downstairs." Pedro took her into his arms. "You'll be safe."

"I'll only be safe with you," she pleaded. "Please don't leave. Don't leave me alone. I'll sleep at the club in one of the offices. At least I know I'll be safe there."

Pedro raised a brow. "I don't think *anyone* is safe there."

"Please let me come." Her eyes pleaded with him.

He relented. "Okay, get your stuff."

She got her things and they went downstairs. Driving to the club, they parked out back and went inside. While Pedro changed, Angelina went in search of Eddie to see if she could sleep in an office.

The night began, but Pedro couldn't quite get into it. With everything that was going on he just couldn't feel good about anything, even his music. He nodded at Sara and Bev, who were there every night, and saw Martine slither up next to them.

Bridie McBall joined the group. She was an up and coming disco singer and had the latest hit that Pedro would be playing later. Dan Slayer, guitarist with rock band Slay Me, was dancing with Wednesday May, the star of the new Star Blade movie, *Killer Revenge*. She was young, she was blonde, and she was hot. Way too young and hot for Dan Slayer who was hitting forty.

Pedro looked around and saw Michael Jackson, Andy Warhol, Bianca Jagger, Debbie Harry and Grace Jones. He still got impressed by the big stars that came to 69.

*****

Stavros meticulously cleaned his gun, taking it apart, using a cotton stick to get into the crevices, and then putting it all back together. He spun on a silencer and shoved in a cartridge. All it would need was one bullet. One bullet to do the job. One bullet to end Pedro Stephanopoulos. He went out to his car and got on his way.

*****

The woman knew what time Pedro got off work in the morning, which was a good thing since she didn't know where he lived. She'd gone back to the brownstone, but they weren't here. She'd gone back to the whore's apartment, but no one was there either. So waiting at the club was the only way to find him. She checked her watch. Five-thirty. One hour left. She set off around the block to waste some time.

*****

Stavros pulled his car up to the alley at the side of the club. He needed to know what the best vantage point was so he could take the best and fastest shot. He cruised by and saw stragglers leaving, but there weren't a lot of people in the street. He looked at his watch. Five-thirty. He cruised around the block.

*****

Pedro finished Bridie's song and did a shout out. "That was Bridie McBall's number one hit, *Rock Me, Roll Me*. Give a big shout out for Bridie!" The crowd jumped and hollered, and Pedro waved her up to the stage. "That's the third time we've played your song tonight Bridie; everyone keeps requesting it. You wanna say something to the crowd?" He held the microphone out to her.

"Thank you all for buying it, loving it, and wanting to dance to it." Her million dollar smile lit up the room. "Thank you all." She waved and left the stage in her skin-tight strapless sequinned jumpsuit and stilettoes.

"Bridie McBall, ladies and gentlemen. And up next is Slay Me's latest hit, *You Do It To Me*, and give Dan Slayer, the guitarist, a big rousing cheer."

"Whoo."

*****

The woman did a circuit of the block and checked her watch. Five-fifty. She sighed. *I should have just stayed in bed an extra hour and then come down,* she thought. She looked toward the stage door then to the cars parked in the alley and out back. Should she hide behind one of them? *I need to take cover when he comes out. I don't want him seeing me.* She glanced at her watch. *May as well walk around the block again.*

*****

Stavros came to a stop outside the club. He had no idea if Pedro would be walking home, if he had a home, or if he'd catch a lift with someone else or take a taxi. He sighed, thinking. *I need another couple of nights to scope the joint out. But no, no, no, Andros wants it done now. 'Now, now, now!'* He had yelled. *'I want it done now.'* Taking notice of the position of everything he looked at his watch. Five-fifty. Sighing, he drove around the block.

*****

Pedro played a medley of Jackson Five songs to end the night to the crowd's delight. He saw Michael shy away into a corner and waved. Michael waved back, and Pedro left a twelve inch running at six on the dot.

The club closed and everyone was slowly escorted out. It usually took about an hour, and staff wrapped things up until the last straggler was gone.

Bev ran over to him and planted her lips on his. "Oh, my God, I love you, Pedro, are you single?" Her arms were around his neck hanging on for dear life.

He disentangled himself and Sara helped. "No, no I'm not."

"Come on, Bev." Sara took hold of her. "You've had a bit too much to drink. Let's get you home."

"I love you, Pedro. I don't care that you're not single. I want to fuck you anyway." She held out her arms as Sara dragged her away.

Pedro laughed, waved goodbye, and went to change.

*****

The woman came back around and saw people leaving. She looked at her watch. Six-ten. *It takes about twenty minutes to do the block, so I might as well stay here.* She wound her way down the alley and hid near a red Corvette and a pile of trash cans.

*****

Stavros came to a stop down the street from 69 and checked his watch. Six-ten. He could do another lap of the block and wait for all of the celebs to get out of the way, but he didn't know what time exactly Pedro left. He idled in place and decided to wait another ten minutes.

*****

Pedro talked with the staff members as they came and went in the staff room. Mike and Leon were some of the last to leave, and Pedro said goodbye. He went in search of Angie and found her in Stew's office, dead to the world on the couch.

He woke her. "Angie, time to go. You've got school, and I've got sleep."

She stretched and yawned. "What time is it?"

He checked his watch. "Six twenty-two."

*****

Stavros checked his watch. Six twenty-two. He slowly moved down the street until the alley came into view and he had a good line for the staff door at the back. He parked and waited.

*****

The woman watched the staff leave. Some were in cars, others walking; one fag of a black man even asked if she was all right and she told him to fuck off and move on. She checked her watch. Six twenty-five.

*****

Pedro said goodbye to those he came across as he walked Angelina through the back of the club.

"Can we go and get some breakfast first? I'm starving." She checked her watch. Six twenty-eight. "I don't have to be at school until eight."

"Sure, what do you want?" Pedro opened the door for her.

"Pancakes with maple syrup, bacon, scrambled eggs, the lot."

"And where are you going to put it all?" He laughed as they walked for the red Corvette.

The woman realised they were headed her way and ducked behind the large trashcans near the front of the car, watching.

Stavros saw Angelina with Pedro. "Fuck!" he swore and jammed his foot on the accelerator by mistake. The car was in park so the engine gunned, but the car didn't move.

The woman looked toward the sound and saw a panic-faced man stick his arm out of the window and aim a gun at Pedro. "No," she screamed and moved to cut it off.

The bullet tore through her and into Angelina. They both screamed and fell to the ground.

"Angie," Pedro yelled, catching her as she fell.

Stavros gunned the car and took off, screeching down the block.

Eddie and a few remaining staff members come running out the back door to see Angelina bleeding in Pedro's arms and another woman lying in the alley only a few metres away.

"What the hell happened, kid?" Eddie yelled.

"I don't know," Pedro sobbed, holding his hand over Angelina's wound. "She just went down, and a car screeched down the road. Help her."

Towels were held to Angelina's arm, and she groaned. "Pedro."

"Angie baby, everything's going to be all right, you'll be fine, just hang in there."

Staff members attended to the other woman. "She's alive," Stew yelled, "but unconscious. Must have hit her head when she fell." He wrapped a towel over the bullet hole. "How's Angie?"

"Hanging in there," Pedro yelled back, holding her tighter. "Come on, Angie, come on, baby."

*****

Stavros belted down the road into screeching turns. He needed to get away so no one could tail him. "What a cock-up. Fuck, fuck, fuck,

251

fuck, fuck!" He banged the steering wheel and headed back to his motel in Jersey. His boss was not going to like this.

*****

They loaded Angelina into the back of the ambulance and Pedro climbed in next to her holding her hand. "You're gonna be okay, baby, you're gonna be okay."

The paramedic took her blood pressure and said, "She's stable and hanging in there."

Pedro stroked her hair. "Yeah, she's hanging in there."

The woman was loaded into another ambulance. "My baby," she murmured, her hand going to her stomach. "Pedro's baby."

Stew overheard her and frowned. This woman was pregnant to Pedro? He didn't seem like the type to cheat on Angelina, but then who knew.

*****

Stavros made the call. "It didn't work."

"What do you mean it didn't work?" Andros said. "You were supposed to shoot him. How did it not work?"

"Because a woman got in the way and she was shot instead… plus…"

"Plus?"

"Angelina was there. The bullet hit the woman and redirected into Angelina."

Silence…

"You shot my daughter?"

"The bullet ended up in her…I think…I didn't shoot her on purpose."

"You shot my daughter," Andros screamed down the line. "How dare you shoot my daughter!" He slammed the phone down. "What's the old saying, if you want the job done right you'll have to do it yourself."

Stavros felt the panic rise. It started boiling in his stomach and slowly crept up his insides to settle in his throat. It choked him, made him unable to breathe. *This is getting out of control,* he thought. *This is nuts, insane, psychopathic. After what he did to Angelina he screams at* me *for cocking up a shooting. No, he's standing on the edge, and someone has to take the fall.*

*****

Hours later, Pedro was pacing back and forth in the hospital when Eddie stepped out of the elevator with Greta Von Burro.

"Pedro, how is she?"

He stopped in a daze and turned. "Still in surgery. They said she should be okay because it's in her shoulder, but even then there's severe bleeding and nerve issues."

"This is a very good hospital," Greta told him. "The best doctors work here."

Pedro flashed a lost smile. "I know. I told them money was no object. Whatever they needed to do, do it. Whatever specialists they needed, get them. They said they're taking care of her."

"That's good." Greta laid a hand on his arm. "She's in good hands."

"Yeah. What about the other woman?" Pedro asked.

"She's being looked at in emergency. Flesh wound, apparently, but knocked her head when she fell. Stew's with her to make sure she gets good care too," Eddie said.

*****

Stew was standing outside the cubicle as the woman was being examined, wondering about the words she'd muttered. "Oh, Doctor," he called to the woman who'd just left the cubicle. "How is she?"

The doctor took a clipboard from a nurse and signed her name. "Flesh wound that will be stitched up. Has a concussion from hitting her head. Some dizziness, fades in and out. We'll keep her in overnight for observation to make sure she's okay."

"Did you check on the baby?"

"Baby?" The doctor's head turned. "Did she say something about being pregnant?"

"She muttered, *the baby, the baby*, when she was put in the back of the ambulance," Stew said.

"Mmm, we'll have to check that out, thanks for telling me." She went back in to the cubicle.

Stew paced, sat, and paced some more over the next twenty minutes while machines came and went and the doctor finally emerged.

"Well, I can categorically say she is not pregnant," she said. "But…" She glanced at the cubicle. "She kept insisting she was. So I'm going to call a psyche consultant and make sure she's checked on through the night."

"Thank you, Doctor." Stew decided to stick around until she had been taken to the psyche ward.

*****

It was another half an hour before the doctor emerged from the operating theatre with news on Angelina.

"Doctor, how is she?" Pedro rushed to his feet.

"She'll recover. The bullet went into her left shoulder. She may not recover full use for a while, but with physiotherapy and time, she should."

"Can I see her?"

"She's being taken into recovery, you can see her once they take her to her room."

Pedro nodded. "Of course. Thank you, Doctor." They shook hands.

Officers Burns and Devron stepped out of the elevator.

"God, not you two," Pedro said. "What is it now? He found out about his daughter and wants to see her?"

"Actually, Mr Stephanopoulos, we heard about the shooting and came to get statements."

"Have you caught the guy who did it?" Pedro asked.

The officers exchanged a look. "Unfortunately no."

"You can start with her father," Pedro told them. "Considering what he's done to her I wouldn't put it past him to try this."

"That's what we were wondering," Burns said. "We've been to the scene and had a good look. Considering your involvement with Mr Poulos, we're wondering if it wasn't *you* the shooter was trying to get."

Pedro frowned. "Me? Why would he…" He nodded when he realised. "Andros is trying to kill me, but got her by mistake because she's not normally there."

Burns nodded in agreement. "If he hates you that much we're thinking, unless you have other enemies, that he took a hit out on you to get you out of his daughter's life."

"Well…" Pedro grinned wryly. "He's the only enemy I have that I know of."

"Then we'll look into that," Burns said. "We'd like to talk to Miss Poulos. We can come back later today."

"Do that," Pedro said. "She's just gone to recovery and won't be out for a while."

Burns nodded again. "Right, now, Mr Monteif, we heard there was another victim. Was she a staff member?"

"No," Eddie said. "Just some woman in the alley. No one knows who she is, but one of our guys is downstairs with her now."

"We'll go and chat with them then, gentlemen, ma'am," Burns turned to go.

The elevator surged to a stop and Stew stepped out.

"Oh, wait," Eddie called to the officers. "Here he is now."

Stew walked over and eyed the cops. "Caught the son of a bitch yet?"

"Not yet, sir. But we'd like a word with the other victim."

"The nutjob?" Stew saw their expressions at his word. "She's just been taken to the psyche ward for observation."

"What's wrong with her?" Pedro asked.

"Mumbled something about a *'baby, Pedro's baby'* when she got carted away," Stew said, watching Pedro's expression.

"Wait." Pedro shook his head. "What do you mean *my* baby? I've only been with Angelina." He saw the curious stares the others gave him.

"That's the rub," Stew said. "The bullet only grazed her arm, and she hit her head when she fell, resulting in a concussion. I spoke to the doctor, told her she had mumbled something about a baby, and she went back in to check. Turns out, she's *not* actually pregnant. Hence the night in the psyche ward because she kept insisting she *was* pregnant." Everyone looked at him. "We've got a whack job on the loose."

"Where's the psyche ward?" Pedro asked.

"Fifth floor," Stew replied. "I've just come from there."

"And Angelina's going to be here on the second." Pedro sighed. "Good, keep her away from us." He turned to the officers. "And keep Andros Poulos away as well. I want an armed guard on Angie's door at all times. If this was an attempt on any of us then who's to say he won't try again."

The officers nodded. "We'll get one down here right away," Burns said, and they left to visit the psyche ward.

*****

Andros stalked around his apartment. "No one gets the better of me," he hissed. "*No one.* I have to do something to get rid of that Stephanopoulos kid, but what? What can I do…what can I do…?" He thought about it. Pedro worked in a club where rumours of drugs and alcohol were rich and rife. He'd dealt in drugs at his own club and knew how to set someone up for a downfall. *Now, where will I get drugs in New York?* He couldn't have them flown in; he'd have to get them from a supplier.

He made a few phone calls to the suppliers he did use and was given a name. Just out of New York on Long Island, was a very wealthy man who dealt in all manner of things who could easily get his hands on a few kilos of coke. He made a call and discussed business. "Good, good," Andros concluded. "I don't know when I'll need it for, but soon, very soon."

"All right, then why don't you come to my house on Saturday night? We are having a little party upstairs while a movie is being filmed outside in the backyard."

"What kind of movie?" Andros's curiosity was piqued. Maybe he could be in it.

"A porno."

*****

Pedro was by Angelina's side when she woke. "Hey, baby, sweetie, how do you feel?" He pushed her hair out of her eyes and off her forehead.

"Weak," she murmured drowsily. "Tired." She licked her lips and swallowed. "Thirsty."

He poured some water into a small cup and held it to her lips. "Here, just a sip."

She drank and lay back on the pillows with a sigh. Looking around the room she vaguely remembered what had happened. Her right hand went to her arm that was in a sling. "What happened? What was that?"

Pedro licked his lips and wondered where to start. "You were shot," he finally said.

Her eyes widened as she turned her head to look at him. "What? What do you mean, shot? By who? My father?"

Pedro gave a brief nod. "We think it might be your father. Who else would it be? But apparently, a guy in a car was waiting for us, and he fired a shot. It hit another woman in the arm and bounced off her into your shoulder." He paused. "The cops think it was me he was aiming for."

"You?" she said. "Why would…" The light dawned. "My father. Of course *he'd* want to kill you." She sighed. "But it got me instead. You said it hit another woman? How is she?"

"Ah, in the psyche ward under supervision." Pedro glanced around the room.

"Why did they put her in there if it's an arm wound?"

"Because she kept saying *'my baby, my baby'*, but she's not actually pregnant. So they're keeping her under observation for the concussion, in case it caused her memory loss, or memory failure, whatever it is."

"Oh, poor thing," Angelina said. "To lose a baby."

"She wasn't actually pregnant, so she didn't lose it."

"Either way, she must be devastated and in need of some mental help."

"Which is why they put her in the psyche ward," Pedro said.

"Well, if that's the best place for her," Angelina said. "Then I hope she gets the help she needs."

"Speaking of help." Pedro changed the subject. "There's an armed guard on your door all day every day until you get out. So hopefully your father won't be able to try anything."

"If he's after you, he won't come near me," she replied sleepily.

"Maybe, maybe not. The other thing is, Greta wants me to shoot a movie on Saturday night, but with everything that's happened, I'm not sure now."

"Do it," she urged, covering his hand with her good one.

"But I—"

"Do it," she repeated. "Don't let this stop you from fulfilling your contract. I'm a bit pissed that I won't get to be there and watch you in action, but I expect a copy for myself so I can watch it. And then we can re-enact it so I get to fulfil my fantasies of fucking a DJ at a party."

Pedro snorted. "I'd say you've already done that one. Just look at the way we met."

She laughed and clutched her arm. "Ow."

"Hey, take it easy." He put his hand out. "Take it easy."

"Do it," she said. "For me."

He gazed into her beautiful brown eyes and saw his forever. "Okay."

TOMAS

Marcus raised his glass. "Cheers to a very important—"

"And lucrative," Violet butted in.

"And lucrative," Marcus continued, "business venture."

"Cheers."

Everyone was at Seralift Manor, the magnificent ten bedroom, ten bath mansion spread across a cove on the glorious Hollywood Beach. Bette, Bertha and Willow to Marie, Beatrice and all of the ladies that Tomas had been training for the last two months were there, plus their partners, husbands, and gigolos, and all of the stage crew at *Seralift Productions*. Not to mention the other talented actors in the movies plus their partners, and friends of Roger and Tomas. It was a huge affair for hundreds of people all decked out in their finery.

Roger and Tomas were resplendent in tuxedos with their arms around each other. Bette, Bertha and Willow were dressed up to the nines in sparkling jewels as were the other ladies. Champagne was flowing freely, and a band played the latest disco on the back terrace facing the water's edge. It was beyond anything Tomas had ever dreamt of going to.

Roger pulled him aside. "Can you believe it's been a month already?"

Tomas shook his head. "No, can you? I can't even believe..." He blushed.

"What?" Roger leant on a sideboard, pulling Tomas into his arms. "What?"

Tomas looked up into the big brown eyes and slid his arms around his neck. "I can't believe we have sex for a living." One month ago he'd made a choice; to make sex movies with his new lover. For all the inexperience, for all the naïvety, for all the things he didn't know and was yet to learn about love and relationships, he knew he wanted to be with Roger. And so he'd made the decision to be with him in movies as well as life.

Roger grinned. "Well, you did say you wanted to do it all day every day."

"Or in our case, all night. I don't want to give up my training unless I have to." Tomas kissed him lightly. "I love you, and I'm so glad I met you."

Roger pulled him tighter until their crotches pushed together. "I love you, too, and I am so glad you came into my life." They kissed, and it deepened.

"All right you two save it for the movies," Marcus bellowed, seeing them pull apart, blush, giggle, and then hug. "You were damn right, Violet. He *is* a talent."

She sighed and sipped her champagne. "Just a pity he's gay. All of my friends want to try him out."

"After watching the steamy fucking these two get up to, so do I." Marcus puffed on his cigar. "He is *one hell* of a boy, and they made *one hell* of a movie together."

"A lethal combination," Violet told Bette who was standing with them. "We're so glad you persuaded him to come here.

"He nearly didn't," Bette replied. "It was that stupid fling with Bertha's Luiz that nearly stuffed it all up. He had to take advantage of poor Tomas and make him feel guilty as hell. Thank God Bertha dumped him and got Tomas to forget about him. Otherwise…" She shrugged. "No Tomas."

They waiter behind them froze. Behind the bleached blond hair, coloured contact lenses, and black rimmed glasses, no one was going to recognise him. Luiz had managed to finagle his way in as a member of staff and had hovered close to Roger and Tomas without anyone noticing. As long as his tray was always full of champagne, no one cared.

He casually glanced at Tomas hugging Roger by the side doors. If Bertha hadn't dumped him, Tomas wouldn't be in Miami? It wasn't his fault the kid felt ten tonnes of guilt for fucking a man. It had been the most wondrous time of his life, spending hours in the sun inside Tomas making love in the heady rays and cool tropical breeze. The feel of Tomas's rod of pleasure against his was magnificent. He'd never met a man so young with so big a rod, and he'd had it inside *and* in his mouth. Oh, God, it was magnificent.

He hardened and quickly left the room. He needed to relieve himself and headed for the private bathroom for guests at the side of the house. He shut and locked the door, unzipped and pulled it out before turning around.

"Hey, it's full in here!" a man exclaimed before seeing the magnificent penis before him.

"I need relief," Luiz told him. "Now."

"Need a hand with that?" The man shook his off and left it hanging.

"If you don't mind." Luiz stepped towards him.

The man turned, bent over the sink, and Luiz entered, thrusting across the finish line to grunts and groans from the man. He shuddered. The man shuddered. Luiz stayed inside and pulled a small vial of white powder from his pants pocket. "Coke?"

The man grabbed the vial, spread some on his left hand and snorted it back. "Oh, God, that's good." He clenched his anal muscles. "Again?"

Luiz examined the man. Average height, long, dirty blond hair, green eyes, good-looking, and a member of Marcus Seralift's stable. "Only if you snort some more." Luiz reached around to squeeze the man's dick.

*****

Bertha sidled up to Bette with her new beau. "Don't they make a charming pair? I'm so glad Tomas found someone of his own."

"Someone who's not yours, you mean." Bette's eyes twinkled.

"I didn't mean that." Bertha grinned mischievously. "Not what I meant at all." She watched Tomas stroke Roger's face as he gazed adoringly at him. "He really looks like he's in love."

"Yes, yes he does," Bette said. "Let's hope he finds some happiness after this fiasco with his brothers and Luiz."

"Speaking of his brothers…" Marcus came up to them. "You'll never guess what I've just found out. Tomas, Roger, get over here." He waved them over.

"What is it?" Bette asked. "You know his brothers?"

"Know?" Marcus laughed raucously. "Wait until you hear."

Roger and Tomas came up to them. "You bellowed," Roger said.

"Tomas, my boy, we've been making movies for four weeks now and have yet to come up with a name for you. Well, I found one. *Tomas Stefan*."

Tomas frowned. "It's just a short version of my name. Nothing different."

"Exactly. *But*…it's also the name your brothers are using." He brandished two 8x10 photos, holding them so the blank backs were facing out and they couldn't see them yet. "Guess who have gotten themselves into the porn industry?"

The blood drained from Tomas's face. "No." His head moved slowly from left to right and back again.

"Oh, *yes*, my boy." With a flourish, he turned the photos around. "Say hello to Carlo and Pedro Stefan."

Tomas looked at the photos of his brothers, slowly reaching out to take them. "My God, Carlos…Pedro." He studied the promotional shots of the brothers he hadn't seen in months. Carlos in the pool, and Pedro with the city of New York in the background. "Where are they? *What* are they?"

"Carlos is in Hollywood with Harry DeVille, and Pedro in New York with Greta Von Burro. Two *very* big producers in their cities."

"Wow." Tomas shook his head in amazement. "I haven't seen Carlos since June when he disappeared, and Pedro since July. They look good. They look healthy and happy. And clearly not in jail."

"Jail?" Marcus asked.

"They fled Mykonos under shady circumstances, and the cops were after them." Tomas moved the photos closer to Roger. "My brothers."

"Good-looking young men. Clearly hot genes run in the family." His hand slid over Tomas's ass. "Very hot genes."

Tomas's blush deepened. "Can I keep these?" he asked. "I don't have any pictures of my brothers."

"Sure, kid, sure. I got copies of their movies too. We'll have to watch them later."

"Are they gay porn as well?" Bette asked.

"No, straight, but fucking hot from the quick bit I saw."

"Carlos always was sticking it to the ladies," Tomas said. "I don't think there were many women left on Mykonos who hadn't had the pleasure of Carlos Stephanopoulos between their legs."

Marcus cocked a brow, and Violet stifled a giggle. "We'd better see that video, then," she said.

*****

The man in the bathroom finished snorting the contents of the vial. "Oh, that's good stuff. Got any more?"

Luiz zipped up his pants and produced another vial. "Snort away my friend, but make it quick. I gotta get back to work."

"Fuck snorting it," the man said and threw the powder into his mouth. "I'll just swallow it. Like I just swallowed you."

Luiz tucked in his shirt. "Yes, you did. And my, what a big mouth you have." He noticed the man change. Just a slight twitch of the face, a look in the eye. He smoothed back his hair. "Gotta go, enjoy." He unlocked and opened the door, sneaking a peek left and right. When he saw no one, he headed back to the kitchen.

*****

"Apparently, Harry and Greta both say they have the hottest star in the porn world. It's going to be the battle of the brothers, and now that we know, we'll be hot on their trail," Marcus told the group.

Murmurs and smashing glass erupted behind them, and they turned to see Jeff Fastwater stumbling into the room, pants unzipped, cock swinging from side to side.

The women gasped in delight, the men snickered at the size. The wait staff dropped their trays at the sight before them. Jeff stumbled, incoherent, wiping his nose and sniffing.

Marcus strode over to confront him. "Put that piece of crap away before I cut it off. This is a respectable party."

Jeff simply sneered at him, sniffing and wiping his nose on his coat sleeve.

"Now," Marcus demanded.

His tone sent Jeff's cock back into his pants as he fumbled with his zip.

"You're clearly on something." Marcus noticed the red, watery eyes as security took an arm each and dragged Jeff away.

Jeff was clearly not in charge of his faculties let alone in possession of a set of balls to man up and keep his habits to himself at a party such as this.

Marcus watched the two guards drag a struggling Jeff to the door where he promptly fell to his knees before falling face first onto the floor. "Oh, for God's sake, get him up." Marcus bellowed.

The guards bent down. "Wait," one said, spying blood coming from Jeff's nose. He quickly checked for a pulse while everyone crowded into the large entrance way. The guard stood and turned to his boss. "He's dead."

Everyone gasped in shock.

"What?" Marcus asked.

"He has no pulse. He's dead," the guard repeated.

Everyone stared in shock.

"Call the police," Marcus bellowed. "Call an ambulance. See if you can help him." He stumbled over to the body, but the guard stopped him.

"No, sir, he's bleeding from the nose, don't touch him." He held Marcus back while the other guard ushered everyone back into the ballroom.

Ten minutes later the police and coroner's van arrived.

"So, what do we have here?" An average height man with salt and pepper curls and a beige trench coat came through the door bearing his badge. "Detective Barden, Miami PD. Who's the victim?"

"Jeff Fastwater," Marcus replied dejectedly. "He's an actor."

"And what are we all doing here tonight?" Barden continued, looking around at the old women and young men.

"Having a party," Violet replied and stepped forward. "Violet Seralift. This is my ex-husband's home, Marcus Seralift. We run a movie production studio, and Jeff is...*was*...one of our actors."

"And what kind of movies do you make?" Barden flipped open his notebook. At fifty-five he'd been hoping to retire soon, but a spate of deaths had kept him working, so it wasn't the first time he'd seen a young person with white powder around their nose flat dead on the floor.

"Adult movies," she said calmly.

Barden blinked and kept his expression neutral. "You mean pornos?"

Violet blinked back. "If that's what you want to call them."

The coroner covered Jeff's body with a white sheet and called Barden over to the side of the room. "Probably an overdose. Too much snorting can cause bleeding, but I'll do an autopsy just to make sure."

"Thanks, Doc." Barden slapped him on the back and walked over to Marcus who sat forlornly in a chair at the side of the hall. "Mr Seralift, can you tell me what happened?"

Marcus looked up, his eyes distant. "What?"

"Can you tell me what happened?"

"Clearly my ex is in a state of shock right now so I can tell you." Violet appeared at his side. "We were having a party when Jeff stumbled into the room with his pants unzipped. He was sniffing and wiping his nose and was very unstable on his feet. Marcus ordered security to throw him out, but when they reached the door, he fell to his knees and collapsed. We called you."

An officer came rushing through the doorway. "Detective, this fell out of the man's pocket when he was put into the van." He handed over a photograph.

Barden took it and looked at it closely. It was of two men on a sound stage, smiling and laughing. And naked. "Mrs Seralift, do you recognise these two?" He showed her the photo.

"Why, yes, that's our sound stage. That's Roger and Tomas."

"And when would this have been taken?"

"Well, that looks like *Big Cock in Little China*, we only filmed that last week."

"And those two men are *where*, now?"

"Here."

"At the party?"

"Yes, in the ballroom." She pointed.

"How appropriate," Barden quipped. "Can you get them for me?"

"Of course." She hurried into the room and returned with the two boys. "This is Roger Dencott and Tomas Stephanopoulos."

"Detective Barden," he introduced himself. "Stephanopoulos… What's that?"

"Greek," Tomas told him.

"Huh! Either of you boys know why this," he glanced at his notes, "Jeff Fastwater would have this in his pocket?" He handed the photo to them.

Roger took it, and they looked at it. "Is that from the movie last week?"

"Looks like it," Tomas said. "Why would he have a photo of it?"

"That's what *I'm* asking," Barden said. "Who was he to both of you?"

Roger shrugged. "Just a co-worker."

"In what sense?" Barden asked.

Roger cocked a brow. "He was in other movies, but we were co-workers."

"Mmm, mmm," Barden mumbled. "What about you, Stephan-popodopolous?"

"Stephanopoulos," Tomas corrected. "I think I only met Jeff last week. He'd been on holiday when I started, and then worked during the day while I worked at night. It was only briefly. In fact, I think it was on the set of that movie." He pointed to the photo in Roger's hand.

"Interesting," Barden murmured, making notes.

"Why?" Roger asked.

"Mmm? No reason. I'll take that photo and get on with it." He retrieved the photo and nodded at Violet. "Mrs Seralift. Mr Seralift." He looked at Marcus. "You going to be all right, Mr Seralift? I'll contact you during the week with details of the investigation."

Marcus raised his head. "What?"

"I'll let you know what's happening during the week, Mr Seralift." Barden left him sitting in a daze.

Luiz had been watching all of it from the background, quietly serving drinks and keeping an eye on Tomas and Roger. He'd slipped that photo into Jeff's pocket while he was snorting, so he hadn't noticed a thing. He waited to see what they would do and saw the confused expressions.

He wanted to run to his Tomas and take him into his arms. Tell him everything was going to be all right if he just came back to him. But he couldn't. Such a shame. He watched them walk back into the ballroom.

"How well did you know Jeff?" Tomas asked Roger. "Would he do something like this?"

"Like what? Collapse at a party?" Roger escorted him to the far side of the room.

Tomas shrugged. "Stumble around with his cock out and then fall down dead from a potential overdose."

"Well, I think that's something you can only do once and not over and over again." Roger grinned.

"Ladies and gentlemen," Violet called a few minutes later. "May I have your attention? Due to the unfortunate circumstances that have occurred, I need to bid you good night and please have a safe journey home. This party is at an end. Please gather your coats and head home. Good night." She left to escort Marcus upstairs.

Bette and Bertha wandered over to Roger and Tomas. "It's sad that young people feel the need to take so many drugs that they lose their life."

"Yes," Bertha agreed. "I'm just glad we're over that."

"But what could have made him overdose at a party?" Bette asked.

"That's what we were just saying," Tomas said.

"And where did he get the drugs? Did he come with them and then take too much?" Bertha sipped on her champagne.

"I don't know. But I think we'd better go," Roger said, seeing the room empty out.

They all agreed and bade each other good night as they collected coats and wandered off to their cars. Tomas had moved in with Roger only two days previously, so on the way home they discussed it some more.

"I wonder if this has anything to do with my car being trashed in August." Roger turned the corner. "I've also noticed that some people have had stuff go missing at the studio. My car, stuff being stolen, now a death. I wonder of it's all connected?"

"Why would it be?" Tomas asked as they pulled into the underground car park. He got out and shut the door. "Stuff goes missing, stuff gets stolen, your car was appalling because it was on private property, and as for Jeff, as we all know, people do drugs and die because of them."

They walked upstairs, and Roger unlocked the door to his second floor apartment. It had beach views, was fully furnished, and was ten minutes from the local shops. "My car was personal," he said, pulling at his bow tie. "No one would randomly walk onto someone's property and trash a car. That was a personal attack, but for the life of me I have no idea who'd want to do that."

Tomas removed his coat and stepped out of his pants. "Well, I don't know, but I didn't know Jeff did drugs, so maybe we should all get together and make a list of everything that's happened."

"Maybe someone's out to get everyone working for Marcus? There's probably some porn kingpin who wants to take over and put him out of business." Roger helped Tomas out of his shirt and shorts. "And I know one kingpin who wants to take over *you.*"

"Except you're still overdressed." Tomas pushed him away and pulled back the covers. "You need to—"

"Done."

Tomas looked over his shoulder. Roger was completely naked and standing to attention. "Perve!" he teased as Roger jumped him.

Luiz slowly walked up the stairs. He kept an eye out for other people and made his way to the apartment on the second floor. Pulling out the master key he'd had made, he opened the door and quietly closed it behind him. Hearing noises coming from the bedroom, he walked over to the door and saw them going at it like rabid dogs. He levelled his camera and clicked a few rounds.

"Mmm, mmm, what was that?" Tomas mumbled. He heard the clicking again. "Wait, Roger, what is that? Roger." He looked over Roger's shoulder and saw the outline of a man holding something in front of his face. "Roger, someone's here, someone's in the apartment. Oh, my God."

Roger's head spun around to see a shadowy figure move. "Hey." He flew out of bed, grabbed his robe and heard the front door slam. Flinging it open he looked out, but only heard heavy steps thudding down the stairs. Racing after them, he came to a stop in the car park before speeding from car to car. He saw no one before going back upstairs.

"Well?" Tomas locked the door behind him.

"I didn't catch anyone. He got away." Roger grabbed a drink from the fridge.

"How the hell did he get in?" Tomas hung the chain up and realised. "Did you put the chain on when we got home?"

Roger thought back. "Nope, just the lock."

"That's how then. We'd better make sure to chain it in future. We don't want to be broken into again. He was watching us, taking pictures of us making love. How many times has he been here? Has anyone else broken in? Has anyone else been following us into our home or taking pictures of us? Oh, my God." The lump rose in Tomas's throat, and he sat on the couch and wrapped his arms around himself. "How many times has he been here?"

"I don't know, but please don't panic." Roger sat beside him and rubbed his back. "Don't panic. Stay calm. You've locked and bolted the door. There's no one here now. It's okay. Stay calm." The softness of Tomas's bare skin aroused him, and his hand drifted up and down. "Let's go back to bed," he said softly. "I want you."

Tomas looked up into passion filled eyes, felt himself rise, and took Roger there on the couch.

*****

Luiz pulled the photo out of the rinse tray and hung it up. Developing the roll of film was easy in his hotel room, he'd done it for a few weeks now. He looked at them one by one. Tomas on the set with Roger, Roger with other men, Tomas being taken from behind, the other man's head cut off on purpose, Tomas with other men. It was a plan, and that plan was in phase three.

Phase one had been to trash Roger's car. Phase two was to take photos on set and steal stuff, and now phase three had gone off with a bang.

The beginning of the end.

He left the photos to dry and walked into the bedroom. Several boxes lay on the bed, each containing photos and vials of D-grade cocaine. So lethal it would kill you if you had too much as poor Mr Fastwater had found out.

Yes, Jeff Fastwater fucked hard and snorted harder. His two loves were men and cocaine. One addiction led to the other and Luiz had played upon that. Jeff couldn't resist cock and took whatever was offered, especially if coke came with it. And it didn't take much to find out. Just a quick search through Jeff's locker at the studio and a search of his apartment showed pictures of young men doing what he wanted them to do. Sucking his cock and snorting his drugs.

Phew! Luiz thought. *One down, so many to go. So many cock sucking perves that deserved to be taken out. And if it means splitting up Tomas and Roger so Tomas will be mine again, then Roger will just be collateral damage.*

PEDRO

Eddie gave Pedro the rest of the week, which was only a few days, off, and he spent Thursday night through Saturday morning at the hospital. In the afternoon he drove out to Long Island to the impressive and indulgently wealthy estate of some rich person. He didn't know who, but he definitely wanted to meet the owner.

After parking next to the company van, he was escorted through the luxuriously excessive interior to the backyard. It was in the process of being set up to look like a private party. DJ booth on the right, a long cabana with flowing curtains that ran across the pool in front of him, and a bar with waiters on the left. It looked like a very expensive pool party indeed.

"Pedro, darling." Greta walked over to him and took his hand. "Come, let me run you through what's happening." She led him to the DJ booth. "You're going to be playing here." They stood overlooking the see-through dance floor that showed the pool's reflection underneath. "There will be lots of hot young women dancing, flirting, sexy, almost no clothes. You'll be here in tuxedo pants and open shirt. You'll give them the look, they'll flirt, there'll be lots of swirling curtains, it will be sexy, it will be hot, it will be fucking good."

Pedro grinned. "Do I get to say anything?"

"Oh, darling, all you need to do is stand there and look sexy."

He laughed. "Is that all!"

"Well…" Greta smiled wickedly. "And get naked and have sex. Let me show you to your dressing room."

*****

Andros took a limousine to Long Island. Stavros wasn't worthy of driving him anymore, so he'd hired a car for the night. They pulled up to the mansion and he gave it a critical once over. *I need to get myself one of these*, he thought. *Maybe I should move to New York and open a club. There are so many opportunities, it's a great city.*

He was escorted upstairs to the lounge area that spread the entire back part of the room and met Nedro Scarvo, an Italian French mix of passion and hatred; for himself and others.

"Andros Poulos," he said, putting out his arms in welcome. "Come, come, we will party, yes."

Andros made his way over to Nedro and accepted the drink the waiter offered. "This is quite a place you have here. I think I might like one of my own."

Nedro laughed loud and long. "Well, you can't have this one, but maybe I can help you there. Come, come, sit and let's enjoy the movie." He pointed to a couple of lounge chairs on the balcony.

"Has it started already?" Andros asked, seeing a group of hot-looking women dancing under the cabana. Cameras were everywhere moving back and forth catching the women in the setting sun.

"Yes, yes. They told me it's a mostly silent movie, so they need more footage than anything."

"And you said it was a porno," Andros said. "I've never seen a porno being made before."

"Sit back and enjoy," Nedro said. "And drink, drink."

Andros raised his glass and kept his eyes on the nearly naked women.

*****

Pedro stood in his pants and shirt having a bit of make-up put on. "Do I need this?" he asked.

"Just to even out your tone and get rid of shine," the make-up woman replied.

"Pedro," Stephanie purred. "It's time to go on. Now, let me fill you in."

"Greta did that this afternoon."

"Well, let me tell you too. We'll tell you when to go on, and it doesn't matter if you make mistakes, just keep on going and we'll edit it out later." She led him to the door. They'd taken over the ground floor for the movie and were exiting through the huge dining room. "You casually walk over, get behind your booth, and start doing your thing. One of us will indicate to you when to pull your shirt out so it hangs, and at some stage we'll let you know when to get down and start dancing. From there you just do your thing."

"My thing," Pedro repeated. "Which is?"

"Being so fucking hot and sexy." Stephanie arched a seductive brow.

Pedro shook his head at the situation he'd gotten himself into.

"So," Stephanie went on. "We're just about ready." She checked Pedro's clothes and undid another button on his shirt, running her hands over his torso. A sigh escaped from between her lips. "Delicious."

"And not yours," Pedro reminded her.

"Ugh, I hate that," she muttered. "Okay, get ready to walk over and...go."

Pedro strolled over to the DJ booth, donned his headphones and got on with it. It was going to be a long night, but at least he'd have fun spinning the discs.

For the next three hours camera crews kept rolling, and somewhere between hours two and three girls disappeared, leaving just three for Pedro to do. He had pulled his shirt out of his pants two hours ago and was slick with sweat. He eyed the beautiful girls on the dance floor waving at him to come over.

In a blur of billowing curtains, he left the booth, danced over to the girls and ground against them. They danced, they gyrated, they removed their clothes in a slow sensual feast for the eyes. His shirt, their dresses, his pants. Their hands slowly pulled down his underpants and he stepped out of them. The gyrating, grinding and dancing continued. The curtains billowed, the cameras moved in, zooming in on the prize it was after.

One girl backed onto him and they kept on dancing. Just like the first time he'd fucked Angelina in the club. He held the girl by the hips as they moved and the other two slithered up and down on him, on each other. He kissed them, touched them, and fucked them one by one.

*****

"Who is that man?" Andros asked from the balcony. "And where did he come from?"

"He's the DJ in the movie," Nedro said. "Some Greek kid called Stephanopoulos."

The realisation hit Andros square in the eye. "*Pedro* Stephanopoulos?"

"Yeah, that's it." Nedro called to the waiter. "Another drink."

Andros boiled with fury. "Do you have that parcel I asked about?" If there was ever a more opportune time to get him back, it would be now.

"Yes. Do you want it now?"

"Yes."

"Okay." Nedro waved over his henchman and spoke in his ear. The man left and came back a few minutes later with a box. "Here," he told Andros.

Andros took the box and looked inside. It was a block of cocaine. "Excellent," he hissed. "I need your help." He told Nedro of his plan, and Nedro passed it on to his henchmen who took the box and left the room.

"Good, good." Andros sat back in his seat. "It will end tonight."

*****

The cameras stopped rolling and Pedro backed off. "You girls okay. I didn't hurt you or anything?"

The girls stared dazedly. Being fucked by an eleven inch cock was oh so mouth-wateringly good.

"Oh…I'm fine," the blonde murmured, her voice husky. "In fact, I could do that again."

"Me too."

"Me three."

"Pedro." Greta came over. "Excellent, excellent. We got some fantastic footage." She turned to the girls. "Get dressed and go home. Excellent job. Pedro darling, get your clothes back on, we're going to do a photo shoot with the city lights as the backdrop. Come."

He picked up his clothes and followed her down the back to an old stone fence. The city twinkled in the distance.

"Get dressed darling and we'll take some photos."

He quickly slid on his pants and shirt before the stylist came over and adjusted everything just artfully so. His shirt was open, collar up. He had make-up reapplied, and the lights lit up his blue eyes.

"Oh, that's perfect," Greta told the photographer. "Put your hands on your collar as if you're pulling it up," she called after a few shots. "That's it. Head down, smile, look hot, look sexy, look like you've just fucked the person looking at you."

The photographer laughed and kept on snapping.

"Look like you want to fuck every woman looking at you," Greta continued until the roll of film was done. "And we're done. Good job, everyone. Let's pack up and go home. Pedro," she called him over. "Awesome job. Get changed and go see that girl of yours. I'll let you know when we do the next one."

"Thanks, Greta." Pedro went back to the house to change.

*****

Upstairs, Andros watched him flirt with the camera and that woman. He'd fucked three women and was probably going home to his Angelina. "Manwhore," he spat and watched Nedro's man come back.

"Is it done?" Nedro asked.

"It is done."

*****

Pedro changed his clothes, thanked the staff, and walked out to his Corvette. He gunned the engine, thrust the throttle, and spun out of the driveway to speed down the highway, wanting to make it back to Angie.

Changing gears, he hit the accelerator, feeling the grunt of the engine beneath him. As he neared the city, he changed speed and hit the brakes…

Nothing…

He hit the brakes…

Nothing…

"What the fuck!" He pumped the brake, shifted gears and slammed the pedal into the ground. "Why aren't you working?" he yelled, speeding across the Queensboro Bridge into the city. He swerved to avoid cars, pumping the brakes all the way. "Oh my God." He saw the end of the bridge. "Oh, my God." He slammed on the brake and spun the wheel.

*****

Andros left soon after Pedro. "I want to see what happened," he told Nedro. "To see if my plan worked."

Nedro slapped him on the back. "I hope it did, and you get that boy out of your life." He walked him to the door. "I hope it goes well."

"So do I," Andros muttered. "So do I."

*****

Pedro's eyes slowly blinked open. Bright twinkling lights flashed before him, voices floated around him, but they were dull, as though he was under water. He heard a siren and tried to move. "Ugh," he groaned. The pain shot through his head like a lightning bolt, making him see stars on top of the bright light.

"Ugh, what happened?" He tried to move his legs, but they didn't move far. He tried to move his arms and could move them enough to feel his head. "Ugh." He looked at his hands. They were slick with red fluid. "Oh, God."

"Don't try to move, we'll get you out," someone yelled and hands came through the smashed window. "Just sit still, we're going to check you out first."

He felt hands go around his neck, pull his eyes down, saw a light flash in them. He felt the rest of him being checked and heard more sirens. "Ugh." He tried to move.

"*Don't move.* We're going to get you out," the voice came again.

Somewhere in the back of his mind he heard machinery, metal on metal, and slowly, piece by piece, the people around him made headway.

A wide hard thing went around his neck, something sharp pierced his arm. He felt something else flow into his veins like a metallic flood oozing through him, *into* him. He groaned again, he moved again. He *was* moved and he was free.

Flat, lying on something cold and hard, he was wrapped and covered. The bright lights twinkled. The people's voices became clearer, yet distant. He groaned. He was moving, feeling sick, dizzy, suffocated by everything around him, on top of him.

"Well, well, well," someone said. "You just can't keep away from us can you, Mr Stephanopoulos. We'll see you at the hospital."

The driver of Andros's limousine saw the flashing lights and hit the brakes, slowing down on the bridge.

"Why are we stopping?" Andros demanded. He was pissed off because he hadn't seen any sign of Pedro or his smashed car on the way back from Long Island.

"Police and paramedics ahead. Could be an accident, sir."

Police? Accident?

Andros rolled down the window and peered out. Could it be? Oh, yes, could it be?

They slowly drove past the accident, and Andros saw the Corvette smashed in half, bent around a pole, and poor little Pedro being put into an ambulance. He smiled. The cold, calculating smile he used for winning. "Oh, yes, little boy," he hissed. "I have won and you are done." He noticed the officers hanging around looked like the ones who'd come to the apartment that night, and then to see him in the hospital to arrest him. "Well, it's not me they'll be arresting for this," he muttered. "Goodbye forever, Pedro Stephanopoulos. You may not be dead, but I hope you go down for life." He rolled the window up and they drove away.

Ten minutes later Pedro was rolled into emergency at the same hospital as Angelina. The officers had directed them there so they would be together. He lay still as he was shunted back and forth from x-ray to emergency before being taken to a room. The brace was removed, the needle was taken out. He was given painkillers. His eyes closed against the stream of lights, faces and voices.

*****

The next morning, Andros read the paper hoping for something about Pedro. But there was nothing. "Guess it's too early for his demise," he said.

*****

Pedro's eyes opened to find Angelina beside his bed. "Hey," he croaked. "You should be resting." He reached out a hand to stroke her face.

"What happened?" she asked, fear, anger and sadness in her eyes. "What happened?"

A small smile slid across his lips. "I don't know. You tell me."

She frowned. "You don't remember?"

His frown replicated hers. "No."

"You crashed your car."

He blinked. He breathed. He blinked again. "What?"

"You crashed your car on the way back from Long Island."

He racked his brain, and slowly the pieces became clear and

connected. "Oh," he groaned. "I'm starting to remember."

"Good. Then you can tell us what happened," Burns said from the doorway. He and Devron walked in.

"You guys are everywhere," Angelina said, adjusting her blanket. She was in a wheelchair and had been brought in earlier when she'd been told Pedro was a patient.

"Well, it seems that the two of you keep popping up on our radios," Devron replied. "We've been told that whatever happens, to stay on your cases."

"Speaking of the case, there was a block of coke in your trunk. Care to tell us where that came from?" Burns asked, tapping his pen on his notebook.

Pedro blinked dazedly. "Coke?"

"He doesn't do coke," Angelina scoffed. "*We* don't do coke or any other drugs."

"Then why did we find a block of it in the trunk of your car?" Devron stood with his hands on his hips.

"Did you also find I had no brakes?" Pedro asked, rubbing his face. "My brakes failed. No matter what I did, no matter how hard I pumped, the brakes wouldn't work. I think that's why I crashed. I couldn't stop."

The officers exchanged a glance. "Where were you yesterday, Mr Stephanopoulos? From the beginning."

"I was here at the hospital with Angie until twelve-thirty. Then I went to Long Island to shoot a movie. I was there until after midnight."

"Where on Long Island?"

"A huge mansion. 1212 Montauk Way. I don't know who owns it. My boss hired it for the movie."

Burns traded a glance with Devron. "We're just going to check on something," he said and stepped outside to radio headquarters. "This is Officer Burns, can you tell me who lives at 1212 Montauk Way on Long Island and if we've had any dealings with him?"

"You got a feeling?" Devron asked, leaning against the wall next to the door.

"Yep."

"1212 Montauk Way belongs to Nedro Scarvo. We have no personal dealings with him, but Long Island police have. Known drug kingpin and deals in anything else you want."

"Thanks." Burns clicked off.

"Well?" Devron asked.

"I've got a bad feeling," Burns said, and they re-entered the room. "Did you happen to meet a man by the name of Nedro Scarvo yesterday at all?"

Pedro thought. "No."

"Why don't you tell us what did happen."

Pedro swallowed. "I got there, was led through what would happen in the movie. Went over it with the producer and director. Ate, worked out, watched them set up, film, talked to the girls in the movie, got dressed, had make-up. Went on stage and filmed until well after dark. Then did a photo shoot, went in, changed and left."

"About what time?"

Pedro thought some more. "I looked at my watch at…ten past twelve when I was getting dressed. So, a few minutes after that."

"And you never met Scarvo?"

Pedro slowly shook his head. "No. I didn't meet anyone outside of the movie. I didn't meet an owner. No one. Why?"

Burns finished taking notes. "Because Scarvo is Long Island's biggest drug dealer yet no one can get him on anything. Now you say you'd never been there before and your boss hired the place."

"That's right."

"Where was your car?"

"Out front next to the company's production van."

"And you didn't go out to it at any time?"

"No."

"Did anyone else that you know of?"

"No. That's not to say no one did, but I didn't see and don't know if anyone did."

Burns sighed. Considering the kid had been at a drug dealer's to shoot a movie that wasn't organised by him, that meant someone else wanted to set the kid up. "You said your brakes failed."

"Yes." Pedro nodded. "I just couldn't slow down no matter how hard I pumped. In fact, it felt empty, light, as if there was nothing there and the pedal just moved up and down."

Burns frowned. He'd heard that before. "You rest, and we'll go and see what the tech boys have found with your car. We'll be in touch."

"What the hell is going on?" Angelina said from her chair when they'd left. "First a shooting, and now drugs and a car crash. Was there anything wrong with your brakes before?"

"No. And why should there be? It's a brand-new car."

*****

The woman was in her apartment. She'd been let out a few days earlier from the psyche ward. What the hell was she doing in there? She ran through the events. Waiting for Pedro, seeing him with that whore, hearing the car, seeing the gun pointed, jumping in front of Pedro, searing pain in her arm and then nothing.

She looked at her right arm. The stitches would need removing and the bandage changed, but other than that she and the baby were okay. Her baby. The baby they'd told her she wasn't having. She'd accused them of lying. They put her in the psyche ward believing the concussion had knocked a screw loose. Well, not only had it *not* knocked a screw loose, but it had made her more determined than ever to deal with Angelina and have Pedro once and for all.

After all, their baby couldn't come into the world with just one parent. She had to put her plan into action as soon as possible. *And no one,* she thought as she remembered the man's face from the shooting, *will get in my way.*

*****

Burns and Devron walked into the building the force used to pull cars apart. They saw the wreckage of the Corvette and Devron whistled. "That must have been some car."

"Yeah, and some crash," Burns replied. The wreckage was laid out,

281

and it was now a mere shell of what it once was.

"Gentlemen, Investigator Grosner. You are here about the Corvette, yes?" the five foot five man in the grey overalls asked. At fifty-five he was balding rapidly and just had a ring of brown hair around his bald spot.

"Yeah." Devron nudged a piece on the tarp. "You find anything?"

"Like a cut brake line, you mean?"

Burns and Devron's heads swivelled to the man. "His brakes were cut?"

"Yep, nothing else. The car is only what, a few weeks or months old. Everything is in pristine condition except for the brake line." He signed off on some paperwork. "I'll get my report typed up and over to you in the next day or two. Anything else?"

Burns shook his head. "No. Thanks for that, can't wait to read it." He and Devron left. "Well, what do you know? *Another* attempt on the life of Pedro Stephanopoulos. What is with that kid that makes Andros Poulos hate him so much?"

"We don't know it *was* Poulos. He was at Scarvo's house for twelve hours," Devron reminded him.

"True." Burns got into their car. "But what reason does Scarvo have for hating him? As far as we know, he's never met Scarvo, but we *do* know Poulos does drugs back in Greece. Both Pedro and Angelina confirmed that."

"Well," Devron said. "Whoever it is, he's a sick son of a bitch and probably won't stop until the kid is dead."

Burns revved the engine. "So, *we'll* just have to stop him."

*****

Greta, Stephanie, Thomas and Carson piled into Pedro's room.

"There you are, darling. We heard all about the accident from Eddie and came to see how damaged you were." Greta laid a bunch of flowers on the table. "How are you?" She glanced at Angelina. "And who's this unlucky girl with the sling?"

"His girlfriend." Angelina raised a brow. "You must be Greta Von

282

Burro, the woman that got him into this mess by hiring a drug dealer's house to film your movie."

Greta arched a brow as Stephanie, Thomas and Carson took a step back. "Drug dealer? Nedro Scarvo? Huh, that's hilarious."

"So is the block of cocaine the cops found in Pedro's trunk after the accident," Angelina spat icily.

The others gasped in horror. "A block of coke, oh no, that had nothing to do with us," Greta rushed to say. "If there was anything going on there we have no idea what it was. We just hire homes for the location. We don't care what the owners do or are."

"And there's the problem," Angelina said. "His car was sitting in a drug dealer's driveway all day and night, and when he leaves there's a block of coke in it and the brakes have been tampered with. Clearly, someone wanted him dead or caught and arrested."

"Whoa, whoa, what?" Greta put her hands up in protest. "Back up a minute. Your brakes were tampered with?"

"We think so." Pedro nodded. "They gave way; I didn't have anything to stop with."

"Jesus." Thomas crossed his chest. "Who'd want a gorgeous specimen like you dead?"

"My father," Angelina said simply. "He probably had Nedro set him up."

"Who's your father?" Greta asked.

"Andros Poulos."

"What does he look like?"

"Five ten, black hair, tan, wears suits all the time. Trim, but well built."

Greta recalled last night when she'd left for her own car and watched a man climb into a limousine not long after Pedro had left. "There was a man fitting that description who left just a few minutes after you," she told Pedro. "I'm sure of it."

Angelina sighed. "Of course it would be. If my father wanted drugs, then he'd find a supplier in New York, and who supplies... Nedro Scarvo."

"Apparently, he cuts brake lines too." Burns stood in the doorway with Devron, having been eavesdropping on the conversation. "Our guy says your brakes were cut. Everything else about the car was fine. Brand new." They walked into the room. "Someone's out to get you, Mr Stephanopoulos."

"My father," Angelina said again. "Was at Scarvo's that night." She motioned to Greta who retold what she had seen.

"It seems your father gets around, Miss Poulos."

Angelina sighed. "He always did."

"He's proving to be a big problem for us too. We're going to have a chat with our superiors to see what can be done about it."

"Deported back to Santorini would be nice," she said.

"Maybe we can arrange that." Burns nodded. "We'll be seeing you." They left, and everyone started talking at once.

"Good heavens, what sort of father do you have?" Carson asked.

"At least you're not hurt, just a few little scratches, we can cover those," Stephanie said.

"Hope the merchandise wasn't damaged," Thomas added.

"I am so sorry," Greta said. "We will check into every owner we hire from in future. No more drug dealer houses. In fact, for the next movie we move into the city into a building with one hell of a view. Oh, we've spliced together the movie already and it is hot, hot, hot."

"Already?" Pedro asked. "I only filmed it last night."

"Oh, please." Greta waved a hand. "It was so hot we spliced it together in no time, but the final movie won't be done for a few days. You'll be able to film next week, won't you? We want to release it after the Porn Star Awards."

"I think we should release it sooner," Carson piped up. "Capitalise on the fact your brother's new movie is out and doing shamelessly well."

"Speaking *of* your brother," Greta added. "We do want to capitalise on the fact he *is* your brother and want to change your name, for the movie, of course, to Pedro Stefan. We might even say on the box *younger brother of Carlo*. How does that sound?"

Pedro exchanged an amused glance with Angelina. "You want me to change my name for the movies?"

"Yes."

He shrugged. "Okay."

"And you don't mind if we capitalise on you being Carlo's younger brother?"

"Well…I am." He grinned.

"Oh, good. We'll get that going next week, and we'll see you next Saturday night. Let's go and leave these lovebirds alone." Greta ushered the others out and left Pedro and Angelina to themselves.

The loved-up duo glanced at each other and grinned.

"Hello, Mr Stefan."

"Hello, Miss Poulos."

TOMAS

Tomas arrived at the studios Sunday morning to find the grounds covered in cop cars and trench-coated detectives. "What's going on?" he asked Roger as he met him at the door. "What's happened?"

"Brock Hardwood is dead." Roger watched the procession of cops moving back and forth like worker ants.

"Oh, my God, what? What do you mean, dead?" Tomas spied Detective Barden talking to Marcus. "What happened? How did he die? Who found him?"

"Don't know, don't know, I did." Roger shoved his hands into his jeans pockets.

Tomas stared at him. "*You* found him?"

Roger's eyes glazed over and he winced. "Yeah."

"Oh, my God."

"Oh, my God, indeed. Mr Dencott, I want a word with you." Barden walked over to them dressed in his usual grey suit and beige trench coat. "I want to know exactly what happened from start to finish. Don't leave anything out." He flipped open his pad. "Go."

Roger sighed. "We were on a break. I was chatting to some of the crew as I'd helped out with the stages earlier."

"You're a member of the crew as well?" Barden interrupted.

"Yes. I help out with lighting, carting equipment, moving stages."

"Ah, multipurpose actor. Move on." Barden waved his pen at him.

"And when it was time to get the next set ready, I went ahead a few minutes earlier and found Brock on the floor. I rushed over, thinking he'd tripped and hurt himself, but…"

"But?"

Roger kicked his lips. "He was cold. So I checked for a pulse and found none." He shifted uncomfortably.

"When was the last time you saw Mr Hardwood?"

"After lunch when we were doing a movie."

"And what were you both *doing* in the movie?"

"He was acting in it, I was stage designer."

"So, a lot of *hands-on* experience?"

Roger eyed the man before him. He came up to Roger's shoulder. "What are you implying, Detective?"

Barden cocked a lip. "Well, you're all gay here, aren't you? Working on movies where you're all having sex with each other, there's probably wild orgies and free flowing drugs."

"Which I don't do," Roger snapped. "I've *never* done drugs, *never* had sex with Brock Hardwood in *or out* of the movies. And I've exclusively been with Tomas for the past month. So what *are you* implying?" He crossed his arms and stared defiantly at Barden.

Barden flipped his notebook closed and eagle-eyed the two boys in front of him. Young tanned, athletic. Everything he wasn't. "Then tell me this, if you weren't involved with Brock Hardwood, why would he have a photo of pretty boy here in his pocket?" He held the picture of Tomas face down on a fur rug with a man coming in from behind. The look on Tomas's face in the photo was of pure pleasure. In real life, standing before the Detective, it was pure astonishment. "Mr Stephanpopolopolous, why would Hardwood have a picture of the two of you doing that?"

"That's not Hardwood behind him, it's me." Roger was angered. "That's a scene from our second movie together, *Mount Cockmore.* As I *said,* Detective, we've been together exclusively for a month. I don't do movies with anyone but Tomas, and he doesn't do them with anyone but me. Is that clear?"

"And again." Barden waved the photo. "Why would he have a photo of Tomas being mounted on him? Did he have a crush? Was he in love with him? Had the two of them been in a movie together? Was Hardwood in this movie with the two of you?"

Silence.

"And there you have it." Barden leant back on his heels.

"He was an extra," Tomas said quietly, clinging to Roger's arm. "But we had no intimate scenes together. Just a party scene."

"Just a party scene. Was this the party?" He waved the photo again.

"No," Roger snapped. "Now we've answered your questions. I need to get back to work." He walked away and pulled Tomas with him, only stopping when the coroner carried Brock's body away.

"What was it like?" Tomas asked, his head following the stretcher being carried out.

"What?"

"Finding the body. What was it like?"

Roger sighed and pulled up his jeans. "Not fun."

"Everyone, may I have your attention," Violet called out. "Please gather round." She waited for the cast and crew to quieten down. "Go home. None of us will be in the right frame of mind for working tonight, and we're probably still in shock, so please, head home, and come back tomorrow." She moved to Marcus's side. He was dazed, moving his head from side to side, and she led him away to their office.

"Not much to do here then," Roger said, eyeing the set where he'd found Brock's body.

"I don't know what I'd do if I found a dead body," Tomas said. "Did anyone say how he died?"

Roger shook his head. "There was no blood, just a bit of powder on his nose."

"Another overdose?"

"Possibly."

"So, what do we do? Go home? Go out to dinner?"

"I couldn't eat."

"You okay?"

"Not really."

"We could just go home."

"No, I…" Roger's gaze wandered. "I need to…I need to get out of here. I'll see you at home." He took off for the car park.

"Roger," Tomas yelled and ran after him, but he was already jumping into his car. "Roger." He slapped the trunk as he took off. "Jesus!" He stood with his hands on his hips. "What the hell?"

"What the hell indeed, Mr Stephanpopodopolous."

"It's Steph-an-op-oul-os. *Nothing else.* It's not that hard to get right, Detective." He suspiciously eyed Barden. "I thought you were all gone."

"Not yet," Barden said. This wasn't his first foray into porn movies, or dealing with fags strung out on coke. He'd been around a while, working hardcore cases involving death, murder, suicide, and now dealing with the same movie production company. Coincidence? He wasn't sure.

"What are you still doing here?"

"Just wrapping things up." He flicked his pen against his notebook. "I see lover boy has left without you."

"He's upset. What do you expect? He found a dead body and needs to deal with that."

"Well, then maybe *you* can help me."

"With what, Detective? What could *I* possibly help *you* with when I turned up just a short time ago? When *you* were already here."

"How well did you know Hardwood?"

"What?" Tomas sighed, wanting to rush after Roger instead of being here with some dumb detective.

"How well did you know Hardwood? Have you talked a lot, about what, did you know he did drugs? Did he know Jeff Fastwater? Have you all worked together? I'm trying to find out why your co-workers are overdosing, Mr Steph-an-op-oul-os," he spelt it out.

"Maybe it's a bad batch of drugs," Tomas replied. "I need to go." He headed for his car, but Barden followed.

He wasn't about to give up. "Have you ever done drugs, Mr Steph-an-op-oul-os?"

Tomas reached his car and turned. "No, Detective Barden, I haven't, and no, I didn't know Brock and Jeff did. And no, I don't know why they had photos of us on them. I have no idea what's going on. Now if that's all?" He waited with his hand on the car door handle.

"I'll definitely be in touch, Mr Steph-an-op-oul-os."

Tomas drove home, keeping an eye out for Roger, but he didn't find him. And he wasn't at home when he got there. Keeping an eye out for anyone suspicious, he went up to their apartment and locked the door behind him. Checking the place, he found no Roger and no intruder. "Jesus, where are you?"

During his confinement, Carlos worked on new ideas for scripts and handed them to Harry when he turned up for the new movie. It was the second meat shop movie they were filming, and once again he'd written it. He was full of ideas and had gotten them down on paper, even drawing little layouts for how sets should look.

Harry read them over in his office while Carlos hit the set.

Today he was working with ethnic beauty Giselle Boudoir. She had a riot of curls tumbling down her back that matched the riot of curls between her legs. She was playing a foreigner visiting Greece. She was in need of meat…

They took their positions…

"And…action."

Giselle walked through the door wearing a see-through white dress and nothing underneath.

"Well, hello," Carlos murmured. "May I interest you in some… meat…?"

Gisele stared dumbstruck by the golden god before her. "Well, I…"

Removing his apron, he came round the counter. "Let me show you today's specials?" He led her to the window display where half a dead cow resided. "It is all *meat…*" Carlos seduced. "From *every* angle."

Giselle licked her lips and put a hand on his chest. "And are *you* all meat?"

Carlos ripped off his uniform. "See for yourself!"

"Oh." She blushed. *"Oh, I need that meat."*

"Of course you do." He ripped open her dress, threw her backwards over the meat, and, spreading her legs, thrust inside.

Her head was lying amidst the remains of the cow, as gross as it was, and she was tilted at an angle so everything was on show in the window. Her breasts jiggled, her arms flailed above her head, her curls splayed across the animal and she groaned in pleasure. He stopped. "Oh, God," she groaned.

"Oh, God indeed," Carlos agreed as he pulled out, pulled her off the meat, turned her around and entered from behind.

She was grasping the meat in front of her, groaning, breasts on display for the camera. It was all a part of the porn. Tits and pussy and cock and mouth, nothing else mattered except those four things. And as long as the cameras zoomed in on female tits and mouth and pussy, and threw in a few cock shots to make women happy and men jealous, then the work was easy enough to do.

And it sold a motza!

When Carlos made her scream it was over.

The *fantasy* was over.

He pulled out, donned his uniform while she adjusted her dress, and once again he offered her meat. Just as if sex had never happened.

And that was that.

"And...cut, print, good job." Andy Merkin, the director, was a dirty old man...more in his perverse sense of pleasure, not his age. He was forty-five and had started from the ground up in the movie industry, but became fed up when he wasn't getting the directing gigs he wanted. That's when he'd met Harry. Harry had seen something he'd done and offered him a job. Now he was making three times more than other movie directors and was getting to pursue his perverse passion on the side.

Sex, drugs and porn movies. It suited Andy down to a T. He got off on watching the sex scenes, as did the other men working there, got to score with a few of the actresses, and met bigwig TV stars, celebrities, and other actors at parties and nightclubs. This world suited him down to a T all right. T for tits. T for tongue. T for take it up the nose or the ass. Either way, it suited Andy Merkin perfectly.

Now his bulging erection showed he'd been turned on, as did a few other bulging pants. He needed to relieve himself and sneaked off to a quiet corner in another room with Suzy, Harry's maid, for a quick back end fuck over a chair. When he was done, he put it in his pants and left the room, and she straightened her uniform and pocketed the fifty bucks he'd given her.

She didn't like being treated like a piece of meat, dear old Suzy Q, as she was known. But at thirty-five she still looked good and had big tits and a big ass that could take a man like a champ. Plus she had a five-year-old son to raise so the money came in handy. How else could she get fifty bucks for five minutes' work? And back to work she went, servicing five more men in the next half hour, earning herself another two hundred and fifty bucks. Score! Three hundred bucks in one day and off the books paid her way through life, and she wasn't about to give it up. Besides, it was only an hour or so once a week. She could deal with that. Couldn't she?

Andy got to work in the editing booth while Harry and Carlos went over the photos from Aneeka's shoot.

"We're definitely using this one, and that will be a poster, that will be on the cover, that will be..." His imagination drifted off as he stared at a photo of Carlos in the pool, upper torso out of the water, his wet t-shirt plastered against his muscular chest, his hair in wet tendrils, his eyes penetrating into the souls of every woman, man, and child who dared lay eyes on them. "We're definitely using this one."

"Those are great photos." Carlos placed them in order. Cabana shots, meat shop shots, pool shots. "I've never done a photo shoot before, but that was well worth it."

Harriet came in with coffee and looked at the photos. Seeing the shots where Carlos was fully naked, she sighed. "If only I could get a taste of that sausage," she murmured. "Am I too old for you dear? You fucked Connie and didn't have a problem." She turned to see a surprised and uncomfortable Carlos slouched on the couch.

He reddened and sat up. "Um, Connie wasn't my boss."

"*I'm* not your boss. I'm only his wife." Harriet sat beside him.

"And I'm not about to go near you." Carlos got to his feet. "Harry, what did you think of the scripts?"

"Great, fantastic." Harry waved his cigar around. "And you'll get full writing credits on them as you will with the meat shop movies. That's why we can now give you a raise and your name will be on the boxes when the videos come out."

"And the movie posters and trailers?"

"And the posters and trailers! Now, what do you think about the Golden God idea? I see you floating down in a white loin cloth to bed the Greek women at your beck and call."

"Corny," Carlos said. "But I'll see what I can do with it."

"Good, good." Harry puffed. "Now I've spoken to a lawyer, and he said our story was a good one. By you admitting to going there and having sex, but lying about doing drugs and then remembering Aneeka lived next door, that should cover any evidence of yours that they find. But the cops are suspicious about the fence even though Aneeka covered that, and they're suspicious about you being out of it for so long. But right now, they can't charge you with anything without proof, and since Aneeka provided them with two other potential killers, you should be okay for a while."

"And he needs to be; the porn awards are next week and he's been nominated for best newcomer," Harriet said.

"Already?" Carlos asked. "I thought they were months away and I didn't stand a chance?"

"Next week," Harry said. "And the ballots closed a week after your first movie came out, so we just scraped in. You're a shoo-in to win."

Carlos grinned. "I'm up for a porn award?"

"Yep, my boy." Harry got up and slapped him on the back. "You're up for an award."

"Will we be going?" Carlos asked. "What about everything that's going on?"

"You leave that to me—" Harry was interrupted by the phone. "Yes."

"Harry," Aneeka's panicked voice came down the line. "I've been broken into and my place has been trashed."

"What do you mean broken into? Don't you have security locks?"

"Of course, and I put my valuable things in the safe when I travel for a job, but someone still trashed it. Equipment, my photos, furniture, art, everything's been trashed."

"Have you called the police?" Harry asked as Carlos and Harriet gathered around, anxious to find out what had happened.

"Of course, they're on their way, but Harry, what if this has to do with what happened next door?"

"Don't consider that until you get some idea from the cops," Harry said. "Get your timeline together, your insurance papers, and anything else they may need. I'll get my private investigator onto it. Call me back after they're gone." He put the phone down and explained what had happened to Aneeka.

"Jesus!" Carlos said. "Do you think it has anything to do with Rosalee? Those men? What if they found out Aneeka took photos of them and trashed her place looking for them?" He paced back and forth. "What if they trash *my* place?"

"What do you have that they would want?" Harry asked.

Carlos thought about it and shook his head. "Nothing."

"Unless they do it to plant evidence," Harry went on. "Get your butt back to your place, Tony will go with you and search for anything that might be incriminating. Go." He ushered Carlos out the door and let Tony know what to do. "Stay on him like glue. Call me." He sighed and sat beside his wife on the couch. "That boy may make us big bucks, but he comes with a bucket load of trouble."

"Yes," Harriet agreed, swirling her pearls. "I wish he would let me deal with some of that trouble."

"Harriet," Harry snapped. "Must you *always* talk about fucking the boy? He's young enough to be your son."

"Aren't they all," she declared. "It's not as though I don't know about fucking, Harry. That's how you met me. I became your first porn star."

"And you were good at it until I decided to marry you."

She cocked a thin grey brow. "Are you saying I wasn't any good *after* you married me?"

Her tight lips and prim grey pantsuit were a turn off for him. "For a while." He got up and busied himself with the photos of Carlos.

"Well…" She stood up. "It's not like it stopped *you* from dipping your pen in the ink. I've had to put up with *that* all these years. So why shouldn't *I* get the pen dipped?" she huffed and stormed out the door.

"Because he's our best asset," Harry yelled. "And he clearly doesn't want you." He mumbled the rest under his breath. "Clearly doesn't want me either. Best to leave that boy to what he does best."

*****

Aneeka didn't wait for the police. She grabbed her camera that she'd had with her, loaded new film and took her own photos. She photographed every room that was trashed, the door locks, and the studio. She took photos of her smashed belongings, artworks, pictures, and documented it all down on paper, writing out a list of what was missing or broken. She checked her safe. All contents safe and accounted for.

The cops turned up an hour after her call.

"I would *hate* to have been injured," she said. "I would be dead waiting for you to turn up."

"Except you weren't harmed, so you're not dead," Detective Star muttered as he and Drew stalked around the house. "And when did you discover there had been a break-in?" He looked down at the floor to see he had stepped on a painted canvas. "If there *was* a break in."

"Do you think I did this myself?" Aneeka's anger rose. "That I trashed my own belongings and expensive photo equipment for the fun of it?" she snapped. "Let me tell you something, Detective Star, you are *not* very good at your job."

"And let me tell *you* something, *Ms* Ne Masta…" He stepped in to lean over her. "I find it highly suspicious that barely a week after your neighbour overdoses and her boyfriend crashes through your fence your house is broken into and trashed—"

"I told you—"

"Yeah, yeah." His temper simmered. "*Gardening* accident." He went nose to nose with her. "I know what you keep saying, *Ms* Ne Masta, but it doesn't jibe with other accounts and now this." He spread an arm out. "Where were *you* when this was happening?"

Aneeka hadn't blinked while standing toe to toe with Star. "I was away on a shoot all weekend. I got back this morning and immediately called the police who *chose* to take their time getting here. Now, I don't know if this is related to what happened next door, it could just be that they saw I wasn't home and broke in. That is up to *you* to determine."

Star hated the fact that a Negro woman so determinedly stood up to him, and he didn't give a flying shit if she was some world-renowned photographer or not. She was still a Negro.

"I see it in your eyes, Detective," Aneeka said. "Your ancestors owned slaves and you hate women, especially *black* women, standing up to you." She boiled inside, but remembered to stay calm, something she had to learn how to do many years ago. "I feel sorry for you, Detective."

He blanched at a black woman telling him she felt sorry for him.

"Sorry that you cannot move with the times like other people."

Now *his* blood boiled. "Who the hell are you to tell me that, you nig—"

"Star!" Drew yelled and grabbed the arm that had risen to hit the woman in front of them. He'd never seen his partner so riled up over a woman, even a black one, and was shocked that he'd raise a hand to one. "Calm down," he said.

Aneeka hadn't even flinched. "Yes, *Detective* Star, calm down, or you might give me a reason to file a complaint of harassment and assault on you."

Star launched himself at her, but Drew got in the way. "Let me go, get out of my way, Drew."

Drew shoved him backwards out the door of the studio, all the way downstairs and out the front door.

Star made racial slurs all the way and insinuations that she was involved with Carlos Stephanopoulos and the suspicious death next door.

The other officers stood in shock, glancing at each other, not knowing what to do. But Aneeka gave them no choice. Taking a deep breath, she said, "All right everyone, have you finished? I need to talk to my insurance officer next. Do you have everything you need?"

The officers took her lead and nodded, leaving her to repair her broken house. Once they were gone, she heaved a sigh of relief and slumped against the door, but saw the mess she'd have to clean up. Dear God, what was she up to her neck in? Did it have to do with next door? If they were after photos, then why not simply go through the studio? Why trash the whole house? Since the whole house was trashed, was it normal crooks looking for a place to do over?

Someone knocked on the door and she jumped. "Oh." Peering through the peephole, she saw it was her insurance broker. She didn't know what she was going to do, but it would have to wait.

*****

Carlos sped back to his apartment with Tony close behind. They made record time, and raced up the stairs before Tony stopped Carlos so he could open the door.

"We need to be careful in case they've trashed your place too." He motioned for Carlos to step back and pulled a small black revolver from the band of his pants. Slowly, carefully, he put his army and C.I.A. training into use. Pushing open the door, he peered through the gap. Seeing no one, he moved the door back, and with his pistol pointed, entered the apartment. Seeing and hearing no one, he silently moved through the two bedrooms, bathrooms and back into the lounge and kitchen. He checked all the windows and balcony doors. When he was satisfied there were no wires, bugs, or explosives, he motioned for Carlos to enter and closed the door behind him. "Sit at the dining table," he instructed. "I'm going to take this place apart."

Carlos nodded and took a seat while Tony explored every nook and cranny, coming up with bloodied drug paraphernalia tucked away behind the toilet in the master suite. He searched the whole place from top to bottom and found a bag of drugs, some bloodied material, and photos of Carlos and Rosalee passed out on her bed before she was killed. He placed them on the table in front of Carlos who started to talk, but Tony quickly put his finger to his lips to silence him.

He went to the phone on the kitchen bench, unscrewed the bottom half to check for bugs and found one. After twisting the cap back on, he called Harry. "Hey, Harry, can you send Mike over to relieve me. I've got a hot date tonight and there are some things I wanna show her…if you know what I mean…"

Harry knew exactly what he meant. "Mike's on his way."

"Thanks, Harry." Tony replaced the phone in its cradle for a few moments before picking it up, unscrewing the cap and removing the bug. He put the phone back together and gathered everything, placing each piece into a coat pocket, so when he walked out it looked as if he had nothing. And if anyone *was* watching, they would think no one had found the incriminating evidence.

Mike arrived twenty minutes later and Tony walked out to meet him.

"Mike."

"Tony. Hot date, man."

"Yep, gotta go and get ready."

"Make sure to get it up then."

"I plan on it."

Mike went inside and Tony left, driving back to Harry's. They studied the evidence on Harry's desk.

Harry tasted the drug. "Cocaine." He checked the pills. "Uppers." He looked at the photos. "She's drugged off her face."

"What do we do with it?" Tony asked.

Harry thought about it. "If I burn it, it might be needed somehow to prove his innocence."

"Or guilt."

Harry sighed. "Or guilt," he agreed. "But I just can't see him doing something like that. He's a good kid, really. If I keep it, it could be found and used against him."

"So, what do we do with it?" Tony asked again.

Harry paced the room. "Lock it up where no one will find it."

*****

The man in the car had watched Carlos arrive with the big bald guy right behind him. They'd entered, and an hour later, another man had turned up, greeting the bald guy as he came out. They exchanged talk about a date and getting it up.

He hadn't gotten it up properly in months. It's not that he hadn't tried. It's just that his boss kept him busy watching Carlos Stephanopoulos. Some big guy with a big dick who got it out a lot. *More than he did.* He didn't know why his boss wanted him watching some porn guy, only that he had to, and supposed his boss had some big plan for the newest porn star. And regardless of what his boss wanted, he'd gone out and seen the movies. He was bored. He'd needed something to do in what little spare time he had. So he'd sat in the movie theatre up the back, getting off to the movie as he was sure everyone else in the room was doing.

Regardless of the reason why he was watching Carlo Stefan, the guy was gorgeous and had a huge dick, and the women he fucked in the movie he'd imagined himself fucking in exactly the same way. After knocking a couple of young girls unconscious, he'd fucked them exactly the same way as Carlo did in the movie.

Of course, he wouldn't be able to do that if they were conscious. They wouldn't want him. They wouldn't even look at him. So he had to find alternative ways of having sex…without paying for it. He'd covered his face and burned the clothes he'd worn so they wouldn't find him even if they looked.

And then there was that pretty young thing called Rosalee.

His cock was hard just thinking about the girls he'd had, and he released it from its nylon prison. "Ah, that's better." It stood, slightly limp, slightly bent in the sun beating its way into the car, seeking release. But he held on, stroking, massaging, pretending he was Carlo Stefan, ready to put his ten inch cock into some young thing's mouth. He felt the warmth of that mouth, the sucking and sliding, a mouth ever so greedy for what he had. For what it wanted. He felt himself peak and come, groaning, tilting his head back, and thrusting his crotch back and forth in the motions.

He sweated and groaned as the mouth sucked harder and he came again.

Tap tap tap tap.

"Oh, yes, tap away," he groaned.

Tap tap tap tap.

He moaned at the interruption and opened his eyes to see a police officer staring at him through the window.

Ah, fuck!

PEDRO

Monday morning, Burns and Devron talked to their captain who called in Detective Gardo. He'd liaised between the drug division and the mob squad, bringing down some of the city's drug dealers and mobsters.

"What have you got for me?" The six feet of Giancarlo Gardo drove full bore into the precinct. He was as wide as a Mack Truck and as angry as a bull in a china shop.

"Nedro Scarvo," was all Captain Shield said.

Gardo stopped, eyes wide. "You got the son of a bitch?"

"Not quite," Shield said. "But you need to hear a story that might help you get him. Burns." He waved the officer over. "Tell him what you told me."

Burns told the whole story, a very detailed story, about a poor Greek boy who had been harassed by his girlfriend's father who just happened to know Scarvo. He told of finding drugs after Pedro spent the night filming a movie and how he'd had his brakes cut.

"But do you have any evidence on *him*?" Gardo asked. "It's all well and good to have people's say so, but we need cold hard facts."

Burns shook his head. "Except for the block of coke, no. But we do have Poulos charged with assault and attempted rape. He's in complete denial that he's done anything wrong, but he *will* do anything to get rid of Stephanopoulos, including cutting brakes and leaving coke in the car."

"Well, that's Scarvo's MO," Gardo said. "We've seen it before. So if they're in cahoots, we'd better put a tail on this Poulos and anyone associated with him."

"He did have a frequent visitor in the hospital," Devron added.

"Put a tail on him too." Gardo made for the door. "And one on this Stephanopoulos kid. Who knows what *he's* up to?"

*****

Andros scoured Monday's paper, but all he found was a small snippet about *Studio 69*'s resident DJ crashing his car. That he was okay and doing fine.

"What? Doing fine! Why isn't he dead, or arrested, or in jail?" Andros reread the article in case he'd missed something. There was nothing about drugs or cut brakes. "Fuck!" He slammed the paper down. *"When the fuck is he going to die?"*

*****

The woman wrote down her plan. The time had come to take the bull by the horns and deal with it herself. Especially now that Pedro was in the hospital.

"With that whore," she spat. "I am alone and not with my baby's father. I am alone and not with the man I love." The fury burned in her eyes. It burned in her throat. It burned in her gut. *I don't know who that man was, but he shot at the wrong person. Oh, if only he had killed Angelina!* If that had happened, she would be at Pedro's side right now. She picked up the photo of Angelina. The face was scratched out, and there was a red target drawn over her.

"Bitch, you are going down!"

*****

Pedro was released, along with Angelina, from the hospital. Greta arrived with a limousine to take them home, but they stopped at the car dealership where he'd gotten the Corvette to buy a Mustang convertible. It was blue; the exact same shade as his eyes.

"Well, I'll let you drive home then," Greta said. "Don't forget, this Saturday we have a new movie."

"Let me know the address and I'll be there," he said, and they drove home in the brand-new car to find boxes of letters and presents from adoring fans. Pedro carried them inside, and they spent the next few hours going through them.

Pedro laughed. "Bev Marie wants me to take her home to Mykonos and fuck her till she dies." He shook his head. "God what a woman."

"Just don't get any ideas," Angelina told him, pulling out a medium-sized box from the bottom. "What's this, it's heavy." She lifted the lid, pulled back the tissue paper and stared…and gasped… and threw the box at Pedro. "What sort of sick joke is that? Get rid of it."

He looked up in surprise at the box and grabbed it. Glancing inside he saw an eleven inch vibrator sliced up with red liquid all over it. "Ugh, what the hell!" He saw photos of Angelina with her face scratched out and a bullseye on her head. There was a bloody piece of paper that he pulled out. "*If you continue fucking your whore she will die. Stop seeing her and you will live. You have one chance. You have one choice. Make the right one.* What the hell! Where's the lid?" Angelina handed it to him and he jammed it on. "Clearly this is someone's sick idea of a sick joke, and we're not going to do anything about it."

"It's not like it's something we can take to the cops. New York's newest porn star gets a sliced dildo as a present. Yeah." Angelina snorted. "They'd really take that seriously."

Pedro looked at her. "Well, I know two people who will take that very seriously."

TOMAS

Tomas sat on the couch to watch TV, and come Monday morning, when he woke, Roger still wasn't home. Making breakfast, he called Bette to let her know he wouldn't be doing the morning sessions and waited. Hearing the clunk of keys in the lock at eleven, he unchained the door just as Roger shoved it open. "Hey." He held the door. "God, you look awful."

Roger breathed in deeply. "Yeah well, I *feel* awful." He dumped his keys on the side table and slumped on the couch.

"Do you want some coffee?" Tomas wandered into the kitchen, watching Roger from the other side of the island bench.

"No, thanks. I've had way too much already this morning."

"Where were you?" Tomas asked tentatively. "I waited up for you. You didn't come home." He curled up beside Roger.

"I stayed with a friend." Roger rubbed his eyes. "Ugh, too bright."

"Which friend?"

"What does it matter?"

"It matters in case I need to get in contact with you, or something happens to you and I know where to find you."

"Like I said, with a friend."

Silence.

"A gay friend?" Tears sprang to Tomas's eyes as he feared the worst. "Were you drinking? Did you stay with a man?"

"Are you kidding me?" Roger asked, peering out from under his hand that shielded his eyes from the light. "Are you accusing me of sleeping with someone else?"

"No, I—"

"You what? Want to get all possessive like a woman and demand to know where I am at all hours? *And so what if I did get drunk?* Big fucking deal. Considering I found a dead body is it any wonder I needed a drink? Jesus." He lay down. "I didn't come home for this shit."

Tomas choked back a sob. "Then why did you bother coming home at all?" He stormed into the bedroom and grabbed his gym bag. "I'm going to work. You can sort your own shit out."

Roger finally realised what he had done. "Tomas," he called as he headed for the door. "Tomas." The door slammed. "Fuck!"

Tomas didn't go to work. He couldn't, not in the state he was in, so he went to the beach and sat crying in his car. After a while, there was a knock on the window. He looked up into the aqua eyes of his first lover. "Luiz?" He wound down the window.

"Tomas, my love. How are you? Long time no see." Luiz knew he had to keep it casual otherwise it would all be for nothing.

"Ah, yeah." Tomas wiped his face. "I didn't know you were still here in Miami."

"Yeah, well, I had been with Bertha here remember, so it is my home. What about you?"

"Yeah, yeah, doing okay, having a great time. At least I was until today."

Luiz leant against the car. "It looks like it." He motioned to Tomas's face. "Except for all the tears."

Tomas sighed and turned away.

"Lovers' quarrel?"

He looked back. "How do you know?"

"A guess. You said everything was okay until today, so it must be personal. You *have* been seeing someone…haven't you?"

Tomas blinked and shifted uncomfortably. "Yeah, yeah I have."

"And he's not treating you well?" Oh, how he wanted to take Tomas into his arms and hold him and love him and fuck him inside and out. His cock ached for him and strained inside of his shorts.

"He's…treated me fine. It's just…" He wasn't sure how much he should mention to Luiz since he'd left him back in Mykonos.

"Just what?"

"Just that he found a co-worker dead on the floor at work yesterday and it's really freaked him out. We were both short with each other this morning."

"Jesus, Tomas. Are you all right? You weren't hurt or anything were you?" He lightly touched his fingers to Tomas's shoulder. The sizzle was still there.

Tomas moved his shoulder to dislodge the fingers. "No. I wasn't hurt. I wasn't around when he died, or when Roger found him. But it was horrible, and must have been even worse finding the body."

"Wow, what happened?"

Tomas launched into the whole story, and Luiz listened intently. "It must have been rough on him, but he had no right to freak you out by staying out all night and not telling you. Talk about selfish."

"No. I get it," Tomas said. "I saw the body being carried away, and I saw another co-worker overdose at a party a few days ago, and that was upsetting, so I get it. He needed time to decompress."

"And he did that with alcohol and sex? Not a very good boyfriend."

"He didn't," Tomas cut in. "He got drunk and stayed with his friend instead of driving home drunk."

"He could've called you to pick him up. But he didn't bother calling you at all?" Luiz asked him. "Some boyfriend you've got. Can't even tell you where he is. Couldn't care less if you were worried."

"That's not the way it was."

"Do *you* know the way it was?"

"Yes…I…" Tomas sighed. "That's all I got out of him before I left."

"You left your boyfriend? After he comes home from an all-night bender doing God knows what with God knows who. I would have stayed and had it out with him. No man does that to me. I would've made him tell me every little thing and then kicked his sorry ass to the kerb."

"Roger's not like that. He wouldn't cheat and neither would I.

We'll sort it out."

"Meanwhile, you're sitting here at the beach crying your eyes out. Yeah, great relationship you two have." He heard Tomas's silence and saw the sad expression. "How about we go for coffee? There's a little café across the street. If you want to talk about it…" He shrugged.

"No, no, but…I could do with a coffee."

They sat for two hours talking about Miami and Tomas's life in it. What Luiz had been doing, back working in the same gym as before, and talking about the spate of deaths, thefts, and their break-in.

"Someone broke into your home?" Luiz asked, shock sliding over his face. He had to keep it real after all.

"Yeah. Roger forgot to chain it, and the person got in."

"Did he steal anything?"

"No, just took pictures." Tomas sipped his coffee.

"Pictures of what?"

"Us."

"Us? You and Roger?"

"Yep."

"Doing what?"

"Having sex in bed." Tomas quickly looked away and buried his head in his coffee.

"You what? He what?"

"He was taking pictures of us in bed."

"Jesus." Luiz pretended to be oh so shocked while seething inside. "The gall of the man."

"Yeah. What a perve. It was horrible. You're in the midst of having sex, and you hear a camera going off and see a man at the end of your bed."

"It must have been so scary. Did you feel violated?"

Tomas thought about it. "Yeah, kinda. And then to have another death on top of it." He sighed. "It hasn't been a good week."

"No, it hasn't," Luiz agreed.

Tomas checked his watch. "I'd better go. I've got afternoon classes. Thanks for the coffee." He got up. "It was…nice to see you again. Good luck with everything." He walked past Luiz and out the door.

Luiz threw money down on the table and followed, watching as Tomas got into his car and drove off. He put his hand up to wave goodbye, but Tomas didn't acknowledge it. He lowered his hand. *So, Roger boy left Tomas out in the cold last night, all on his little lonesome. If only poor little Tomas knew what his beloved Roger got up to. Naughty, naughty.*

*****

Tomas arrived at Bette's in time for lunch and told her all about his fight with Roger and running into Luiz.

"I hope he doesn't suck you in like last time. Stay away from him," Bette said over lightly baked lemon salmon and delicately boiled potatoes and asparagus. "He's bad news for you, Tomas."

"I know." Tomas sipped crystal water from a crystal glass. "We just talked about what's happened since being here in Miami."

"Including his running into us at *Sexe et Faveurs*?"

"Oh." His face fell. "I'd forgotten about that. Because I haven't seen him since, and so much has happened, I'd forgotten."

"Well, I bet *he* hasn't." Bette sipped her champagne. It was champagne all the time, any time of the day, morning, noon and night for Bette. She lived on the stuff, and only the best would suffice. "I bet he remembered every little moment you were together and still wishes he had it again."

"That's not the feeling I got today. He's back at the gym he used to work at, and he seemed okay. He didn't try anything with me."

"Just as well. You don't want him to ruin your relationship with Roger, do you? That would be such a pity if you did all because of a scoundrel like Luiz Manning. You stay away from him, Tomas. I have a feeling in my waters that he's up to something bad."

Tomas laughed. "You and your waters. I'm going to get ready for our first session." He turned to Webster. "Delicious as always."

Webster nodded his appreciation.

The rest of the day sped by quickly. The women wanted to talk about Tomas and his movie career, the latest death, and how they were dealing with it. All gave him advice on how to talk to Roger, leaving him more confused than he was that morning. He rolled into the studio car park at seven and found Roger on set getting everything ready. Biting his lip as he nervously walked over to him, he watched for some form of emotion. "Hey."

Roger looked up. "Hey." His attention turned back to the table he was fixing.

"Are we going to talk about it?"

"Nope."

"At all?"

"Nope."

"You're kidding?"

"Do I look like I'm kidding?" Roger asked, placing a lamp on the table and moving a chair.

Tomas huffed. "No, but then I guess I was kidding myself thinking I was ready to move in with you and have a relationship." He stormed off.

"Tomas," Roger called. "Ah, Jesus."

Marcus had been eyeing the whole thing. "Problems?"

"No!" Roger spat. "Just leave it."

"Will it interfere with your work later?"

Roger sighed. "I dunno." He stormed off in the opposite direction to Tomas.

An hour later, they were both on set ready to perform. You could have cut the tension with a knife, and the awkwardness between them was palpable. They stood on opposite sides of the set not looking at each other and trying to ignore everyone else.

"Take your places," Marcus yelled, sitting in his chair. "I hope you two drop the crap when the cameras roll. In three, two, one, action."

Roger and Tomas worked their lines, did their actions, and came together as they were supposed to. Albeit awkwardly and childishly. There was no chemistry, no zing, no whiz-bang between them and finally, Marcus called cut.

"What the hell is wrong with you two? What's happened to fuck you up?"

"Ask Roger, coz I sure as hell don't know." Tomas grabbed the blanket from the bed and wrapped it around himself. "And he sure as hell isn't telling me." He sat down with a flounce.

"Dencott? What the fuck is going on? Time is money."

Roger stood to attention with his hand on his hips, naked in front of all. "Nothing."

"Bullshit."

"A guy died here. *A co-worker.* And we all just move on as though it didn't happen and it only just happened three days after Jeff. It's freaking the fuck out of me," Roger yelled.

"And now we're getting to the root of the problem," Marcus said. "We're *all* freaked out. I've got two dead actors to replace. How do you think *I* feel? It's *not just you*, it's *all of us.* We've lost two family members and now have to replace them. But I have no time to sob and whine, we have to get on with it, and that *includes you.*"

"But I'm the one who found the body."

"That includes you," Marcus repeated. "Now sort your shit out so we can get on with it. Time is money. You've got five minutes; sort your shit out *now!*" The crew left the sound stage and they were alone.

"Tomas."

"Roger."

Roger sighed. "I'm sorry. This is all my fault." He sat next to Tomas on his side of the bed. "I'm sorry. I just…haven't been handling any of this well."

"It's understandable."

"Yeah?" Roger looked at his lover. "Then explain it to me coz I don't know where I went wrong."

Tomas covered Roger's hand with his. "You found a dead person. That would have freaked anybody out. And you clearly haven't been dealing with that well, which is *understandable.*"

Roger moved his head slowly. "I can't believe another one is dead. First Jeff, now Brock, ugh." He buried his head in his hands. "Ah, I haven't been dealing with this and getting drunk didn't help." He sat up and grabbed Tomas's hand. "I'm sorry. I'm sorry I took off. I'm sorry I didn't call. I'm sorry I snapped at you. I'm sorry I didn't tell you I was staying at Freddy's."

Relief washed over Tomas. "You were at Freddy's? Why didn't you tell me?"

Roger shrugged a shoulder. "It wasn't a big deal. I was drunk, and knew I wasn't going to be driving, so Freddy let me bunk in his spare room. I didn't think that was a big deal."

Tomas rolled his eyes. "It isn't. *You not calling* to tell me all of this *is*. I was worried. If I'd known you were sleeping it off, I wouldn't have been."

Roger had the decency to look ashamed. "Yeah, fair enough. I'm sorry. I really haven't dealt with this well, have I?"

"Nope." Tomas smiled. "So, while we're sharing, I went to the beach this morning after our fight for some air, and Luiz popped up."

Roger stared incredulously. "You're kidding? *He's still here? In Miami?* I thought he'd buggered off after that club incident."

"So did I, but no. He's still here. We went across the road to a café and had a coffee. I left a couple of hours later."

"How was he?"

Tomas exhaled. "He *seemed* okay. Didn't go on about what had happened. We talked about our jobs, being here in Miami. He *really* seemed okay."

"That's a strange one then. Should make sure it's the only time you see him if he's that much of a weirdo. Are we okay, though?" He kissed Tomas's hand.

Tomas smiled at the gesture. "Of course we are. Just please tell me in the future so I know you're safe and I don't have to worry, *especially* since some weirdo broke into our apartment."

Roger nodded. "Fair enough." He gazed into his lover's eyes. "I love you. And I was such a dickhead. I'm sorry."

"I love you, too. And yes, you *were* a dickhead. Apology accepted."

"Good to see you two worked out your lovers' tiff. Now, let's get back to work," Marcus bellowed from his director's chair.

They turned to see everyone back at their stations.

"Better get back to work," Roger said, and they got into position.

"Okay boys, take it from the top. Three, two, one, action."

Roger cornered Tomas in the fake bedroom set. His fingers trailed up Tomas's arm to his shoulder and down his lean torso to his cock. They stroked, massaged, held, while lips and tongues continued in slow motions. Roger led him to the bed and laid him down across the fur cover. He lay on top, kissing his way up Tomas's body to his mouth, delighting in touching and tasting.

Tomas closed his eyes and arched upward as Roger invaded his neck, sucking him like a vampire, thirsty after a thousand years of drought. "Ah," he breathed, sliding his hand up Roger's side. "Ah…"

Roger made his way down and enveloped him, getting a hard sucking in of breath in return. The fake fireplace and overhead heaters made the room hot and steamy as Roger lay between Tomas's legs, leaning up on one arm while his hand joined the two of them together.

Tomas's left hand joined in while his right held onto Roger's arm. Their hands wrapped around their muscles, slowly rubbing them together, bringing their balls into the fray with back and forth motions.

Roger moved in slow fluid rocks so his package pushed against that of the man beneath him. He breathed. It always exhilarated him to touch his lover in this way, on screen and off. To see Tomas beneath him, lithe, lean, and in such perfect paradise made his heart pound and his cock hard. He kept control of himself. Small thrusts against his lover's testicles, his hand rubbing one cock against the other, fingers slid around the other's.

He watched Tomas close his eyes and arch, his breath coming in small gasps as they both approached climax. Roger moved a little faster, with longer, harder thrusts and Tomas lifted his legs to wrap around his lover's waist.

Roger slid over him and thrust until the end. Staring down, he watched Tomas's face. With the few lovers he'd had, none were like Tomas. Exotic, beautiful, perfect. The most amazing, giving, taking lover he'd ever had. His fingers slid up his body, up his neck and to his cheek, and Tomas opened his eyes as Roger extended fully onto him, his face above his lover's. *I love you,* he mouthed.

I love you, too, Tomas mouthed back, and Roger took him in a kiss.

Marcus knew better than to yell cut at a moment like this, so he silently got out of his chair and waved the crew away. They often let them go, the end result was always hotter than when they'd done the deed as they always did it again or more. They made for great extras on the video. He glanced back and saw them still joined in the throes of passion and wrapped around each other as they went full on into it. He left them to it, knowing Roger would deal with the cameras when they were done.

"Ah," Tomas gasped against his lover's mouth. "Oh, God, come, come inside me."

Roger moved in perfect rhythm until he gave Tomas what he asked for, and he covered his mouth with his own. They kissed, not letting go, not parting until they were done when they lay still in the quiet.

"I see Marcus and the crew have left." Roger gazed out over the sound stage as his fingers lazily made their way up and down Tomas's side.

A huge sigh of contentment left Tomas. "They always do. They know it's better to just leave us alone as they get better footage."

"Mmm," Roger murmured against Tomas's cheek as he nuzzled his way down to his collar bone and onto his nipple. "Mmm." He buried his face on Tomas's chest. "Mmm."

Tomas slid his hand over Roger's back while the other held his head there. "How long do you want to stay?"

Roger kissed his way across the splendid layer of dark hair to his other nipple. "Forever."

Tomas smiled. "We can't stay here forever. Although, all night could work." His hand slid down between them and squeezed. "How about now?"

Roger's head shot up. "What about forever?" He devoured Tomas for the rest of the night.

*****

Tomas made it to Bette's the next day where all of the ladies were pleased to know he'd sorted things out with Roger. "You'll soon know how well we got back together when *Big Cock Avalanche* comes out. That's the movie we made last night."

"Hot is it?" Marie asked. "How do you feel about doing the same with women?" She stretched her legs by spreading them apart as she sat on the ground. "I'm very flexible and *love* cocks."

Tomas blushed, swallowed and looked away. "I'm sure you do Marie. But we're not interested."

"Shame." She moved into the splits. "Very flexible," she added.

"Don't worry about Marie," Bette said. "She's a whore from way back."

"Aren't we all darling?" Marie rolled onto her back with her legs still splayed. "I'm flexible because of *you,* Tomas."

"Oh, for Christ's sake!" Bette exclaimed. "Shut your damn legs *and* your mouth." She turned from Marie's shocked expression to Tomas. "I'm so glad the two of you worked it out."

Tomas smiled. "So are we, Bette. So are we."

PEDRO

"That's some gift," Eddie said when Pedro showed him the box. "Wouldn't put too much thought into it, kid, but if you're worried about this and everything else, get yourself a bodyguard." They were sitting in Eddie's office before 69 opened.

Pedro sighed and sat down across from him. "I don't want to get a bodyguard."

"But with this Poulos guy trying to kill you, maybe you should. And this crazy whack job that thinks she's pregnant with your baby, what about her?"

"I don't know." Pedro ran a hand through his hair then rested his head in his hands. "I don't know anymore. I just want to be left alone."

"Well, you won't be, and you aren't. You work here, you're doing porn now, and someone's trying to kill you. It's time to hire bodyguards for both of you. Look…" He spun through his Rolodex. "Here's the name of the company I use when I need extra protection. Think about it." He handed the card over.

Studio 69 opened, and Pedro did his thing. The news had travelled far and wide about his accident, and all of the regulars were there. Bev, Sara, Martine. Even Bridie dropped by to say hello. Diane Von Furstenberg, Dyan Cannon and Jerry Hall cornered him for a chat and asked how he was. He was very moved that so many people were interested in how he was and was very grateful for all he had. But what he had was being threatened, and he needed it to stop.

TOMAS

That night, Luiz walked into *Wood*, a local gay hangout. He knew Tomas and Roger wouldn't be there, as they were working, but a few of their co-workers were, and he spied Brent Woodcock on the floor dancing up a storm. Making his way around the room he kept an eye on Brent, who was dancing with another man, one Luiz didn't recognise. He also didn't see crew or staff that he knew personally so believed he was safe with what he was about to do.

Dancing his way through the crowd, he came up behind Brent. Moving with the crowd, he danced around the couple until he was behind the dancing partner and then eyed Brent off over the man's shoulder, making sure to keep contact at all times. He did this for half an hour, throwing little waves and smiles in Brent's direction. When Brent took a break, Luiz followed him into the bathroom, greedily eyeing off his cock while he took a leak.

Nine inches of glorious hard cock.

Nowhere near as big as Tomas, but it would have to do.

"My, Grandma, what a big cock you have," Luiz said playfully from beside him at the urinals.

Brent caught on to the meaning. "All the better to fuck you with, little red."

"Would you?" Luiz said breathlessly, forgetting about peeing and letting his hard-on free. "You're so hot and fuckable. I've seen your movies, but never imagined I'd ever meet you in…the flesh…" He glanced down at the muscle still in Brent's hand. "It's magnificent."

It stiffened.

"It clearly likes compliments." Luiz reached out and gently touched it.

It hardened even more.

"And it clearly likes a man's hand around it." Luiz looked into Brent's green eyes. "What about its owner? Does he like having a man around it?" he breathlessly quivered. "Can *I* be around it?"

The next thing Luiz knew, Brent was hauling him out of the toilets, out the back door, into the alley and behind a dumpster. "Drop your pants," he demanded, and Luiz obediently obliged. He took it hard and fast as Brent entered, thrust a few times, and withdrew.

"Oh, God," Brent gasped. "That was good. Oh, God, that was good." He zipped up his pants, leant against the wall, and lit a cigarette. "Oh, I love quick fucks."

Luiz pulled his pants up. "What about long fucks? Mouth fucks? Blow job out of the question?" His fingers slid to Brent's crotch.

"Have at it," Brent said, and Luiz got to work.

No man could resist a blowjob. Getting your cock sucked was the best thing next to sliced bread. And if the person doing the job got it right, the man at the other end got everything he wanted and then some. But this time it was Luiz that wanted something. He withdrew his mouth.

"Mind if I have a drag?" He nodded at the cigarette in Brent's mouth.

He held it out for Luiz to inhale and then stuck it back in his mouth, watching while Luiz performed the trick of blowing smoke rings onto his penis. "Awesome," Brent crowed. "Do it again."

Luiz obliged and took another drag. Once the smoke was gone, he sucked Brent until they were both done. He wiped his mouth and got to his feet. "You into more than cigarettes?" He leant against Brent's six foot muscular frame. "I've got a stash of stuff in my car. Maybe we could go somewhere…private." Luiz's hand took hold of Brent and cajoled until he heard yes. "Good, let's go to your place."

Half an hour later, they were spread out on Brent's king-size fur-covered bed, in his well-furnished apartment. Luiz had just given

Brent what he'd given him and was flat on his back next to the porn star.

Brent snorted more of the coke Luiz had brought. "This is good shit, man." He flung his head back. "Oh, God, this is good shit. Fuck me again. Give it to me up the ass again. Fuck me with that your sword of yours and give it to me *hard.*" He snorted another line, and Luiz obliged, reminding him to keep snorting throughout. He went slowly, allowing line after line to go down, and when Brent's body started jerking he finished off, and Brent lay dead.

Three down, more to go.

He withdrew, rolled Brent over, jerked him off until he came over the pictures Luiz held. Oh, yes, to a normal person it would look as if Brent had downed drugs and got it off over pictures of Tomas Stephanopoulos. A jilted lover? A spurned nobody? Who knew, but that's how the cops needed to see it.

Brent's dead eyes stared at the ceiling, his long golden-brown locks spread out around him, his right hand holding his penis, his left the photos. The drugs spread out beside him with vials, a mirror, razor, and sprinkling of coke all sat there waiting for the cops to find.

Luiz stared down at the scene and took photos. He walked around to make sure everything else was intact before dressing, singing a little ditty in his head as he went. *'How much wood could a Woodcock cock if a Woodcock could cock wood.'*

With one final check and a wave goodbye, Luiz turned off the lights and left.

PEDRO

Pedro called Angie before leaving work Wednesday morning. "Anything you want me to pick up on the way home?"

"Breakfast?"

"You got it." He stopped at the little café down the road from their apartment and was home ten minutes later. "Breakfast!"

Angelina crawled out of bed, her arm still in a sling, her hair a wild mess. She was taking the week off Juilliard, although, at the rate she was going she'd get booted out before she graduated. "Yum, I'm hungry." She grabbed a fork and dug into the scrambled eggs.

"How did you sleep?" Pedro opened the two cups of coffee.

"Badly," she mumbled around her food.

Handing over a cup, he said, "Here, get this into you. You want a painkiller?" He fussed over her, making sure she had what she needed before sitting at the island bench and eating. "I talked to Eddie about the package, and he suggested getting bodyguards. I said I'd talk to you."

She finished eating a mouthful of bacon and eggs and swallowed. "For both of us?"

Sipping his coffee, he found it hot and strong just the way he liked it. "One each. Unless you want two," he joked. "What do you think?" He watched her face for any indication of a yes or no.

After eating another mouthful and drinking some coffee, she said, "Isn't it a bit late for bodyguards?" She pointed to her arm before grabbing the strip of bacon he was about to eat. "The damage has already been done." She popped the bacon in her mouth.

"But maybe we, I, can stop even more from happening. What do you say? Do you want a bodyguard?" He silently implored her with his charismatic eyes. "I love you, I want to keep you safe. And you're right; too much damage has already been done. So let me protect you from now on."

Her lips moved up into a smile. "You know I can't resist you when you stare at me with those big blue eyes."

He batted his long black lashes. "Please!"

Her laughter floated around the room. "As long as I can have a woman."

After breakfast, Pedro made a call to the company Eddie recommended and arranged for two guards who would be at his door at six.

At six p.m. he opened the door to find a man on one side and a woman on the other, standing like sentinels outside the door. "Hello, hey, come in and we'll have a chat."

The man was Pedro's height, with a big build and cropped black hair. The woman was average height, with blonde hair pulled into a bun. They both wore suits.

"Right, I'm Pedro Stephanopoulos, and I guess you will be my bodyguard," he told the man.

"Mark Monroe, ex-special forces, black belt in karate, weapons expert." The man shook Pedro's hand.

"Great," Pedro replied. "Do you have a problem with hanging around a club all night and the apartment all day?"

"If that's the job, sir, that's what I'll do."

"Great." Pedro nodded his enthusiasm. "And this is Angelina," he said as she walked into the room to see their new guards. "You'll be guarding her," he told the woman. "So far it's just here at the apartment, but she'll be back to school next week and we'll need to let the school know to expect you. And you are?"

"Sara-Michelle Dubois. Fifth Dan black belt and weapons specialist." She nodded.

"Great," Angelina said. "I got a woman. I hope you won't be bored here all day and night. I'm taking the week off and don't go anywhere."

"Wherever you need me to be that's where I'll be."

"Great, well…" Pedro grabbed his bag. "I need to go to the club. Now we won't be home until six-thirty in the morning, and then I sleep all day. So I don't know how that's gonna work out. If you do tandem watches, one sleeps while the other works…"

Mark gave a curt nod. "That's how we do it, sir. If that's what you need."

"Okay. Well, then we'd better get going." He kissed Angelina goodbye and left with Mark. "I've never had a bodyguard before, so I have no idea how you do it, or how this is supposed to play out."

"First thing's first," Mark said as they entered the underground car park. "I inspect your car before you get in it." He circled the Mustang, checked underneath the hood and got down under it. "All clear. Second thing is, I drive." He held out his hand.

Pedro opened his mouth to say something but rethought his decision and quickly handed over the keys. "Any reason why you get to drive my new wheels?" He slid into the passenger side. "I only just got her this week."

Mark slammed the door shut, making Pedro wince. "Because if we need a quick getaway, I know how to out-manoeuvre them. I know New York like the back of my hand. I know which roads to take if I have to get you out of the club or your apartment. I know how to get you to where you're going in the shortest time and if the people who are after you are from out of town or out of the country, then they don't have the knowledge and I've got the upper hand."

Pedro grinned. "I'm impressed."

Mark remained poker-faced. "You should be!"

*****

Andros had no one else to turn to, so he called Stavros. "Where are you?"

"In my motel."

"I need to see you. Come to my apartment now."

Twenty minutes later Stavros stood in Andros's apartment. "What now?"

"What now is that I need you to stake out 69, so you can get information on Pedro and Angelina. When they go out, what sort of car they have since the old one's obviously not working. Who comes over. I want to know every little detail, so I can plan my revenge."

Stavros inwardly groaned. *Not again, fuck he's bonkers.* "When do I start?"

"Now," Andros said, looking at his watch. "He'll be at 69. I know Angelina's taking the week off Juilliard, but I still have no idea where they live, so follow Pedro home and find my daughter."

"Yes, Mr Poulos."

"And Stavros…"

"Yes, Mr Poulos…"

"Don't cock-up this time."

*****

The woman held the little baby onesie in her hands. She smelt it, drawing in a breath slowly, breathing in the scent of new clothing and new baby. Her baby. Hers and Pedro's baby.

She didn't have long to go, it was only a matter of a few months, if that, but she needed supplies, she needed a new home, and she needed Pedro. She needed the father of her baby to provide for her. *And when he sees his newborn and holds her in his arms he's going to know that this is where he belongs,* she thought. *With us.*

Caressing her stomach, she spoke to the baby. "Not long now, Bubba. Daddy's coming to see us. He's gonna be with us real soon." She picked up another picture of Angelina with her face scratched out and sneered at it. "Bitch, your days are numbered."

She placed the photo into a gift box with her note and bloodied onesie. It would be posted later, or left somewhere they would find it. So easily find it. Like maybe outside their apartment door.

*****

Stavros knew Pedro didn't knock off work until after six so he slept until five. Getting up at the crack of dawn on a crisp fall day was not what he wanted to be doing, but he did it anyway. He drove into New York and hovered on 54th street near the alley. He checked his watch. Six-twenty. He waited. Not long now.

He watched celebrities exit the club and noticed a red-haired woman lingering near the alley. He frowned. She was the same woman in the alley that night. The one who'd gotten in the way of his clean shot at Pedro.

He watched her. She was slowly making her way down the alley to hide behind the trashcans she'd emerged from that night. In fact, now that he thought about it, she was the same woman from down the road outside of Angelina's first apartment.

Now what does she want and could she cause trouble? She saw me that night, what if she remembers me? He watched her hide and saw Pedro emerge from the back door with a man. The man checked over a blue Mustang convertible before motioning to Pedro to get into the passenger side. He got behind the wheel, and they left.

The woman came out from behind the cans and ran for the alley as he slowly drove off behind Pedro. In the rear-view, he saw the woman hail a taxi. They drove down 8th Avenue and turned onto Central Park West before pulling into an apartment complex.

Stavros pulled over just past it, making sure to get the number. He watched as the gate to the underground parking closed, and a guard checked that it was locked. There was a doorman and check-in screenings. He watched a taxi drive slowly past with the woman in the back, her head frantically moving around for a look at where he lived.

Interesting. What sort of threat was she?

The taxi drove off with her looking longingly out the back window, and he followed at a safe distance, all the way back to her tacky apartment where she climbed out and went inside. He made a note of the address and drove off to see Andros.

"Well," Andros demanded when Stavros walked in the door.

"Where do they live?"

Stavros pulled out his notebook. "On Central Park West, but he had a guy with him who checked the car over before they left. And he drove it. It's a Mustang, blue, but we might have another problem."

"What's that?" Andros tightened the belt on his robe. It was seven-fifteen a.m., and he was not used to being up this early.

"The woman, the one that got in the way of the shooting, she was there again. And I remembered I'd also seen her outside of Angelina's apartment the night you were there. It looks like they have a stalker."

Andros poured himself a cup of coffee. "Interesting. Their new place, where is it from here?

"Across the park."

He sipped his coffee. "Interesting. Very interesting."

TOMAS

Brent Woodcock was found on Friday morning, after police had the real estate agent let them in. The smell hit them like a ten tonne brick in the face, and they found the body covered in flies, and God knows what else.

When Brent hadn't shown up to work for two days or returned calls, Marcus had called to report him missing. And now, this is what the cops found.

Detective Barden slowly walked into the bedroom, a handkerchief over his mouth, and stood at the foot of the bed. He looked down at the body of Brent Woodcock, porn star, and realised why boys like him got into movies like that.

Big dicks.

He felt his shrivel at the mere sight of it, and speaking of it, he noticed photos in the left hand. Sidestepping his fellow officers who all stood around checking out the view, Barden made his way to the side of the bed for a closer look at the photos. "Interesting."

"Sir?" one of the officers asked through his own handkerchief.

"Hurry up and get the coroner here. I want these photos cleaned and packed up." He quickly covered his mouth again.

"Sir." The officer couldn't wait to get out into the fresh air and neither could Barden.

"Everyone out until the coroner's done," he yelled. "Tape the door shut and put two guards on it. No one enters until the coroner does."

An hour later, the coroner was done.

"Same as the last two," he said, putting his instruments in his bag. "Drug overdose."

"Which is obvious," Barden said.

"It looks that way, but won't be confirmed until autopsy. I'll give you the details in a couple of days, Jeremiah." He slapped him on the shoulder in passing.

"Thanks, Doc." Jeremiah Barden thought he'd seen it all, yet now he had a spate of porn star deaths on his hands. Ah, if only the good old days still existed. He picked up the Ziploc bags and put each photo separately into them. "Don't want to get them all covered in juice." He took one last look and let the coroner's people do their jobs.

PEDRO

Saturday rolled around and Pedro got ready for the movie. He opened the door and asked Mark and Sara-Michelle in. "I need to head off to work, but not at the club."

"Sure," Mark said. "Where are we going?"

"Downtown to a building to film a movie."

"Okay then. What kind of movie, and what kind of security do they have?"

A brief frown crossed over Pedro's face. "Well, it's filming on the roof, so I guess they'll have their own or use the building's security."

"And what kind of movie?"

Pedro winced. "A porn movie."

Mark's eyebrows slowly moved up his forehead, and Pedro wasn't sure if he was going to laugh. But strict business won out, and Mark's expression was back to normal. "Okay then," was all he said.

"And I'm coming too." Angelina walked out of the bedroom with her bag and coat.

"No, you're not. You're going to stay here," Pedro said. "It's safer."

"No, I'm not," she told him. "I missed the last one, so there's no way I'm missing watching this one being made." She turned to Sara-Michelle. "You don't have a problem with pornos do you?"

Sara-Michelle tried to hide a smile. "No, ma'am."

"Good, it's set. We all go together."

"Oh, my God, this is so embarrassing," Pedro muttered as they gathered their things and left. They arrived at the old office building half an hour later, and after security checks, walked out of the elevator to see the whole roof had been set up like a party. Cabanas, flowing curtains, DJ booth, lights, waiters. Basically the same concept as Long Island.

"Pedro, darling." Greta and Stephanie came toward him. "We're going to have so much fun." They stopped at Angelina and the two bodyguards. "And what are you doing here?" Greta asked Angelina.

"Watching," she replied. "You didn't think I wouldn't be interested in watching my boyfriend do a porno, did you? I can't wait."

Greta frowned and turned to the others. "And they are?"

"Bodyguards," Pedro said. "Eddie suggested we hire them."

"Yes, that's a good idea," she said. "With everything that's happened you need protection. Let's walk you through what will happen." She led him onto the dance floor, and the others followed.

"The girls will be here, you will be in your DJ booth, you'll come down and start flirting with the girls. When you are having sex the camera will circle around you, and there will be one above you here." She pointed, and they all saw a camera suspended above them. "You will be standing on a record. It's a stage that's painted to look like a record that we will bring in during the movie. We'll get some awesome above shots of the three of you on the spinning record."

Pedro nodded. "Sounds cool. I hope it looks good too."

"It will. Now, let's get you downstairs and dressed."

They followed her down to the top floor, and found everyone scurrying around like worker bees. Sound and engineering were all working off to the right, and to the left was the dressing area full of beautiful women getting changed into skimpy dresses and clothes. Tits and pussy were everywhere, and Mark had the decency to look away. The girls didn't care, they just wanted Pedro.

"Pedro, darling, come and see what you're fucking later."

"Come and fuck this now, Pedro." A blonde bent over and aimed her ass at him.

He grinned cockily. "Gotta go to work, babe," he told Angelina.

"Don't worry, babe, I'll be watching," she replied.

He laughed and walked over to the women where he was swamped. They quickly had his clothes off.

"Girls," Stephanie yelled. "Leave the merchandise alone. It's for later." She escorted Pedro away from the horde to a quiet spot for him to change.

Angelina and their guards stood off to the side watching it all go down. Within half an hour they were back on the roof watching the cameras roll, standing with the other crew behind white curtains so they weren't noticed on camera. There was a screen set up in front of them so they could see what was being filmed, and so far, it was all women in the setting rays.

Pedro finally walked out in his tuxedo pants and white shirt and climbed behind the booth. He danced, he sang, he flipped records into the air and caught them behind his back before flipping them onto the players. He pulled trick after trick and Greta loved him for it.

"God, he's hot," Greta said.

"He certainly is," Angelina muttered in agreement.

"Not much of a porno yet," Sara-Michelle said.

"Just you wait," Greta told her. "Wait until he takes his clothes off."

Yes, Angelina thought. *Just you wait.*

The city lit up the skyline and the stars came out to play. Pedro's shirt came out of his pants, and he came down off the stage. Women surrounded him, but one by one he waved them off until just the two remained. Blonde twins with big tits. They were standing on the spinning record stage and started undressing each other. A dress came off, his shirt came off, a top came off, his pants came off, a skirt came off, the underwear came off.

"Jesus fucking Christ," Sara-Michelle muttered, her eyes going wide.

Angelina smiled. "Yep!"

They watched Pedro fuck one twin while sucking the other and then he changed partners. Groping, licking, gyrating occurred before they went down to their knees on the spinning record.

Not long after it was done so was he, and to a resounding applause he slipped his pants on and left the stage.

"Whoo, that's my man," Angelina called as they emerged from behind the curtain. "That was fucking hot! Can we keep that record stage?" she asked Greta.

"Um, sorry, we'll need it for future use," she replied, stunned that Pedro's girlfriend wouldn't have a problem with him doing porn. "You seemed to enjoy it," Greta said to her.

"Why wouldn't I?" Angelina looked at her. "I get that every single day. I'm secure in our relationship, so if he wants to follow his brother into this…"

"Have you seen Carlo's movie?" Greta asked.

"Last month when it came out," Angelina said. "Have you *seen* his brother? Phwoar! If I wasn't with…" She trailed off at Pedro's expression.

"Me? You'd what?" he asked, a cocky grin on his face. "Do my brother?"

"Well…" Angelina blushed. "You have *seen* your brother…right?"

"Oh, God." He laughed. "Just as well he's on the other side of the country."

"And have you heard? He's nominated for quite a few Porn Star Awards," Greta said.

Pedro raised a brow. "Really? No, I haven't heard. But then I haven't read up on the awards, so don't know much about them, or how they work."

"You'd better." Thomas walked over to them. "Because you'll be nominated next year so get ready." He eyed off Mark whom he hadn't noticed before. "And who are you?"

"Mark Monroe, bodyguard." Mark nodded. He knew fags from a mile away and wasn't interested.

"Bodyguard huh?" Thomas preened, moving closer to the tall brute of a man. "I wouldn't mind a good bodyguard," he flirted.

"Then get one that's interested in fags," Mark muttered loud enough for only Thomas to hear as he narrowed his eyes at the male before him. "Because *I'm not interested.*"

Thomas stepped back, shocked at the words. No one else had heard or taken notice as they were too busy talking about the porn awards. He turned and left, leaving the others wondering what had gone down.

"What happened?" Pedro asked Mark.

"I told him I wasn't interested in his advances," he replied, his face stone-cold hard. "Apparently, he doesn't like to be rejected."

Pedro frowned and glanced from Mark to Sara-Michelle who remained poker-faced, to Angelina who looked puzzled.

"We should go," Angelina finally said and turned to Greta. "Thank you for letting us stay. It was fun."

"Oh, thank you for coming," Greta replied, waving them off.

They made it downstairs for Pedro to change then went down to the car park. Mark checked the car, and they piled in.

"So, what *was* that about?" Pedro asked on the way home. "Coz whatever you said it upset him."

"As I said." Mark kept his eyes on the road. "I rejected his advances. Not my problem if he couldn't deal with that."

"It just seemed like a strong reaction to someone saying, I'm not interested."

"Sometimes people overreact." Mark pulled into the underground parking for their building. "If you're not strong enough to understand and accept the fact some people just won't be interested, then you should stop asking them."

"Fair enough," Pedro said. Climbing out, he pulled the seat forward and helped Angelina out of the back. "So, what did you think of the movie?"

"I'll tell you when we get upstairs," she whispered with a giggle.

"Can't you tell me now?" They entered the lift and went up.

"Tell you later."

They got off on their floor and walked toward their door.

"Hold up." Mark put up a hand, and Sara-Michelle drew her gun "We have a situation." Mark waved them back. "I'll check it out." He slowly moved toward the door to get a closer view of the object sitting in front of it. "It's a box. A gift box."

Angelina drew a sharp breath. "Not another one."

"What do you mean another one?" Sara-Michelle asked her.

"We got a gift box in some fan mail the other day, and it contained some not very nice things," Angie told her.

"Monroe," Sara-Michelle called. "It could be ugly fan mail, be careful."

Mark crouched and checked for wires and small devices before flipping up the lid. Pulling back the tissue paper he saw photos of Angelina with her face scratched off and a target on her head. Underneath was a bloodied baby onesie with a note. "This is sick," he said.

Pedro moved to his side. "Stay back," he told Angelina and held out his arm. "What is it?" He bent down and looked inside while Mark pulled out the note.

"You're out of time. Make your choice. Our life or her death. Your baby's life hangs in the balance. Can you really say no to our baby?"

"Is that blood?" Pedro asked.

Mark sniffed it then touched a finger to it and tasted it. "Sauce with something else." He looked at Pedro. "You, my boy, have a stalker."

Pedro stood up. "Great, that's all I need."

"Let's take this inside shall we." Mark picked up the package while Pedro opened the door and then waved Angelina and Sara-Michelle inside.

"What is it?" Angelina asked, dropping her bag and coat on the kitchen island.

"Another one of those gifts," Pedro said as Mark dropped the box next to her bag on the counter.

"A pretty bad gift," Mark said. "You still got the other one?"

Pedro went to the hall cupboard, dug it out of the box of fan mail, and laid it next to the new one. "Same person?"

Mark examined both parcels. Same kind of box, same wrapping, same kind of note. Finally, he said, "I think it's from the same person. Now, who could this woman be?"

Pedro shook his head. "I have no idea. I came to New York with Angie. We've been together since…" He remembered back.

"You've got something?" Mark saw his faraway look.

"No." Pedro came back. "It couldn't be…she was brunette…"

"A woman can dye her hair," Sara-Michelle said.

Pedro breathed in sharply. "On Santorini, at the club, there was a woman. Brunette hair. She attacked me one night after the show. I was on the beach, I'd just had a swim, and she was standing in front of me naked. I told her I wasn't interested and walked away. She shoved me onto the sand from behind, rolled me over, ripped my pants open and tried to…" He made small hand gestures. "…you know…"

"Jump on your love muscle," Angelina stated with a straight expression.

Pedro blushed and glanced away. "Yeah. That's what we're calling it today?" he asked her before continuing. "But I pushed her off and ran for it."

"You know," Angelina said. "Now that you mention it, there was a woman who followed me home and attacked me. She had dark hair, and it was in the early hours of the morning. I karate kicked her, and she fell to the ground and called me a whore."

"Would you recognise her if you saw her again?" Mark asked. "Either of you?"

Pedro shook his head. "It was night-time."

Angelina shook hers as well. "It was dark and I didn't get a good look."

"Okay. What about since being here in New York?"

"Besides my father?" Angelina said. "Nope."

"Mmm," Pedro mumbled. "There could be…"

"What?" Mark asked. "Tell us. It could be vital to stopping this woman."

Pedro sighed and looked everywhere else but Angelina.

"What aren't you telling me?" she asked. "Spit it out."

"Ugh," he groaned. "The night of the shooting, there was that woman who was in the alley. She was shot too."

"The one that ended up in the psyche ward?" Angelina asked.

"Right, well, Stew was there when she was loaded into the ambulance, and according to him, she muttered, *'my baby…Pedro's baby'…'*"Pedro winced at the words.

Angelina's brows hit her hairline. "She what?"

"Don't look at me like that." He shook his head and put his hands up in protest. "I have no idea who she is or what she's up to. But when Stew told the doctor about it, she was examined, and *she wasn't pregnant*, so they put her in the psyche ward for observation in case the blow to her head knocked something loose."

"And maybe they were already loose," Mark said.

"What do you mean?" Pedro asked him.

"What if this is the same woman?" He pointed at the gifts. "This woman from Santorini becomes fixated on you, getting you to fuck her to get her pregnant." He waved a hand at Angelina. "She hates you so attempts to do something, and now she's popping up here in New York leaving gifts about 'Angelina must die for your baby'. I reckon it's the same whack job and we need to find her."

"How do we do that?" Angelina asked.

Mark checked the boxes. "I'll dust for prints, eliminate ours, see who else's is on this stuff. Take more notice of who's hanging around now. I'm looking for a woman with red hair."

"Oh, my God." Pedro snapped his fingers. "I bet it's the same woman at the club that night. She got into a fight with Martine Krevnokov, but she got her in a headlock and security threw her out. Oh, my God, I forgot about that."

"Wow," Angelina said. "She really is in our life."

"And now it's time to get her out," Mark said.

TOMAS

On Sunday morning, Barden had three files on his desk. Three files containing cases of three porn stars all dead of apparent overdoses. All had sex beforehand. But then what did one expect from men who fuck for a living. And all three had copious amounts of cocaine in their systems. The reports on the cocaine had it at D-grade level. Not so much coke, but a whole bunch of other stuff mixed in with it. Ecstasy, laundry powder…some had bleach and a bunch of other stuff Barden couldn't even pronounce. He hadn't come across this kind of coke before, although, it wasn't the first time he'd seen impure cocaine.

It was time to talk, and he knew who to.

Twenty minutes later, he stood in the studios of *Seralift Productions*. "Mr Seralift, three of your stars are dead. All of them from drug overdoses. All had sex before or during, so someone else is involved and that's why I need to question you all."

"About what?" Marcus bellowed. "Whether they get drugs from me? Was I the one to give it to them? I don't run my place that way; we are clean cut, and everyone found doing drugs is automatically fired." He paced up and down in front of Barden. "You can get your attack dogs in here; you will *not* find coke or any other drug in my studios, including in lockers and change rooms."

"How well did you know Mr Woodcock?" Barden asked, closely watching Seralift's expression.

"As well as can be expected," Marcus huffed. "I check their

credentials, hire them, and make movies. That's all I have to do with it."

"Do you sample them, Mr Seralift?"

"Sample what?" Marcus stopped and stared the man down. "Sample what, Detective?"

"Your workers'…*credentials.*" Barden remained unblinking. Marcus Seralift was not about to get the better of him. He'd dealt with far worse.

"*I do not fuck my stars,*" Marcus bellowed, realising everyone in the studio had turned to watch. He lowered his voice. "I don't fuck them. I don't supply them, and I certainly don't allow them to do drugs. *You got that!*"

Barden backed off. "Fine. I want to talk to Dencott, he here?"

Marcus turned. "Over there. Dencott, get over here."

Roger warily wandered over. "What now?"

"Brent Woodcock died in his apartment a few days ago. He was found holding photos." He held up a bag with the photo in it. "It seems he had ah…" He cleared his throat. "Masturbated over them."

Roger screwed up his face. "Ew, God." He looked at the photo and saw Tomas with a cock in his mouth.

"Any ideas, Mr Dencott?"

Roger sighed and took a closer look, finally giving a shrug. "It could be from one of our movies."

Barden cocked a brow. "You don't know?"

"As I told you last time, Detective, Tomas and I are exclusive. We only star with each other in movies, no one else. So it has to be me he's deep-throating."

"Mmm," Barden mumbled. "Why would Woodcock be getting off over pictures of Stephanopoulos? He's *your* boy isn't he?"

Roger crossed his arms. "He's my *partner* if that's what you meant."

"Yeah…that's what I meant. So why would Woodcock have photos of lover boy and why did he masturbate over them?"

"Look, I don't know. We only knew each other through work and haven't worked together for months now," Roger growled.

"You worked together?" Barden eyed him suspiciously. "In what capacity?"

Roger rolled his eyes to the ceiling and threw his arms down beside him in frustration. "We made a couple of movies together. Fucked in them. Happy now?"

"So, Woodcock could be jealous that you have a new toy boy?"

"I highly doubt it," Roger said. "We worked in the movies, nothing happened in real life."

"Didn't date, or fuck for fun after the cameras stopped rolling?"

"No," Roger snapped. "I'm done talking ,Detective." He stormed off backstage leaving Barden alone.

*****

Luiz watched the scene unfold from the shadows. Poor Roger, feeling the heat from the detective. *Well, three deaths are on your shoulders and there's more to come. So get ready, Roger, the fun is about to blow you away.*

He watched Barden leave and followed in the shadows, spying Roger sneaking out to his car and taking off in the opposite direction.

Luiz hurried to his own car out on the street and took off after Roger. "Now where's he going?" he muttered, following Roger all the way to Brent Woodcock's apartment building and watched him park in an alley and make his way inside. Fifteen minutes later, Roger came out and left, driving off to Brock Hardwood's place.

Luiz parked down the street. *Now, this is getting interesting.*

He watched Roger run in the back way and emerge fifteen minutes later. And off he went to Jeff Fastwater's house, and once again, fifteen minutes later he was in and out.

All three places. I wonder what he's up to. He followed Roger out to the Glades where he watched him stop by a waterway, get out, look around, and rip something up into a million pieces and throw it into the water. Luiz waited until Roger had left, then went in search of those million pieces. Once he'd collected all he could, he went back to his motel room and spread the pieces out on the table. It took him the rest of the afternoon to put the photos back together. There were twelve altogether, and in four were Roger and Brent.

"Ah, interesting," Luiz muttered. Roger in compromising positions with all three men. Pulling out a roll of tape, he stuck them together and examined them closer. *Very* compromising positions. *Now, was that in their movie or after hours?* He studied them, trying to remember if the sets were stages at the studio. *Not that I remember.* He glanced over his own photos, but none of the sets looked the same.

"Ah, after hours. Well, well, well. I bet he doesn't want lover boy or Detective Barden seeing these." *No, no, no. If anyone saw these photos, Roger's life would be over. Suspicion would fall squarely on his shoulders, and he'd be put in the spotlight for the three deaths. Oh, yes, it would all fall squarely on Roger's shoulders, and Tomas would have no choice but to leave him and come back to me. Oh, yes, he will come back to me.*

*****

Barden sat behind his desk staring at the files. They were spread out, along with photos, reports, and a whole pile of witness statements. And what did he have to go with them?

Zip. Zilch. Nada.

His cop instincts told him there was more to this than overdoses. There was sex, there was porn; they were all from the same production house. Something extremely fishy was going on here, and he couldn't put his finger on it. He checked the list of people involved and decided to do some digging.

Two hours later, he had a list of felonies and reports involving most members of *Seralift Productions*, from misdemeanours to jail time. The studs of the *Seralift* stable had pasts as bad boys. And one report, in particular, intrigued him.

It was the report of a Mustang convertible being trashed back in August. It seemed Mr Dencott had some bad luck, then there was the spate of thefts he'd heard about when eavesdropping…not that they were newsworthy. Little things, personal items, photos, jewellery had gone missing at the studios, and now there were three deaths.

An idea started forming in his mind. Either someone was out to destroy *Seralift*, or someone was out to deal with the stars of the productions.

Why would you want to kill porn stars unless you were some kind of religious zealot who hated fags? If straightening them out didn't work, killing them did? That was some mentality. He wrote the theory in his notebook.

The next angle to investigate was why did all three have pictures of the new kid Stephanopoulos? He was a good-looking rooster, new to the game, but had kept to himself. Yet here were all three dead studs with pictures of him. Did they take them or did someone else take them…oh…someone else took them. But who?

He went back over the list of employees past and present, all the way back to the very beginning of *Seralift* and their manly productions. "Anthony De Milo, Cade Caldwell, Evan Williams, Luiz Manning, Nick Michaels, Roger Dencott, Van Michaels," he muttered at random down the list. Plus new boy Tomas, the three dead, and a bunch more. Jesus, they went through them like he went through underwear. What was their secret?

He tried connecting names with Tomas, but except for Roger, he couldn't. Stephanopoulos was new in town, and Dencott had just passed his two year status. The rest had been around for years. Unfortunately, the dots just weren't connecting, and he needed fresh air.

*****

Tomas didn't eat much at Bette's the next day. The morning sessions were slow, and now he wasn't hungry. There was something going on in the pit of his stomach, and he didn't know what. His energy was down, and his taste buds were flat. He pushed his plate away.

"Not hungry?" Bette cut a piece of succulent chicken breast with lemon butter sauce and roasted cashews. Three small garlic butter potatoes were the side dish.

"No." He took a sip of juice and leant back in his seat. "I don't feel…like I normally do." Closing his eyes, he took a slow deep breath.

"Are you sick?" She gazed at his face. "Your colour isn't up to snuff."

A slow exhale. "I'm not sure. I don't feel like I normally do. A bit down." He shook his head. "Something…I don't know, I can't put my finger on it."

"Maybe you're coming down with something?"

"Maybe, although, I don't get sick."

"Ever?"

"Not since I was a kid."

"Maybe you ate something that didn't agree with you?"

"Yeah, maybe."

But that evening he stumbled into the studios.

"Whoa, take it easy tiger." Roger caught him. Noticing the pale colour and weakness, he helped him over to Marcus's chair "You okay? Have you eaten?"

"Not since breakfast." Tomas collapsed. "Ugh, I don't feel well."

"You don't look good either." Roger checked his eyes. "We need to get some food into you, and you need a good night's rest."

"What the hell!" Marcus bellowed. "Get that germy-looking kid out of my chair. Do I need to disinfect it now?" He stared at Tomas. "Ain't no way you're working tonight. Take the night off and if you're not better tomorrow take the rest of the week off. Roger, get him home."

"Come on, you." Roger hauled him to his feet. "I'll get you home." Leaving Tomas's car in the lot, Roger drove home and tucked him into bed. "I'll go and get you some hot soup from down the road." Fifteen minutes later he was back, and Tomas was downing chicken soup and dumplings.

"Feel better?" Roger sat beside him on the bed eating Moo Shu pork.

Tomas thought. "Yeah, I do. My stomach's got food in it. I'm getting some strength back. I feel okay."

"Well, try not to go without food again. Your blood sugar must have been low. You need to keep your strength up. Finished?" He collected the rubbish.

"Yeah. There's enough left for tomorrow, so don't throw it out." Tomas stuck the lid back on. "Put it in the fridge."

"Don't waste anything do you?" Roger said, heading into the kitchen. He chucked the rubbish and put the soup in the fridge. "Jesus, the milk's hit its use by date, better throw that out." He poured it down the drain and threw the carton into the bin. "Hey, you'll need a new milk tomorrow," he said, walking back into the bedroom where he saw Tomas fast asleep. Pulling the covers up around his shoulders, he kissed him on the cheek and whispered, "Sweet dreams, my sweet prince."

PEDRO

It took a couple of days for Stavros to finally resolve the issue that was going on between his orders from Andros and his guilty feelings. He wasn't sure if spying on Pedro and Angelina was even right. His conscience was getting the best of him, and he wasn't sure what to do about it.

Did he follow through with the orders, or walk away? And if he did walk away, what would Andros do to him? If he *didn't* walk away, two young people would be dead.

He paced across his hotel room. He knew where they lived. Knew where they worked. Knew how far by foot their apartment was from across the park. Knew which path to take to not be seen. Knew which path to take to get there quickest.

Yes, he had done all the legwork, the dirty work, while Andros sat back in his luxurious apartment and waited while his lawyer got him off his charges.

Stupid bastard!

Unless he bribed his way out, there was no way he'd be leaving for Santorini. Unless he paid every person up the food chain, he'd be sent to jail. But then Andros Poulos was a wealthy man. If he wanted to pay a thousand people off, he could quite easily do so with drugs, money, sex; anything they wanted he could *and would* pay them off with.

He didn't know when he was supposed to do it. Kill Pedro that is.

And he didn't know *how* he'd be asked to do it, but he knew without a doubt his boss would walk away scot free with clean hands and he'd be left paying for it with his life. His hands would be the dirty ones. He looked down at them. They were clean, reasonably anyway. They already had the shooting on them; did he want anything else to mar them and make them dirty?

"Argh!" he cried and rubbed his forehead. "I don't know if I can do this. I really don't know." His pace picked up. *I can't kill those two kids.* The first time had been bad enough and that hadn't worked, but wounding that woman and Angelina had scarred him. Never mind the fact that Andros had gone off on him for shooting his daughter.

His daughter. *Puh-leeze! That's if she's even his daughter considering what he did to her. Ugh, my stomach. Hearing what that bastard did to her from his own lips. So proud of the abuse. Not caring that she is only an eighteen-year-old girl that he raised as his own.*

He bit his lip. It had sickened him to the pit of his core, and he'd wanted to kill Andros there and then. But he had refrained. Oh, how barely had he refrained. He knew something needed to be done, but didn't know what.

The phone rang…

TOMAS

Tuesday morning, Tomas felt better, so they had breakfast at a local café. At work, everyone noticed how much better he looked.

"You've got your colour back *and* your appetite," Bette said over lunch.

Tomas nodded. "I do. I feel good again, so maybe it *was* a bad meal."

"It certainly wasn't from here." Bette laughed.

"Of course it wasn't," Tomas told her. "Geez Bette, I wouldn't know *what* to think if you were poisoning me," he joked.

"Oh, darling." She giggled delicately with a hand to her mouth. "Why would I kill you? You make me money."

*****

That night after work, Tomas and Roger grabbed some groceries from the local market before going home.

"I really don't know why you drink that stuff. It's unnatural," Roger commented on the homogenised, unflavoured, unsugared milk that Tomas was putting away.

"It's the healthiest milk there is," he replied. "How do you think I stay in such great shape? By having healthy milk in healthy cereal every morning!"

"God, I don't know how you do it," Roger complained as he sat on the stool under the island bench. "You eat so healthily it's sickening."

Tomas pulled a face. "But *you* certainly don't mind reaping the rewards."

Roger frowned. "What rewards?"

"The reward that is my long, lean cock that all of those healthy foods go towards making."

"Yes," Roger agreed. "That is true. And I'd like to go and play with that cock now."

From the shadows on the street, Luiz watched the living room light go out. He'd seen them buy their groceries and knew he had to go in again. Looking left and right, he slipped across the street and inside, up two flights of stairs and to their door. Sliding his key into the lock, he tried the door, glad that Roger had forgotten to chain it. Moving inside he went into the kitchen, removed the carton of milk, replaced it with one of his own, and quietly slipped back out with no one noticing he'd even been there.

He paused and breathed. He'd heard the sighs and giggles, the gasps and groans, and it absolutely killed him to hear it. He wanted Tomas all to himself and had to wait it out until he could make his move. But the time was coming and coming soon. So soon, in fact, it was just a day away.

Carlos stayed indoors for a week until it was time to film another movie and got ready for the porn star awards. Everyone had been partying hard at Harry's that day, and they all got dressed, drank, ate, fucked, and were merry right up until it was time to go.

Harry, Harriet, Carlos and Tony piled into Harry's limo, while everyone else piled into two others.

"So, my boy, turns out we're up for quite a few awards, including best cock, best script, best director, best actor, best newcomer, best actress…"

Carlos's eyes widened. "That's almost all of them."

"Yes." Harry grinned. "Almost all of them."

"What are these porn awards like then?" Carlos put the window down a little and peered out into the night.

"*Big*, in more ways than one." Harriet giggled.

"Bulging," Harry added.

"Horny," Harriet continued.

"Yep, everyone's horny, hot and hard." Harry's grin grew larger. "It *is* the porn awards after all."

They cruised down Santa Monica Boulevard and slowed down to form a line of limos all waiting to deposit their guests at *The Pussycat Theatre* where the awards were held every year. They chatted until it was time to alight.

Harry stepped out first to thunderous applause and then helped

Harriet. The two stood, waving to fans and cameras like some big movie stars, and then moved aside for the real star.

Carlos bounded out of the car waving, blowing kisses, and hearing fans scream wildly for him. Flashlights popped, men *and* women called for him, and one young man broke loose to come screaming toward him, lurching at him, grabbing him around the waist.

Tony did his job and quickly bent the man's fingers back to release his grip, then twisted his arm behind his back and pushed him into the waiting arms of security.

"Carlo, I love you," the young man screamed, tears pouring down his face. "I love you."

"Jesus," muttered Carlos, stunned at the attack. "You didn't tell me it was going to be like this." He pushed his hair back which made his fans scream louder.

Harry let out a great big thunderous laugh. "Carlos, my boy…" He put his arm around his shoulders. "You're a star now!"

With Tony following up the rear, Harry led Carlos and Harriet up the red carpet and into the theatre.

The red extended inside with carpet, velvet walls, disco balls, couches with feather boas and whips, mannequins with costumes of spikes and chains, not to mention sex toys liberally sprinkled around. They made their way past other stars into the auditorium and took their seats in the middle of the room. The theatre itself was full of old wood and velvet curtains, velvet covered chairs, and bright lights.

After ten minutes the lights dimmed, the curtain rose, and the annual Porn Star Awards began with a rousing musical act that performed while sucking dildos and blow up dolls. The disco ball lights twinkled, the speakers blared, and Carlos sat in stunned amazement.

Ackroyd Ackerman came out to present the first award to thunderous applause, waving to the audience. "Thank you, thank you. I love you, too." He was one of the oldest porn stars at forty-nine, but looked twenty-nine, and came with a twelve inch cock. He was one of the best in the industry.

"And the first award is…Best Male Newcomer to the industry. And the nominees are…" He read the names while footage of the actors rolled across the screen behind him. "Milos Pensuala, Archer Target, Bennon Frankme, Dale Rideher, what a great name that is, and last but definitely *not* least…Carlo Stefan."

The crowd went wild at every name, especially Carlos's.

"And the lucky winner is…" Ackroyd ripped the envelope open excitedly. "Carlo Stefan," he yelled and applauded wildly. He had a big thing for Carlo as he swung both ways and wouldn't mind giving it to him sometime. *I must ask him if he's interested in me,* he thought.

Carlos sat in shock as the crowd thundered around him, staring dazedly at the two Harrys.

"Go on, my boy, go and get your award." Harry pulled him up from his seat and Tony stood in the aisle, his eagle eye on the lookout as Carlos stumbled his way down the stairs and onto the stage to collect his silver penis award.

"Oh, wow." He accepted it from Ackroyd, who kissed him on the mouth. "Oh, um, oh, ah." Ackroyd let him go, and he turned to the microphone with a frown. "I…" He shook his head and glanced over the adoring audience. "I'm in shock.…I…I never thought I'd be here in Hollywood receiving an award." He looked at it in his hand. *"A big silver penis award."* The crowd cheered. "For liking sex so much." More cheering. "I love women…" He threw a glance at Ackroyd. "I love acting, I love writing, I love being *with* women, and now I get paid to do all of it and you all get to see it."

"All ten inches," someone screamed from the crowd.

Carlos blushed. "Yes, about the size of this." He held up his award. "Thank you so much. Thank you." The hot Latin woman who had brought the award on stage led him backstage to be interviewed. He stood on a platform in front of cameras and reporters, answering questions while more awards were announced, including Andy Merkin for Best Director of the Cabana movie that was Carlos's first.

Carlos answered questions the best he could, but Tony soon stepped in and led him back to his seat as Best Producer was announced.

Harry won it for Cabana, and dragged Carlos on stage with him, huffing and puffing on his cigar to accept the award.

"Thank you, thank you. I couldn't have done it without this cock here." He pulled Carlos close. "Without it, I wouldn't be here this year. Thank you." They went backstage and were told to wait as Best Cock was being announced.

Ackroyd took to the microphone again. "And now…we come to my favourite award where I get to see if young Hollywood measures up to old Hollywood." He dropped his pants for all to see his twelve inch cock and read out the nominees to thunderous applause. "And the nominees for Best Cock are…Centurian Masters, Villa Vion, Richard Head, Marcos Du Mont and my personal favourite whose cock I can't wait to see in person is… Carlo Stefan…"

"Jesus," Carlos muttered as Harry slapped him on the back. "Is this guy for real?"

"Yes. And you…" Harry pointed at him. "Have to drop your pants out there and show them why you won Best Cock."

"I haven't won yet," Carlos said.

"Carlo Stefan!" Ackroyd yelled out.

"You have now, go show 'em." Harry slapped him some more, and Carlos walked out to a standing ovation of screams and wolf whistles. He waved and tried not to look at Ackroyd's cock hanging for all to see as he was presented with a gold penis award. Gold, for best cock.

God love Hollywood!

"Get it out, get it out, get it out," chanted through the crowd and Carlos embarrassedly glanced at Harry in the wings. He waved at him to drop his pants, and reluctantly, he placed the award on the small lectern and dropped his pants.

"Whoo," screamed through the crowd and he quickly pulled his pants back up. "Okay, okay, thank you for the adulation and the award. It's going on the bedside table." He waved and quickly left the stage. "*That* was embarrassing," he told Harry and went to keep walking, but was stopped.

"You're up for more awards in a minute."

Ackroyd went on to announce Best Actor, Carlos again, and Best Movie, Cabana, which Harry and Carlos both went on stage for. That was it for them, and they made their way back to their seats as the final performance came on stage.

"What now?" Carlos asked, hanging on to the three cocks in his hands.

"Now we go and party," Harry said and led the way out to their limo.

The club was already packed with people and had more outside waiting to get in. They were quickly led through the back door and made their way to the private roped off area. Alcohol was flowing, drugs were being snorted or injected, and sex was happening on the dance floor.

Roller-skating women delivered drinks; roller-skating men delivered the drugs. With the pulsating beat of the music and the twirling lights of the disco balls, Carlos found himself lost in the atmosphere and the alcohol.

The rest of the crew turned up followed by everyone else that had been at the awards. Men and women congratulated Carlos, and Ackroyd tried for a cock-off.

He pulled his out. "Come on, show me yours, let's compare."

Carlos backed away. "No, thanks." He turned around to find himself in the arms of Vivian. "Viv." He picked her up and spun around to the beats of the music blaring at them from all angles.

"Well, hello there, Mr Best Cock. Tell me, is your award bigger than you?" She laughed as he put her back on her feet and slipped her arms around his neck, tossing back her long brown hair.

"Same size, I think." He laughed. "Where have you been? I haven't seen you in ages." He held her close and thrust against her as they swayed to the pounding music.

"I've been away, darling. Photo shoots in Paris, Milan, London, Tokyo." She hooked a leg up to his waist and thrust back.

His hands grabbed her and held her tight. "How about coming to my place. We can spend the night together."

"After the trouble you've gotten yourself into? I'm not sure I'd be safe alone with you."

He frowned. "How do you know about it?"

"Harriet, darling."

The frowned deepened. "How about your place then? I miss you, Viv." He twirled her around and slid a hand between her legs to find she didn't have any panties on.

"How about here, darling," she said in his ear and slid a hand down to unzip his erection.

Under the tribal beating and dizzying lights, they made their way together on a rhythmic beat all without missing a step until the music slowed down and they remained joined through a slow dance with Carlos massaging her firm ass and Vivian clenching her well-trained womanhood. Their tongues entwined and they stayed that way for five more songs before reluctantly parting and walking up to their private party for a drink.

"Viv, how are you, my dear." Harry got up to give her a kiss.

"Good thanks, Harry."

"I see you've done some sampling of the Best Cock of 1977."

"Not the first time, Harry." Viv laughed.

"Guess not," he replied.

"We're gonna get a drink and go." Carlos came up with two champagnes.

"Not without Tony you're not," Harry said, and Carlos noticed him standing nearby.

"A bodyguard? How very celebrity of you." Viv sipped her drink.

"I need to keep my boy safe now, don't I," Harry replied. "So, if you two leave, take him with you." He threw himself back into the melee.

Carlos downed his drink. "Ready?"

"Ready." Viv led him by the hand and they walked out into the quiet air of downtown L.A. Tony flagged their limo down, and they headed for Viv's luscious Hollywood Hills home where Tony did a perimeter check as they went in.

"Wow, great looking place." Carlos eyed the antiques and art on the walls, tables, and pedestals.

"I like expensive things." She led him to the enclosed backyard where the pool was lit, and the spa was already on. Slipping out of her dress she helped Carlos out of his suit and shirt.

He picked her up and dipped into her before dipping into the spa. Holding her up over the side, his long even strokes thrust her back and forth.

"Oh, God, oh, God, Carlos. Oh, God, I've missed this," she gasped as the hot bubbling water slapped against her ass.

He gave one last stroke and lifted her to him, delving into her mouth and tasting the champagne. It was so good to be with her again; a woman who wanted him for him and not because he could give it to her. He tasted her neck, her breasts, her nipples.

"Ugh," she groaned and tightened her inner sanctum, clenching him, keeping him there, and hardening him.

He sucked harder.

She clenched harder.

They came together.

Lying on a poolside lounge afterwards with a towel over them and more champagne inside of them, they stared up at the stars.

Carlos told her his side of everything and Viv offered her opinion. Then she told him everything she'd been doing, and they made love until the sun came up.

He stroked her soft, dewy cheeks. "I love you, Viv," he said.

She moved her head back in shock. "What?"

He laughed. "Don't panic. I've loved you since I was fourteen and you were on my bedroom walls. You're my dream girl. And then I met you, and you were everything I thought you were and then some. Beautiful, sassy, vibrant. Great in bed."

"And out of it," she quipped.

He laughed again. "And out of it." His fingers slipped down her throat to her breast and played with her nipple which hardened in an instant. "You're beautiful, and I love you. I just wanted you to know that. I don't expect anything from you, and you won't get anything else from me. Unless you want it. But I just wanted you to know." He kissed her lips before his mouth latched onto her erect bud.

She sighed. Completely relaxed, completely free, completely happy. "I love you too," she murmured and arched into his mouth. "Oh,

God." She enjoyed the freedom she had with him. To be the sexual nymph she was. No other man had pleasured, pleased, or fulfilled her like he did, and she'd been so glad that Harriet had let her know about him. Because once she'd tasted him, she didn't want anyone else to occupy her pussy. It was for him and him alone, and she'd missed him terribly when she was away, not even realising he'd get personally involved with someone else. But he had and now more trouble had followed. Was he worth it considering how he filled her? Of course he was, but he was still so young. Sixteen years her junior. But then, they *were* in Hollywood where age doesn't matter, especially when surgery for looking younger was becoming big business. As long as he kept those ten inches up and at attention that was all she needed.

Cock.

Cock was all she needed. But the body it came with wasn't bad either. She wrapped her legs around that body as he entered her, sliding in like he owned the place.

She looked into his eyes. He owned her, every time. This place was his and his alone. No one else had been in it since him, and no one else would be in it after him. That's why he needed to stay. This place was his and his alone. Did she dare keep a younger man? It was not as though he needed her money. Did she dare keep a porn star for a lover? It's not like he fucked too many others outside of work. It had only been Rosalee, but that didn't last. No, there would never be another for her as long as Carlos Stephanopoulos fucked her senseless all night every night like now. Oh, God, oh, God, oh…God…

They slipped into a semi-conscious state and stayed that way all day, drifting in and out, making love, sleeping, lying in the sun, drinking in the pool, the spa, on the lounge. They stayed that way all day.

*****

Aneeka was in her studio looking at her recent photos. She hadn't seen or heard from Carlos, Harry, or the cops since the break-in and had wondered if they'd be back. The insurance company had her claim on the go, and she'd installed a better security system than the one she had.

She glanced out the window to the house next door. The police had come back and removed the tape. A company had come and cleaned it out of furniture, and any evidence of drugs, and now there was a for lease sign on the front. The rental company hadn't waited long. The poor girl wasn't in her grave yet.

She picked up her camera to give it a polish and made sure there was a film in it, then methodically went through each piece. Around midnight she went downstairs to make a cup of tea, a ritual she did every night if she was still awake at twelve.

Getting the kettle on the stove, she got a sachet of her favourite herbal tea out and placed it in a mug. While waiting for the water to boil, she went through the house making sure the windows were closed and the doors were locked. She noticed her neighbours had all gone to bed because the only lights on were hers and the street lights.

On hearing the kettle whistle, she poured water over the sachet and let the fumes waft up to her nose. Just the scent of it made her calm. Sitting at the table, she read a magazine and saw an ad for Carlos's new movie which featured one of her photos.

"He *is* gorgeous," she murmured and had been quite hypnotised by his blue eyes when taking the photos, especially the ones in the pool where his eyes were the focus. After finishing her tea and putting the magazines away, she saw her rubbish bin was overflowing and decided to take it out. She tied the bag up, unlocked the back door, and stepped onto her porch going over to the side fence where her bin was. *Better not forget rubbish day this week.*

The back light went out, and she turned at the sudden darkness, a chill creeping down her spine. "Damn light bulbs," she muttered. "There must be one that lasts longer than this." She hurried up the stairs, across the porch, and managed one foot in the door before she was grabbed from behind with one arm around her waist and one arm over her mouth with a rag that smelled sweet…sickly…sweet…

PEDRO

"What have you been up to?" Pedro asked Wednesday morning after getting home. Dumping his bag on the end of the bed he saw Angelia reading a magazine. He glanced at his watch. "Six-forty and you're awake reading a magazine."

She looked up. "I don't have school today. I'm taking a break, two days on, one off, two days on, so I'm waiting for you."

"What are you reading?" He flopped on the bed beside her and peered at the article. "Carlo Stefan, the hottest new cock in the business. Ah, Jesus!"

"I've been reading up on your brother." She flipped the magazine over to reveal the cover. "It's *Porn Star Monthly* from last month. It has stories on the nominees for the awards and your brother is up for a lot—"

"He always was," Pedro muttered.

She giggled. "As best male newcomer, his movie is up for best movie, best director, best producer, and he's up for best cock and best actor. You know he wrote some of the Cabana movies. There's four or five of them, and it says here he got a pay raise for writing them. Babe…" She closed the magazine. "Maybe you should get into writing *your* movies? You'd get a pay rise. Ask Greta about it."

Pedro stared at the magazine and his brother's blue eyes. Just like his. Just like their mother's. He swallowed, but teared up anyway. "Oh, God, I miss them," he sobbed.

Angelina wrapped her good arm around him, resting his head on her chest. "Shh, it's okay. I know you do baby, I know you do."

He sobbed until he was done and then freshened up. A shower did him good, and breakfast would be even better. Hearing Angie in the kitchen, he spied the magazine on the bed and sat down to flick through it. He read snippets about his brother on several pages until he came to the story. The picture was of him in a pool, soaked through wet. He grinned. It would get all the girls wet. If there were a wet t-shirt contest for guys, he'd definitely win hands down. He read the story.

'I miss my family like crazy. One minute we were all together on Mykonos and the next I'm in Hollywood making movies. My two little brothers have flown the coop to go and do their thing, and I haven't seen them since June. Four months isn't long, but it feels like forever.'

Pedro felt the tears again. Wasn't he in the same boat right now? He'd left in July and not gone back. Reading the rest of the article, he saw there was no mention of why he'd left. He thought about it. *I wonder why the charges were dropped. I guess I won't know unless I see him.*

*****

The woman lay in bed trying to keep cool. It was mid-October, but the heat still lingered some days, not to mention the noise outside. How could people sleep with that racket outside?

Rolling over, she stared at the corkboard with all of Pedro's pictures on it. What had become of Andros Poulos? She had seen him go into Angelina's apartment last month, but had followed Angelina so had no idea what had happened since.

Except that someone was trying to hurt her Pedro. Was it Andros? Had he ordered a hit on Pedro instead of taking his whore of a daughter home? Maybe she should track him down and have a little chat with him. He clearly wasn't doing his job as her father. He should have taken her by the ear and dragged her home by that fancy private jet of his. But no, he'd stuck around and Angelina had been bruised. Had he done that to her? Had he taught her a lesson? She hoped so.

Sitting up, she swung her legs to the floor. *Oh, Pedro, I need you. Why won't you come to me and our baby? Our baby needs you, we need you. That whore doesn't. And don't you know he's trying to kill you? How can you be with a whore whose father is trying to kill you? I wouldn't do that to you. I wouldn't hurt you. I love you.*

She went over to the board and stroked the photos one by one. "I love you, I would never hurt you. I need you to be a father to our baby." She kissed one of the photos. "I love you, you will be mine. Soon, very soon. We will be together very soon. Not long now, baby." She stroked her stomach. "Not long now until your papa is here and we will be married and be a happy little family." She felt the baby move. "Oh, yes, little one. We will be a happy little family soon. Very soon indeed. Just a matter of days and daddy will be leaving that whore he's with and coming home to us."

She left the board and slipped out of her nightshirt. It was Pedro's, and she'd taken it on one of her many visits to their first apartment. He didn't seem to miss it, and it smelled of him still. It made her feel closer to him, that he was closer to their baby.

Stepping into the shower, she thought about her plan and how she was going to execute it. Yes, the plan had to go off without a hitch. Because if anyone got in her way it would be damaging to all involved and she couldn't have anything happening to Pedro before she got to him.

Down on the street below, Stavros was gazing up at the apartment wondering what he was going to do with her.

Twenty-five feet away, Mark was wondering what he was going to do with them both.

Stavros had been given the address by his boss. Not Andros, who was just a small time boss, but his big boss. He'd been given a plan, a plan that involved a lot more than what Andros had made him do. He'd been given clear orders and had to follow them to a T. He had to get the woman out of the way and then Andros out of the way. And he'd been told by any means necessary.

He glanced up and down the street and spotted the man that had been with Pedro looking up at the same apartment. "Fuck! What's he doing here?" He took off in the opposite direction and made it down the street to his car. Seeing Mark in the rear-view, he took off.

"Not so fast, buddy boy." Mark was parked right behind him and drove off, not wanting to lose him. Following at a safe distance, he tailed him to Jersey to a small hotel, and pulling up to the curb, watched the man go inside. "Well, now. What are you up to?"

*****

Pedro stared at the ceiling. It was eight-forty, and normally he'd be asleep. But today he couldn't. Something was wrong. He felt it in his bones. He wasn't sure if it was Carlos's article, or the fact he had left in such a rushed way. But it wasn't *just* the fact they had all left. It was something bad. Something bad was going to happen. He didn't know what, he didn't know when. He just knew soon.

He heard Angelina in the lounge room. She was studying on the couch, keeping as quiet as she could, but he still heard her. Still heard the page of her book being turned. Still heard every intake of breath, every sigh.

"Jesus!" He rolled out of bed and sat up. Ah, the life of a DJ. Work all night, can't sleep all day. And he certainly wasn't interested in taking pills. He'd learned a bad enough lesson on Santorini when he'd found his juice was being spiked by Andros. No, he wouldn't be taking sleeping pills.

But it kept nagging. *Maybe I should go home and see my parents? Is that it? But then Andros would just follow me there.*

No, he had to sort this out, whatever it was, and he had a feeling it was coming soon.

*****

Greta sat looking at the photos of Pedro. "My, God, he's gorgeous." The shots from Long Island had turned out beautifully, and she put a

359

few aside to be used for promotional posters and video covers. "Speaking of…" She grabbed the video of the movie and popped it into the VCR. She sped through until they got to the sex. "Oh, God, you do it so well," she murmured.

Pedro's eleven inches was one inch bigger than his brother, and she wondered if they'd ever measured off against one another. She'd seen Carlo's movie, and while it was hot, Pedro's was hotter, classier, and tasteful.

She'd heard him briefly mention a middle brother and wondered if he was like them. "Oh, yes, this movie will be the talk of the town at the porn awards next year." They had just been, and Carlos had won almost all of them. "Oh, yes, Harry, I'm going to beat you next year. I'm going to beat you with Pedro Stefan. He's got two inches in height and one inch in cock on your boy." An idea came to her. *Well, maybe that idea will work once Pedro finishes his movies. I'll have a little chat with him.*

TOMAS

Tomas cracked open the milk and drank straight from it.

"We do have glasses, you know," Roger quipped. "They're those things there." He pointed to the ten clear glasses sitting on the kitchen shelf. "Or have you not seen one before? A glass I mean."

"Ha, ha." Tomas poured milk over his cereal. "I'm the only one who drinks it, so what does it matter?"

"True," Roger said, whipping up Eggs Benedict. "I'm not much of a milk lover anyway, so I'll leave that to you."

"You really should try it." Tomas offered the carton. "It's not that bad."

Pulling a face, Roger said, "No, thanks. I'll stick to my eggs and toast, and coffee straight and black."

"Clearly not how you prefer your men," Tomas teased.

Roger laughed. "Straight no, black, not so bad."

"You've had a black man?" Tomas's interest was piqued, having forgotten about seeing Roger working with a black co-star.

"Yes." Roger inhaled a whole forkful of eggs and wriggled his brows.

"So, it's clearly not true then."

Roger stopped eating long enough to ask, "What?"

"Once you've had black you never go back." Since Roger was Tomas's second, Luiz his first, he'd never been with a black man. Not even in a movie.

"I'm with you, so obviously not."

PEDRO

Mark kept an eye out for the two stalkers Wednesday night while Pedro was at work. It all went off without a hitch. Bev, Sara and Martine were front and centre as always, other fans stopped by, but no one tried anything. Standing just offstage near Pedro, he certainly copped an eyeful.

Men on men, women on women, sex, drugs, snorting, drinking. "Fucking hell," he muttered when two men with nothing but leather cock covers on walked by. He rolled his eyes. *The fucking jobs I have to do.* His eyes moved around the room looking for stage jumpers. The security at the door kept unmentionables out, and the extra security standing guard at the back door kept trespassers away.

So far, so good.

*****

The woman wrapped one last parcel. This time it was a dead doll with the eyes poked out and the face scratched off. It had long black hair and was covered in blood. With it was a note.

She took a cab down to their apartment and watched from down the road. "Please stay here and wait," she told the driver.

Seeing no guard at the door, she slipped in quietly and walked up seven flights of stairs. Peering around the corner, she saw no one on guard at their door. She slipped her shoes off, tiptoed along in stockinged feet, and laid the box at the door.

Smiling, she quickly ran back to the stairs, grabbed her shoes, and ran down to the lobby where she put them on, flew past the guard, who was back, and out to the taxi. "Drive," she ordered.

*****

Stavros turned down the alley beside 69. If he was going to fulfill the plan his boss had given him, then he needed to get his shit together.

"Fuck!" He saw the security guards and drove by. If they stopped him, he'd say he was taking a short cut. But they didn't, so he looked for a place to park away from the door.

If he was going to do it, he had to do it right. No cock-ups this time. He had to be close enough to the door of Pedro's car so he could get the job done without being seen, blocked in, or stuck. He needed a quick clean getaway and needed it all to go smoothly.

Turning down 8th Avenue, he decided to leave it until the following morning, knowing he'd have a better chance of scoping it out in daylight and without the guards.

*****

Andros knew he had to put his plan into action within the next two days. He was due in court next Monday. He had no idea why; something to do with assaulting his daughter, but he knew the plan needed to happen now.

He sat staring out into the beautiful October night. It was lovely this time of the year. The air was crisp in his nostrils, the wine crisp in his mouth. Yes, it was very nice here indeed. *I'll have to consider holidaying here during fall more often. A nice summer home in the Hamptons, a fall home in the city. Yes, very nice indeed.*

Gazing across the park toward their apartment, he wondered what Angelina was doing. Had she thought about him? He knew she'd had the day off school, he knew she had a bodyguard as did Pedro. Now, it was just a matter of getting them in a place together where his plan could come to fruition. "Let's hope Stavros does his part," he muttered.

*****

Pedro had to deal with a drunken Bev Marie.

"I luv you sho mush," she slurred. "I don't get drunk over just anyone ya know."

He laughed and removed her arms from around his neck. "That's nice to know Bev, but look at all the gorgeous men here in their short shorts and rock-hard abs. You can have your pick."

"I did have my pick." She weaved against him on the dance floor during a break when he'd gotten down with the crowd to dance. "I picked you."

"Why?" he asked. "Why me?"

"Because you're young, gorgeous and have a huge cock."

"And how do you know that?"

"Look at you." She eyed him up and down. "You pack a lot into those shorts, and now with your movie being released, I can't wait to see it in action. But really…" She slobbered on him. "I want to see it in action now." She grabbed his shorts, but he grabbed her hands and waved the security guards over.

"Time to go, Bev, you've had a long one."

"Will you come with me?" She was escorted away. "*Come* with me, Pedro, make me come."

"Bye, Bev." He waved and smiled at Sara and Martine, a few others gathered around, and he danced through the twelve inch with them until it was time to get back on stage. He ended the night a few hours later with another twelve inch and walked off. "Oh, God," he cried as he walked into the staff room. "Those women are ca.ray.zy!" He pulled on his t-shirt.

"You don't know the half of it," Mike said, tying a shoe lace. "They will snort anything, drink anything, suck anything."

"Such as?" Pedro asked with a raised brow.

"My cock," Mike said.

"You're kidding?"

Mike laughed. "I've had quite a few offers, but have been a gentleman and refused them all."

"Well, that sounds *so unlike* you." Pedro pulled on his jeans. "You went hell for leather when we first opened."

"I did, but then I met someone special." Mike slammed his locker shut and grabbed his bag. "And she's pretty damn special."

"Ah, sweet on someone. Who's the lucky girl, and how long's it been happening?" Pedro slid into his sneakers.

"Maggie."

Pedro looked up in surprise. "Angelina's Maggie?"

"Yep." Mike's grin was ear to ear.

"Since when?"

"Since your brother's movie. We got talking and…" He shrugged. "It happened."

"Well, good for you." Pedro high-fived him. "When are you seeing her again? Maybe we can double date."

"Not sure. I got next week off, but she's got a test at school, so maybe this weekend."

"I'll tell Angie and see if she can set something up."

"Okay. See you tomorrow." Mike walked out.

Pedro picked up his bag and met Mark in the hallway. "Time to go home. I'm beat." They left, and Mark did the usual check of the car before driving home. The parcel met them at the door.

"Ah, geez, not another one." Pedro stopped as Mark investigated.

He picked it up and removed the lid. The bloodied doll and note lay inside. *"Your time is up. If you have not chosen us and our baby by Friday night, the whore's life will end."*

"What the hell?" Pedro took a step back. "I am so sick and tired of this, Mark. When will it stop?"

"Friday."

"What?"

"She says it will end Friday. So we have two days."

"Do you know who she is?"

"Yes."

"Then why haven't you stopped her?"

"With what? I'm a bodyguard, and she hasn't physically threatened you or come near you."

"She was here…tonight…with Angie here."

"Yes, but no harm was done."

"We don't know that."

Sara-Michelle opened the door. "What's going on? I can hear you inside." She saw the box. "Fuck! When did that come?"

"Is Angie okay?" Pedro asked.

"She's fine." She shook her head. "I heard nothing all night. I have no idea when that was delivered."

"The problem is, it *was* delivered. That means she can still get into the building even with the guards and security. And that's not a good thing," Mark said.

"So, what do we do?" Pedro stared at the box.

"We keep the two of you together in the same place at the same time. Two of us protecting you is better than one. If she wants you, she'll get all of us. Four against one are not odds in her favour."

"And what about *our* odds?" Pedro asked.

"I'll make sure those odds get better. Far better than hers," Mark replied.

Pedro sighed. "This needs to end."

"It will."

TOMAS

Once the sun went down Wednesday night, Luiz put his plan into action. He was after another victim, and it had to be tonight. *Oh, yes,* he thought, *tonight it's all going down.* He made his way to *The Bat and Balls*, an Aussie pub that catered to gay men. It was a few years old, had become a big hit with the locals, and was the place for gay Aussie men to hang out when they were in Miami.

Luiz walked through the door and looked around, spying the man he was after sitting with friends at a table. Pushing his red hair out of his face, he went up to the bar and ordered a beer. Keeping to himself as he casually looked around, he tried to remain inconspicuous.

"Anything else, mate?" the blond Aussie bartender asked.

Luiz looked him over. "How about you? You gay?"

The blond hunk laughed. "I am, but taken."

"Pity," Luiz commiserated. His gaze wandered around, noticed his target, and kept on wandering. *Have to play it cool and casual.* He checked out the décor, the brunet hunk at the end of the bar, and the black guys at the far table. *Mmm, black…* God, black men had great cocks, great big hulking pythons of love they were, but Tomas's was better.

The men saw him looking and gave him a nod. He gave a saucy cocked brow in return before turning his attention back to the man he was there for. The man looked in his direction and Luiz quickly looked away, blushing, before coyly looking back. The man was still staring; a smile on his face as he checked out what Luiz was packing in his tight jeans.

Luiz gave a coy shrug of the shoulder. The man kept staring. Luiz asked the bartender which way to the toilets, and with a glance over his shoulder, walked down the hall and into the small bathroom. He didn't have to wait long as the man soon followed.

Aiden Head had been with *Seralift* for two and a half years, not long before Roger started, and they had starred in a movie together. Now, Luiz wanted Aiden to star in *his* movie.

Aiden locked the door and leant against it. "I saw you checking me out."

"Was I?" Luiz murmured, slowly unzipping his pants.

Aiden eyed his crotch. "Yes. Yes, you were, and now I want to see what you've got." He moved over to Luiz, pushed him against the sink and finished unzipping his pants. Pulling it out, he moved it in his hands.

Luiz groaned, collapsing against the sink. "Oh, God, oh, God that's so good." He loved it when hands other than his own manipulated his cock. "Oh, God, fuck me."

"Not yet." Aiden unzipped and pulled his own out. "Let's get to know each other first." He pushed against Luiz and manhandled them both.

Luiz's hands joined in a mad frenzy of cockfighting. They thrust against each other in a mad dance of lust until each came.

"Ah," Aiden groaned, letting his head fall back. "Oh, God that was good."

"Is that all I get?" Luiz whispered, massaging Aiden's manhood until he hardened again. "Is that all I get? I want more. I want you. I want you to fuck me up the ass." He turned around and guided Aiden into him. "Now." Holding onto the sink with one hand he grabbed Aiden's right hand and brought it around to his package, rubbing it all over as Aiden thrust inside him. He was long, strong and powerful and hit all the right spots. They came in a frenzy at the bathroom sink.

Aiden finally stepped back, but Luiz grabbed his jacket. "I want more. I want more of you. I want you in my mouth, up my ass, inside of me. I want to be inside of you. Come with me, let's leave and go somewhere else." Luiz's hand slid down to Aiden's crotch. "Let's go somewhere where we can indulge all night."

Aiden stared glassily at the redhead in front of him. "I want you to fuck me too. Let's go." He zipped up, and they made their way out the back door. They barely made it to Aiden's car before they were fucking on the back seat like wild animals.

"Oh, God, oh, God." Luiz bounced up and down. He wrapped Aiden's hands around his cock, moving them up and down as Aiden thrust. "Oh, God, oh, God fuck me," he yelled. "Fuck me." They climaxed and relaxed. "Oh, God," Luiz panted. "You don't stop." He rolled onto his back, spread his legs and pulled Aiden down on him. "Can we make it to your place?" he whispered in his ear.

"We can try," Aiden whispered back and climbed over the seat to gun the engine. They made it to his place, up the stairs, and into the bedroom before ripping each other's clothes off and humping on the bed.

"Oh, God, oh, God," Luiz cried as he rammed it home. "Oh, God." He collapsed onto Aiden's back. "Oh, God, you're good. So, so, good. A big cock and a tight asshole just right for the taking."

"Take them all if you like. You're the best fuck I've had in years." Aiden pushed up and moved so he was free of Luiz. Digging around in his bedside drawer he pulled out a small bong and lighter. "Want some?"

"No," Luiz said. "I've got my own shit if you want to give it a try?"

Aiden stopped puffing. "Like what?" He blew out smoke.

"Coke." Luiz fetched the small kit from his jacket pocket and brandished a vial. "Want some? It's good shit."

Aiden licked his lips. "I'll tell you what. You smoke this bong, lie back and enjoy, and I'll snort coke right off your cock."

Luiz sizzled inside. "Why fucking not?" He took the bong, lay back, and smoked while Aiden spread a line of coke along his dick. He snorted, he licked, he sucked.

Luiz groaned. "Oh, God, that's good." He was so relaxed he'd almost forgotten what he was there for. "Again."

Aiden spread, snorted, licked and sucked again, and Luiz held him there, enjoying the hot tongue around him. "Oh, God, you suck good. Oh, God." He felt himself coming. "Swallow, swallow, I'm coming. Oh, God, oh, God." He climaxed, and Aiden took it. "Oh, God, you're good. More coke?" He rolled Aiden onto his back and lay on top, sprinkling cocaine in Aiden's nose. Rocking back and forth, he felt the manly strength of the man under him. "You're so fucking hot," he murmured into his nipple. He bit and pulled. "So, fucking hot. More coke?"

He poured the rest of the vial into Aiden's nose and made his way down to his cock. He swallowed him whole. *So fucking good*, he thought, lost in dreamland, sucking on a cock as if he'd never had it before. When he was done, he moved back up and sat on it. "More coke? I have another vial." He moved up and down slowly. Oh, God, he was enjoying this. It was so, so good it seemed like such a pity to kill him. He looked at his watch. He had a few hours of play time left. And play he did, until Aiden was out of his mind on a drug overdose four hours later.

"Come on, baby, we're gonna take a trip." Luiz dressed and cleaned up, keeping all of the essentials within arm's reach. He wrapped Aiden in a robe and helped him down to his car, then quickly ran back up to grab his things. Glad that Aiden lived in a house and not an apartment.

He drove to Roger's building, quietly drove into the underground garage and left the car parked lengthways. Making sure no one was around; he slid over Aiden and opened the passenger door.

"Come on, baby. We're home now." He glanced around and checked his watch. He had a couple of hours until they started leaving for work and he had to be out of there now. He smacked Aiden's face to wake him up. "Come on, baby, time for another line of coke."

"Mmm," Aiden mumbled, struggling to wake.

"Come on, baby." Luiz unscrewed the three vials and tilted Aiden's head back, holding his mouth open while he tipped the powder in.

"Mmm." Aiden tried to struggle as Luiz held his mouth shut, his eyes staring into his as the coke hit his adrenaline, dissolved, absorbed and sped to his heart. "Mmm." He grabbed Luiz's hand that was holding his mouth, but all he saw was black. His hands fell. He stopped struggling. All power left him.

Aiden Head was dead.

Four down, one to go.

Luiz quickly scratched, *Roger, I love you*, into Roger's car with Aiden's car key and then hauled his body out of the car and laid it between Roger's and Tomas's. He stuck a few photos of Tomas into Aiden's hand, opened his robe to display the whole package, and spread the coke vials around Aiden's body. He had to make it look like a suicide *or* murder. Either way, Roger was going to be hauled in for this one way or another.

He gathered his own things, wiped down the wheel and handles and anything else that might have his prints on it, and glanced at his watch. He saw it was five a.m. on the dot.

Because he'd cased the joint, he knew the first tenant left for work at six-thirty, so it would be just an hour and a half before Aiden was discovered. Tomas and Roger were up at seven, so only two and a half hours away. If only he could stick around and watch the festivities, but alas, he couldn't. Sneaking out of the car park, he silently ran a few streets then walked the rest of the way back to the pub where he'd left his car. It was five-thirty. Not long now.

*****

George Cauldwell was an average man.

Average in every sense of the word.

He was average height, average weight, average in looks, demeanour and stature. He had an average job in an average company, doing average things. But for the next two months, George Cauldwell would not be average at all.

George hit the alarm and threw back the covers. It was another average day in the Cauldwell home. Average décor, average life. He showered, put on his clothes for work, and had a breakfast of cereal, fruit and juice. All so average.

At six-twenty on the dot, George Cauldwell stepped outside his apartment, locked the door, and walked down four flights of stairs to get to his car in the underground park. He saw a black car parked in front of the two fags' cars and kept on walking. Unfortunately, it meant he was blocked in and wouldn't be able to back out of his parking space.

"Goddamn it," he swore and eyed the car. There was no one in it, and the passenger side was open.

Walking around the back of the car, he spied a slipper and then a foot. And coming to a stop between the two fags' cars, he saw the body that foot belonged to; a gorgeous above-average young man with a tight torso and a big dick.

George Cauldwell stared at the man's body. He'd dared not look at a naked one for the last two years, had been too afraid of the feelings it stirred up, but now, one was on full display, right there in front of him, in *his* parking garage.

"Sir, sir, are you all right?" he called while eyeing off the cock and balls and licking his lips. Oh, how he wanted to touch it, feel it, taste it. "Sir." He leant down to feel for a pulse at the neck; the beautiful long neck that belonged to the beautiful long body that provided him with the beautiful long cock that his eyes wandered over.

He hovered inches above it. The beautiful long cock that looked so delicious he could taste its sweetness. His tongue peeked out to wet his lips and kept on going until George Cauldwell had that juicy long cock in his mouth.

Oh, my God, it's so good, he thought, sucking and tasting and licking. His average mouth left it behind and licked its way up the long beautiful body until it came to its mouth, where it tasted and licked and sucked. *Oh, my God I'm in heaven.* He sighed and decided he couldn't keep it in any longer.

Taking off his clothes, he lay full out on the dead body of Aiden Head. George Cauldwell didn't care that he was dead, just that he wasn't resisting.

After devouring the front of Aiden where he backed onto his dick and rubbed a dead man's hands over his ball sack, he rolled the body over and entered him from behind. "Oh, God, oh, God, you're so good," the very average George Cauldwell told the very above-average Aiden Head. "Oh, you're such a good fucker, so good." His hands explored every inch of Aiden's body and made Aiden's hands explore every inch of him. "Oh, God, you're so good."

George rolled Aiden back and rubbed his balls up and down the long, strong torso of the young man beneath him. He lengthened out and went back to kissing the mouth, the mouth that now lay perpetually open in a frozen state. When he was finished tonguing a dead man, he sat on his face and put his cock in Aiden's mouth. "Oh, yes, suck it, suck it, oh, God, yes, suck it," George cried out. He moved Aiden's head in opposite motions, hardening and coming. "Oh, God, oh, God," the very average George Cauldwell cried.

He waited until the tingling died down before sitting backwards and taking Aiden up the back passage again. He enclosed Aiden's hands around him and rubbed as he moved on a dead man's dick.

His hands slid up and over his own body, touching himself, masturbating, fucking a corpse. In fact, if anyone had been watching the scene, it would have been a very crazy and debauched scene indeed. A man, very much alive, fucking a man that was very much dead, in between two cars with a third one parked across. Some people would have merely thought two fags were getting it off in the underground parking. To those that knew, which only two did, the scene would be seen for what it was.

And now there was about to be a third person to see the scene that way from the start, especially when it took him only an instant to realise what was actually going on.

The very average George Cauldwell came and slid down onto Aiden's body.

"Ahem."

George's head flew up into the shiny gold light of a detective's badge. "Oh, my God," he cried and tried to cover himself.

"Detective Barden, Miami PD. What do you think you're doing?" He slid his badge back into his pocket, staring down at the naked middle-aged man on top of a dead body.

Oh, yes. The very average George Cauldwell was about to be very average no more. In fact, he was about to become very *non*-average. For the world would soon find out what a raving necrophiliac George Cauldwell was.

"I, ah…" George covered himself with his shirt. "It's not what it looks like."

Detective Barden smirked. "I'm sure it's *very much* what it looks like. You're a guy who fucks dead bodies. And now it's *my* dead body. Get up and get dressed." He watched while Cauldwell quickly put his clothes on and stood in front of him.

George saw the police car in the driveway and the two officers leaning against it. "Am I…under arrest?"

"Of course you are." Barden led him away. "You've disturbed a crime scene and had sex with a corpse." He turned Cauldwell around while he was cuffed. "Did you kill the corpse?"

"What? What, no, no." The very average George Cauldwell's eyes widened. "I didn't kill anybody. I just found him there…"

"And took advantage of the situation," Barden interrupted.

"No, no." George vehemently shook his head.

"Yes, yes," Barden replied. "And now I have a crime scene. Take him away. I'll charge him later." He watched the very average George Cauldwell be placed into the back seat of the car, head shaking left and right, eyes wide as if he was on coke. He noted the pale complexion and short brown hair. Yep, it's always the average ones. He saw George stare out the back window as they drove away, then called for reinforcements. He walked back to the scene and crouched, spying vials under the cars. Turning his head to the right, he spied something on Roger's car. *Roger, I love you.*

"Well, well, well, and now we have a connection. How nice of him to spell it out for me." He checked his watch. Six-fifty. *Nah, we'll let the kids sleep some more.*

The ground crew and coroner rolled in ten minutes later. "Doc." He nodded. "Got another one."

The doctor looked down at the body. "The scene has been disturbed."

"Oh, it certainly has." Barden rocked on his heels, his hands in his pockets. "Found some perve having sex with the body."

Doc looked up in surprise. "You're kidding?"

"Nope."

"Jesus bloody hell, a necrophiliac!"

"Yep."

"I hope he didn't do too much damage." He set down his bag and opened it.

"Don't know. Hopefully, you can tell me if he did." Barden watched Doc pull out several instruments and kneel over the body.

Doc shook his head. "It's compromised." His eyes found the vials under the car. "And full of drugs I take it." He used tweezers to pick them up and put them into an envelope. "I'll get them analysed." He noticed the scratching on the car. "Ah, got a suspect have we?"

"Dunno yet, Doc. I'll get 'em on the way out I suppose." He watched him finish up and cart the body away before examining the third car. "No wallet, no ID, nothing." He dug around in the glove compartment and found several business cards. *Aiden Head, Seralift Productions.* "Ah, Mr Head was a fag fucker. That tells me everything." He checked his watch. Seven-fifteen. Time for business. "Come with me." He motioned to two officers and made his way up to the second floor.

CARLOS

Carlos managed to make it home, even though he'd wanted to stay, but Viv had another shoot to go to in New York and needed to leave. So he'd stumbled through the house and out to the car that was now there with Tony behind the wheel.

"Tony, man. Have you been here the whole time?" Carlos slumped into the back seat.

"No, sir. I was relieved and came back with this car. Home, sir?"

"Thanks, Tony."

Carlos rested his eyes behind black shades on the drive home and didn't take them off until he walked inside his apartment. Only then did he see the mess that lay before him.

"Tony," he yelled. "Tony."

Tony came hurtling through the door and saw the overturned dining set, lounge suite, broken prints, smashed glass and half-open balcony door. He whipped his gun out and stalked toward the other rooms.

Carlos waited.

"Clear. You'd better come see this."

Carlos followed the trail of destruction into his bedroom where he saw the upturned bed and strewn sheets. "What?"

"That." Tony pointed.

On the mess that was the bed lay a photo of Aneeka, bound to a chair and gagged with today's paper held under her face. The note that came with it read, *'We want the photos she took. We want you. Get us those photos and all negatives, or she dies. If you call cops, she dies. If you take off out of town, she dies. If you don't do as you're told, she dies. We want photos. We will call at 3:30 p.m. Tell anyone, she dies.'* The words were crudely written, the paper ripped from a ruled notebook.

"We'd better call Harry," Tony said.

TOMAS

Tomas and Roger were finishing up with breakfast. Roger with his eggs and toast, and Tomas with his cereal.

"What did you want to do this weekend?" Roger asked. "I thought we'd get away for a couple of days. We could head north or go out to one of the islands."

"Sounds good," Tomas said. "Do we get a holiday from the studio? It's nearly two months now, and we make movies most nights except for the weekends."

"And you work all day. You can give that up now you know. You're making good money. Do you really need to keep working out old ladies?"

"If it weren't for those old ladies I wouldn't be here," Tomas admonished him. "And *we* would not have met."

Roger pouted. "True, but you spend all day, every day with them. It's not for the money."

"I like training." Tomas dumped his bowl in the sink and turned around. Pain seared through his gut. "Ah." He grasped the kitchen counter. "Oh, God."

"Tomas." Roger ran around the island and held his lover. "What is it? What's wrong?"

"My stomach. Oh, God," Tomas gasped. "The pain."

Roger helped him to the sofa and sat beside him. "Is it left or right?"

"What?" Tomas gasped through the hazy fog.

"If it's your right side, it's your appendix."

Tomas screwed up his face in thought. "No, oh, uh, it's all over." He wrapped his arms tighter around himself and felt the pain subsided. "Oh, God, I think it's passing." He breathed in and out slowly as Roger rubbed his lower back.

Three knocks sounded on the door.

Roger's head flew to face the door and back, while his hand kept rubbing. "Are you okay yet?"

Tomas breathed and slowly unfurled. "Yeah. The pain's going. I'm okay."

"What the hell *was* that?" Roger asked, staring into the face of the man he loved.

Tomas didn't look good. His pallor was a little grey; eyes a little dull.

Three more knocks sounded on the door.

"Just a minute," Roger yelled, before turning back Tomas. "Someone's impatient."

"Go answer it, I'm okay." Tomas sat up and gently stretched. "I'm okay."

Roger ran to open the door. "What," he barked before running back to the couch.

"Am I interrupting?" Barden asked, seeing a sick-looking Stephanopoulos and a doting Dencott on the couch.

"Yes, you are." Roger looked up. "Detective. What do we owe the pleasure to?" He kept rubbing Tomas's back. "Now's really not the time."

"So I see." He stood in front of them while the two officers waited at the door. "Not feeling well, Mr Stephanopoulos?"

"Not really," Tomas replied, warily eyeing the man off. "I've been off-colour for a while."

"Coming down with something?" Barden studied the two.

"Probably. Is there something you wanted?"

"Yes. Do either of you know Aiden Head?"

Roger's eyes narrowed. "Why?"

Barden noticed the change in Roger's expression. "Because he's dead."

"What!" Roger and Tomas said at the same time.

"Another one?" Tomas went on while Roger stayed quiet and looked away. "What happened?"

"Oh, the usual…drug overdose." Barden kept his eye on Roger until he looked up.

His eyes widened. "You don't suspect *me* do you?"

"Just asking if you knew him, Mr Dencott. He *does work* for *Seralift Productions.* Have the two of you made a movie together?" He watched closely.

Roger looked down. "Two years back after I first started. It was only the one. That's all we ever did. We'd do a movie with one actor and move on to the next, so it wouldn't get stale."

"But that's not how you do things now. You've told me several times the two of you are *exclusive.*" He glanced at Tomas who was looking strangely at Roger. "Are you telling me that's a recent development since Mr Stephanopoulos has joined the stable?"

Roger heaved a sigh. "That's what I'm saying. Marcus saw the chemistry between us and knew I never wanted to work with anyone else, so I suggested it to him that we make movies exclusively. After seeing the footage he got, he agreed wholeheartedly."

"I'm sure he did." Barden saw Tomas's eyes never leave Roger's. "That must make you feel…*special,* Mr Stephanopoulos. That you're… *exclusive.*" He made the quote marks with his fingers.

Tomas finally looked up. "Ah, yeah, yeah it does. I don't think I'd be doing this if I wasn't working with just Roger. I wouldn't feel comfortable otherwise."

"Fucking other men?" Barden asked.

Tomas's eyes narrowed. "That's right."

"Had *you* met Aiden Head?" He kept his eyes trained on Tomas. "What was he like?" He rocked slightly on the balls of his feet.

Tomas shrugged. "Met him once in passing. He seemed okay."

Roger got to his feet. "What's the point in all of this, Detective? Every time one of our own has died you've come bearing photos. *So where are they now?* Am *I* a suspect, or did Aiden just take too much blow? Why are you here?"

Barden produced the photos and held them up for the both of them to see.

Roger stared. "That one looks like the movie we did two years ago." He pointed to the one on the right of him deep-throating Aiden on the back seat of a car. He looked at the one on the left, of Tomas being taken in a classroom. "That could be our movie from last month."

"Yet, your face is not in the photo," Barden replied. "In fact, anytime there's a photo of Mr Stephanopoulos in the throes of passion with someone you claim is you, your head is cut out of it. Why would that be, Mr Dencott?"

Roger shrugged. "How the fuck would I know? Maybe whoever's doing this wants you to think Tomas is cheating on me. By not revealing the whole picture it throws suspicion my way."

"And why would someone want to throw suspicion your way?"

"Again, how the fuck would I know?" Roger stormed over to the window and saw multiple cop cars in the street. "What's going on?" He turned. "Why are there five cop cars on the street and two officers in our doorway?"

"Because, Mr Head was found in the underground car park of this building, Mr Dencott."

"What?" Roger and Tomas cried out.

Tomas struggled to his feet, and Roger rushed to his side to support him. "He was found here? Downstairs? When? How?"

Barden noted their surprise. "We got a call about a suspicious looking scene in a car park and came for a look. We found the body of Mr Head lying between your two cars with three vials of coke."

"What do you mean he was lying between our cars?" Roger spat. "What the hell is going on?"

"It would seem Mr Head felt lovelorn and drove over here this morning, took an overdose, and died for the sake of love," Barden told him. "*Your* love."

Roger watched Barden's face and frowned. "What? What do you mean...?" His voice trailed off, and Tomas laid a hand on his chest. He covered it with his own as he looked at him. Tomas was confused and sick.

"It seems Mr Head was in love with you, Mr Dencott. He used his keys to scratch, '*Roger, I love you*', into your car."

"What!" exploded out of Roger. "*That bastard scratched my car? Was* he *the bastard that did that a couple of months ago too? Was it him?*" He wildly paced back and forth. "I'll kill him. *I swear to God I'll kill him.*"

"Did you, Mr Dencott?" Barden asked.

Roger stopped, hands on hips, staring at Barden. "What? Did I what?"

"Kill him?"

"Don't be absurd." Roger moved over to him. "*I didn't kill anyone, least of all Aiden Fucking Head.*"

Barden raised a brow. "Yet here he is, in *your* car park, next to *your* car, after scratching that he loved you into it. And yes, I found that report about your car, nasty business that was. Four tyres, sugar in the tank, needed a complete overhaul.

"Did he do that, too?" Roger asked. "Did he give it a second try?"

"Were you lovers, Mr Dencott?"

Roger blinked. "What?"

"Were you and Mr Head lovers?"

Another blink. "No. I told you we did one movie together years ago. We were never lovers. I never fuck my castmates outside of work."

"And yet, here you are with Mr Stephanopoulos." He glanced at Tomas. "Who doesn't look so good."

Roger moved to his side. "Sit down." He sat beside him. "You okay?"

Tomas shook his head. "I don't feel good."

"The pain's come back?" Roger rubbed his back.

"No. I just feel a bit light-headed." He covered Roger's hand with his. "I'll be okay."

"Plan on killing another lover, Mr Dencott?"

Roger's head turned sharply. "What? I didn't kill anyone and I sure as hell wouldn't kill Tomas. I love him."

"Of course you do, because you *never* fuck castmates out of work."

"Mmm," Roger mumbled. "It was different this time. We met and got together before Tomas started working for Marcus."

"Introduce him, did you?"

"No. I think that was Violet who'd found out about him through Bette Olander. Are we done?" He sighed and attended to Tomas.

"Afraid not, Mr Dencott. I must insist on you coming down to the station for a full questioning. We need to go all the way back to the beginning."

"What?" Roger protested. "You've *got* to be kidding me?"

"Are you refusing to come down to the station of your own volition?"

"Yes, I bloody well am," Roger said.

"Then, Mr Dencott, I am arresting you on suspicion of murder. You have the right to remain silent, anything you say or do will be used against you in a court of law. You have the right to an attorney. If you cannot afford an attorney, one will be appointed to you. Do you understand these rights as they have been read to you?"

"What? You can't be serious?" Roger clung to Tomas as the officers came over and produced cuffs. "You're arresting me for murder?"

"On *suspicion* of murder," Barden corrected and indicated for the two officers to take him.

They hauled him to his feet, put his hands behind his back, and cuffed him.

"I can't believe you're doing this, Barden. I'll have your guts for garters before the end of the day." Roger struggled as he was taken out of the room.

"Roger, Roger, don't do anything rash. I'll call Marcus. Roger, I love you," Tomas called weakly.

"I suggest you call an ambulance instead, Mr Stephanopoulos. You look ill." Barden frowned.

"I'll be all right, Detective, it's just a bug." Tomas's steely look of determination was all show, for he was a quivering mess on the inside. He waited for Barden to leave and close the door before collapsing on the sofa. "Oh, God, oh, God. I feel, oh, God. Get a grip, Stephanopoulos. Your man's in trouble, and he needs you." Taking a deep breath, he phoned Marcus and told him what had happened. Marcus promised to get their lawyer down there immediately.

Next, he called Bette to cancel all sessions until further notice and told her what was happening. She promised to round up the troops if they were needed.

He grabbed his bag, made his way slowly downstairs, and caught a cab to the station, where stumbled inside to the front desk.

"You okay?" The clerk stared at Tomas.

"I don't feel good," he replied. "I'm here for Detective Barden. He brought a friend of mine in for questioning."

"Sure. I'll just give him a call." The officer made the call and directed Tomas to his office.

"You really need an ambulance, Mr Stephanopoulos," Barden said upon seeing him. "Do you do drugs, Mr Stephanopoulos?"

Tomas frowned. "No, I don't."

"Then what's making you sick?" Barden sat on the corner of his desk.

"I don't know." Tomas struggled to think. "Food poisoning…I don't know."

Barden frowned in concentration. "Lover boy's in with the lawyer. He was here within minutes of us bringing him in."

"Good," Tomas muttered. "Can I get some water?"

"Sure." Barden hit the cooler and was back in thirty seconds. "Here. So what have you been eating that would make you sick?"

Tomas sipped the cold water, feeling it slide down his parched throat. "I don't know. We had some Chinese the other night, we eat breakfast at home, I eat lunch at Bette's, and then we have something at the studio."

"Eat anything out of the ordinary?" Barden made notes in his book.

"No." Tomas shook his head. "I try to eat healthy food. Roger jokes about the food I do have. It's always the healthiest I can find. He hates my milk."

"He doesn't drink it?"

"No. Only I do." His eyes felt like sandpaper. "I want to see him."

"Not until he's finished with his lawyer, and then we talk to him.

So it will be a while." He watched Tomas close his eyes, his hand drop the cup, and his head slump before he collapsed onto the floor. "Get an ambulance," he yelled into the station before tending to Tomas. "Wake up, damn it."

Ten minutes later the ambulance arrived and carted him away on a stretcher.

Barden burst into the interview room. "What poison have you been feeding Stephanopoulos?" He slammed his hands onto the table.

Roger and his lawyer jumped. "What?"

"What poison have you been giving the kid?" Barden repeated, leaning closer.

"I have to protest," the lawyer jumped in.

"I don't, I haven't," Roger cried.

"Bullshit," Barden yelled. "Stephanopoulos just collapsed in my office and he's been taken away by ambulance to the hospital. He's clearly not well, and I want to know what he's been fed."

"Nothing." Roger stood and slammed his hands on the table as well. He leant in close to Barden so they were nose to nose. "I haven't poisoned anyone, let alone my boyfriend. I love him; why would I want to hurt him?"

"What about the milk?" Barden went head to head. "You don't drink it?"

"No, because it's shit stuff and I'm allergic to it."

"Or is it because you poisoned it?"

"I'm done with this garbage," Roger said. "I want to go to him." He looked at his lawyer in a panic. "I want to go to him."

"Well, you can't," Barden sneered.

"Well, someone has to," Roger cried. "He can't be alone."

"So he won't die?" Barden asked.

"What? No! So he's not alone," Roger replied. "I want to go to him."

"No. You'll stay here until we're done and that kid is well enough to talk. Is there anyone else to call?"

Roger thought about it. "Call Bette Olander. She'll go," he told the lawyer.

"Fine," Barden snapped and shoved a finger at Roger. "*You* sit down. You're going nowhere." He raced back to his office and hailed the officers from before. "Get back to Dencott's place and get the carton of milk from the fridge. Get it to the hospital lab. I think there's poison in it and they can test Stephanopoulos. I think the poor kid's being put out of commission." The officers nodded and left.

Barden went back to his desk and laid out the paperwork. Dencott was getting rid of previous lovers so that Stephanopoulos didn't find out? Or so they didn't talk? But talk about what? What was Dencott hiding?

CARLOS

"What the fuck is happening here?" Harry bellowed. He paced across his office and back. "Your girlfriend gets killed, and now Aneeka is kidnapped all because of the photos. *What* photos?"

"Photos of Carlos's girlfriend's house and the two intruders," Tony stated.

"And now that means they're all combined." Harry was pissed. Pissed off that the golden Adonis he'd put so much money into was causing him so much trouble. "Is trouble your middle name?" he asked. "'Cause that's all you've caused me."

"I had nothing to do with this," Carlos yelled. "Aneeka took those photos, she told the cops those guys killed Rosalee. That had *nothing to do with me.*"

"Well, who are they and what do they want?" Harry continued.

"I don't know," Carlos yelled back. "I have no idea who they are, or what they want, or why they killed Rosalee. I...don't...know!" Carlos was frustrated and overwhelmed. His life had been turned upside down since that night in Mykonos, and now it was continuing. What the fuck was going on?

"What do we do?" Tony asked. He had stood straight and tall the whole time, not moving. Army training.

Harry paced. Harry puffed. Harry waved his hands in the air. "I don't know." He picked up the note and read it again. "Photos. They want photos. Where are those photos? What the fuck do they want them for?"

"Because they're photos of the men that killed Rosalee and tried to frame me for it," Carlos said. He wiped his face and leant against Harry's desk. "They don't want anyone knowing they were there."

"*Why* did she have to take photos of them?" Harry asked.

"And tell the police and give them copies," Carlos added. "I was there when she told them she had photos. It was the day after, and she gave them to them after I left."

"So, if anyone was still lurking around, they would know about them."

Carlos nodded. "Probably."

"And that's why her house was trashed," Tony added. "They must have been looking for them."

"Did she still have them?" Harry paused thoughtfully, puffing on his cigar. "She made copies to hand over but did she make more?"

"Don't know," Carlos said, crossing his arms. He'd been nothing but trouble, and now he was feeling guilty for bringing this upon everyone.

"But she should still have the negatives," Tony said. "Does she have a bank vault, a safety deposit, house safe? Does she keep personal stuff somewhere special?"

Harry thought. "I know she puts her valuable stuff in a safe in her home when she travels."

"Where is it?" Tony asked.

Harry thought some more. "In a small hidden room…" His eyes narrowed. "Between her studio and the…stairs. Under the stairs." He frowned. "Something to do with the stairs."

"Okay, here's the plan," Tony said, checking his watch. "It's twelve now. We'll go and search her house. Do you have a key or know if she leaves one out?"

"No, no, I have one for emergencies." Harry pulled out a huge keyring full of about a hundred keys from his desk drawer.

"Right, we'll go search and be back at Carlos's by three-thirty. Then we'll take the next step."

"What's the next step?" Carlos asked.

"Doing what they want," Tony said, taking the key Harry gave him.

"What about an alarm system?"

"Ah," Harry faltered. "She had a new one installed, but if they got her, they probably cut it or something."

"Do you know the code, just in case they didn't?"

"Uh…" Harry paced again. "It's uh…uh…uh…" He tapped his forehead. "It's something to do with…6547." He snapped his fingers. "6547."

"Right," Tony said. "Let's go, Carlos, we need to find those pictures." He started for the door but stopped. "What's the safe code?"

Harry shrugged. "Probably the same code. I think she uses the same one for everything."

"Not a very safe thing to do," Tony replied. "Come along, Carlos."

They drove to Aneeka's and walked up the stairs to the porch with Tony on guard for any strange vehicles or lurking strangers. He unlocked the door and stepped inside. The alarm pad blinked to his right and he quickly tapped the code in. Closing the door made it blink green.

"I'll check the place out first, see how they got her." Tony went straight for the back door and found the light globe untwisted, and a pot plant knocked over. He walked over to the back gate and found it unlocked and a cut padlock on the ground. "Mmm," he mumbled.

Going back inside, he shut and locked the door, and they went upstairs to her studio. Tony measured walls and layouts and started pushing wall panels. He pulled objects, shifted prints and finally heard a click.

The wall panel slid aside, and they saw a small room with two huge safes, one on either side, that would have been neatly packed away under the stairs in the hallway.

"Nice," Tony said. "But which bloody one?"

Carlos hovered behind him. "Try both. It's one-thirty."

Tony got to work with the safe on his left and used the same code as the security system. It opened, and he quickly pored through the paperwork and small boxes. "No negatives." He closed the door and locked it then turned his attention to the second safe. Same code, same time to open it.

There were boxes of negatives neatly filed away by date. He quickly found the box, and they both checked through it, finding the right negatives in a few seconds.

"We've got them, let's go." Tony put everything back, and they hightailed it out of there and back to Carlos's not even noticing the two men following in a car.

One hour later the phone rang.

Carlos jumped. He'd been expecting it, but they had been sitting in silence so the sound was incredibly loud in such a small quiet room.

"Answer it," Tony said.

After taking a deep breath, and wiping his sweaty palms on his pants, Carlos picked up the phone. "Hello."

"Ah, Carlos Stephanopoulos himself," the voice said, the Greek accent coming through. "Do you have the negatives and photos?"

"Yes."

"Good. You're to take them to Venice Beach Pier. You are to go underneath and leave them in rubbish bin."

"What if I don't?"

"Then she is dead."

"Why are you doing this? Why did you kill Rosalee?"

"Because we were told to."

Carlos's eyes widened and he looked at Tony who was listening next to him. "What? What do you mean you were told to?"

"It doesn't matter, you need to leave the photos in bin under pier. Leave them and walk away. Go there now. Now, Mr Stephanopoulos, now and do not tell police."

The phone went dead.

Carlos breathed and stared at the phone in his hand.

"He didn't tell us if they'd let her go, though." Tony grabbed the phone and disconnected the call. "And that could be a problem." He called Harry. "They want us to deliver the photos to a bin under Venice Beach Pier, now. How fast can you get men down there... Right... Right... Right...we're off." He replaced the phone. "Let's go."

"But they said tell no one," Carlos stated, following Tony out the door.

"They said don't tell the cops, Harry's men aren't cops." Tony bolted down the stairs with Carlos on his heels.

"We could get her killed," Carlos shouted, running after Tony to the car.

"Get in," Tony snapped. "And keep your bloody voice down." They sped off. "Look, they could kill her anyway whether they have the photos or not."

"God." Carlos ran a hand through his hair. "Why the hell is this happening?"

"Let's go over this," Tony said. "You get involved with Rosalee, then these thugs kill her and try to frame you, and when they find out photos were taken by the neighbour—"

"How did they find out, though?" Carlos butted in. "Really?"

"They probably kept an eye on Rosalee's house to see who came and went. If they spotted Aneeka talking to the cops and handing over photos, they may have looked into her, found out what she knew, put two and two together, and figured she may have seen something. So they grabbed her."

They pulled into the car park at the wharf. "Right, listen closely. You give me five minutes to get into position, and then get out and slowly go down to the bin and leave the package. Then get the hell out of there and back here. You got it?" He saw Carlos's stunned expression and grabbed his arm. "You got it?" he demanded, snapping him out of his trance.

"Yeah." Carlos swallowed the lump in his throat. "Yeah."

"Right." Tony opened the door and looked around. "Give me five minutes, check your watch."

It was ten past four.

Luiz had watched the proceedings from the street as Roger was taken away, and followed Tomas as he'd taken a cab to the police station, then followed the ambulance to the hospital. Putting his plan into motion, he'd gone back to his hotel and changed into the outfit he would need to blend in.

He parted his hair on the side and slicked it down before packing up his toiletries. Today, he was leaving, never to return. Today was the finale of his plan. All phases were accomplished, the end was nigh, and time was up.

Shoving his toiletry bag into his case, he picked up a picture of Tomas. He'd taken it in Mykonos when they were on the small island, away from prying eyes and Tomas was asleep in the afterglow of their lovemaking. His face was soft and serene as he slept, dreaming of things he'd done and was going to do. Dreaming of happiness such as he'd never known.

He kissed the photo. "God, I love you, Tomas. And now that Roger is gone we will be together, for always." He tucked the picture into his pocket and walked out to his car, depositing his case in the trunk. He returned to collect some blankets and a box of food, then shut the door and put them in the front seat of his car. Leaving the hotel, he drove to the hospital and parked near the closest entrance possible.

*****

Bette, Bertha and Willow made it to the hospital and stood guard outside Tomas's room. He was strung up with tubes and machines so there was no way anyone was going to get their Tomas, even if they had to fight off any attacker.

They watched as blood was drawn, and officers arrived, handing over a carton of milk which the doctor took away. They waited while Tomas was given drugs and the doctors came rushing back. They watched as the doctor ordered ten milligrams of some medication and then inserted it into the drug bag. And they listened while the doctor told them Tomas had been poisoned over a period of time. They sighed in relief when they found out he was going to be okay. And when he was moved from the ICU to a private room they took a break.

Willow went off in search of food, and Bette went in search of a phone to call Roger's lawyer. Bertha went in search of the ladies' room and when she was done walked back to Tomas's room. As she turned the corner into the hallway, she saw an orderly pushing a patient into the lift at the other end of the hall. The patient *looked* like Tomas, and she stopped. *Why would...?* She looked up at the orderly, and while she didn't recognise the blond hair, she definitely recognised the aqua eyes.

"Oh, my God," she muttered as the doors closed. She hastened to Tomas's room to make sure it was him before pounding down the hallway in her jewelled orthotic slip-ons to the nurse's station, colliding with Bette and Willow. "He's gone," she shrieked. "Tomas Stephanopoulos has been taken. He's been kidnapped."

The whole hospital went into lockdown, and Bertha ran for the lift. "Come on," she yelled to Bette and Willow. "I know who took him."

"How do you know?" Bette asked on the way down.

"Because I know those eyes anywhere," she said.

They bolted out of the hospital and in the direction of the other entrance, seeing Tomas being loaded into the back seat of a car as they rounded a corner.

"Stop, thief, kidnapper," Bertha yelled, catching him by surprise.

He slammed the door and climbed into the driver's side before screeching out of the driveway and down the road.

"Oh, no, he's getting away," Bertha cried.

"But I got the licence plate and car make and model." Bette flashed the paper she'd written it down on. "Let's call Roger."

They hastened back to the public phone booth and called the station, asking to speak to Roger's lawyer.

Barden stayed with Roger while the lawyer took the call. He had a silent stare-off with him as they waited, hoping he'd say something. He didn't.

The lawyer came back in. "Stephanopoulos has just been kidnapped by a man dressed as an orderly. The women got the make, model, and plate of the car. The officers are checking it now, but they say they know who did it."

"What?" Roger stormed to his feet. "Someone kidnapped Tomas? Who? Who took him?"

The lawyer looked at him. "Some guy named Luiz Manning."

"Luiz?" Roger felt the wind blow out of him and slumped into his chair. "I thought he was out of Tomas's life."

Barden frowned. *Why does that name sound so familiar?* He quickly left the room and went back to his desk, poring through the papers until he finally found it on a list for ex-members of *Seralift.* Luiz Manning. Slapping the paper, he muttered, "Knew I'd heard of you before." He barged back into the interview room. "*Who* is Luiz Manning to you?"

Roger looked up in a daze. "What?"

"*Who* is Luiz Manning to you?"

Roger shook his head in frustration. "No one. Not personally. I've never met him, but have heard all about him."

"So, why would he poison and kidnap Stephanopoulos?"

Confusion set in. "What? Why would he poison…?" Roger vaguely asked.

"Well, unless *you* poisoned the milk lover boy drank, I'd say Manning did it to get you out of the way so he could take him. I had officers get the milk from your place and take it for analysis. Nerium Oleander. It makes you weak and sick, but only kills you after a large enough period of exposure. So who is he?"

Roger warily eyed the detective. "He was Bertha St John's fiancé for over a year. When they were in Mykonos over the summer he met Tomas, and they had a fling except Tomas didn't know he was Bertha's fiancé. They both dumped his sorry arse and came here. Luiz only turned up once at a club that I knew of until the other week when Tomas came across him at the beach. They had coffee in a café and talked." He shrugged. "That's it, as far as I know."

It was all starting to fit together for Barden. "Was Luiz the spurned lover?"

"I suppose," Roger said. "Look, what are you doing to find Tomas? He's sick, he needs care and needs to be in a hospital, not dragged off somewhere by some nut job."

Barden waved his hand. "Don't worry about it. We've got an APB out on the car. We'll find him. Would you put it past this Luiz to try and set you up for four murders so Tomas would be free for him?" He laid photos of all four dead porn stars before Roger on the table.

Roger thought about it. "I've never met the guy, but from what Tomas told me he was very controlling and obsessed on Mykonos. He followed Tomas to an island and kept him there overnight."

"Against his will?"

Roger blushed. "Well, no, that I know of."

"Mmm." Barden sat down. "So, what we have is a spurned lover who wants nothing more than his lover back and will stop at nothing to *get* him back."

CARLOS

Tony left to get into position, and after waiting five minutes, Carlos followed. Making his way down to the sand, he walked underneath the wharf and looked around for the bin. He found it, and placed the package inside. Glancing around, he had turned to go back when a sharp pain stabbed through his head, and all he saw was black.

"Quick, grab the photos," a man said and started dragging Carlos toward the water. "Have you got them?"

"Yeah."

"Then help me."

The two men quickly carried Carlos to the water where they had a small inflatable boat. They dumped him on board, revved the engine, and sailed away, glancing back to see Tony and several men running toward the water.

"We've been seen," one man said.

"And there are cops," the other said. "We said no cops."

They watched the cops take down Tony and roared off into the distance.

"What the fuck are you doing?" Tony yelled. "They've got a hostage."

"Yeah, yeah," Detective Star said, clicking the cuffs shut. "And what hostage would that be?" They started leading him up the sand toward the stairs.

"Aneeka Ne Masta," Tony spat. "You've just stuffed up a hostage negotiation." He struggled and managed to push Star away. "And now they have Carlo Stefan and you've got me in cuffs, you dick wank."

"Who do you think—" Star dived at him, but Drew held him back.

"What do you mean they have Ne Masta and now Stefan?" Drew asked.

"They kidnapped Aneeka Ne Masta because she'd taken photos of them coming and going from Rosalee's house. She fingered them, and they broke into her house looking for the photos. *They're* the ones who trashed her place, and they wanted Carlos to get them and deliver them."

"How did you get into her house? Did you have the damn code?" Drew asked.

"Yes," Tony sneered. "*And* we got the negatives. We were in the middle of the hand off when you dick wanks fucked it up. And now they have Stefan."

Star lurched at him. "Well, if you hadn't been lurking around maybe we would have caught the guys we've had under surveillance since we found out about them."

Drew got between them.

"You had them under surveillance?" Tony asked incredulously. "Then you know who they are and where they have Aneeka?"

"Of course, we know where they are, but it's not like we're gonna tell you," Star raved.

Tony roundhouse kicked him. "She could be dead because of you," he screamed and got taken down by ten cops as Drew helped Star to his feet. He was hauled away. "She could be dead because of you, Star. How's your boss gonna deal with one of his detectives letting the thugs keep a kidnap victim?" He was taken up to the van and shut inside.

"You okay?" Drew asked, gaping at Star.

"Just fine." He spat blood out. "Let's lock that prick up."

But an hour later, Star was left red-faced after a dressing down from his superior after *he'd* had a chat with Harry DeVille.

"*You knew* where they were and where they were going, but you didn't know they had a world-famous photographer under lock and key?"

"Um, no sir," Star muttered, shifting from one foot to the other.

"How goddamn incompetent are you, Star?" Captain Ward yelled, his veins popping out of his temple as his face turned red. "I should demote you." He thrust a finger in Star's face. "But I'll wait to do that *until* you have told Tony Vega everything you know about the two men in those photographs and *what you've done* with them under surveillance. You will tell him *everything* and then help him find Ms Ne Masta *and* Mr Stefan safe and sound." He looked from Star to Drew and back again. "*Both of you.* Is that understood?"

"Yes, sir."

"Good, now Vega is ex-army and C.I.A., and I trust *him*, not *you* right now, so you do what you're damn well told." Ward strode around his desk. "Get out."

The detectives hurried back to their desks to find Tony poring over paperwork.

"I want to know everything you know. Who are they, where they're from, and how long they've been here? What they eat, where they shit, and who they've fucked. If you don't know, find out," Tony said at the two brooding men. "Let's get started."

Star slumped into his seat, crossed his arms, and refused to talk.

Drew did it for him. "After we received the photos from Ms Ne Masta we tracked down their license plate but found it had been stolen two weeks earlier. As luck would have it, a man was picked up down the street from Stefan's getting himself off in his car. It was a different car than the one outside Ms Brentworth's place, but the man fitted the description. After he was charged with indecent exposure we put a tail on him. We've been tailing him and his partner since. From Stefan's place to Ne Masta's, back to their hotel, which we've checked into. They used aliases. The man we picked up is Dimitri Yustoff, of Greece. We have passports and driver's licences."

He handed the papers over. "But he's been using different names wherever he goes. We also tried to connect him with some assaults; three women, attacked by an unknown assailant. We wondered if it might be one of them. He was seen masturbating at a Carlo Stefan movie a few weeks back."

"Who hasn't," Tony said, looking at the photos of the man. "Do you know when they could have taken Aneeka?" He continued dealing with Drew.

"In the early hours of this morning," Drew said. "They were out and about, but we lost them in the back streets, and when we realised they could be going back to the scene of the crime, we headed over there."

"They weren't there?" Tony asked.

Drew's eyes dropped. "No."

Tony paced back and forth. "The first thing we need to do is get to the hotel room, get a team to Aneeka's and Rosalee's and Carlos's to find out if they've been back. If they think we're searching for them they may think of hiding in the most obvious place on the grounds it would be the last place we'd look. Do you have surveillance on them now?"

"We did have. They went to the marina and rented a small boat. But they didn't bring it back, so we've lost them."

"Here's what we're gonna do. We're gonna hit 'em hard. We're gonna take out every place we can think of and wait. We're gonna put out an APB on all the cars we know they drive, *and* on them. Get their descriptions to every cop in the city. They have two hostages now. They either haven't gone far and have changed their car, or they've already gone. Get cops to every car rental company and flash their photos, someone will recognise them." He looked down at the paper in his hand. "For their sake, they have to."

*****

Carlos came to, tied up, gagged, and lying next to a body on a bed. The blindfold offered no ability to identify it, but he hoped it was Aneeka. He heard two men arguing in Greek and struggled to listen.

"We have to do what he says."

"But what is it he wants?"

"I don't know?"

"But he asked us to kidnap these people."

"We just do, we do not ask questions."

"But we could be in big trouble now."

"We stick it out and wait for him to call."

"What does he want with these people?"

"I don't know, but he told us to get those photos."

"We shouldn't have been so obvious. We should have done it at night then no one would have seen."

"But we didn't, and now we're trying to fix the problem."

"But the cops could find us."

"We wait for his call."

"But—"

"End of discussion!"

They fell silent, and Carlos lay back to rest. What a grade A cock-up this all was. Aneeka got kidnapped because she saw them in Rosalee's yard, and what was he kidnapped for? And where were Tony and Harry's guards? And where was he…?

*****

Teams of cops swarmed every part of town; Carlos's apartment, Aneeka's house, the hotel where, surprise, surprise, the men had left without paying, the movie theatre, take out joints, car rental shops, and any small marina or dock up the coast.

They found the boat with blood in the bottom.

But that was all.

Nothing more; nothing less.

They kept surveillance teams in every place and moved on, hoping someone would remember something.

Had anyone seen two men carrying an unconscious porn star up the beach to the car park? Had anyone seen suspicious behaviour in the neighbourhood?

Harry put every man he had out to talk to people they knew, letting them know that Carlos had been kidnapped and if they saw anything to call him immediately. The gay community rallied, the porn community rallied, and all put ears to the ground for information while keeping the news to themselves.

Harry refused to call Carlos's parents, figuring, why disturb them with news like this when he hoped he could find Carlos and bring him home, because when push came to shove, he had grown quite fond of the boy and considered him almost as a son.

TOMAS

Luiz floored it out of the city and up the coast. He had to get the hell away from Miami and Florida so the cops couldn't get them. There was no way he was going down for all of the crimes he'd committed. Oh, no. Roger could take the rap for those while he sailed home free with Tomas.

He glanced over his shoulder. "Okay, Tomas? They gave you your meds, so you should be okay soon." He leant over and covered his lover with a blanket as he slept. "You rest, you need it." Knowing they had Roger in custody offered him some relief, and with luck, time to get as far away as possible.

He crossed the border into Georgia and debated which way to go. Across country would be good. He headed for Alabama and made it into a little town in Mississippi by nightfall. Crawling through the one horse town, he found a room in a seedy hotel, and under the blinking neon lights, carried Tomas into the room and closed the door.

*****

The man crawled to a stop outside the motel. He'd been tailing the car since Miami when he'd seen the man dressed as an orderly wheel Stephanopoulos out of the hospital and dump him in the back seat of his car. He'd taken off when recognised by three old broads and he'd followed since. He thought about how he could execute his plan and drove around the corner to find another way in.

*****

"Have you found him yet?" Roger stood up as Barden came into the room.

"Not yet. But Manning has to stop for sleep sometime," he said. "We'll find him. We've got officers checking every motel now."

Roger slumped into his seat with a sigh. "I should be out there looking."

"And where would you look?"

"I dunno."

"Then there's not much point you being out there because you'll only get in the way."

"But he needs me!" Roger yelled.

"What he *needs* is a hospital and real cops to find him," Barden replied. "Now, we have spoken to Ms St John, and there wasn't a whole lot she could tell me about Manning. She met him as a trainer, and it seems he trained her in the bedroom as well. They got engaged, and she broke it off when she found out he'd," he checked his notes, "seduced poor young Tomas with his sharp tongue and deft fingers. Not to mention his sizable cock that could do wonders." He grimaced and shut his notebook. "Gross. We've put out a description of him, but it's possible he's done a dye job on his hair and probably has Stephanopoulos covered over. We're doing everything we can."

*****

The man pulled to a stop at the back of the motel and turned off his lights. He had to be quick and quiet. No one could know. Pulling his gun from his pants, he rolled on the silencer and picked up his lock pick. He popped the trunk and left the car.

*****

Luiz was busy changing clothes and washing up. He needed to get Tomas out of the hospital gown and into something more appropriate. *Like me,* he thought, after taking off the gown and seeing Tomas naked on the bed. *Oh, God, how I've missed you.* He enveloped him whole, sucking the cock that had started it all. *Oh, God, how good it is.* He got a groan in return and swallowed when Tomas came.

He worked his way up his lean body and passionately kissed his mouth. Tomas responded weakly, and Luiz took advantage, rubbing their cocks together, sliding his hands all over. His leg was over Tomas as he explored the body he'd wanted for so long, and when he was done with the front, he rolled him over and started on the back. "Oh, God." He slid inside and tried to keep himself in check. "Oh, God, oh, God, oh, God," he squealed. Moving back and forth he was in pure heaven and heard not a single sound except for the beating of two hearts. He couldn't help himself, he sped up, thrusting wildly into the man he loved, so encapsulated he didn't notice the door open and close.

"Oh, God, oh, God, oh, God."

"Oh, God indeed," the man said.

Luiz's head spun around to see a man holding a gun and a bullet coming for his forehead.

Five down, none to go.

Luiz's blood splattered and he slumped backwards off the body of his lover, his eyes staring at the ceiling, his mouth in an o shape. O for orgasm? O for ecstasy? O for terror?

No one would miss Luiz Manning. Not his mother, Sheila Manning, who lived alone in New York with the exception of a couple of cats. She hated his guts and had disowned him at seventeen upon finding out he was a fag who fucked the underage neighbourhood boys, and so he'd run away to Miami and joined a studio making porn movies. And his sperm donor father, whom his mother had met in Santorini twenty-six years earlier and had a holiday fling with, certainly wouldn't miss him. No, Andros Poulos had never acknowledged his illegitimate son, or paid for him, and never would.

For Andros Poulos *never* acknowledged his illegitimate children.

No, no one would miss Luiz Manning at all.

The man rolled Luiz all the way off and grabbed the clothes on the floor, slipping a hoodie over Tomas's head and pulling track pants up his legs. He noted the sizable package and moved on, tying sneakers onto his feet. He hefted Tomas over his shoulder and looked out the window before opening the door. Looking left and right, he silently closed it behind him and walked back to his car where he lifted the trunk and placed Tomas inside. All he needed now, was to get to Chicago.

CARLOS

The phone rang.

"Hello…yes…all right…yes…okay…yes…okay…bye."

"Was that him?"

"Yes."

"What did he want?"

"He said to wait till dark and kill the woman, burn her and her photographs, and bring the boy back to him."

"All the way to Greece?"

"No, he's not in Greece."

"Then where is he?"

"Here in United States."

An intake of breath. "He's here?"

"Yes."

And we're supposed to take him where?"

"He did not say."

"But how do we know where to take him?"

"He said to call him when job was done."

"And we have to take him in the car?"

"Of course, we cannot fly."

"But what if we are caught?"

"If we are careful we should not be."

"But surely there are people looking for us now."

"I'm sure, but we must leave under cover of dark."

"And where do we dump body?"

"There is old quarry on way. We dump her, burn her and leave."

"On way to where?"

"On way out of town."

At ten-fifteen the next morning, the police rolled through town looking for a car. They found it in the *Shady Seeds Motel* parked out front of room 29. After knocking, they had the attendant open it and found the body of Luiz Manning dead on the bed. There was no sign of Tomas Stephanopoulos except for the hospital gown he'd been wearing. The officers radioed in and called their coroner.

*****

Barden heard the news fifteen minutes later, right after he heard the APB for a Carlo Stefan. Formerly Stephanopoulos. "What?" he'd muttered as he listened. Could they possibly be? He made calls to L.A. and found out that yes indeed, Carlo Stefan, formerly Carlos Stephanopoulos of Mykonos, was missing, feared kidnapped, and the police were on the hunt.

The man who had Carlos was headed east. Barden dug an old map out of his desk and spread it out. With a red marker he circled L.A., and moved east along the main highway, and then circled Miami and headed north. He left the lines unfinished, but circled a big space of the country. They could be going anywhere.

*****

The man pulled into a gas station. He'd driven all night and made it across Tennessee, but needed gas and food. Not to mention a hot shower and a pussy to fuck. He needed to lay his own cock in a good accommodating whore, and he couldn't wait. But first, he had to take care of this one little thing.

Standing at the counter paying for his food, he glanced out to see the man from the car behind looking strangely at his own. Walking outside, he found out why. Tomas was banging on the inside of the trunk, yelling out for help.

He didn't panic. He simply looked at the man, pulled his jacket aside to show his gun, and proceeded to get in his car while the man's pump flooded over. He drove away while the attendant came running out.

*****

An hour later, Barden got a call about a man being trapped inside of a trunk, yelling for help, and the owner of the car had a gun. The licence, TGS 333, had been checked and the plate stolen, but a description had been taken, and now there was an APB out for him. Barden uncapped his red marker and circled the town Luiz had been found in, the town the new guy had been found in, and connected the dots.

He was moving north.

He followed the main highway and came to a stop. He finished off the other line and found they could be heading in the same direction. He went to see Roger in his cell. "Does Stephanopoulos have a brother?"

Roger lazily sat up. "What?"

"Do I *really* need to repeat myself?"

"No." Roger sighed. "Two. Carlos and Pedro."

"Who also happen to be porn stars?"

Roger stood up, intrigued by where the conversation was going, and moved over to the bars. "What? Why? What's happened?"

"It seems that both brothers are in the porn industry and both have been kidnapped."

"What!" Roger exclaimed. "You're kidding."

"No. I've been in contact with L.A. Carlos has been missing for nearly twenty-four hours."

"Fuck," Roger said. "So, where are they going?"

"After detailing it all on a map, my gut tells me one place."

*****

The man pulled up behind an old dump site on the outskirts of some clunky little town in Kentucky. It was midnight, and he needed rest.

"Let me out, help," Tomas yelled pitifully, banging on the trunk.

"Ugh." The man got out, opened the trunk, and stuck his gun in Tomas's face. "Shut it, and you won't be dead."

Tomas lay back, shielding his eyes, dazed, confused and scared as hell. With everything that had happened, he had no idea what was going on, and he was sick, tired, and hungry. "Water," he croaked through dry lips.

The man slammed the trunk, dug through his supplies of food, and opened the trunk again. "Here." He handed over a sandwich and can of soda. "Now shut up." He slammed the trunk and settled back in the driver's seat.

Tomas greedily ate the sandwich and drank the soda. *Who the hell is he?* With a head that was pounding, he curled up on his side with his arm under his head. He didn't know what the hell was going on, but he wasn't about to find out in the trunk of a car.

*****

"Where?" Roger asked. "Where are they taking him?"

"Chicago," Barden said, proud of his detective skills and putting it all together. "Does he know anyone in Chicago?"

Roger thought about everything Tomas had ever told him and shook his head. "No."

Barden lost his wind. "Well, I'm flying out there to see what the cops know. You can stay here until I learn something." He left with Roger calling out behind him. After a quick rest at home and a four hour flight to Chicago, he was in the captain's office talking about the case.

PEDRO

By Friday, Pedro was so on edge he was snapping at Angelina.

"What the fuck is going on?" She pulled him up on his behaviour after school.

"I'm sorry." He took hold of her arms. "I'm sorry. I'm just…"

"Scared about what's going to happen," she finished the sentence.

He looked into her eyes. "What do you know?" he asked slowly.

"That that psycho bitch left another present and it's all going to end tonight. Yeah…" She nodded. "I heard you all in the hallway yesterday."

"Jesus, Angie." Pedro swiped a hand through his hair. "We were trying to keep that from you."

"Why?" she demanded. "The bitch wants me dead, I have a right to face her and defend myself. Besides, *we* have bodyguards."

"But *we* don't know when she's going to strike or what she'll do," Pedro reminded her.

Angelina moved her left arm. "Can't be any worse than what my father did."

Pedro sighed. "Aw, babe, come here." He enveloped her in his arms. "I'm sorry you have to go through all of this because of me."

She pushed away and whacked him on the arm. "It's not because of you, you idiot. It's because of my father. So how bad can *she* be?"

"I just hope we don't find out."

*****

The woman had packed up her things. She didn't have much, so it all fitted into her suitcase and large overnight bag. Between her clothes and the baby's things, she was leaving with more than she'd come with, and it was all happening tonight.

She would be moving into Pedro's tonight. That whore would finally be out of the way, and Pedro would be all hers. Hers and the baby's.

She left the apartment forever, taking a taxi to Pedro's place, arriving just as they left. She told the cab driver to continue onto 69 knowing that it would soon be happening. She'd be in Pedro's arms and soon be Mrs Stephanopoulos. She was so lost in her dreams she didn't see the car following.

*****

Stavros had prepared his kit, packed his bags, and checked out of the hotel. He wouldn't be hanging around anymore, he had his orders to do the deed and get the hell out of there, and he had two days to get to his destination.

He drove into New York and waited down the road from Pedro's, watching as they drove off, surprised to see four people in the car, but not surprised to see a red-haired woman in a taxi drive past and follow the Mustang.

He followed the taxi.

*****

Andros dressed. It wouldn't be happening for hours, but he wanted to be ready. A slick light grey suit with black shirt and silver tie was going to get him into 69. He was going to see for himself Pedro's debauched lifestyle and was going to stick around until the deed was done.

*****

Mark parked opposite the back door, and he and Sara-Michelle ushered Pedro and Angelina in quickly. The sun was setting, casting shadows amongst the buildings, and Mark came back out to scour the alley. He checked behind trash cans, over fences, and around other cars. When he was satisfied, he went back inside.

*****

The woman paid the taxi driver and climbed out. It was a quarter to seven, and she would be waiting outside for him when he finished work. Maybe even sooner.

She spied the Mustang, but kept walking down the alley. It was ridiculous to think a pregnant woman should be carrying her own case and bag, but she had to get it done.

Moving past the car, she found a safe spot behind an old brown clunker, put her luggage down, and sat on her case to wait. She pulled a sandwich out of her handbag. It was going to be a long night.

*****

Stavros crawled to a stop in the street and saw the alley was free and clear of guards. Shifting gears, he cruised past the back door and found a nice tree to park under. He had a long wait ahead and decided to go for some food. Checking the alley, he got out, locked the car, and then walked in the opposite direction.

*****

The woman saw the car cruise by and park under a tree. Saw the man get out and walk away, and knew that was the man that had shot at them. She thought about calling the police to have him arrested, but that would put her in it. She thought about slashing his tyres, but then what if they needed a getaway car? Munching on her sandwich, she thought about it some more.

*****

Andros rolled up to the club at ten p.m., went inside, had a look around, sipped a drink, and left. Sitting in his limousine, he waited for the festivities to roll around.

*****

Stavros looked at his watch. Ten p.m. He left the café and slowly walked back to his car. He spied the two guards at the door and wondered how to proceed. Carefully crossing the alley, he walked, hunched over, to not be seen, completely missing the woman who had seen him coming and hidden between two cars.

He slid down to the Mustang, got on the ground, got underneath and cut the brake line. Being just as careful when he left, he slid down the alley toward his car only to be caught by her.

"What are you doing to Pedro's car?" she whispered furiously.

Startled, he covered her mouth with his hand and took her to the ground. "You be quiet or I'll shoot you again." He opened his jacket to reveal a gun. "Scream, and you die."

Her eyes widened and she nodded.

He removed his hand. "Now, what are you doing stalking Pedro Stephanopoulos?"

"I'm not stalking him," she whispered. "We're going to be together. I'm having his baby, and we're going to be together tonight."

"You do know Angelina's here?"

That took her by surprise. "No, no I didn't."

"And their guards."

A steely look of determination came over her face. "*I will be* with Pedro tonight."

"Then you'll also have Angelina's father to deal with."

Now she was stunned. "Mr Poulos is here? At the club?"

"Yep."

"Is he here to take that whore home?"

"Possibly, but then I'd say he's here to kill Pedro." An idea was forming in his mind. Andros Poulos needed stopping, and he had been given the task. But maybe he could keep his hands clean and get this girl to do the dirty work.

"What do you mean, here to kill Pedro?" she spat. "He was supposed to come and take his whore home, *not kill my man.*"

"Well, that's what he's planning. You see that limo across the road from the alley?" He nodded toward it, and she turned to stare. "That's his car. He's just waiting for Pedro to get into his car and kapooh." He made an explosive sound and moved his hands apart to demonstrate a bomb blowing up.

"He's going to blow Pedro up?" Her eyes flooded with tears.

"It will go off shortly after. It has to warm up," he lied. "I was hoping to stop him, but he has my family locked away and is threatening to kill them if I don't co-operate."

"He wants you to kill Pedro?"

"Yes."

"No. I won't let that happen. Tell me what I can do."

 CARLOS

Waiting until dark, the men loaded Aneeka and Carlos into the trunk, threw their bags in next to them, emptied their hotel room and drove out of the parking lot.

They weren't noticed.

Why would they be? It was a seedy part of town, bordering the outskirts, derelict houses, hotels, and bars. Everyone was either blind drunk or off their face on drugs.

No, they weren't noticed.

They took a circuitous route out of town, driving south out of L.A. until they found the exit that would take them back north. It was going to be a long trip, but they had to do it. Bypassing L.A. on the highway, they headed further north and took another exit back. But this one wouldn't take them completely back to L.A., it would take them out to the desert, past one horse towns and that empty quarry they needed.

They kept an eye out for cars following them and pulled over when there was too much traffic, pretending to have a break in case someone was watching. They swigged beer and cola and eventually pulled back onto the desolate highway and drove up the empty road to the quarry, coming to a stop away from the entrance where no one would see them and the fire they were about to start.

They got out, looked around, popped the trunk and hauled Aneeka's body out, carrying her a short distance to lay her down on the cold gravel and rocks.

The fresh air helped her come to, and she breathed. "Mmm," she mumbled behind her gag. "Mmm." She kicked her legs. "Mmm, mmm."

"Shut up," the short man said and gave her a swift kick in the side.

"Ahh," she screamed behind the gag. "Mmm, mmm."

"I said, shut up," he shouted.

"Knock it off, Petrov," Dimitri Yustoff said, coming over with a can of gas and matches. He'd left the trunk up and didn't see Carlos struggle out.

Carlos had spent the whole car trip untying his hands, but pretended to be out of it when they'd stopped and opened the trunk. They'd only grabbed Aneeka, so he was safe, and he'd quickly pulled off the leg rope, blindfold, and tape. He slid over the side of the trunk and hid around the back of the car out of their way. Watching them pour the fluid over Aneeka he heard her muffled cries. "Fuck!" He had to do something, and do something he did when he saw them light the match. "No," he yelled and bolted toward the two men.

Dimitri dropped the match in shock and Petrov's eyes went wide.

Carlos saw Aneeka roll away from them as he came crashing into both of them.

Petrov went down like a lead balloon, but Dimitri pushed himself away and ran for the car.

Aneeka screamed behind her gag and Carlos punched Petrov, who was beneath him, until he was dazed and then raced over to her, ripping off her gag and blindfold.

A shot rang out.

Dimitri had gotten his gun from the car and was shooting at them.

Carlos dragged Aneeka further away and she quickly sat up, pulled her legs through her arms, and started pulling the rope around her wrists with her teeth.

"Go get them," she said.

Carlos ducked and weaved his way to Dimitri and tackled him. "Why did you do this?" he yelled. "Who told you to do this?" The gun was knocked away and they struggled. "Where were you taking us?

Ugh." Dimitri had landed a punch to the chiselled jaw of Carlo Stefan. Carlos rolled off, but quickly sprang up.

Aneeka finished with her bonds as Petrov came to and she saw he was lying in the same spot she had been. Swiftly moving over to him she kicked him in the side. "Let's see how you like it," she said when he was curled into a ball. She scrambled looking for the box of matches that had been dropped and flicked one alight. Seeing the terrified look in Petrov's eyes, she tossed it into the petrol around him.

He went up like the Fourth of July, and the scream that left his throat was the guttural noise of pure hell. He rolled, and rolled, and rolled, managing to dampen the flames.

Carlos and Dimitri stopped fighting long enough to see what was happening, and that's when Carlos felt the pain in his head.

Dimitri hauled the unconscious body into the trunk, slammed the lid shut and ran to the driver's side. Firing off the rest of his bullets he saw Aneeka go down. He got in, slammed the door, gunned the engine, and sped off back to the highway to continue on to the next town to make his phone call.

Aneeka gasped. "Ah, fuck!" came out through gritted teeth. Her hand tightly grasped her right arm where the bullet had hit, and it burned like a mother. The only thing she could do was go into meditation mode.

She breathed, in and out, in and out. Slowly, surely, her breathing regulated and the pain subsided.

Unlike the pain of the man ten feet from her.

Petrov groaned. The pain, the searing pain. He'd never been set on fire before and didn't appreciate being set on fire now. Rolling had managed to put it out, but he could feel the melting skin, the burning of his lungs. He was barely able to breathe, and it tasted like ash and smoke. Seeing her stand over him, the gorgeous black woman they had been told to take, he didn't know why they needed to get the guy with the big cock because all they'd needed to do was threaten the woman for the photos. But no, the cockhead he worked with had decided to take her and that's all there was to it. Now here he was, lying in some God forsaken hole in the ground, melting like the witch in the Wizard of Oz, and the woman they'd kidnapped was standing over him. His partner had taken off on him, and he was not going to get back home to see his wife and child. *That's what happens when you live a life of crime,* he thought. *I always thought it was a joke, that saying. Crime doesn't pay. Well, it certainly won't be paying this time.* His eyes drooped, and he was down to his last gasps of air.

Aneeka knelt down beside him, blood pouring from her arm wound, and she laid her hand on his forehead. "It's all right," she soothed. "You will be with the creator soon. You will be at peace soon."

Her calming words made him feel better as he slipped away.

Seeing his eyes close and hearing the death rattle, Aneeka stood, breathed deeply and set off for the highway. She needed a phone, she needed food, and she needed a stiff drink.

*****

Dimitri sped down the highway looking for a phone booth. He needed to make his call, needed to call his boss, needed to find out where to dump the body in the trunk. Why couldn't they have just killed them both? He banged the steering wheel with his fists. Hard calloused fists. All the years he'd worked for his boss, and nothing had ever been a cock-up like this. Sure, he'd kidnapped people before, and sure he'd killed people before, but all of this had been a cock-up from start to almost finish. And now he had to drive to God knows where to get rid of the body in the trunk. He shook his head. This thing, this plan, was getting worse and worse.

Seeing a gas station in the distance, he checked the gas gauge. He needed to fill up the old bomb of a gas guzzler, so he pulled in. Casually gazing around while pumping gas, he was on the lookout for cops, feds or suits. He saw no one and went inside to pay. He grabbed some candy bars, soda, and chips, handed over his money, peered around and walked outside. He parked beside the phone booth and made his call. "I've got him, where do I bring him?"

"Did you dispose of the woman?"

"Yes."

"And did everything go smoothly?"

"…Not quite…"

"What do you mean…not quite?"

"We lost Theodopolous."

"…And how did you do that?"

"The woman got loose and set him on fire."

"…But you still have him…"

"Yes."

"Then bring him…"

Dimitri listened and hung up. Peering around before leaving, he failed to notice the man pumping gas that just happened to be an off-duty cop who still had his APB in his car.

The man leant in and checked the photo. Yes, the same one, and after finishing with the gas went in to make a phone call to his superiors before paying and following.

*****

Aneeka hiked back to the highway and started walking. She didn't like the idea of hitchhiking but had to get a lift to the nearest phone. With no headlights in sight, she had to keep moving and pushed on against the night.

*****

Carlos woke to a pounding headache and a bumpy road. "Ugh," he groaned. "Where the hell are we?"

Thunder cracked overhead making him jump. "Great, now it's gonna rain." He felt around for something to break out of the trunk with and found some loose tools. Forcing them into the cracks and crevices of the trunk, he tried to pop it but couldn't, so he smashed out the lights instead, hoping a cop car would pull the driver over for not having brake lights. He lay back. *I hope Aneeka is okay. Can she make it on her own? It's a long walk to civilisation.* He rubbed his head. Another crack of thunder made it worse because of the electrical waves flowing through the car. *I wonder where Tony is?*

*****

Tony had been at the cop station with Drew and Star when the call came through about the sighting of Dimitri Yustoff at a gas station. They made a beeline for their cars and got on the road even though it was nearly two hours away. The off-duty officer had said he'd continue following the car and report in periodically. They hit the gas and waited for his call.

*****

Aneeka kept walking. She'd rather walk than hitchhike with some of the crazies around these days. But her arm was killing her, and she didn't see any lights in sight. Breathing deeply she kept walking, trying to piece the puzzle together. She still couldn't figure out why they had kidnapped her. If photos were all they wanted, just ask. No need to trash her place, or take her against her will. And who was the person behind it all? They had not only taken her, but Carlos as well. Why did they want him? Did they need him for something? Did they want to frame him for Rosalee's murder again? Maybe inject him with drugs and plant a suicide note that was also a confession? Confessing that he had killed Rosalee when he hadn't?

Her head pounded to a different beat than her arm, so she breathed slowly and deeply. *What I wouldn't give for a drink and maybe some aspirin,* she thought. She kept on walking, one foot in front of the other. How far now? How long had she been walking? She tried to picture the highway, but didn't know which highway she was on. After pounding up a hill she stopped. There, in the distance, the bright lights of a city. "Ah," she said. "Vegas!"

The thunder cracked overhead.

*****

Dimitri pushed through. The most direct way to get past Vegas was through Vegas, so he hit the strip and kept going. *God, I wish I could stop just for one game, one drink, one woman,* he thought, eyeing off the women walking the streets. He hadn't had a fuck in weeks and had been tempted to do damage to the black woman, but he had refrained, although, he had allowed himself to touch her. She was unconscious, just how he liked them, and he'd had a suck of her tits, but nothing else.

And then when they got the porn king he couldn't help himself. He had to have a look at the great cock in person. It was long and strong and sturdy, and he'd held it, feeling the weight in his hand.

Mmm, he'd thought. *Not much heavier than mine.* Now he had the king of cock in his trunk. He drove out the other side of Vegas and kept going. It was going to be a long drive and would take a couple of days, but he had to get there, and since Theodopolous wasn't there to help with the driving, he was going to have to do it all himself. Which meant no sleep. Just sugar, fresh air, and coffee.

*****

Aneeka came across the gas station, saw it in the distance, and broke into a stumbling run. There was no way she was giving up now with help in sight, and she ran as hard as she could.

The station came closer.

She ran faster.

The gas station attendant walked outside to check on something and saw a black woman running at him.

"Help me, please help me," Aneeka yelled. "I've been shot." She ran into the station and fell just as a car came screeching in.

*****

Harry stormed around his office while Harriet, Connie, and Viv sat on the sofa. "How long does it take to find someone, God in blazes?" The phone rang. Harry grabbed it in a second. "Yes."

"He's heading to Vegas at this stage," Tony said. "No word on Aneeka or Carlos, but one of the men has been identified."

"Okay, keep me informed." Harry replaced the phone and resumed his pacing. "He's been taken to Vegas."

Harriet fluttered her handkerchief. "What is going on Harry? Why would someone do this?"

"I don't know, but I won't rest until I find out."

*****

Tony had to stop for gas, but Star and Drew hadn't, so they left him and kept going. He took a minute to call Harry then jumped in his car and raced off, knowing he'd easily catch up.

*****

"What the hell!" Drew flew out of the car and ran to Aneeka's side. "Ms Ne Masta, are you all right?"

Star bailed up the attendant. "What did you do? What did you do?"

"It wasn't him," Aneeka said. "It was the men and one's dead. They tried to kill me, set me on fire. But Carlos tackled them, and it ended up being one of them that was on fire. The other took off with Carlos. He shot at me." She looked at her arm. "He got me."

Five cars pulled in behind them.

"Where did all of this happen?" Drew put his coat around her.

"In a quarry," she said. "Back that way. He's still there."

"Get cars back to the quarry and look for him, boys. It's one of the men we're after," Star barked, hands on hips and thinking he was in charge.

Drew helped Aneeka to her feet as Tony slammed into the station. "Aneeka!"

"Tony." She ran for him and he enveloped her in a bear hug.

"Are you okay?" he asked. "Harry's mad as hell about this."

"No, I'm not," she said and showed him her arm. "I've been shot."

Tony examined it. "Just a flesh wound, let's get it wrapped up." He led her inside and Star and Drew followed.

"Start from the beginning and leave nothing out," Star demanded as Drew questioned the attendant.

"I was taken from my own backyard," Aneeka said as Tony bathed her wound with products he'd grabbed from the store's shelves. "My eyes and mouth were covered, my arms and legs bound. They held me somewhere and demanded the photos I'd taken. I wondered what their interest in the photos was, and realised they must be the men in them. They knocked me out, and I only came to when they put me on the ground in the quarry. I fought, Carlos got my blindfold off, and I untied myself while he was fighting one of the men. The other one ended up on fire because he was lying in the petrol they had poured on me. He must have rolled onto the matches because he went up in a ball of flame," she lied as the rain came pouring down hard outside.

They all looked out the window for a few moments.

"Do you have any idea why they want a porn actor?" Star asked.

She looked up at him as Tony finished wrapping her arm. "No."

"Any idea where they're going?"

"No."

"All right, Vega," Star said to Tony. "Get her back home safely and we'll see after the actor."

"You've clearly forgotten Star that *your* superior put *me* in charge. *Not you*," Tony reminded him.

Star flinched and went beet red.

"You do as *I* say," Tony continued. "*We* will go after Carlos. Aneeka, do you want to go back?" He looked at her for her answer.

"No." She shook her head. "I want to continue. I want to know what's going on."

"Then you'll come with me," Tony said, helping her stand. "Have we heard from the off-duty cop yet?" he asked Star who just stared at him with a look that could freeze Satan in hell and then shatter him into a million pieces. It didn't faze Tony, who'd faced worse.

"Word is he just called in. They pulled into a fast food outlet and are continuing on their way," Star finally said.

"To where?"

Drew came over. "He's in Utah at the moment. Who knows where he's going."

"Okay, let's take the same road he's taking and keep up," Tony said. "Stock up on food, water and whatever you need. Let's get on the road. I'm going to call Harry, sit tight," he told Aneeka and went to make the call.

When his back was turned Star bolted for the car and jumped behind the wheel.

Drew followed and jumped in after him. "What are you doing? We have to wait."

"The hell we are," snarled Star and they skidded out of the station. "Who does that pompous, no good, low-down son of a cock sucking bitch think he is?" Star spat.

"The person in charge," Drew replied. "Shouldn't we wait?"

"Fuck waiting. I'm a cop," Star ranted, stepping on the gas. "I'll do whatever the fuck I want and to fucking hell with that cock sucker."

"Until Ward gets on your case and demotes you."

Star seethed, the rain poured down, and Drew hung on.

Tony got through to Harry. "I've got Aneeka, she's okay. She was nicked by a bullet, but she'll be fine."

"Oh, thank God." Harry slumped in his chair. "What about the boy?"

"Still got him."

"Get Aneeka back here."

"No, she wants to continue so I'm taking her."

"Take care of her then."

"I will."

"Keep me updated."

Tony hung up and made his way back to Aneeka. After leading her to the car, he made her comfortable and was pissed that the detectives had taken off, but not surprised that Star was acting out. He sped onto the highway in the same direction with two cop cars after him.

"Pair of fucking idiots." He slammed the wheel. "His boss threatened to demote him and he still acts like a cock."

"What did Harry say?" Aneeka changed the subject.

"Thank God you're okay and to take care of you and find the boy."

"He's hardly a boy."

"To me he is," he spat. "A selfish, inconsiderate little asshole who doesn't think twice about anybody but himself."

"So, like you when you were that age." Aneeka flashed a grin.

Tony's jaw tightened. "I *was not* like that when I was his age, and what would you know about it, anyway?"

"I've heard stories."

"Not from me you haven't, and not from anybody else."

"And why do you think that?"

He glanced at her. "Because *nobody* knows about my past."

*****

Back at Harry's, everyone heaved a sigh of relief except for Vivian who felt sick to her stomach. She stood up. "Uh, excuse me. I feel sick. It must be all the stress." She fled to a bathroom and promptly threw up in the toilet. When she was done, she flushed and rinsed off. Patting her face with cold water at the sink, she thought about the mess that was happening right now and said a quick prayer that Carlos was found alive and well and came home safely.

She dried her face and opened her purse for her compact, seeing the stick at the bottom of the bag where she'd thrown it that morning.

The stick from the pregnancy kit.

*****

Rain bucketed down through Vegas into Utah, and the pounding on the trunk was not helping the pounding in Carlos's head. He was cramped. His legs bent at odd angles, and something was digging into his back. He shifted, trying to find a more comfortable position, but his five-ten frame didn't fit well in the trunk of a car.

I wonder how long we've been driving for… His eyes closed as the rain came to a stop.

The off-duty officer pulled in at the rest stop, staying out of view of the other car. There were tables, a phone, a picnic bench and barbecue, and he went into the toilet block for a quick check. Seeing no one else, he called in to his boss. "We're at a truck stop in Colorado. I'm still following and have no idea where he's going. I'll need to stop for gas at the next station, so I'll let you know where."

Dimitri slept with one ear open and a gun in his hand. *Thank God for quiet nights and good hearing,* he thought and wound up his window.

PEDRO

Friday night went off like clockwork. Sara-Michelle kept Angelina in Stew's office, and Mark kept a watch over Pedro. Come six-thirty in the morning everyone was ready to go home, including Stavros and the woman.

Stavros sat up in his seat. Any minute now. He woke the woman sitting beside him. He'd allowed her to sleep in his car, her luggage on the back seat. She stirred. "It's showtime. Now we get our revenge."

She sleepily nodded, wiped her eyes, and stepped out into the cold dark alley. The sun was not yet up, even though the light was changing shades, so the alley was cast in haunting shadows. She slipped down the alley as Stavros quietly got out and deposited her luggage next to the tree. He popped the trunk, but kept it down and then got back in the car, ready for the moment.

Mark came out first and checked the Mustang over. He got in, gunned the engine and pulled out into the alley, but alighted, leaving the door wide open and the engine running, while he went to open the club's back door for the others.

Across the street from the alley, Andros rolled down his window to see what was happening. With butterflies in his stomach, he exited the car, closed the door and stood to watch. He wanted to see their faces when they saw him because it would be the last time for any of them.

*****

At the police station, Burns and Devron got a call about a limousine sitting outside of 69 all night. They thought nothing of it until tracking it down and seeing it was rented by Andros Poulos. They called Gardo and got him out of bed. "He's at 69, his daughter's got a restraining order on him, and he shouldn't be near Stephanopoulos," Burns said.

"Right, get down there. I'm on my way."

*****

The Mustang sat idling in the alley as Pedro, Angelina, and Sara-Michelle stepped out of the club.

Something inside the woman snapped, and it snapped again when she spied Andros standing at his limousine. "No one's going to kill my Pedro," she mumbled and started screaming. "He's here, look, it's Andros Poulos, he's here!"

Pedro, Mark, Angelina and Sara-Michelle looked from the screaming woman who was running up to them on their left, barely recognising her as the stalker, to Andros Poulos on their right staring at them with a smug then confused expression on his face.

"Get back inside," Mark yelled, the Mustang forgotten.

But it was not forgotten by the woman. She jumped into the driver's seat, revved the engine and gunned it down the alley. She passed a stunned Mark.

He stopped in surprise and looked back to see everyone still standing there, then whipped his head around to watch and took off running.

The woman raced full speed for Andros, who stood shocked to the spot, and rammed right into him, smashing into the side of the limousine.

The top of his body flew backwards, arms outstretched like Jesus on the cross, his head hitting the roof of the limo, his bottom half pinned between both cars. Gravity got the better of him and he slumped onto the hood of the Mustang.

Dead.

The woman had smashed her head against the steering wheel and driver's window. Her neck was broken. Her eyes stared wide and lonely at the floor beside her.

No one in America would miss Barbara Weston; the young Australian girl who went to school with Carlos back home and was royally rejected by him. The young girl who had reconnected with him in Mykonos, even though he hadn't recognised her. The young girl who was put in her place by model Vivian Villiers and dumped by Carlos after a good fucking. She'd gone crazy after that; after he'd left the island. She latched onto Pedro, hoping he would be the father of her baby. The baby she was never actually having.

No, no one in America would miss Barbara Weston.

Mark skidded to a halt in shock at what lay before him.

Stavros had turned the car on and stepped out, leaving it running, leaving his door open, pulling the trunk up as he passed. The sound of the crash had muffled it all.

"Daddy," Angelina yelled, pulling out of Pedro's arms and bolting for the car.

Sara-Michelle ran after her as Pedro stood in shock. Staff members came from the back door, saw the carnage, and ran to help, leaving Pedro alone.

This suited Stavros perfectly, and he shoved his gun into Pedro's back. "Don't say anything. Just do as you're told, and you won't get hurt."

Pedro glanced dazedly at him as he was pulled around by the arm and led down the alley.

Burns and Devron pulled up behind Gardo on West 54th.

"Well…" Gardo strode over to the wreckage. "Looks like we don't have to worry about Poulos anymore." He eyed the body and watched Angelina on the other side of the car. "After what he did to you you're *still* crying over him?"

She stared up through tear-filled eyes, unable to say anything.

Mark pulled out of the Mustang's driver's window and turned around to come face to face with Gardo and the officers. "You'll find this woman to be a stalker. She was stalking Pedro and sending *little gifts* if you know what I mean."

"Wonderful," yelled Gardo. "Two birds with one 'stang."

"Except I think there's a third." Mark looked down the alley. "Pedro?" He noticed a man turn around as he was smacking Pedro over the head and dumping him in his trunk. "Pedro," he yelled. "Quick, someone's got him." He raced down the alley with the officers on his tail, missing the car by inches as it sped down the alley. "Fuck," Mark spat, getting the license plate and memorising it.

Gardo screeched to a halt beside him. "*You* get in," he told Mark. "You two..." he directed the officers, "get your car and follow."

Mark jumped in, and they took off.

Burns and Devron radioed for backup at the crash site, made it to their car, and raced down the alley. Gardo came through on the radio five minutes later.

"We're after a black Cadillac Seville, license PMS 333, on Broadway...wait...it just turned onto the George Washington Bridge into Jersey." He shoved the radio back. "Now, tell me...who are you and what the fuck is going on?"

Mark gave him a sideway stare. "Mark Monroe, ex-special forces, black belt in karate, weapons expert. Hired as a bodyguard by Pedro Stephanopoulos after everything that Andros Poulos had done to him."

"No surprise there." Gardo gunned it down the highway. He saw a cop car roar up behind with sirens and lights going and radioed through. "Whoever is behind me cut the lights and sirens."

They turned off and then a voice crackled over the radio. "It's Burns and Devron, sir."

"Go on," he told Mark.

"It also turns out Mr Stephanopoulos was being stalked by one Barbara Weston, the woman in the car. So between her and Poulos, there was a lot of damage going on."

"And the guy we're following?"

"Small time crook who gets hired by whoever needs him. Andros had him shoot at Pedro, but the woman and Angelina got in the way. Now I think there's someone bigger involved. Clearly, someone who wants Pedro Stephanopoulos."

"Any idea why?"

"Not a one."

"Any idea where he's headed?"

"Not a one."

*****

Back at the club, Eddie thanked God they'd been closed as the clean-up was going to be horrendous and take too much time. There was dealing with cops, giving statements, and waiting for the tow truck to come and clear the mess away. But that wouldn't be until later in the day, and he hoped they'd still be able to open, albeit with their stand-in DJ. Fuck knows what the hell was going on with Pedro, and why someone would want to take him! *Fuck.* He ran his hand through his receding hair. *Just another thing to deal with.*

After Angelina had given her statement to the officers, she was taken home by Sara-Michelle. She walked in, sat on the sofa, and stayed there, sitting in shock. Sara-Michelle made tea, but it sat cold in front of her as she hadn't touched it. Didn't want it. Just wanted Mark to find Pedro and bring him home. She just wanted Pedro and nothing else.

Sara-Michelle stepped aside and called her boss, fearful for her co-worker whom she had a slight crush on. "Any word on Mark?"

*****

Gardo sped down the highway, but kept a safe distance from the car. It was now daylight, and he was going to need to stop for gas.

Burns and Devron had stopped earlier and were ten minutes behind. He radioed every other cop car and police unit to be on the lookout and to stay close behind, but not scare him.

"He's just pulled into a gas station on Highway 80 in Pennsylvania," a cop called in.

Gardo slowed down. They were on the same highway and would catch up quick. Within minutes they had the station in sight and slowed down further. The car drove out and back onto the highway. Gardo drove in for gas and radioed in. "He's just left the station. We need to fill up, keep an eye on him." Five minutes later they were back on the road doing double time to catch up.

"Any idea where he's going?" Gardo asked Mark.

"Not yet."

*****

Stavros put the pedal to the metal. He needed to get the kid out of his car as soon as possible. The longer he was in there, and the longer he was in America, the more trouble he'd be in.

He bit into a sandwich he'd grabbed at the station. He was starving, but couldn't stop to eat. Needing to be at his final destination that night, he made it into Ohio around lunchtime.

CARLOS

When the sun's rays hit the horizon, Dimitri woke, and after taking a quick leak, he took off for the main road. He knew where he was going, but the man behind him didn't. He had plenty of places to lead him, but not much time to do it in. He had another day, maybe two, to get to his destination, so if he stopped for gas and food and nothing else, he should make good time.

Driving into the first gas station he came across, he got out to pump his own gas, keeping an eye out for the car which he saw pull in front of the toilet block. He casually leant on his car giving a periodical glance over his shoulder. After racking up a thirty dollar bill, he added to it with coffee and bagels and took a few minutes to watch the tall, lanky man get his own food, and gas up.

He threw his rubbish in the bin and took off for his destination.

The off-duty cop called in. "I'm at a small gas station in Nebraska. It's a little town, not much, gotta go." He jumped in his car and followed.

Two hours behind were Star and Drew, Tony and Aneeka, and five cop cars. Occasionally there'd be reports on the car from officers seeing it drive by. They radioed in and back to L.A. Ward had set up a map to keep track of his movements with red tacks. "He's heading cross country," he radioed the detectives. "Probably Iowa and Illinois next. I'll get in contact with Chicago PD in case he comes their way, and they can keep an eye out."

"What if he's heading for New York?" Star asked on the two-way. "Or takes a right or left and heads in a different direction?"

"Then we'll be ready," Ward said. "Sit on his tail and close in. Out."

Star hung up the handset. "How long are we meant to follow?"

"As long as we have to," Drew said. "Not that it matters."

*****

Aneeka woke from her restless sleep and looked around. Stretching, she winced, having forgotten about her arm.

"You okay?" Tony asked. "There's some water and aspirin if you need it."

She smiled. "What would I do without you?" She cracked open the aspirin, swallowed three and washed them down with water.

"A damn sight better than what's happened with Carlos Stephanopoulos," he said. "There's been nothing but trouble since that boy came to town."

"And yet, somehow I don't think it's his fault." She sipped more water.

"Huh?" Tony grunted. *"How is it not his fault?"*

"Because I think someone is doing it *to* him like they did it to me."

He glanced at her. "What makes you say that?"

"Why did they take me? Because I caught them on camera and told the police. Why did they try to set Carlos up? Because someone wanted him in trouble. So who is doing this? Who is behind it?"

Tony sighed. "Dunno. Maybe Harry's investigators have found something out."

TOMAS

"I think my guy's headed here, but I don't know why and I don't know where." Barden stood looking out at the grey clouds. It was ten o'clock in the morning.

"What could possibly be the point of bringing the kid here?" Captain Wallace asked. In all his forty years on the force, he'd never heard of such things, even though Chicago had been labelled a mob town. "And you say his brothers have been kidnapped as well?"

"Apparently." Barden turned around. "I got news of New York before I came here. But so far, neither L.A. or New York know where the kidnappers are headed."

"So, how did you figure it out?"

Barden smiled. "I just connected the dots."

*****

The man woke and checked his watch. Ten a.m. "Fuck." After taking a leak, he took off for the nearest gas station and kept an eye out for cop cars, but fifteen minutes later he was on his way with no trouble. He had Indiana and Illinois to get through, and the paper predicted rain.

The service attendant made a call. "I just seen that car you're afta, you know, the brown seedan…yep…yep…gas und food…he took off down the high heading north… Yep…yep…yep sir, thank you sir, yep sir, bye."

Feeling proud of himself that he had called in a wanted car and the potential reward it would pay, he didn't see the two fifteen-year-old kids sneak in the back door, or come up behind him. They raised their arms and blasted his brains out with their guns. He fell dead to the floor.

There would be no reward for Hector Veddler today. After all, no good deed goes unpunished.

The two kids raided the till, piled junk food into their bags, and took off the same way they'd come when a cop car pulled in. The cops were stopping to chat with Veddler to get a statement. But they were too late and called in a dead body instead.

*****

Barden kept in touch with his officers back in Miami. He also listened to the calls over the radio about the car being seen at a station, and then the call for the body of an attendant.

"Think he doubled back to get rid of a witness?" Wallace asked.

"Nah. I doubt he has the time." Barden marked off his map. "Oh, he's definitely headed here. Only two states to go."

One by one, they trailed across the countryside into Iowa to reach the border of Illinois where Dimitri stopped for gas. He was close now, not far to go, but he needed gas and food and a leak and a fuck. He parked around the back of the station after filling the tank and quickly ate the burger he'd bought, slurped down his drink, and kept an eye out for a female who might be up for it. He saw no one but the guy in the car. The one that had been following him since Vegas. He watched the man go into the station and took the opportunity to pop the trunk to check on the porn star. He nudged him.

"Ugh," Carlos groaned, his hand moving slowly up to his head. "What's…what's happening?"

"I'm done with you, Mr Ten Inch Cock. I am *so* done with you," he hissed and slammed the lid shut. "Don't worry, not long now and then *he* can take you."

*****

"You'd better step on it, he's made Illinois." Ward's voice popped up over the radio. "I've called the Captain, they know not to stop him at any time and to let him go. We need to find out where he's going."

"Why are we not nabbing him if he has a body in the trunk?" Star asked.

"Because there's a reason this is happening, so there must be bigger fish to fry. Besides, I take orders too, you know."

Star hung up. "Why in fuck's name is this happening?"

"Don't know, but it's your turn to drive." Drew pulled over into a station and the others followed. They wasted no more than five minutes getting gas, food or taking a leak, then it was back on the road at more speed.

*****

Harry got off the phone with his investigators.

"Well?" Harriet asked, running her pearls through her hand.

"They're on the trail. They've checked back in Mykonos, nothing there. They've checked back in all the places the cops have been, nothing, but…" He waved a finger. "They have found out something very interesting. There is a private plane registered to a Greek company out of Athens that flew into O'Hare Airport three days ago."

"Is that important?" Connie asked. She had camped out at Harry's since this started.

"Well…" Harry paced. "It may or may not be. But, since it's from Athens, and Carlos is from Mykonos, I wonder. Of course, the CEOs could just be here on business, but there's a name that's popped up that we know from Carlos's last lot of trouble."

"And who's that?" Viv asked, clutching her handkerchief to her mouth.

"Gustoff Dropopolous."

"And who's he?" Harriett asked.

"The man at the resort that claimed Carlos raped two women and then shot one."

Connie's eyes widened. "Oh, my God. That means I could have seen him."

"Did you?" Harry asked.

She shook her head slowly. "I don't think so."

"Did *he* see *you*?"

Another shake. "I don't think so, otherwise he might have attacked us at the pier and he didn't."

Harry stood in front of her. "Well, the fact that he's still around is highly suspicious, and my men are on it. I'll let Tony know the next time he calls in."

"What will he be able to do?"

"Pass it on to the cops," Harry said.

*****

Dimitri headed into a massive storm as he crossed Illinois and hoped it didn't slow him down. He had to stop to make a call and take a leak. "All that damn coffee and soda," he muttered and stopped outside of the next gas station he came across. He took a leak and entered the phone booth, keeping an eye out for the car. "I'm nearly there, where do I go?"

"The airport."

"Which one?"

"O'Hare."

"And then what?"

"We deal with it."

"What time?" He looked at his watch.

"Eight-thirty, sharp."

He sighed. "I'll do my best."

*****

Tony believed they'd made good time and phoned Harry during a break. Learning of the name Gustoff Dropopolous, he asked Star and Drew if they'd heard of it.

"Don't remember that one," Drew said, pumping the gas.

"And it wasn't the name of either man involved in the kidnapping," Star added. "So who is he?"

"Someone of interest," Tony said. "Let's get going."

PEDRO

Angelina still sat on the couch. It was past lunchtime, and she just sat and stared. Even when the officers who'd taken her statement came to see her for a follow-up. Even when her lawyer had come to see her about the charges against her father. She'd just sat and stared. There was so much going through her mind.

Why had her father done this? Why had the woman done what she'd done? Wasn't *she* the stalker? Why had she changed her mind and killed her father instead? Why? Why? Why was this happening?

She relived the scene. Walking out of the club, a woman screaming on their left and seeing her pointing to their right. Seeing her father with his smarmy Cheshire cat grin standing next to his limousine, as though he had no worries in the world. As if nothing mattered. Hearing the Mustang gun it down the alley. Seeing it smash into her father. Seeing his dead body.

She finally moved.

Moved into the bathroom to throw up.

*****

Stavros made it into Indiana mid-afternoon and stopped for more gas. He looked around. He knew someone would be after him, but so far saw no cars that had been behind him the whole time. He checked his watch. He'd need to step on it to make it on time. Consulting a map, he found a shortcut to take.

*****

Gardo and Mark were only five minutes behind and catching up, until needing to stop for gas. "I just saw a black Cadillac Seville, licence PMS 333, turning off the main highway onto some backroad," came through on the radio.

Gardo got out to pump gas. "It's gonna be hard to follow him now."

Mark alighted and spread the map on the roof of the car, following the back road to its destination. "Chicago."

"What?" Gardo hung up the pump.

"The road leads to Chicago." Mark folded the map. "Let's go."

*****

Pedro came to in the trunk. His head was splitting with pain and he groaned. "What the hell?" Breathing in, he choked on oily rags and dirty clothes. He felt about and found he was lying on something rectangular. His fingers traced one side and found a handle. It was a suitcase.

The car sped up and crossed some sort of grid, making the pain in his head worse. *"Where the hell are we? What the hell's going on?"* He vaguely remembered a gun in his back and a man telling him they needed to go. He didn't say where, but the shocking aftermath of the accident had made him unable to get his wits about him. But now he could, and he started looking for a way out.

Knowing the type of car he was in, he knew there was a lever on the inside so you could open the trunk. He felt for it with deft fingers and found it. Holding onto the trunk lid, he carefully popped the release and lifted it several centimetres to see they were on a back road in the country. The car slowed, and he held the trunk down.

"Damn it," he heard the man say. "I've got to get to hair. I've got to get to hair. Time's running out."

Alarms sounded, and the roar of a train thundered past. Pedro took his chance. Lifting the lid, he looked out. It was late afternoon, and the train continued past. He held the trunk while he slipped a leg out, allowing his body to slide with it, rolling out onto the road. His feet hit it first, and he paused before pulling the trunk down until it locked into place.

The train kept going and the noise killed his head, but it was coming to an end, and he needed to get out of the way. He looked around and scrambled for the bushes on the opposite side of the road so he wouldn't be seen out the window or in the mirror. He made it with seconds to spare as Stavros took off.

He lay panting. "Oh, God, my head." He rolled into a sitting position and saw a car coming down the road. "Hey." Waving, he climbed unsteadily to his feet. "Hey." He fell onto the road and Gardo came to a skidding halt.

"Pedro," Mark yelled, getting out and running to him, hauling him to his feet. "Are you okay?"

Gardo flung open the rear door, and Mark helped Pedro in, then climbed in after him. "What the hell happened to you, kid?" Gardo stepped on the gas, and the door flew shut as he left.

"Shoved in a trunk at gunpoint." Pedro told his story, and Mark gave him a bottle of water. "Oh, God, my head," he sighed. "Angie… where's Angie?"

"She's okay," Mark calmed him. "Sara-Michelle's with her."

Pedro relaxed. "That's good. How is she about her father being dead?"

"Relieved I should think," Gardo said, flooring it. "Any idea where he was taking you?"

Pedro gave a slight shake of his head, but even that was too much, and the sharpness of the pain rattled around. "When we stopped for the train I heard, 'must get to hair, must get to hair'. I have no idea what that means."

Mark looked at Gardo's reflection in the rear-view. "O'Hare!"

TOMAS

In the afternoon the floodgates opened. He'd made it to Illinois and just needed to get to Chicago, where his boss was waiting to take care of the package. Considering some of the other jobs he'd taken on in the past, this one wasn't so bad. He only had to do away with one prick that got in his way, and the other was sleeping in the trunk.

He flicked on the radio and spun the dial around until he found an easy listening channel that played old songs he liked. Not the disco crap that was currently all the rage. He couldn't stand it and didn't know how anyone could. It all sounded the same and had no real meaning. The words were a bunch of mumbo jumbo and made no sense. He sang along to a *Carpenters'* song. Now this one had real heart. At least it had meaning.

The sky grew darker as he approached Chicago.

PEDRO

It was pouring with rain as Stavros drove through Illinois and into Chicago. He had time to get to the airport, but wanted it all over and done with now. After driving through the city, he made it to O'Hare, passed through the gates and into one of the private hangars. The plane was waiting. He pulled to a stop and got out.

A man stepped out of the plane. "You are early."

"I wanted to get here early so this was all over and done with."

"Where is he?" The young man of Greek heritage descended the stairs, buttoned up his suit jacket, and smoothed his hair.

"In the trunk." Stavros removed the key from the ignition and hurried around to unlock the trunk. He stepped back beside the car. "Ready and waiting."

The man walked over and lifted the trunk, looked in and lowered it. "Where is he?"

Stavros's face fell. "What do you mean where is he? He's in the trunk." He moved back to the trunk, lifted the lid, and looked inside, seeing nothing but his luggage and dirty rags. "But he…but I…he was in there."

"But where is he *now*?" The man levelled his gun at him.

"I…" Stavros shook his head in disbelief. "No, please, I had him, I had him." The bullet seared through his body under his ribcage. "No," he rasped. "I had him…" He slumped into the trunk.

TOMAS

It was dark when Barden looked out the window, even though it was only early evening. The storm covered the city and blocked out all light. He checked his watch. Seven. Where was he? He looked at his map and knew they couldn't be far.

An officer ran into the room and handed over a piece of paper.

"What is it?" Barden asked excitedly, leaning on Wallace's desk as he read it. "What does it say?"

"They've found Pedro Stephanopoulos and are headed to O'Hare."

"I knew it," Barden crowed. "Let's go."

They flew downstairs and into their cars, racing to the airport. The storm picked up and pelted them all the way until they made it under cover and spoke to someone in charge.

"Are there any planes leaving tonight?" Barden asked. "Private planes, I mean."

The manager called in the list and found there was one plane destined for Athens that had to leave tonight.

"That's it!" Barden exclaimed. "Stephanopoulos is Greek. If all three brothers are coming here that has to be a connection. Where's the plane?"

The manager checked. "Hangar 33."

After getting directions, they took off and saw a car scream past them in the same direction, pulling into a hangar. Barden, Wallace and ten officers followed in the shadows, raising their guns, and surrounded the car as the man got out. "Hold it right there, police."

The man, stunned that he had been found, put his hands up. "What's going on? What have I done? Did I run a red light?"

"Open the trunk," Barden yelled. "Open it." He motioned for an officer to pop it and found Tomas Stephanopoulos dazedly looking up at him.

"Hello," came quietly out of Tomas's mouth as he peered up.

"Mr Stephanopoulos, welcome back." Barden and Wallace helped him out, but he fell to his knees. They propped him up on the trunk lip. "Still sick, I see."

"What is this? I did not know there was someone in my trunk," the man said, knowing there was only one way out. "What is going on? Have I been set up?"

"You know full well what's going on," Barden told him. "You killed Luiz Manning and took Mr Stephanopoulos. Why did you do that? For *whom* did you do that?"

"Luiz is dead?" Tomas mumbled, his brain foggy and his stomach sick.

The man eyed everyone around him and pulled his gun out of the back of his pants. Shots were fired, but before he could run far, a bullet from Barden's gun had flown into the back of his head. He hit the floor. Dead.

"Ah, geez." Barden stood over the body. "Another one snuffs it." He waved a hand at Tomas. "Let's get him out of here. Get some food into him."

After soup and sandwiches, Tomas was brought up to speed. He shook his head. "Luiz was behind all of this? Just to break up Roger and me to get me back? It seems too incredible to believe."

Barden spied trench-coated feds from across the airport. "Mmm, it does." He watched them keep on going and wondered why they were there.

"Barden." Wallace pulled him aside. "They're here. I just heard it over the radio; they're all here and headed for that jet."

"Let's go," Barden told the others before turning to Tomas. "*You* stay here and keep warm. We're going to find out what's going on."

"No." Tomas stood up. "If I was kidnapped by someone else for a reason, I want to see for myself and find out what's going on."

"It's safer if you're out of the way." Barden didn't have time to argue. "Besides, you're weak and sick, so stay here." He took off with Wallace and the officers.

Dimitri cruised toward the city of Chicago. Rain bucketed down so he had to slow down, but he knew that gave the others a chance to gain on him. "Damn it." He banged the steering wheel and looked at his watch. Seven forty-five. He had forty-five minutes to get to the airport. Glancing in the rear-view mirror, he saw the car behind him had moved closer, but also noticed something strange. There was a car cruising on each side of the car going at the exact same pace. Never ahead, never behind. Three cars abreast on the highway. He didn't like the look of that. Glancing back at his watch he pressed the accelerator.

Carlos came to as the rain belted down on the trunk. The noise deafened him, making him grab his pounding brain. "Ugh, God." He groaned. "Where are we? Why am I still in the trunk?" Breathing deeply, he decided enough was enough.

"Fuck it! I gotta get 'em off my tail." Dimitri sped up, heading into the heart of the city. "I gotta lose 'em and lose 'em now." He'd skirted the airport because if he'd gone straight there, they would have followed and found not only him but his boss. And he couldn't risk it. Veering left then right, dodging traffic and pedestrians, he sped through the city.

*****

"We're heading for Chicago, now," Star told Ward. "Are the cops on his tail?"

"They're keeping an eye on him and following, trying to clean up the mess."

"Well, we're nearly there, any idea where he's going?"

"Not yet, but hurry up."

Tony heard the conversation on his two-way. He was only a hundred yards or so behind the detectives and sped up. That was the thrill of the chase; he was going and closing in.

"Whoa." Aneeka grabbed the dashboard. "Guess there's no point asking you to slow down?"

"Nope. Just hang on."

*****

Carlos was being tossed around in the trunk, but managed to find a metal bar that he could get his fingers around. He braced himself with one foot and started kicking at the back seat with the other. They swerved left then right, and he kicked again, and again, and again. The seat gave way, but not all the way. He rested as they swerved around a corner.

*****

"He's headed north out of the city," blasted over the two-way.

"Nearly have him now," Star and Tony said at the same time. "You're going down cock sucker!"

*****

Dimitri was trying not to panic. It was eight oh five and he had twenty-five minutes to get the cock sucker in his trunk to the airport, but needed to get the cops off his tail. He looked in the rear-view. There were flashing lights behind the three cars. "Fuck it! Fuck it, fuck it, fuck it." He slammed the wheel and did a screeching turn down the next main road he came to, having no idea where he was, but saw planes landing and taking off in the distance. He changed lanes and thunder clapped overhead, covering the sound of Carlos finally kicking through the back seat.

Carlos rested, listening to the man mutter and heard the word cops. *God, are they behind us? Is that why he's driving like a mad man?* He quietly pushed the seat aside and carefully crawled through, inch by inch. First his arms, then his head and chest. He pulled his legs up as they swerved around a corner and waited until the car had settled before pulling them out. He lay on the back seat listening.

"Gotta get to the airport. Where the fuck is O'Hare?" He wildly swung the wheel and Carlos grabbed the armrest. "Gotta get to the airport. Gotta get to the airport. Where the fuck is the turn for the airport? What the fuck? What the fuck is…no, no, no." He banged the wheel. He'd seen the cars with sirens and flashing lights bearing down on him, in front of him as he glanced in the rear-view, bearing down from behind him. Sweat dripped down his face, his back, his sides. "No, no, no," he yelled.

Carlos took his chance and popped his head up to look. Seeing the cop cars, he took his chance at exactly the same time the man saw him in the rear-view.

"No," he yelled as Carlos leant over the seat and grabbed the steering wheel. "No." The wheel lurched back and forth, sending the car careening across the road and back. "No, get off me," Dimitri yelled, letting one hand off the wheel to punch Carlos in the face. "Get back, let go of the wheel."

Carlos hung on. "No! Tell me who you are and who you're working for. Who told you to do this?"

O'Hare came up in the distance.

So did the cop cars.

"Fuck you and your ten inch cock, you cock sucking asshole," Dimitri yelled as they both wrenched the wheel and smashed through the bridge railing into the cold Illinois water.

*****

Star and Drew could only stare in shock and amazement as the car flew off the bridge no more than a hundred feet in front of them, and Star could swear he saw two faces in the front seat. They screeched to a stop at the gaping hole in the railing.

"No," Aneeka screamed.

They had all been tearing down the road, closing in on the car, lights flashing, sirens blaring, in the pouring rain when they saw the car go off the bridge.

"Fucking hell," Tony yelled. "Hang on." He screeched to a halt behind the detectives, and they all raced out of their cars to stare over the railing.

*****

The last thing Carlos saw was the bright lights of the cars in his face, blinding him. He and Dimitri hung on to the wheel as the car crashed through the barrier and into the cold water below. Letting go of the wheel, he pushed backwards, away from the windshield as it crashed in.

Water engulfed the car, flowing over Dimitri and Carlos as he pushed back to the back window. He needed as much air as possible, but the car was filling up fast.

Dimitri struggled and found his jacket caught on the door, but yanking it, he couldn't get it free. His lungs burned, his head pounded, and tugging on his jacket wasn't getting him out of there.

Carlos took a deep breath before water flowed over his head. Once the car was under, he moved to Dimitri and yanked his arm. The car lights flickered, but Dimitri saw Carlos point upward. Dimitri tugged his jacket, but couldn't break free.

Carlos started yanking it off him, and Dimitri realised what he meant and slid his arms out of the jacket.

The car settled on the bottom of the river and Carlos pushed Dimitri through the windscreen and followed him out, pushing and pulling him to the surface.

Dimitri pushed him away, kicking off and swimming for the surface.

Carlos didn't bother following him; he needed air now. Living on Mykonos for the last ten years had afforded him good swimming skills and the ability to hold his breath for four minutes, but this was hitting his limits. He no longer saw the man, but saw the lights as he surfaced. "Argh." He gulped in air.

"Carlos," Tony and Aneeka yelled out. "Carlos."

Sucking in huge gulps of air he looked up and saw everyone holding their flashlights down on him. They waved towards their right, his left, and he saw the bank only metres from him. He swam for it in the pouring rain and freezing water, using every water skill he had and what little energy he had left to get him there.

Tony and Aneeka ran for it with Star and Drew and all the cops after them. They ran across the bridge, over the side, and down the bank to haul a shivering Carlos out of the water. Tony whipped off his jacket and put it around his shoulders. "Carlos. Carlos, are you all right? Are you hurt?"

"No." Carlos coughed up some river water. "I'm okay." They helped him to the bridge. "Where is he? The driver." He frantically looked around. "Where is he?" he yelled.

"Get your flashlights down to the bank and start searching," Star yelled. "Get over the other side and look for a body."

Tony checked Carlos over for cuts and damage.

"I'm okay." Carlos pushed his hand away. "I'm just…"

"Yes?" Aneeka took his face in her hands.

"Tired and hungry." He smiled softly.

"Let's get you to the car. We're gonna get you home." Tony and Aneeka led him back to their car.

"There's no body." Star raced up to them. "No body, nothing. He either floated off down the river, or got out on the other bank. So if he did, where the fuck is he heading?"

A plane flew overhead.

"The airport."

Everyone looked at Carlos.

"What did you say?" Tony asked.

Carlos looked at him. "The airport. O'Hare. He had to get to O'Hare."

"Let's get to O'Hare," Star yelled. "Everyone to the airport."

Tony bundled Carlos into the back seat, and Aneeka piled in after him. She clung to him as they belted down the highway and onto the road that led to the airport.

"Did he say anything to you?" she asked. "Who he was? Why they wanted you? *What* they wanted?"

Carlos shook his head and rubbed it when pain surged through it. "No. Once we had left that place where they were going to kill you, I was in the trunk and in and out of it. God, I need something for this headache." Tony threw aspirin and a bottle of water into the back seat and he grabbed them and downed three.

Since Mark and Gardo knew where Stavros was going, they hit the sirens and lights. Burns and Devron were right behind them, roaring into Chicago's O'Hare Airport. It poured with rain, thunder clapped overhead, and lightning lit up the sky. But it didn't stop them.

"There's no way I'm staying here on my own." Tomas ran weakly from the room and followed the others down the hall and out into the blinding rain. They made their way back to the hangar, but kept going. In the distance they heard sirens, and on the other side of the hangar was a plane with the engine already running. Running through the hangar, they skidded to a halt as the plane on the tarmac prepared for take-off.

Gardo sped through the airport and headed for the private terminals, knowing there was no way the kidnapper was taking a public flight, and belted past one after the other until they came across the one they were looking for.

"Is that it?" Barden yelled over the thunder. "Is that the plane we're after?" They watched the plane and saw trench-coated feds coming their way.

"Here's trouble," Wallace said, seeing the feds hunched against the rain as they stormed towards them.

Barden saw Tomas behind him. "You were supposed to stay inside," he yelled.

"Not on your life," Tomas yelled back and turned to the right as sirens screeched to a stop in a hangar down the lane.

Gardo, Mark and Pedro piled out of their car to find the driver dead and hanging out of his trunk.

"Shot through the stomach," Mark said and rolled the kidnapper back as thunder exploded overhead. "He must have been here for a private jet."

"I'm coming," Dimitri yelled, running through the back of the airport to the hanger that held the private plane that would take him back to Greece. "I'm coming." He saw it on the tarmac, stairs down, waiting in the pouring rain. "Wait for me, I'm coming." He'd made it to the other side of the river bank and managed to grab a taxi to the airport, finding a back way in when he'd shoved a gun in the driver's face. Time was running out, and he needed to get on that plane. His breath was leaving him. After dealing with the fight, the crash, and shivering, which he was not used to, he didn't have much left. He saw a man stick his head out of the door. "I'm coming," he yelled, waving his arm.

"Look." Pedro pointed to a man running past the other end hangar, and Gardo and Mark looked up in surprise.

"Guess we're not the only ones after that plane and whoever the hell's on it," Barden told Wallace and Tomas, watching as a man, waving and yelling, ran across in front of them following the plane. "Who the hell is that?" The trench-coated feds got closer.

The man popped his head back into the plane, and a few seconds later his boss popped out and looked in his direction. A look as black as the night they were in crossed his face and he receded into the plane. The rotors revved, the first man popped back out, and a look of surprise flitted across his face.

Dimitri looked behind him and saw the flashing lights. "No," he yelled and ran faster.

The man on the plane held out his arm, and a small flash went off.

Dimitri Yustoff fell dead on the tarmac.

"Oh, my God, did you just see that?" Carlos said, leaning forward in his seat. "They just shot him."

The stairs closed, the rotors buzzed, and the plane took off for the runway.

Pedro, Mark, Gardo, Burns and Devron were off and running for the door and made it to see a small jet taking off and three cars speeding past.

"Stop it," Star yelled. "Get in front of it. Get in front of it."

"I've got my foot on the floor," Drew yelled back, speeding down the back road and past the dead man.

"What the blazes is going on here?" Wallace yelled as the three cars screamed past.

Drew screeched to a halt.

"What the fuck are you stopping for?" Star screamed. "After them…after them."

"It's too dangerous," Drew yelled. "We'd never make it, and there are too many other planes here. It's too dangerous."

Tony slammed on the brakes behind them and they piled out.

Carlos ran back to the man and rolled him. "That's him. That's the man in the car."

Thunder cracked overhead, and they watched the plane take off.

Carlos, Tony, and Aneeka walked over to the detectives as Star was still screeching. The rain poured down, soaking them to the skin, plastering their clothes to their bodies as the plane flew off into the middle of the thunderous sky.

"What now?" Carlos asked.

"Mother fucker," Star screamed, kicking at his car's tyre. "Mother fucking son of a cock sucking bitch."

"What now?" Carlos repeated more firmly.

Drew glanced at him. "Find out who was on that plane, why they were here, what they wanted with you and where they're going."

Carlos sighed. "Is that all?" He pushed his hair back with both hands. "What a fucking cock-up."

"Looks like we're not the only ones after someone," Gardo said and lifted his collar. "Come on boys; let's see what we've got." The five of them ran for the group on the tarmac.

The feds caught up to Barden, Tomas and Wallace. "What do you lot want? You shouldn't be here." He looked past them. "Who the hell are they?"

They all turned to see a small group of cops running for the cars on the tarmac.

"Don't know, but I guess we'd better join them." Barden took off with Tomas right behind.

Gardo, Mark and Pedro made it half way before seeing the other group heading in the same direction from another hangar off to their left.

"What the hell!" Gardo skidded to a stop with Burns and Devron behind him, guns drawn. Mark and Pedro stopped a few paces ahead.

The two groups stopped and eyed each other off.

Star, Drew, Tony, Carlos and Aneeka lost sight of the plane and Star finally exerted all of his energy by giving the tyre one final kick and bending over, hands on knees. "Mother fuckers," he gasped, hating the stitch that was now in his side. He stood, not straight, as his back was also killing him. Huffing and puffing he walked around the group and stood by Carlos, looking past him back toward the hangers.

Tomas was looking over at the group to their right and spied a familiar profile as that group looked at them. "Oh, my God…oh, my God…" He pushed his hoodie back for a better look, and seconds later took off running for the man in the other group.

"Oh, my God," Pedro murmured as the man ran for him. "Tomas!" His brother flew at him and grabbed him in a bear hug.

"Pedro." Tomas hung on for dear life.

"Tomas. Oh, my God," Pedro cried, hugging him back. "Tomas!"

They didn't let go, staring as if they hadn't seen one another in years. The cops all gathered around giving each other the eye, and the boys finally noticed they were being watched.

"Ah, this is my brother," they said at the same time.

"So, who's that then?" Gardo and Barden asked in unison, pointing to the first group of cops that had come tearing into the airport. They eyed each other suspiciously.

The boys turned to look in the pouring rain, arms still around each other, wiping the water from their eyes for a clearer look.

Star saw a group of cops, feds and other people with two young guys at the head of the pack standing on the tarmac looking at them. "Hey," he said to Carlos and pointed toward the group. "Friends of yours?"

Tomas and Pedro saw the trench-coated man nod and point in their direction.

Carlos warily turned and recognised the two young men in front of the group instantly.

"Oh, my God," Pedro and Tomas murmured, not believing who they were seeing. They knew that face anywhere. Knew the man the way they knew their own brother.

"Pedro, Tomas." Carlos knew his brothers in an instant and ran for them as they did for him. They met in a big group hug. "Oh, my God!" he cried. "You're here, you're here. Are you okay?" He grabbed Pedro's face. "Are you okay? What are you doing here?" He grasped Tomas's shoulder. "What are you doing in America? Oh, my God, how are you?" He engulfed them again.

"What are *we* doing?" Pedro laughed. "What about you?" He hugged his older brothers fiercely, not wanting to let go.

"Oh, God, I've missed the two of you," Tomas mumbled into Carlos's shoulder as he dug his fingers in, not wanting the moment to end. "You've been gone too long, and I missed you both so much."

"Ah, my little brothers," Carlos murmured, longing for their carefree days back on Mykonos. "Where have *I* been? Where have *you* been? Why are you here? *How* are you here?"

"Friends of yours?" Star repeated from behind them.

The boys parted reluctantly. "My brothers," Carlos told Star before noticing the group now standing around them. "And something's clearly going on."

"Detective Gardo, NYPD." The trench-coated six foot Mack Truck sized detective flashed his badge. "We were tracking a man heading for that plane."

"So were we," another trench-coated average height man said. He flashed his badge. "Detective Barden, Miami PD."

"Star, LAPD." He nodded at Drew. "My partner. We were tracking that man." He pointed to the dead body on the tarmac. "Guess he was heading for that plane too."

"Then I guess we have something in common," Gardo said.

"Yeah, like being soaked to the skin," Barden said. "How about we go find somewhere warm and dry to chat, shall we."

With Carlos hanging onto his brothers, and Tony, Aneeka and Mark behind them, they were all shunted into the airport where they were met by security. But all the detectives and officers had to do was flash their badges, of which there were many, and the security guards had no control over the situation. The guards called the manager and showed everyone to a large boardroom where they were given towels and coffee by the girls that arrived along with the manager.

Everyone started talking at once.

"Now, where the hell have you two been?" Carlos demanded, keeping a hand on each of his brothers' shoulders.

"New York."

"Miami."

"Wait a minute." Pedro stopped him. "You don't get away with it that easily. What about you, Mr Hollywood Porn Star with the new hairdo?" His eyes went to his brother's hair. "Why didn't you let us know you were leaving or what you were doing? You just up and left after that shooting."

"You can't talk, little brother," Tomas reminded, eyeing him off and sliding an arm around his own waist as his stomach twinged. "You took off and became a porn star of your own. I saw the pictures."

Carlos watched the two of them. His younger brothers. God, it was so good to see them again. He frowned and looked at Tomas. "Wait. What did you say?" His head turned toward Pedro. "You're in…"

Pedro blushed. "Yeah, yeah. Not that I can talk. It seems I'm following in my big brother's footsteps. I've followed you into the big bad world of pornos."

"Pedro." Carlos's frown was still in place as he took Pedro's face in his hand. "Why?"

Pedro shrugged. "Well, when I saw you doing it, I thought, why not."

"But you're still young. You're only twenty, you have your whole life ahead of you, and that's not you anyway." Carlos's hand slid back to Pedro's shoulder.

Pedro gave a shake of his head. "It's not so bad. My movies are classier, more tasteful, and have better producers." He raised his brows in amusement. "And then I had my own troubles, so back to Carlos since it all started with you. Why did you just up and leave and not let anyone know where you were, or what you were doing?"

Carlos took a deep breath. "I had to. I had to get out of there. I have no idea what the hell that was about."

"What *was* it about?" Tomas asked. "You were called a rapist and murderer. Mama and Papa were sickened by it." He shook his head. "What did *you do,* Carlos?"

"Nothing." Carlos vehemently shook his head. "*I did nothing.* I did *not* rape anyone, and I certainly didn't shoot anyone."

"Then why didn't you stay?" Pedro asked. "Why didn't you stay and fight it?"

"Because I think the gunman was aiming for me and got the woman by mistake. Connie heard the shots, got me inside her room, and told me to meet her by the dock. I raced home and got my stuff and left the letter. Did Mama get the letter? The cops didn't get it did they?"

Two heads shook no.

"Mama got it," Pedro said.

Carlos sighed. "Good," pause, "Connie and Vivian got me out on the ferry to Athens and then on a private jet to L.A. Harry, uh, my new boss, sorted everything out." He turned to Tony who was hovering nearby. "It was all sorted out, wasn't it? Uh, this is Tony, he works for Harry and has been my bodyguard for a few weeks," he told his brothers.

Tony stepped closer. "There was nothing to sort out because it sorted itself out."

Carlos frowned. "What do you mean nothing to sort out?"

"The cops were all over the house," Tomas added.

Tony shrugged. "By the time Harry got me on the case it had been sorted. The cops said it was a case of mistaken identity and a lovers' tiff that had gone awry. You were just in the wrong place at the wrong time."

"If that's the case then, why did all of this happen?" Carlos asked him.

Another shrug. "Dunno," Tony said. "We thought it was a bit strange."

Tomas thought about it. "That's kinda what happened with me. Stuff started in Miami, but all of a sudden it changed gears. I'm brought here, and now this."

Pedro nodded. "Same with me. Now, I'm here." He motioned to Mark. "My bodyguard, Mark Monroe."

Carlos nodded at him and looked around. "Well, there's a hell of a lot of cops for whatever *is* going on, and it all has to do with that plane and who was on it."

"So," Star started as the detectives gathered round. "What have *you* boys been up to and what are your parts in all of this?"

"Searching for a kidnapper," Gardo replied, shrugging off his trench coat and laying it over the closest chair. "Turns out, my kidnapper not only worked for Andros Poulos, the man who was after *my* Stephanopoulos, but someone up the food chain." He downed the remains of his first coffee and picked up another from the tray on the table. "Looks like we got a big fish to fry here somewhere." He looked at Star, Drew and Barden. "Any ideas?"

Barden shook his head and wrapped his thick cold fingers around his coffee cup for warmth. "I have four dead drug-riddled gay porn stars, a spurned ex-lover, and a flat out raving necrophiliac to deal with, so whoever the guy was that took *my* Stephanopoulos, we found him and ended up shooting him before getting any information." He sipped the hot brew in his cup and let the molten liquid slide down his cold, sore throat.

Gardo raised his brows and grinned. "Is that all you had?" he asked, and Barden wearily grinned back.

Drew sighed, crossed his arms, and half sat beside Barden on the table in the middle of the room. With a glance over his shoulder at the three brothers, he said, "Our Stephanopoulos seems to have caused a hell of a headache. A dead ex-girlfriend, a kidnapped photographer, and two dead henchmen. Ours caused trouble for weeks."

Star snorted. "Is that what you call it?" He called his partner out. "That little cock sucker has been the bane of my existence for weeks, and that's more than *mere trouble*." He shifted position and snarled across the room at the brothers, slamming his hands onto his hips as the rest of the cops and Feds hovered around the table, chatting and warming themselves with coffee and blankets. "He's a little cock sucker that needs to be taught a lesson."

Drew warily eyed his partner. He'd never seen him so angry over anyone, but the last few weeks had turned Star into some sort of raving maniac out for revenge on everybody.

Gardo's eyes narrowed. He knew types like Star. Hot-headed like himself, but also angry and full of resentment at his lot in life and the fact minorities and people who didn't seem to work hard for anything always got more than him. Arrogance, narcissism, and self-loathing all rolled into one. Cops like Star thought the world owed them and got pissed off when it didn't deliver.

Barden stayed quiet. He was a people watcher from way back, and after flying around in the freezing fall winds and rain during the investigation, he was running low on energy. And Star was not someone he wanted to get into a row with when he was not running at his peak. He knew better than to confront men like Star, knew to stay out of their way and let them self-destruct all in their own time.

Just down the side of the room from his seat at the table, a black-suited Fed eyed everyone. He was a trained profiler, and knew exactly what everyone in that room was just by reading their body language, and hearing the words out of their mouths.

Well now, let me see, he thought. *The three brothers have no idea what's going on as their actions and speech portray. They're hugging and holding and speaking and acting like they haven't seen each other in the months they've been apart. Their body language speaks of nothing else but truth, some fear, and an utter lack of information.*

The two men standing behind them are stoic, hard-backed, like they have a rod up their ass, military trained maybe. Trained in more than that, martial arts, know how to handle guns and deal with crazed people. But how did two kidnappers get past them? His eyes travelled up and down Tony and Mark who caught him out when they stared back. He smiled slightly, knowing full well they knew what he was and did. So they hardened even more against his eyeball invasion. *They're good*, he thought. *They would probably hold up well against torture techniques.*

His gaze roamed around the room to the many cops there as part of their job, having tagged along in the three car chases for the kidnappers. Now they hung around to see those cases out until the end. *And that's all they're doing*, he surmised, watching two officers called Burns and Devron in particular. *But they're making mental notes. Look at the way their eyes are taking everything in. They're watching everyone closely, studying body language and listening to words being said. Yes*, he thought, *those two want to go somewhere and be something, and they're on the lookout for it.* He eyed Devron's six feet of hard-muscled blackness. *Not sure he'll get far being gay, though, closeted or not. But I think he'll give it a damn good go.*

And then there were the detectives. They were only there to claim a win. With one in particular, Star, there for the glory only. He knew men like Star, and he needed to be told by a higher authority, not that that always stopped him. *Like now*, he thought. *He's been threatened with suspension over this case and yet has doggedly gone after the criminal with every ounce of anger he has.*

The suit eyed Star up and down. *He may be good at what he does, but he can be a son of a bitch doing it. And his poor partner Drew. A weak man, or maybe polite and well-mannered are the words for him. Rarely let's his temper flare and is always stopping Star from making a mistake. Sadly for you, though,* the suit scratched his chin, *it could be the downfall of your career unless you stop partnering him.*

Then there was Gardo, who knew his position in life and had worked damn hard for it. His size and bulk held him in good stead and helped make him what he was. A formidable opponent when it came to crime. He knew all about Gardo's track record. And a damn good one it was. Nine out of ten crims caught and the only real one not yet captured was Nedro Scarvo. The suit took a sip of coffee. *The one criminal so many cops wanted, and Gardo was yet to catch. I doubt he's going to let retirement stop him from trying.*

And Jeremiah Barden is a slow burner. He spent his years working his way up dealing with Miami crime, and now the gay scene that's currently thriving. Four dead porn stars and a necrophiliac! How I'd love to help him with that one.

His attention turned to the stunning African American woman walking into the room. *Now,* he thought, *how does she figure into things?* He liked women of style and class, and this one had it, even if she was a Negro. It didn't matter to him. While he'd never been with a black woman before, he had no qualms in admiring the beauty of them. And this one was definitely a beauty. Regal, tall, slim, and in control of every man around her.

His head swung back at the mutterings down the table and saw the black fury sweep over Star's face as he stared at the woman across the room, hands on hips, brows so far down they were joined between his eyes. *Ah, look at that. The anger, hatred, and resentment are so evident, and then there are all those other things I'd like to get into,* he thought. His eyes swung from Star's facial expression to watch the woman approach the brothers.

"Carlos, I've just called Harry to let him know we are safe. Vivian was there as well." Aneeka came up behind the three brothers.

Carlos turned to her. "Thanks for that. I can't wait to see Viv again."

"I'm sure she feels the same way," Aneeka replied warmly, looking the boys up and down.

"Boys, this is—"

"Aneeka Ne Masta, one of the best photographers in the world." Pedro reached out to shake her hand. "Pleasure."

"And it is a pleasure to see such good genetics run in the family." She shook hands with both brothers. "No wonder you're all famous."

"All?" Carlos asked. "Who?" He turned to Tomas with a crestfallen expression. *"Not you, too?"*

Tomas blushed softly, a small smile coming to his lips. "I found my way into it through someone I met."

"Ah, Jesus, Tomas!" Carlos managed before being interrupted.

"All right, all right, listen up porn brothers," Star yelled over the commotion, thinking he could *and would* take control of the whole situation. For that was what Star's personality was all about. Being in control. And when he wasn't…look out. Carlos frowned at the phrasing as Star continued. "We've all had a little chat, now we wanna hear from you three. From the beginning, shall we." He downed his coffee and slammed the cup onto the table.

Carlos sighed and looked around the room. There were cops, Feds and detectives. He leant against the edge of the cupboard behind him with Pedro and Tomas to his right, all three of them standing with their arms crossed.

Aneeka, Tony and Mark stood to his left.

"I have no idea how this started except that someone wanted to frame me for the murder of a friend," Carlos started.

"I meant," Star interrupted with an impatient wave of his hand. *"The beginning.* As in, that little rape and murder crime you were wanted for but somehow, *someway,* the case suddenly disappeared, and it's all a case of mistaken identity. Start from Mykonos and go from there."

Carlos's frown deepened. Where the hell is this going and what does it have to do with what's happening now?

"Same goes for you two." Star pointed to Pedro and Tomas. "One at a time."

The brothers exchanged looks.

With another sigh, Carlos started again. "I was a masseur by night and was on to my second customer when the previous customer suddenly popped up and called my current customer a whore and asked *how could she?* I turned and saw a man with a gun with the woman, and took off running when the gun went off."

"Masseur, huh?" Star harrumphed almost triumphantly, so ready to burn the porn star to the ground with his attitude. "You were *more* than a masseur. You were a cock for sale. You fucked the women for money." His contempt was evident, and so was his 'I've got him now' grin. His eyes quickly went around the room to see that his fellow officers were watching the porn star with interest. *Oh, I've so got him,* he thought.

Carlos burned with fury inside. "So what if I did?" he snapped. "Are you *jealous* of my ten inch cock and the amount of women it's had, detective? Or the fact I get paid thousands to fuck hundreds of women you can only *dream* of fucking yourself?"

Snickers went through the room, and Star reddened like a sun-drenched tomato, growing redder still when his fellow detectives joined in the laughter with sidelong glances and sniggers.

"Either way," Carlos continued, seeing his discomfort. "There *was* no rape, and I *didn't shoot anyone.*"

"How did you get off Mykonos?" Barden asked from his spot on the table where he sat sideways so he could see all three brothers. He marvelled how a half Greek could not look Greek. Unlike his brothers, Carlos had no visible Greek in him whatsoever.

"I had help from friends," Carlos told him. "They got me on the ferry, then on a plane to Hollywood, and I stayed with one of them for a while."

"What happened then?" Gardo straightened his blazer and shifted closer to Barden. He wanted his own clear view of the brothers so he could try and figure out how one little boy called Pedro could get himself into so much trouble. And now he was finding out it had to do with his two older brothers. *Ah,* Gardo thought. *That's brotherly love for ya. The family that plays together, and gets involved with crime together, stays together.*

"Everything was supposedly taken care of by my new boss, and things were fine until the day I went into Rosalee's house. I had called her about having lunch, and she said she wanted me to come over. I did and found her naked. We had sex, and I got hit over the head with something. When I came to I was tied to a chair, and there was a man having sex with her, another was standing to my right, watching. They made me watch her being raped then they injected her and hit me over the head again. I blacked out and came to when the sirens were coming, and I stumbled out the back door and over to Aneeka's."

"I knew that fence wasn't a gardening accident," Star yelled across the room, surprising everyone as he pointed his thick, calloused accusatory forefinger at her.

Aneeka didn't move except for one brow that arched itself into position. "Very astute of you, *detective*."

His eyes narrowed at the insult, and his hands moved for his hips. He knew from psychology training that to make yourself look bigger and more threatening you put your hands on your hips and puff your chest out. Clearly, that didn't work on this woman. And he hated it.

"I slept most of the day and came up with a story to tell you," Carlos went on, ignoring Star and his childish tantrums. "After that, Aneeka was broken into, *I* was broken into, then Aneeka was kidnapped and so was I. And now we're here." Carlos spread his hands. "With thirty or so cops and Feds and my brothers involved."

"Okay, that's your story. Pedro, tell everyone yours," Gardo said and grabbed another coffee and a sandwich.

Pedro glanced at his brothers before starting. "I didn't think too much *was* happening. I worked in a club on Santorini for Andros Poulos. He owned it. All I was doing was minding my own business, and then I found out I was being drugged. He had his assistant put it into my drinks when I was working."

"Pedro," Carlos said. "Are you all right? You didn't keep taking them, did you? Mama and Papa didn't raise us to do drugs."

"I know, I know," Pedro replied with a small wave of his hand, blushing and hating being chastised by his older brother in front of so many cops. "I didn't know he was doing it, but when I found out, I stopped drinking anything they brought me." He shook his head. "I ended up sleeping with his daughter, and he found out. He threatened to kill me, but Angelina hit him over the head, and we took off for Athens and went on to New York where she was going to be attending Juilliard. Everything was okay until he attacked Angie. She took a restraining order out on him and he was arrested and charged. I crashed my car and ended up in the hospital with cops telling me they had found drugs in my car."

He glanced around the room as Carlos stood a little straighter and turned towards him. "Turns out Andros had set me up, stashing the drugs and cutting my brakes so I'd have the accident. After that, we found out I had a stalker, she jumped in my new car and drove it into Andros Poulos and killed him. That's the last thing I saw before being shoved into the trunk of a car by a guy with a gun. I managed to escape and was picked up by you and Mark." He motioned to Gardo and his bodyguard. "We made our way here, and now here we are with my brothers, finding out all about what actually happened."

"It seemed Andros Poulos was in cahoots with Nedro Scarvo, Long Island's resident drug kingpin. One of his cohorts was the one who stashed the drugs," Gardo said. "And then there was the guy who worked for Andros Poulos. He grabbed the kid, and we followed him here to Chicago, not knowing where he was going or what he was doing. He didn't make it to the plane. He was killed when they found the kid had escaped."

"Yeah, well," Star muttered, leaning on the back of a chair and crossing his legs as he stood beside his peers. "So was ours, join the club. Next."

Everyone stared at Tomas who glanced around at all of the eyes staring at him.

"That's you, lover boy," Star added.

Tomas blushed and cleared his throat. "I was a personal trainer at the same resort Carlos worked at. After both he and Pedro had left, I decided to pack my bags and leave as well. Some of the guests I trained lived in Miami and they offered me a place to stay and help to get my career off the ground. So after getting involved with someone I shouldn't have, I moved there and was immediately welcomed with open arms. After a few weeks, I met Roger who…" He briefly glanced at his brothers with a slight movement of his head. "Introduced me to the world of porn."

Carlos groaned. "Oh, God, I really can't believe you too."

Tomas kept going, but he was rapidly declining in every way, shape and form, especially his breathing and strength. "Everything was going well. We moved in together and were making movies, but things were happening. Roger's car was damaged by some vandal, things were stolen from the studio, and then other actors were being killed off. Roger was fingered—"

"I'm sure he was," Star muttered.

Tomas reddened and shifted uncomfortably. "And he was arrested. I'd been feeling unwell for a few days and collapsed. I ended up in the hospital, and that's when I was kidnapped and taken away. The rest is hazy because I was so sick, but I ended up here at the airport with Barden pulling me out of a car and telling me what had happened. Turns out, a guy I met on Mykonos decided to kill off anyone I worked with or got involved with. As for the other guy, I have no idea who he was or what he wanted." He noticed Pedro looking at him strangely and frowned, feeling his stomach lurch.

"Tomas, are you okay now? You don't look so good." Carlos leant past Pedro, to intently examine his brother's face.

Tomas swallowed and blinked slowly. "I'm weak, but okay. I think. Apparently, my milk was poisoned, and I was slowly ingesting it day by day. I got the cure in the hospital. I'll be okay...I hope..." His strength slipped further, and his breathing laboured.

"We need to get you checked out again after the ordeal you went through," Carlos said, reaching out to him. He turned to the cops. "Can we get a doctor to check him over?"

Barden nodded. "I'll get the airport doctor in."

Carlos thought about it. "All three of us have been set up for, or affected by, crimes we didn't commit. What the hell is going on? Because clearly, *something is* going on?"

The black-suited man finally stood. "My name is Special Agent Payday from the FBI." He flashed his badge around. "I suggest you gentlemen," he told the four detectives, "tell your stories now." He put his badge away and waited.

Star rolled his eyes at the interruption from some FBI bigwig that had nothing to do with it. "I suppose I'll go first. We first caught wind of Carlos Stephanopoulos when we were called to a house. We found the body of Rosalee Brentworth on her bed, naked, injected, surrounded by drugs. Her place was turned over, there was no sign of a break and enter, and the only two things out of place was the broken side fence to Ms Ne Masta's house and the car parked out front. This we found out belonged to Mr Stephanopoulos. Ms Ne Masta gave us a detailed description of the two men she had seen in Ms Brentworth's backyard, and we found Mr Stephanopoulos at her house the next day. We kept a tail on him, as well as the two men."

He shifted position to make himself look like the most important man in the room. "But we found these men to be using aliases to hire cars, motel rooms, etc. We wanted to link one of them to several assaults that happened, but had no hard evidence. We did get one of their prints and photo, plus a passport and ID when he was arrested for indecent exposure just down the road from Mr Stephanopoulos's. His name was Dimitri Yustoff. We kept an even closer eye on them then. Not long after, we followed the men to the Venice Beach Pier where we arrested Mr Vega for interfering in a sting operation."

Tony mumbled under his breath. He moved and sneered at Star, flexing the biceps of his tightly crossed arms.

Star snidely glanced at Tony. "*He* informed us that Ms Ne Masta and Mr Stephanopoulos had been kidnapped. Once we had details and put out an all-points bulletin, an off-duty cop spotted Dimitri Yustoff on the highway to Vegas, and we followed. All the way here to O'Hare. Clearly, he was catching a flight. Clearly, they didn't want to wait for him. And now here we are." He spread his hands. "Wasting our time sharing when we could be catching them at the other end."

"Do you know which company that plane was registered to, or who *owns* the company?" Payday asked, knowing what the answer would be.

Star's face reddened. "No, not yet."

"Well, *we do,* so wait your turn," Payday said, sliding his hands into his pockets. "Gardo, you're next."

Gardo put down his coffee cup and stood. He'd been sitting through the boys' explanations and Star's diatribe and now took centre stage. Burns and Devron were behind him, ready to back up the story and add their bit if needed. "Mr Stephanopoulos first came to our attention after the assault on Angelina Poulos. Her father had done the deed, but blamed the kid, clearly wanting him to go to jail so he was free and clear. But Angelina filed charges and Poulos was arrested. After that, we had the drugs and cut brakes, plus the shooting outside of *Studio 69*, New York's hottest nightclub where Mr Stephanopoulos works as the resident DJ. He was standing with Angelina and another woman when a car drove by and a shot was fired. Both women were injured, but survived. Mr Stephanopoulos got away scratch free."

Carlos looked sharply at his brother. "You forgot to mention that!"

Pedro had the decency to look sheepish. "Did I?" He nonchalantly shrugged a shoulder at his scowling brother.

"We kept an eye on Mr Stephanopoulos and found out he had a stalker who then proceeded to kill Poulos the other night outside of 69. He was kidnapped by our small time crook in those few moments, and we followed them here to Chicago, but we couldn't track down his name, although, I guess we will now. A very tangled web it all was, and I'm sure, *still* is." He grabbed another coffee from the fresh tray of drinks the airport staff brought around. "Someone is definitely out to get you boys."

Payday spoke up. "Barden, your turn."

Jeremiah Barden straightened from his spot on the table and slowly glanced at every face of every person in the room as he spoke. "Tomas Stephanopoulos first came to our attention when we were called to Marcus Seralift's home for a dead body. A porn star, dead of a suspected overdose, which was nothing unusual. What *was* unusual is that it was the first of many. Three more actors from *Seralift Productions* all died in the same way, and *all* had their fingers pointed at Mr Roger Dencott, Mr Stephanopoulos' partner *on* screen and in real life."

Devron's interest perked up at that tidbit of information, and he eyed Tomas with renewed interest. A *gay* Greek God. *Mmm, the Greeks are definitely tasty looking indeed,* he thought as his lips laid themselves on a fresh cup of coffee he imagined was hot hard Greek cock. *Pedro's tall and white and gorgeous, but Tomas is dark and brooding and gay. Just the way I like them.*

Pedro and Carlos turned their heads to look at Tomas who reddened. He clenched his jaw, and his eyes swept the floor. His sexuality had never been discussed with his family, and it was embarrassing for them to find out this way. Not to mention all the cops who were staring. His jaw clenched harder, and he hugged himself tighter.

"It came to the chase when the fourth body was left in the underground car park to their apartment. I arrested Dencott for it, and Stephanopoulos collapsed in my station. He was rushed to the hospital and we found he had been poisoned. I managed to put two and two together and realised his milk was what had been tampered with. We rushed it to the hospital for analysis, and he was given the drug to counteract it. That's when Luiz Manning took him from the hospital and absconded with him. We found Manning's body in a seedy hotel room with a bullet through the forehead. Stephanopoulos was gone, but after a report from a guy at a gas station hearing someone in a trunk yelling for help, *and* seeing the driver flash his gun, I knew it was them and followed them here to Chicago. I kept track on the radio and heard about the other boys and what was going on. We found Tomas not long before the rest of you got here. We had to shoot our guy dead as he tried to make his getaway." He glanced at the other detectives with a cocked brow. "All three brothers kidnapped and brought here to Chicago. Coincidence times three?"

"Tomas," Carlos said quietly. "Are you all right now?" He reached across Pedro to squeeze his brother's arm, but Tomas swiftly moved past him and walked out the door.

"Tomas?" Carlos said in surprise, standing. Glancing back at everyone he said, "Let's take a break, he's clearly still not well." He followed him out the door with Pedro hot on his heels. They found Tomas halfway down the hallway leaning against the wall, breathing heavily and looking quite sick.

"Tomas," Carlos called. "Are you still feeling sick? You need to see a doctor. What about having some food and drink? That might make you feel better." But one look at his brother's shame-filled burning face and he knew exactly what it was about. He softened and held Tomas's face in his hands. "Oh…Tomas. Are you okay? Because *it's* okay." Shaking his head, he added, "I always wondered. You weren't into girls, but I was never sure if you were into boys either."

Tomas's face crumpled into tears and he slid down the wall until he was crouching. Wrapping his arms around his head, he sobbed.

"Tomas." Carlos went down to the floor and held his brother tight with Pedro right there beside him.

"It's all been a lot for you, being poisoned and all. You must still be so weak and sick. Maybe you need to go back to the hospital to make sure you're okay." He rubbed his brother's back. "As for being gay, that's okay. We don't hate you, we don't anything. You're our brother, we love you." He kissed his head and pulled back.

Tomas rubbed his hands over his face and through his hair. "I've never mentioned anything, never said, never thought, but Mama…"

"*She* knows?" Pedro asked, sliding his arm around Tomas's shoulder.

"I told her," Tomas said, finally looking up. "She…she was okay with it after a few moments, but Papa…"

"Does *he* know?" Carlos asked.

Tomas shook his head. "I didn't tell him, and I doubt Mama has but…oh, God, if he finds out… What will he do? We're Greek. Greek men aren't gay, they're manly and masculine and straight." He replicated their father's words. "How many times have we heard stuff like that over the last few years?"

"I'm sure Mama will bring Papa round," Carlos said. "Once they find out we're all alive and healthy it will be okay." His smile was lopsided. "This Roger guy, does he make you happy?"

A bright smile slowly lit up Tomas's face. "Yes."

Carlos smiled and nodded. "Good, *but*…what about the person you were involved with but shouldn't have been? And this Luiz Manning? Are they the same…? What…?" He swallowed. "What was going on there?"

The smile disappeared from Tomas's face and he closed his eyes. "Yes, they're the same person. Luiz was…my first…I didn't know who he was, just that I was intensely attracted to him." His head bowed, ashamed of the whole thing. "I only found out after it happened…that he was engaged to one of my clients, and I vowed to end it…but he followed me out to one of the islands and we…" He shuddered. "We spent the weekend together. I didn't want it to end, but I knew what I was doing was wrong, and so I confessed the whole thing to Bertha St John who told me she knew all about his bisexuality and that we should both dump him."

Ragged laughter tore from his throat. "I saw him once in Miami before I met Roger, then once more when we had a coffee at a café. Then all of the murders, and Roger getting arrested, and me getting sick…I never for the life of me thought it was *him* doing it." He glanced up under hooded eyes. "I never thought anything like that would ever happen."

Carlos kissed the top of his head. "Well, it's over now. He's dead, and you're with a man you love. Does he treat you well?"

Tomas lifted his head, a silly smile on his face. "Yeah. Yeah, he does. I love him so much." His emotions flowed over his face like a waterfall, and he heaved a breath.

Carlos saw those emotions and nodded. "Good. I can't wait to meet him."

Tomas suddenly frowned. "Oh, my God, I should call him. I wonder if Barden has had him released yet."

"I have." Barden walked up to them, and the boys helped a weary Tomas stand. "Just now during the break. I told them to hold him there because I'd let you know and you might want to call. But right now, you're needed back inside."

They walked back into the room, supporting Tomas as they went, and stood where they had before.

"So…" Payday stood when he saw them enter and walked over to a whiteboard on the end wall where he picked up a black marker to start laying out the issues. "What we have here is a case of connect the dots."

He drew three circles down the left side of the board. "We have three brothers. All accused of crimes or connected to them. All attacked by thugs." He drew three smaller circles to represent the thugs to the right of the first three and drew connecting lines.

"What we know is, someone pulled off all three crimes against the boys, but we don't know who." He drew a big circle on the right side of the board.

"We know that all of the thugs involved were coming here to Chicago to catch a plane." He drew a plane and connected lines to the thugs. "Do they work for someone? Do they work for the same company? Did they know each other? Did they all complete their missions? No. What we *do* know is that plane is registered to Brickam West Imports here in Chicago."

He drew a circle to the right of the plane and wrote the initials BWI in it then added a connecting line. "What we know is that company is owned by Freeman Imports, a global company that operates around the world." He drew another circle to the right with the initials FI and another line. "What we know is Freeman Imports is owned by Papadopoulos Exports in Athens, Greece, and that is owned by Stefano Papadopoulos who lives in Athens." He finished connecting the dots and added the initials SP to the large circle on the far right of the board.

Carlos frowned. Where had he heard that name before?

"And who's Stefano Papadopoulos?" Star asked, his arms going from his hips to being crossed in front of him. He hated being out of the loop and his arrogance over the matter had gotten the best of him.

"A very wealthy businessman with many pies containing many fingers," Payday said, putting the marker down and brushing off his hands. "We've been looking into him for some time."

"What for?" Gardo asked. "Does he run mobs? Drugs?"

"All of the above and then some." Payday walked back to his seat at the table and grasped the back of his chair. "We have managed to track down every limb of the tree, the *family* tree, from Papadopoulos." He stared at Pedro. "To Andros Poulos, who, at one stage, was his stepson."

Pedro glared back in surprise. "What?"

"Yes." Payday returned the look. "I couldn't believe it either, especially when I just put it all together during the break."

"What together?" Star asked, now downing his fifth coffee. He needed another toilet break and was getting pissed off that he wasn't up to speed because some FBI twat wasn't telling him anything except when making a grand declaration to the whole room.

Payday tried to hide his amusement. *Ah, men like Star. Arrogant assholes who think they know it all.* "That Papadopoulos is also connected to the murder of Luiz Manning in Miami. You know why?" He watched Tomas. "Because Luiz was Andros's illegitimate son that he never claimed."

That surprised Tomas, and he stood a little straighter.

"And finally..." He turned to Carlos. "Papadopoulos is behind getting the charges against *you* dropped. Apparently, the shooter was taken care of. Not to mention the kidnapping."

"But why would he do that?" Carlos asked. "We don't know anyone by the name of Papadopoulos. Why would he get us out of our legal troubles?"

"Are *you sure* you don't know him?" Payday asked, searching his face intently. "There must be *some* connection somewhere?"

"If there is I don't know it," Carlos snapped and rubbed his head. "The name is vaguely familiar, like I've heard it somewhere, but can't place it."

"*Think, damn it!*" Star thumped his large fist on the table. "If you're caught up in this—"

"Enough!" Payday yelled, and Star stopped and stared. "*You're not in charge* Detective Star. *None* of you are. Whereas *I am.*"

"But I—" Star started.

"Are just a cop, and *I'm* an FBI agent," Payday said. "*I* have jurisdiction."

The pain was banging around in Carlos's head like a hammer. "Ugh, I can't think."

"You have to," Payday went on as he turned back to him. "Whatever you know, or have heard, *we need* to know it too."

Everyone in the room was staring at him, muttering, focussing their attention. Star was giving him the evil eye. Gardo and Barden were watching. Payday was staring intensely. It was all too much. "No, I can't, not here, not now. My head is killing me." He dropped the towel from around his shoulders and stormed out of the room.

Tony moved after him, but Aneeka stopped him. "Let me," she told the room. "He needs a few minutes of peace and quiet." Tony nodded, and she followed Carlos down the hall to the floor-to-ceiling window. "It was too much for you to handle in that room." Her voice was low and soothing.

Carlos sighed. The pounding had subsided with the quiet. "Yes, too much."

She massaged his neck and the back of his head. "Just relax," she soothed. "Let it all go. Let the stress leave your body. The tiredness, the fear, the problems. Let it all go. Let it all wash away on a wave of warm salty ocean. Warm and soft and enveloping you as you float along."

Carlos breathed deeply and let everything go.

"Remember back," Aneeka went on. "Remember the voice, the person, whoever it was. Wherever it was that you heard the name, Papadopoulos. Just listen to the name being said and let your mind remember everything else around it."

Carlos's mind drifted back.

"Papadopoulos you have no right to be here. I owe you nothing. Get out of my shop and don't come back."

"You don't get to tell me what to do Stephanopoulos. You're just a lowlife little scum at the bottom of the pool. I have more, I own more, I am more than you'll ever be."

"And I don't care."

"No, you wouldn't. You have your foreign wife and your half-breed sons—"

"Don't you ever call my children that!"

"Or what? You'll kill me?"

"I won't need to."

Silence.

"What does that mean?"

"It means that I won't be the one to deal with you... He never liked

you, in fact, he *hated you."*

"Are you threatening me…with him?"

"Do I need to?"

The meat store formed in Carlos's mind. He'd been seventeen, working one afternoon when his father had a visitor at the back door. He'd never seen who it was, but definitely heard the voice.

"He won't do anything to help you and your half-breed—"

Thwack!

The thud was heard through the store making Carlos jump. He knew his father had just slammed his meat cleaver into one of the wood boards on the table out back.

"I told you not to call my sons that."

Silence.

"Mmm…well don't get on the wrong side of me, Stephanopoulos. You won't win."

"Neither will you."

Carlos's eyes flew open, and there was a sharp intake of breath. Turning on his heel, he sped down the hallway to his brothers who were standing there waiting, huddled together for warmth and comfort and support.

"What's going on?" they asked together.

"We're leaving," Carlos replied.

"Where are we going?" Their expressions showed their surprise and curiosity.

"Home!"

"And where would home be these days?" Payday asked as the detectives gathered in the doorway.

"Mykonos," Carlos said. "We're going home tonight. But we need a private plane, no names, and we can't land in Athens."

"Why not?" Payday asked, intrigued by the sudden change in plans and Carlos's behaviour. Clearly, something was going on.

Carlos stared at him. "Because *he* can't know we're home…and we also don't have our passports."

"All right, what's going on?" Star demanded. "Who do you think you are, giving the orders?" He slammed his hands onto his hips as was his habit.

"*He's* not," Payday told the hostile Star. "*I* am." He now turned to his men. "Get a private plane ready. We'll fly into Mykonos. Tell no one. No names, no credentials. Nothing."

"Who do you think—" Star started with a waving finger.

"The FBI," Payday told him before encompassing the rest of the group. "The rest of you are dismissed. You can all head back to your hometowns. The FBI has official control of this case. We'll keep your captains informed of what's happening so you can close your cases." After a moment of confused, but relieved expressions, he turned back to Carlos. "Tell me why Mykonos? Why home? You remember something; you remember where you heard the name."

Carlos glanced at the others then beckoned Payday down the hallway out of earshot. "Seven years ago I was working in my father's meat shop when someone turned up at the back door. My father said his name, Papadopoulos, and then he threatened my father. But they also mentioned a *he*. No name, just *he*." Carlos shrugged. "I think we should go home on the sly and find out from my father, then go and see Papadopoulos to find out what's going on."

Payday nodded thoughtfully. "One step at a time. We'll get to Mykonos then Athens. But first…" He looked down at Carlos. "We need to make sure you blend in with us." They walked back to the others where Star, Drew, Gardo, Barden and Payday's men were waiting. "Take these boys to the menswear store and get them suits, they need to look like us, and I'll call the doctor in to check on this one." He pointed to Tomas, and his men nodded and led them away.

Aneeka stepped up to Payday and spoke with the natural allure she always used to get what she wanted from men. "We will be going too, Agent Payday, but we also don't have our passports, money, clothes or bags. Will the FBI be gracious enough to pay for the things *we* need?"

Payday generously eyed her up and down then gave Mark and Tony a cold once over as they were of no real interest to him. "Go and get some things from the pharmacy and a change of clothes. We'll foot the bill."

She smiled graciously, gave a nod of her head, and held his hand between both of hers as thanks. "Thank you, Special Agent Payday. Thank you very much." Turning on her heel, she took off for the pharmacy.

Tony and Mark stayed. Turns out, they knew something of each other, and while they had never met, had heard many stories of past battles.

"Do you know who Carlos works for?" Tony asked Payday.

"And Pedro?" Mark added.

"Harry DeVille and Greta Von Burro along with Marcus Seralift are the porn kings and queen of the business." *Ah yes,* Payday thought. *I know all about them.*

"Harry wants me here all the way, protecting his asset, so I'll be coming," Tony said.

"And Pedro hired me personally, so I'm in," Mark added.

Payday nodded. "I don't like it, but then if they have the two of you to protect them, we won't need to."

Tony and Mark nodded. "That's our job."

*****

After towelling down and being fitted for a suit, Pedro took a few minutes to phone Angelina. "Babe, it's me. I'm in Chicago. I'm okay."

"Oh, my God, Pedro," Angelina cried down the line. "I was so scared. I haven't heard anything. The police haven't called me, and Sara-Michelle hasn't heard from Mark, although, she's on the phone now. I didn't know if you were alive or dead or okay…" she sobbed.

"Angie," he murmured. "I'm okay. But I can't come home to New York yet. We need to go home to Mykonos to sort this shit out. Something big is going on and the cops, and Feds, and FBI are involved. And you'll never guess what. Carlos and Tomas are here as well. Someone wants to cause trouble for all of us, and this needs to be dealt with. The FBI are taking us home to sort it out."

"Oh, God, back home. I want to come. Please don't say no. I love you. I need to come over there."

"Look, I have no idea what's going to happen." Pedro glanced over his shoulder to look around the airport. The phones were about twenty feet from the men's shop, and Mark and Tony had arrived to keep an eye on them. "I know Carlos's friend Aneeka is coming; she's getting a hotel room in Athens, paid for by the FBI no less, and she told me to give the address to you and to wait for her there if you decided to come."

"Oh, that's good." Angelina sighed. "There's so much I have to tell you. To *say* to you. I love you, and I never want to be apart again."

"I never want to be apart from you. I love you, Angie. I'll see you in a day or two in Athens. If you don't hear from me don't worry, we'll be taking care of business. It's the *Elegance Hotel*, and ask for Aneeka Ne Masta. And can you bring my passport, papers and money, and a suitcase with clothes?"

"Okay, I'll bring everything. I love you."

"I love you, too. Bye." He hung up and saw Tomas with his back to him on the other phone. He gave his shoulder a quick squeeze as he walked past.

Tomas acknowledged Pedro's touch and nervously twirled the phone cord around his fingers. "Roger, it's me. Are you okay?"

"Me! What about you? You were in the hospital sick and dying. Are you okay? Have you seen a doctor? How do you feel? Are you hurt? Did that bastard do anything to you I know it was Luiz who killed off our friends and tried to set me up for their murders the lying stinking bastard." He finally took a breath.

"I'm fine," Tomas interrupted, feeling the burn of passion for the man he loved being so worried about him. "A bit weak and woozy, but the doctor's going to check me over in a minute. Look, the reason I'm calling, besides to hear your voice, is that we have to go home to Mykonos. Carlos and Pedro are here with me, you'd never guess what the hell's going on in a million years, but it's very confusing, and there's too much going on to explain it all over the phone."

"Do you want me to fly over?" Roger asked. "I can pack a case for you and bring it with me."

"That would be great, and bring my passport and legal papers. I may need them. A friend of Carlos is getting a hotel room in Athens that you can go to. I don't know how long this will take, or what it's about, or who's involved, so ask for her at the counter."

"Okay, let me just get a pad and pen…okay, give it to me."

"It's the *Elegance Hotel* in Athens under the name Aneeka Ne Masta."

"The famous photographer?"

"Yeah, we'll all meet up there." He glanced up and saw Carlos waving him over. "I gotta go. I love you."

"Love you too."

"Bye." Tomas hung up and went for his fitting.

An hour later, they were boarding a private jet for Mykonos. Aneeka, Tony and Mark took seats across the aisle from the boys who looked remarkably different in suits and ties. Their hair was slicked down, and they had dark glasses to conceal their identities. It was going to be a very long flight, and they had much to catch up on.

"So…" Carlos directed a stare at Pedro. "Angelina?"

A goofy smile spread across Pedro's face. "Yeah."

Carlos laughed. "Are you in lurve?" he teased.

Pedro's smile got bigger. "Yeah."

"Is it serious?" Tomas asked. He'd never seen his brother serious about any girl, and no girl had put a grin like that on his face before. But then he *was* only twenty.

The smile spread from ear to ear. "Yeah…what about you? Is it serious with Roger?"

Tomas frowned slightly then thought about Roger, and the same goofy Stephanopoulos grin spread across his face. "Yeah," he said softly.

Pedro's head moved up and down. "Finally, our brother is happy with someone. It was a long time coming, bro. We didn't think it was *ever* gonna happen. Guess we just needed to let you figure it all out on your own. Especially *who* you were going to be with."

Tomas looked into his brother's eyes. "Yeah, it took a while. But I found him."

"Good," Pedro said then turned to Carlos. "Now, big bro, who the hell is Viv?"

Carlos blushed.

"Ooohhh," Pedro teased. "*Clearly* someone special. A girlfriend? A lover? A wife?" Carlos looked up sharply, and Pedro leant forward in his seat. "Oh, my God, she's not your wife, is she? Did you get married and not tell Mama and Papa or us?"

Carlos sighed and waved his hand. "No, little brother. I didn't get married…but…" He thought about Viv and felt the heaving of love in his chest. "She is *definitely* someone very special indeed."

"Serious?" Tomas asked from his seat next to him.

"Very," Carlos replied, his gaze drifting out the window.

"*Very.*" Pedro leant back. He was sitting facing them and watched Carlos's face. "It really *is* serious. Just look at the loved-up expression on his face," he told Tomas. "*Very* loved-up indeed."

"Just can it and let's get down to business." Carlos pointed a finger at Pedro. "*Your* story from start to finish and don't leave anything out. I can't wait to hear how *you* got into the porn industry."

Pedro sat back and stuck his feet up on the armrest between his brothers. When they stared disdainfully at his feet, he said, "Hey, it's gonna be a long story."

Half an hour later, Carlos was shaking his head. "Pedro, Pedro, Pedro. You always did get yourself into trouble, and fucking the boss's daughter was what started it all off."

Pedro shrugged. "I couldn't help it. I was high on drugs, and she was offering herself to me…I took her and *kept* on taking her. Besides, she's hot and gorgeous, and I love her."

"Did she encourage you to start in the business, or are you still using me as an excuse?" Carlos asked.

Pedro shrugged and pulled a face. "If you can do it why can't I? Besides, it pays well, and I get to do what you do, write my scripts and earn more money."

"Is that what you *are* doing, or what you'll *be* doing and *still* using me as an excuse for it?" Carlos joked.

"Who knows?" Pedro grinned. "Maybe *one* day I'll stop using you as an excuse. One day when I'm old and grey and have more money than you. Like I have a bigger cock than you." The expression on his face was cockier than the tone of his voice.

"Ouch," Tomas said with a glance at Carlos. "Burn."

"Yeah, yeah," Carlos grumbled. "Not funny." He changed the direction of the conversation. "I still can't believe Barbara Weston turned her psycho attentions to you. After what she did to me, Papa hit her with a legal letter. But clearly, that didn't stop her."

"Yeah." Pedro moved his head up and down. "That was some pretty weird shit. What she did to me on the beach in Santorini, moving on to Angelina and what she did to her. The gifts she sent were seriously sick. But less about me and more about Tomas." He turned his attention to his brother.

Tomas shook his head. "Uh-uh. Let's hear about Carlos's time in Hollywood." He turned *his* attention to his older brother. "Let's hear how you won the best cock award."

Carlos groaned. "It's all a part of the industry as you boys will soon find out. Has the world seen what you have to offer yet?"

Pedro's grin went from ear to ear. "Oh, hell yeah."

Tomas's grin was not so wide. "Well, half of the world has seen it."

Carlos looked at him. "We'll make Papa come around if he has a problem."

The grin left Tomas's face. "He *will* have a problem, though."

"But he'll get over it," Pedro added. "We'll make him."

Hours later, during a stopover in Barcelona for fuel and food, they were delayed by a series of events. First, they found out Papadopoulos wasn't even in Athens, two, the authorities kept them in a small room at the airport until Payday sorted the legal side of things out, three, their plane needed repairs, and four, there was a worker's strike at the airport, all delaying them by many hours. But finally, they were back in the air and touched down in Mykonos in the early hours of Monday morning.

"Argh." Carlos arched his back after exiting the plane. "Definitely not enough room for long legs."

Pedro breathed in the air. "God, smell that. Good old Mykonos."

"Right, now, we have our plans. We'll separate once we get past the local cops," Payday said.

"They'll recognise us," Pedro said. "I went to them after Carlos left.

They'll know me for sure."

"Then hang at the back of the pack, and hope they don't notice." Payday walked ahead of the team. With six other feds, there were thirteen of them in total, and after a few minutes of to-ing and fro-ing with the local police, Payday waved them all on. They split into three groups; Pedro with Mark and three agents, Tomas with three agents, and Carlos with Tony, Aneeka and Payday. They would take different routes to the Stephanopoulos home, and the agents would stand guard while Payday went inside with the brothers.

Payday checked his watch; 3:30 am. Leading the way, he took directions from Carlos and they all arrived at their parents' house within fifteen minutes.

One of the agents stepped forward and pulled out a lock-picking kit. Since none of the boys had their keys, it was the only way to get inside. Carlos turned the handle and the door slipped quietly open. Seven of them stepped inside and closed the door behind them.

The boys went into their parents' room, and each took a side. Turning the bedside lights on, they covered their parents' mouths. "Shh," they whispered when they woke.

Jenny's eyes grew wide at the sight of her children, and Spiros frowned at the invasion.

"Shhh. Come into the lounge and don't turn the lights on," Carlos whispered. "It's important."

Spiros nodded, and the boys let them up. After grabbing dressing gowns, they turned off the lights and followed them into the lounge.

Payday flicked on a lamp, and Jenny and Spiros saw him, Tony, Aneeka and Mark.

"What's going on?" Spiros demanded.

"Keep your voice down, Mr Stephanopoulos, we don't want your neighbours to know we're here." He flashed his badge. "I'm Special Agent Payday of the FBI, and we need your help."

Jenny was smothering her boys in hugs and kisses. "Help with what? My boys are home, that's all that matters." She ran her hands through Carlos's hair. "I love it. You look so mature."

"*Our* boys are *criminals*," Spiros spat with venom. "Especially you." He eyed Carlos. "*What* did I teach you?"

"Papa—" Carlos started.

"Mr Stephanopoulos," Payday said sharply, catching Spiros's attention once more. "Your sons *are not* criminals, they have all been set up by Stefano Papadopoulos, and we want to know why." He saw Spiro's eyes widen at the name and Jenny stopped fondling the boys. "Who is he to *you,* Mr Stephanopoulos? And why does he want to set your sons up for crimes they did not commit?"

*****

It was four in the morning in Athens, and Marta Effidopolous sucked Gustoff Dropopolous's cock. Before he came, he spun her around and took her from behind as she held onto the bed sheets, half standing, half kneeling.

He thrust, and it was over within thirty seconds. Letting her go he pushed her to the bed, eyeing her as he zipped up his pants and she rolled onto her back, spreading her legs.

"Need more?"

He eyed off the tits and open pussy, and his tongue went to work.

*****

Spiros stared at Payday. "What do you mean, he set my sons up?"

"Exactly that," Payday replied and told him of the links to Papadopoulos. "Your sons are innocent of every charge against them. They have committed *no* crimes, Mr Stephanopoulos. Now, your son Carlos remembered an incident from when he was seventeen. He was working in the meat shop when Papadopoulos visited. Do *you* remember?" He watched the play of emotions cross Spiro's face.

Spiros glanced from Payday to Carlos and back before he finally spoke. "Stay away from Papadopoulos. He's dangerous."

"But *why* does he have it in for your sons?" Payday asked.

Spiros warily eyed his visitors. He hadn't seen, or heard from Stefano Papadopoulos since that day over seven years earlier. "Just leave it."

"We can't, Papa." Carlos went to his father's side. "This man has set us all up. He set *me* up for rape and murder. His stepson, Andros Poulos, tried to kill Pedro, and *his* illegitimate son kidnapped Tomas after poisoning him—"

"Oh, my God, what?" Jenny cried, one hand flying to her mouth, the other to Tomas. "Spiros," she pleaded.

Carlos glanced from her to his father knowing something was up. He went on. "All of the people involved in this are connected to Stefano Papadopoulos. *Who* is he and *why* would he be doing this? To *you*, to *us*? What did *we* ever do to him?"

They all waited with bated breath.

Spiros looked at his wife's distraught face, sighed, and finally said, "You were born."

*****

In Athens, Stefano Papadopoulos was walking downstairs to the kitchen. He was hungry and wanted something to eat. And maybe he'd wake up Maria, his maid, to service him while she was making him food. He may be seventy-five, but he could still get it up occasionally, with some work. But that didn't stop him wanting to plant it in a woman, and Maria would do. She was in her fifties, with a brat of a daughter he figured was his, so he would never touch her. The mother would have to do.

He passed the kitchen on his way to Maria's room and heard noises coming from the girl's room. The light came underneath the door, and he quietly slipped over and listened.

"Ugh, Gustoff, you are good," Marta said. "You know what to do with your tongue."

Stefano opened the door quietly and peered through the gap. Marta lying naked, sideways, and spread-eagled on her bed with Gustoff, his bodyguard, between her legs. He arched a brow and licked his lips, feeling the stirring in his groin.

"When we tell people we got married?" she asked, wincing at the pain of having her insides sucked out.

He stopped. "What?"

She put her head up and looked down at his face hovering above her bushy thatch. "When we tell everyone we got married? I told you if you helped get rid of Consuela I would marry you and make you heir to Papadopoulos fortune and that happened. He's seventy-five; he's not going to last much longer."

Stefano stood to attention. *What was that about Consuela?*

Gustoff stood up. "I think we should not tell anyone. I think we should keep it a secret."

Marta sat up. "What do you mean you want to keep it a secret? What am I giving it away for? You said you were all for it?"

"I changed my mind." He buttoned his shirt. "That mess was enough. I can't believe I let you get me into that mess."

"You got what you wanted," Marta spat. "Fucking me."

"Yes, and at the time I had no problem shooting Consuela and blowing that Carlos kid all for your daddy's fortune. The fortune you don't even know you'll get," Gustoff said. "You're just the bastard child. He either doesn't know about you, or he denies you exist. You will get nothing. Look at you, shut your legs, you're just a whore."

"You didn't have a problem the night we killed Consuela. You fucked me senseless." Marta's eyes shot daggers at him. "I'll inherit everything, and I'll make sure of it."

"Is that so?" Stefano stepped through the door brandishing the revolver he always carried in his dressing gown pocket. He closed the door behind him to block out any noise. Not that it mattered as he had a silencer on it. "*You* killed my fiancée? *You* killed Consuela? You told me that Carlos Stephanopoulos had killed her, but it was *you*?"

Marta and Gustoff backed up against the bedhead. "No, no, we didn't," they pleaded. "It really *was* him," Marta cried. "He was raping her; we stopped him."

"Stopped him?" Stefano said. "*You're* the ones who involved him in the first place. *You're* the ones who killed her. *You're* the ones who took her from the protection of this house to Mykonos to be corrupted by your vile, wicked ways. Just look at the two of you. Both whores and you made my Consuela a whore too."

"No, no, we didn't," they pleaded.

Stefano fired bullets into their stomachs. "Yes, you did. And you made me believe another person was responsible. Just as well I found out that he wasn't. Oh, yes, I've been sitting on that all these months." He watched their painful, but surprised expressions as they lay dying. "Do you know what the hilarious part of all of this is…?" He waited as they pleaded with their pain-filled eyes. "You're actually brother and sister."

*****

"There's someone I need to talk to," Spiros said. "All of you need to leave while I make the call."

"If it has anything to do with Pap—" Payday was cut off.

"It does, but it *must* remain private," Spiros said and waved everyone out. "It must be private." They all went and sat on the balcony to watch the sky lighten for the new day, and a half hour later, Spiros came back out. "It is done."

"What is?" Payday asked, getting to his feet.

"Papa?" Carlos said, standing. "What's going on?"

Spiros took a moment. "We're going to Athens to see Papadopoulos."

"I can't let you do that." Payday put up a hand in protest.

"You can't stop me," Spiros told him defiantly. "This is something that has to be done. I'll get dressed. We'll leave on the ferry." He escorted Jenny into their room to get dressed.

"What the hell's going on?" Pedro demanded of Carlos as they stood beside Tomas at the railing.

Carlos shook his head and glanced at his brothers. "I have no idea, but I think we're about to find out."

*****

In Athens, Stefano quietly called for his henchmen to remove the bodies of Marta and Gustoff. They were of no consequence to him and would not be needed. He closed and locked the door once the bed

492

had been removed and all belongings were taken. The room was empty once more. He went down the hall and entered Maria's room, removed his robe, and laid it over the chair beside the bed and climbed in beside her.

She startled, but calmed when she saw it was him and lifted her nightgown to accommodate his needs.

All of them.

*****

In Mykonos, Jenny pulled her boys aside for last kisses and hugs. She hadn't seen them in months, and there was no way she was letting them go again without getting her fair share.

"I love you," she told Carlos and squeezed him tight. "As the oldest, you need to look after your brothers. Promise me that."

"I will, Mama," he said, hugging her back fiercely.

"Now, Aneeka told me of the change in plans and that you've all invited some people to come. Who's coming for you?" She pulled back and glanced up at her son. "Someone special I hope."

He smiled. "Very special, Mama."

"Good." She stroked his cheek and moved on to Pedro. "My baby," she murmured, getting a kiss before he grabbed her in a bear hug. "You shouldn't be involved in stuff like this. You're way too young."

"I know, but I'm not a boy anymore, Mama."

"You are to me." She kissed his cheek and pulled back. "You'll always be my baby."

"Mama." He blushed. "I'm twenty now."

"Doesn't matter, you're not an adult yet, so you're still my baby. Always have been, always will be." She moved on to Tomas. "Are you okay?" She took his face into her hands. "You've been so sick and don't look that good."

"I'm getting there," he said, hugging her tightly.

"Do you have anyone special coming?" she asked for only him to hear.

He pulled his head back to look at her and smiled softly. "Yes."

"So, you've found someone?" Her heart soared.

"Yes."

"Is he good to you?"

Tomas's smile broadened. "Very."

"Good." Still hugging him, she looked at her other sons. "Now, you two, I expect you to look after him because he's been so sick *and* because he's your brother and it's what the three of you do. He needs love and care."

"Yes, Mama," they said.

"Good. Now make me proud."

Tomas bent down for another hug, and she kissed him on the head.

Aneeka stayed behind with Jenny as they would meet the men later in Athens. Spiros, the boys, Tony, Mark and the FBI went to the airport to take the plane as it would be faster than the ferry Spiros had suggested. They made sure it was fuelled, climbed aboard, and took off with Tony behind the stick and Mark as co-captain. The trip would take them about thirty minutes.

*****

In Athens, Stefano delighted in all the pleasures that was Maria Effidopolous. His loyal servant for thirty years, taking care of his house, his needs and his sexual appetite, she served in all ways, every way, to please her master. And please him she did. Just a pity she had to fall pregnant and have a bitch of a bastard child.

He came and slowly rocked to a stop, then with a groan of satisfaction rolled off her. "Ugh. Good, as always."

"Is there anything else you need?" She laid a hand on his chest.

He smiled. "No, no, that will be all." He stood, donned his robe, pulled out his gun and fired one shot into her stunned face.

Blood spattered everywhere.

"Well, that is that." He called to his henchmen to clear up the mess. "Help is so hard to find these days. Maybe I'll get a lovely young girl to come work for me."

*****

It was seven o'clock when they flew into Athens and landed at the airport. After hiring cars, they drove to the most expensive part of town and up the driveway of Stefano Papadopoulos's home.

His house was a luxurious one, what one would consider a mansion. Perched high above the city it spanned fifty acres of lush greenery and had twenty-five rooms and a garage big enough for a fleet of cars.

They alighted and slowly made their way to the door.

*****

Aneeka and Jenny made their way to the *Elegance Hotel* that morning and booked in, ordering champagne, drinks and food to be delivered.

"Oh, this is lovely," Jenny said, casting a glance at the rich, luxurious décor of the lobby. "We hardly ever come to Athens. There's no real need to."

"That seems like such a pity," Aneeka told her. "The city is beautiful. I've been here several times in the last few years for photo shoots. I always make time to play tourist and see the sites."

"Oh, yes, we've done the tourist things too, bringing the boys here when they were younger so they could learn about their heritage." They stepped into the lift and went up to their suite. "Spiros wanted them to learn about his half too."

"Of course he would. It's a part of them. Especially Tomas. He looks very much like his father."

"Yes," Jenny told her as they entered their suite. "He does take after his father in looks, but Carlos always intrigued people the most since he doesn't look Greek."

"Yes." Aneeka put her brand-new handbag on the sofa. "That seems to be the thing that people mention most. The fact he looks nothing like a Greek."

Jenny laughed. "Yes. He's gotten that his whole life, poor thing."

After freshening up and settling in, Aneeka called Harry's room to let them know they were there, and shortly after, Harry, Harriet, Connie and Vivian entered the suite.

"Jenny, this is Harry and Harriet DeVille, Connie DeLuca and Vivian Villiers." Aneeka introduced them as they came through the door. "Everyone, this is Jenny Stephanopoulos, Carlos's mother."

They all shook hands, and Jenny asked, "Which one of you got my son into porn?"

Viv and Connie flushed at their parts in it, but Harry guffawed. "Well, I'd like to think that he got *himself* into it. After his sexual endeavours on Mykonos, I'd say the boy was ripe for the picking."

Jenny arched a brow and narrowed her eyes. "I know my son, all three of my sons, have healthy sexual appetites, but that doesn't mean they're ripe for the picking by old fart Lotharios like you to be used for making money by getting their clothes off on the big screen." She lifted her chin in defiance. "I don't approve of what you've done with him, or what he does via his own choices when it comes to working, but I *will not* have you take advantage of my son. *Do you understand me?*" Her tone hardened as she eyed off the man before her. She moved her glance to Harriet. "Or you."

Harry lowered his cigar and stared at Jenny, open mouthed. In all of his years as a porn producer, he had never come across a parent. And he was feeling the bite on his ass from the sass of the fiery Australian woman in front of him. He now knew where Carlos got it from.

Harriet quaked in her boots. As a woman of older years, she had always, at least for the last couple of decades, seen herself as a motherly figure to the boys they hawked. But now that she was up against a mother, the *real* mother of one of her boys, she was feeling highly inadequate.

"You will *not* take advantage of my boy, *do you understand me?*" Jenny looked from one to the other, waiting for their replies.

Harry and Harriet glanced at each other before replying, knowing it was the only thing to do. "Yes, ma'am."

"Good. Now go and sit in the corner and say nothing until you're spoken to," Jenny told them. "You *are not* the important ones here, my boys are." They skulked away, and Connie followed, smirking at the dressing down she had just seen.

Vivian jumped in nervously, wanting to know about Carlos. "How is he? I haven't spoken to him since before the kidnapping and I'm so worried."

Aneeka stopped grinning at the two Harries' discomfort due to the smart as a whip Jenny Stephanopoulos to quickly fill her in without going into detail. "He's fine. They are off doing their man thing and will be back later. You'll see him then."

Viv sighed and held her clutch purse in front of her. "That's good. I can't wait to see him. To tell him I love him and want to spend the rest of my life with him."

That surprised Jenny. That her twenty-four-year-old son was having a relationship with the forty-year-old model, Vivian Villiers. "Am I to understand you and my son are a couple?"

Viv blushed. "Ah, um, sort of. We, ah, need to talk about it, but we have seen each other since he left Mykonos and I do love him." She waited breathlessly for Jenny to stop staring with her eagle eye. *She'll be okay with it, won't she? I do love her son, that's the only thing that should matter. Oh, God, how I love him so.*

Jenny narrowed her eyes and homed in, holding out an arm in the direction of the bedroom. "*Ms Villiers*, let's have a chat." She led her into the room and motioned for her to sit on the bed.

Vivian gracefully tucked her dress under her and sat, making sure to keep her clutch in front of her stomach. She didn't want anyone knowing until she told Carlos. She looked up at Jenny who stood pacing in front of her.

"Ms Villiers," Jenny started.

"Please, call me Viv," she jumped in.

Jenny arched a brow at the interruption. "Ms Villiers," she said icily. "Am I to understand that you met my son on Mykonos before this trouble began?"

Viv shrank back at the death stare coming from her potential in-law. "Um, yes," she said. "A few days beforehand."

"And were you one of his conquests?" Jenny stopped pacing and stood in front of her, arms crossed. They knew all about Carlos and his women, in fact, she despised it, having not raised him that way. But Spiros had always argued it was the Greek in him and that the boys should bed who they wanted until they got married. Jenny disagreed, glad that they had at least remembered to use protection. She hoped.

"Um," Viv faltered and blushed. "Not quite."

"Then tell me, how did you meet my son?"

Viv took a deep breath. "I had been holidaying on Santorini and came to Mykonos for a while. I was at the bar the day a young blonde girl called him out in front of everyone. I intervened, and she ran off. Carlos went off duty, and I followed him to talk. We...um..." She blushed furiously.

"*Talked...a lot...*apparently," Jenny said. "But then my son did that with *a lot* of females. You're not the first, you know."

"But I hope to be the last," Viv said quickly. "Now, I know I'm older than him, and believe me it's something I've thought about, but the way he makes me feel when we're together it's..." She shrugged lightly. "Magical."

Jenny laughed. "Yes. We've heard that line many, many times. Our Carlos sure knows his stuff in bed. Seems to be a Greek thing according to his father." She sat beside Viv on the bed. "You know you're *far* from being his first? There have been many, *many* women *and girls* before you who all thought Carlos was the one for them."

Viv felt her cheeks burn knowing she was just one of the possible hundreds, if not thousands, of women Carlos had bedded. She looked down at her lap. "I know," finally came out of her mouth. "There was a long line of women before me." She looked at Jenny. "But I'm hoping I'm the last in that line. I know I'm older than him by sixteen years, Mrs Stephanopoulos, but I love him. And I think being with an older woman may settle him down. But that's just my hope."

Jenny examined the woman before her. Gorgeous, slim, and painfully in love with her son. She started feeling inadequate. "Do you think the age difference will be an issue for you? That he may leave you for a younger version of you one day?"

Vivian glanced away as her fingers nervously played with the tassel on her clutch. "I've thought about it. What will he think of me when we hit our tenth, twentieth or thirtieth wedding anniversary? What will he think of me if I grow old and fat and grey?"

"And?"

Viv sighed, shrinking into herself slightly, almost in defeat. "I will hope and pray that you and your husband have raised him well enough to not think that way and to love me until my dying day *regardless* of how I look."

Jenny felt the spark in her chest, and a tear sprang to her eye. "You really love my son *that* much?"

Viv's eyes teared up as she looked at Jenny. "Yes."

*****

Spiros rang the bell and saw Payday take out his badge. "Put that away. We'll have a problem if you don't."

Payday eyed Spiros and saw he was serious. He slipped it back into his pocket and kept on wondering about the relationship between Spiros and Papadopoulos.

A young maid answered the door. "Yes?"

"We need to see Stefano Papadopoulos," Spiros told her.

"Of course." She led them into the entrance, and they were taken into a spacious room off the back of the house. "May I tell him who's here?"

"Spiros Stephanopoulos."

"Of course." She left, and five minutes later Stefano Papadopoulos came storming into the room.

"How dare you set foot in my house, especially this early in the morning? I've already sacked the maid for letting you in."

"And probably fucked her as well," Spiros muttered under his breath, but his sons heard and eyed him suspiciously.

Stefano stopped when he saw more than just Spiros standing in his lounge room, and the blood drained from his face when he saw the brothers. "You...!" He was deathly white. "You..."

"Yes…us," Carlos said. "Alive and well and in your house."

"No," Papadopoulos muttered and grabbed the back of a chair for support.

Payday moved forward, but Spiros held him back. "Don't speak," he hissed, and in a confused state, Payday stood back.

"We're here to deal with this, Stefano." Spiros stepped toward him. "Why have you set up my sons? What is your deal with them?"

"Sons," Papadopoulos spat, coming back to life. "Half-breeds! That's all they are. Half-breeds that deserve everything they get. And besides, I didn't set them up for anything. That was everyone else's doing. I *saved* them. *I* saved your brat Carlos from murder and rape. *I* saved your brat Pedro from that pathetic, stupid ex-stepson of mine, and *I* saved your brat Tomas from *his* stupid illegitimate brat, Luiz. So don't you stand there and tell me *I've* set them up. Because whatever *they did get, they* deserved."

"And what is it we deserve?" Carlos asked, getting a clear view of the old man with such hatred for them. "We don't *know* you. We've never met you, and until recently we'd never heard of you, or had anything to do with you."

"No." Stefano straightened. "But that stupid stepson of mine was as stupid as his mother was. Thank God she was only my second wife and I got rid of her when I was done with her. As for him, he thought he was a drug kingpin, he did. That had nothing to do with me, but when I found out what he'd done, I did something about it."

"What?" Pedro asked, more confused by the minute. "Why? What did you do to help me? Why would you do *anything* to help me?"

"Because my stupid stepson had plans for you that interfered with the plans *I* had." Stefano's grip tightened on the chair. He could feel the rage inside like a hurricane whirling around. The veins bulged in his neck, and his heart was going faster than it should have been. *All because of Spiros fucking Stephanopoulos and his half-fucking-breed brats. And who the fuck are those other three?*

"And what plans were they?" Pedro asked, feeling tiny cold tendrils of terror rise up through his chest.

"Death," Papadopoulos said.

Pedro's brows made a slight move into a frown before settling back into their normal position. "Then you may as well have let Andros do the job."

Stefano sneered. "Except I wanted the job of making your lives a misery myself."

"And your fiancée…was *she* collateral damage?" Carlos asked. "Sending one of your goons to do the job and frame me for it?"

Stefano shrugged and felt a little more relaxed. "I cannot claim that. I have only just found out that my maid and her husband took Consuela to Mykonos, and involved you in that with the idea to set you up and make it look as if someone else was at fault and they were not. They have been dealt with."

Payday opened his mouth, but Tony's hand on his arm and a warning look made his mouth close.

"Of course they have been," Spiros said. "So, let's get down to the bottom line, shall we. What do you want with my sons…?"

*****

Angelina flew into Athens with Greta Von Burro and arrived at the hotel. They were taken straight up to Aneeka's room by a bell boy who carried their bags, and there she met her lover's mother.

"Mrs Stephanopoulos, what a pleasure meeting the woman who gave birth to the gorgeous god that is Pedro." Greta held out her hand to shake, but retracted it when she saw Jenny's icy gaze and unmoving hands. She saw Harry and Harriet shrinking back into the corner and wondered what was going on.

"Ms Von Burro," Jenny spat. "The woman who turned my baby boy into a sex machine for the world to see. Definitely *not* nice to meet you."

"Uh," Greta mumbled. "Well…" She wiped the sweat from her palms in pretence of smoothing her skirt. She'd never met a parent either, but after seeing Harry in the corner, she realised she was in for a grilling.

"*What possessed you* to ask my baby to do pornos for you?" Jenny asked, staring her down. "*He's twenty for Christ's sake,* barely legal in some states, and I'm sure barely legal in America. But no, you had to snatch him from his cradle and make him yours. Yours for the world to see and manipulate and use for your own benefit. Get off on it do you?" Jenny moved closer. "Get off on seeing him naked, did you? Want him for yourself? Hoped that you could take him for a ride like the DeVilles wanted to take Carlos?" She waved an arm at the shrinking Harries in the corner. "You disgust me," she went on. "Don't *ever* think that I will be happy with what you've done. Don't *ever* think that I will support it because I won't. I will *never* support porn let alone my sons being in it. *Do I make myself clear?*" She waited for the stunned expression to slide from Greta's icy Swedish face.

Greta gulped. Never had she been reamed out before for anything because no one ever went up against the iciness of Greta Von Burro. And so never had she ever been reamed out for being a porn producer, but then she had never come across a woman as fierce as the one before her.

"Well?" Jenny demanded.

"Um, yes, um, Mrs Stephanopoulos, very clear."

"Good, now go and sit in the corner with your cohorts." She sent Greta scurrying to the corner with her tail between her legs, as she had Harry, and turned her attention to the very young girl with her left arm in a sling. The girl looked frightened. Having backed up at the attack, she had nearly fallen over the suitcase and cabin bag she'd brought with her. "You must be Angelina Poulos?"

"Um, yes Mrs Stephanopoulos," Angelina nervously breathed, taking a small step forward. "I wasn't sure if I'd meet you here…or not…" She quickly wiped her hand on her pants before shaking hands with Jenny.

"And you're dating Pedro?" Jenny said, holding on.

"Um, oh, ah, yes," Angelina said. "We, uh, met at the club he worked at and started dating, and then he came to New York with me."

Jenny examined the girl's face. Nervous, young, but old enough for Pedro? She tilted her head. "And what do you do?"

Angelina blinked slowly, her brain working even slower. "Ah…I'm a student at Juilliard…in New York."

Jenny relaxed. "Oh, you're a musician, how wonderful. With Pedro being a DJ you both have that in common. Tell me about the last few months." She led Angelina to the bedroom and started the grilling she'd already put Vivian through.

"Tell me, what do you think of my son?"

Angelina sat on the bed and smiled. "I love him."

"Why?"

"What?" Angelina became momentarily confused.

Jenny smiled at the girl, who was younger than her baby. "*Why* do you love him?"

Angelina smiled, relaxed by the question. "Because he's amazing. He's gentle and kind and caring, and he loves me for me and not who I am…" She glanced away. "Was."

"Yes, I heard about your father. I'm sorry."

Angelina glanced out the window as tears came to her eyes. "I'm not sure I am."

"Understandable," Jenny said. "But what does that mean for you and my son?"

Angelina wiped her eyes. "I don't know what you mean?"

"Do you expect him to take care of you? Will you continue at school? What will you do now your father's dead?"

Angelina shook her head. "I hope to continue school, and I have no idea what I'm going to do now my father's dead. I suppose I should talk to our lawyer while I'm here in Greece."

"But what for you and Pedro? What sort of life will you have, do you want?" Jenny studied the girl beside her. She was way too young to deal with the issues that were going on. Especially the ones concerning her father.

"I don't know, Mrs Stephanopoulos." Angelina looked at her. "All I know is I love him and that he is my forever."

*****

In the lounge room, Greta sat next to Harry on the sofa. "What the fuck was that all about?"

Harry looked at her. "You're kidding, right?" When she shook her head, he continued. "That was a mother who is pissed off at us making her babies take their clothes off and fuck for a living."

"But that…she…" Greta took a breath. "I have never come across a parent before. That was *not* something I want to do again."

"Then don't get on a mother's bad side," Harriet said. "Why do you think we avoid parents at all cost?"

"But this time it couldn't be helped," Harry said, puffing on his cigar. "Carlos started off with trouble and has ended with trouble. And to sort it all out, we had to come here."

"And now we've met the parents," Harriet said.

"Oh, no," Connie said from her position on a couch. "You haven't met *Spiros* Stephanopoulos yet."

*****

Stefano shrugged again. "To kill them."

"Of course," Spiros said again. "You want them out of the family."

The others turned to stare at him.

"What else?" Papadopoulos asked. "We can't have half-breeds taking over the family business."

"Except they wouldn't be," Spiros barked. "When I moved to Australia I was disowned. I only moved back when my father died."

"Yes, except I can't be sure of that," Papadopoulos said. "The old man hasn't said who'll take over the business and except for you, I'm the only one left."

"Doesn't mean he'll leave it to you," Spiros told him. "He could get rid of it completely and leave it to neither of us."

"Wait," Carlos interrupted, holding his hand up. "The two of you are related?"

Papadopoulos chuckled. "You haven't told them?"

"Have you?" Spiros snapped back. With a deep sigh, he glanced at his sons. "Stefano is your grandfather's brother-in-law."

"So…our great-uncle-in-law…" Pedro slowly worked out.

"Yes, by marriage," Papadopoulos said. "Smart, for a half-breed." He scored a filthy look from Pedro in return. Not that he cared.

"So what the hell is going on? What has your relationship with our father got to do with us?" Carlos asked.

"He doesn't want you taking over the family business when his father-in-law dies. He's not blood, but you boys are. And it gets handed down to his blood relatives, not in-laws," Spiros said.

Carlos was confused. "We don't want the family business. We have our own lives, and money, and jobs."

"As fuckers on the big screen with ten inch cocks. Hardly a job," Papadopoulos scoffed.

"What even *is* the family business?" Pedro asked, just as confused as everyone else besides his father and great uncle.

"You name it they do it," Spiros said. "Sex, drugs, prostitutes, counterfeit shit. Anything and everything. Guns…money…"

"Definitely not something we want to be involved with," Carlos said.

"Not the way it works in this family," Papadopoulos spat. "When the old man dies it will go to your father, then you."

"Giorgio knows I don't want it." Spiros scowled.

"Then it goes to your half-breeds, and that's why I wanted the luxury of killing them myself. So they don't get to inherit. It belongs to me and me alone." Stefano whipped out the gun from his smoking jacket pocket.

Payday, Tony and Mark whipped out theirs and stood in front of Spiros and the boys.

"Ah," Stefano said. "I wondered who you three were. Armed guards? Assassins? Bodyguards? Undercover Feds?" He shrugged. "Doesn't matter, I have my own. Get them," he yelled at the doorway.

But no one came in except for one bulked-up muscle man in a blue suit wheeling a shrivelled up old man in a wheelchair.

*****

Roger finally arrived in Athens with Marcus and Violet Seralift, Bette

Olander, Bertha St John and Willow Bertran, and went straight to the hotel. He was greeted by Aneeka and Jenny, who Tomas had told him all about. Glancing around, he saw people he knew of, but had never met. Once the introductions with Jenny were made, Marcus and Violet were given the severe tongue lashing from her about getting her child into the porn industry.

"Who in God's name do you think you all are?" she asked them, turning her head to include the two Harries and Greta in her question. "Who in the hell gave you permission to make children do naked movies?"

"They're not children, and it's not like they didn't make a choice," Marcus started before Jenny cut him off with her icy glare.

"Oh, I know they made a choice, especially Carlos and Pedro, but Tomas is different," she said. "He's quiet and an introvert; this is *not* something he would have gone into willingly."

"Well, he was certainly willing to fuck my fiancé," Bertha muttered from her recently acquired spot on the sofa.

"What did you say?" Jenny's glare turned on her and Bertha withered into her seat. *"I know all about your fiancé,"* she spat with a pointed finger. "The arsehole who took advantage of my son while *engaged to you.* That made him absolutely gut wrenchingly sick, so don't you *ever* bring it up again, *especially* in front of my face." She turned back to Marcus. "So high and mighty with your fancy clothes and fancy homes all paid for by men and women taking their clothes off and baring all for the world to see. You should be so ashamed and disgusted with yourselves, but *clearly* none of you are. Have you *ever* thought about the families of these boys? What *they* think, what *they* feel, what *they* want? Or is it all about the exploitative means of making a quick buck from young and naïve boys and girls who don't know any better, who are taken with all the glitz and glamour of being in a movie. *Regardless* of what it is?"

She turned her back to them with a huff and crossed her arms. "Go and sit in the corner with *them* and keep your mouths shut. You may be my son's bosses, but that doesn't give you the right to waltz in here and expect open arms and a welcoming hug." They quickly moved to the corner with the others, mouths open, yet stunned into silence.

And all had quaked in their shoes having never dealt with a parent before.

Jenny heaved for air a few times, her heart pounding with the adrenaline. Sighing, she turned her head to Roger who was also quaking after her diatribe. "Do you love my son?" she asked quietly. Searching his face, she saw pure joy and happiness flood over it when he talked about Tomas.

"Yes. Oh, yes. I love him, Mrs Stephanopoulos. I've never felt this way about anyone, and Tomas is it for me." He felt weak at the knees just talking about his lover, but his stomach was clenched in knots at what was about to happen.

Jenny breathed and smiled. "Good, now come this way." She led him into the bedroom and motioned for him to sit. "Tell me, how did you meet?"

"Uh." He sat on the bed. "At a club one night. He was dancing with Willow Bertran when he caught my eye. I went over to the bar and chatted to him. He was…" A smile crept over his lips. "Mesmerising."

Jenny took note of the smile. "So, it started from there?"

"Yes. He then came to the studios with Bette to have a look at what happens in movie making, and I ran into him, surprised that he was there. He was scared of what was going on because we were…well… we were filming a steam room scene."

"Ah," Jenny said. "That would *not* have helped him."

"No, you're right, it didn't. He bolted, and I followed. I knew something was going on and got it out of him by talking. He opened up, and the grief eased. We started hanging out and then…things happened."

Jenny smiled at his happiness then brought up *that* subject. "You know about Luiz?"

The smile disappeared. "Yes. Do you know what Luiz did?"

Murderous anger washed over her face. "Yes. And I'm glad the bastard is dead."

"So am I."

"I'm sure you are. I heard you'd been arrested for the murders.

How are you holding up?" She took in his features as he spoke.

He nodded briefly. "Okay. Glad I've been freed and will be reunited with Tomas."

Jenny gave him the once over. "I hear your Australian accent. Where from?"

Roger was mildly surprised. "Wollongong. Did Tomas tell you?"

She shook her head. "I only got the bullet points of what's happened."

"Well, I've been in America for two years. Decided to try my luck at the movies."

"And that's how you got into pornos?"

"Ah." He laughed lightly and wiped his palms on his jeans. "I was auditioning for normal movies and somehow found my way to Marcus Seralift who offered me a job. I was having sex with girls in them for a while…but knew I couldn't continue."

"Because you're gay?"

He looked her square in the eye. "Yes."

"How long?"

"Mmm," he blinked, "close to ten years I think."

"So, you would have helped Tomas deal with his sexuality then?"

Roger nodded slightly. "Yes…when we met he was clearly still traumatised from Luiz, but we talked a bit, and he wanted to love and be loved regardless of which sex it was with. It just happened that he chose a man to be with."

She nodded, and a soft smile came to her lips. "Thank you for that. I wasn't sure if I'd be able to help him. And his father certainly wouldn't have."

Roger watched her. "Will he have a problem with it now? If he does, it could hurt Tomas more than anything."

"Not if I can help it," she said. "No one hurts my babies. Not even my husband." She tilted her head. "Are you safe? Do you use protection?"

"Always, every time, even in the movies."

"Good. I want my baby safe. Did you get him into pornos?"

He blinked slowly and sighed. "I'm not sure."

"What do you mean?"

"Well, the ladies that arrived today knew Violet and took him to the club where we met. Bette then brought him to the studios and he met Marcus. Next thing, he and I are talking about making movies because he wanted to know the ins and outs and how I could do it." He looked down, feeling a bit embarrassed. "I asked him if he'd ever thought of making a movie with a lover, and one night at the studio after I'd filmed one, we re-enacted the steam room scene. I wanted to make the memories happy ones so he wasn't affected by Luiz anymore. It worked on that part, but Marcus and Violet saw us and wanted Tomas to join the company."

"He obviously did."

He looked up at her. "Yes, but not right away. He put some serious thought into whether he could do it or not, and he decided to do it so we could spend more time together. For us, it's not about the movies; it's about being intimate every day. The closeness, the moments we're together, the cameras are forgotten, and sometimes the crew walks out and just leaves us alone to do our thing. It's not about the *making* of a movie; it's about spending as much time together as possible. It's about the time we spend making love and being intimate. It's about me loving him and him loving me. When we're together, in that moment, it's the most beautiful, peaceful moment ever and we never want it to stop. That's why we do it, to spend as much time together as possible."

"'That's how you feel about my son?"

The smile came back, flying across his face until it was ear to ear. "Yes. I love him *so much*, Mrs Stephanopoulos. He is the man I want to spend the rest of my life with."

*****

In the suite, Marcus and Violet were reservedly greeting everyone else. "Harry." Marcus shook hands with him after Harry had stood. "What in blazes was that?"

Harry guffawed. "We were just talking about that. Her babies are *not* to be messed with."

"Well, fuck me," Marcus said. "I thought we were here to support her sons, but it looks like Mama Bear has her claws out."

"I wouldn't be too smarmy if I were you," Greta told him. "She reamed us all out."

"And here I was thinking I was too old and too done with bullshit." Marcus sat beside Violet on the sofa.

"Not to be told off by a parent you're not," Violet told him. "I wonder what she's saying to Roger?"

Harry turned to Viv. "What did she do to you?"

Viv came out of her dream world. "Mmm? She asked me about my relationship with Carlos and whether I loved him."

"Is that all?" Connie asked. "I'm surprised she didn't pick me off. After all, I had him before you."

Viv wearily looked at her. "Don't remind me."

Greta glanced at Angelina who was shrinking into her spot on the sofa, looking fragile and tiny. "What about you? What did she say to you?"

Angelina lifted her head. "Pretty much the same thing. I get it. From the way Pedro talks about his family, they're all really close. His mother was bound to defend her babies."

"Except they're not babies anymore," Marcus said. "They're full grown men who can look after themselves."

"Can they?" Harry asked. "Look at all the trouble they've gotten themselves into. Even before we took them on."

"And can you believe we all took on a Stephanopoulos brother?" Marcus added. "Imagine the money we're going to make when we advertise the shit out of that detail."

Greta arched a brow. "Pedro did mention another brother to us. Clearly, that is Tomas, and we had come up with the idea of maybe getting all three into a movie at some stage. What do you think of that?"

Marcus and Harry both looked at her. "Have you *seen* Tomas?" Marcus asked.

"In a picture," Greta said. "So I can't wait to see him in real life."

"You know he's gay, right?" Marcus added.

"When you have three incredibly hot brothers with massive cocks in a porn movie getting naked and fucking other people, what's it going to matter?" Greta said.

*****

"Stefano," the old man said, and Papadopoulos spun around.

His eyes widened. "Giorgio I…wasn't…expecting you. What are you doing here?" He smoothed his jacket, but still held onto his gun.

"Put it away, Stefano." Giorgio waved a withered old hand as he moved into the room. "Spiros."

"Giorgio." Spiros wearily eyed the scene before them.

"Gentleman. Put your guns away." He looked at Payday, Tony and Mark. "There is no one else coming in. My men took care of your men, Stefano. So we shall wrap this up fairly quickly," Giorgio said before spying the boys. He blinked in wonderment. "My great-grandsons. Let me see you."

The boys looked to their father who gave a stiff nod, and they stood around him.

"Ah, Tomas, you look just like my son, Giorgio, when he was young. Pedro, you have the mix. Your grandfather and father's head of hair and jaw, and your mother's eyes. And Carlos, you look like Jenny. How is she, Spiros?"

"Fine," he muttered. "With no thanks to what Stefano has been putting this family through."

"Yes, yes, so you told me, which is why I've come to pay him a visit."

Stefano glanced from Giorgio to Spiros. "What you told him? And just what *have* you told him?"

"Everything," Spiros replied.

"And now I'm here," Giorgio said. "Paying you a little visit to straighten things out."

Stefano preened a little. "Well, you haven't done that before. I'm honoured."

"Don't be," Giorgio said. "I won't tolerate my boys being set up for

511

murder, especially by my hateful bastard of a son-in-law."

"But I—"

"Don't interrupt," the old man thundered. "I always hated you. The way you married into the family and used my daughter for your own benefits. What you did was appalling."

"What do you mean *what I did*?"

"You killed her," Giorgio bellowed.

"Now, just a minute," Stefano said. "I did not."

"You drove her to it with your philandering ways because you couldn't keep your cock in your pants."

"I never—"

"Yes, you did, stop denying it," Giorgio rasped, coughing and spluttering. "You cheated and clawed your way to the top, and when she couldn't give you the child you desperately wanted to continue the bloodline, she died of a broken heart. And then you got stuck with Andros's mother. What was her name? Caterina? You got rid of her soon enough, and Consuela went the same way."

"I had nothing to do with that." Stefano put a hand up in defence. "Nothing."

"Maybe not, but that bastard child with your housekeeper did."

Stefano nodded. "And I've taken care of that."

"I bet you have. Just like you took care of my Giorgio. My son."

Spiros's eyes narrowed at that little tidbit of news. "You! You had something to do with my father's death?"

"Ah...well..." Stefano smoothed his hair. "As much as I'd like to take credit for that...ahhhh..." He fell to his knees, blood seeping from his right knee cap. "What the bloody hell did you do that for?" he screamed and grabbed his leg.

Giorgio shot him in the shoulder, the gun hidden by the blanket across his knees.

Payday went for Stefano's gun and kicked it out the way.

"Stay back," Spiros warned him. "Don't get involved with this. The less you know or do, the better."

Payday nodded, but kept his gun handy.

"What have you done?" Stefano screamed, bleeding all over the expensive ten thousand dollar rug he was lying on.

"What I should have done a long time ago," Giorgio said and raised the gun. "For my Giorgio, for my Marishka, and now, for my great-grandsons." He fired one last bullet. It landed between the eyes of Stefano Papadopoulos.

Silence.

No one would miss Stefano Papadopoulos. He had no children, he had no wives. All he had was his mansion, his businesses, and his money. The mansion and the money would now go to his next of kin. No, no one would miss Stefano Papadopoulos.

"Giorgio," Spiros finally said, eying his grandfather.

"Go, go," the old man replied wearily, dropping the gun into his lap. He was tired, and knew it was almost time. He had waited all of his last decades to deal with Stefano and should have way back then, but had left it until it was almost too late. He gazed up into the faces of his grandson and great-grandsons. "We'll clean up the mess. Go, go."

Spiros urged the boys toward the door, and Giorgio grasped his hand weakly as he passed. He pulled him down to whisper in his ear. Spiros nodded and followed the others out the door.

*****

All seven of them entered the suite half an hour later, in a morose, sombre state.

Jenny was waiting and gave her boys a hug and a kiss as each came through the door. Tony, Mark and Payday stood to the side of the room, but Spiros stayed beside her, casting a wary eye over the people surrounding them.

Carlos spied Viv over his mother's shoulder. "Viv." He ran to her, swept her into his arms and spun around. "Oh, Viv." He held her tight. "You're here."

"I'm here." She laughed. "Of course I'm here." They kissed and walked over to the side of the suite for a quiet moment.

"Angie!" Pedro took Angelina in his arms and carried her tiny frame to the other side of the room away from prying eyes. "God, I missed you." His lips found hers, and the passion stirred.

She pulled away and blushed. "Your parents are here," she whispered.

"So," he whispered back and grinned.

"Roger!" Tomas rushed over to him and hugged him. "I'm so glad you're here."

Spiros saw it and frowned. "Do *not* tell me my son is—"

"There is nothing wrong with that, and *you will not* have a problem with it," Jenny said forcefully in his ear.

"But he is a Greek—"

"He's also Australian!"

"Ugh." Spiros gave in with a defeated bow of his head.

Carlos and Pedro curiously eyed the man who had stolen their brother's heart, but kept to themselves, lost in their own moments with their other halves.

"Mr Stephanopoulos." Harry, Harriet, Greta, Marcus and Violet moved up to them. "Pleasure to meet you, fine young men you have there. Fine young men indeed."

Spiros eyed all five and knew exactly who they were and what his wife had done to them. "I know," he said. "Yet look what you've done to them. Put them naked on the big screen."

"Yes, well," Harry harrumphed, glancing at his wife, Marcus, Violet and Greta. "We only show what God *and his parents* gave him." He slapped Spiros on the arm and got a stony look in return. His hand retreated, and they skulked back to their corner.

"You did a number on them, didn't you?" he asked his wife as he continued to eye them off, skulking in the corner of the suite.

"You better bloody believe it!" The Australian came out in her.

"Good!"

"That went well," Violet said sarcastically walking beside Harriet.

"What did you expect?" Harriet replied. "A thank you?" They sat back on their sofa.

"No, but do you see how gorgeous the boys all are. We *need* to do a movie with all three of them." Greta eyed off Tomas's dark features.

"Mmm," Marcus murmured, seeing all three in the flesh. "You

may be right, Greta, you may be right."

Thinking about the mega bucks they would bring in, Harry nodded in agreement.

Jenny stood watching her family. The boys were back home, they had partners, and were happy. They had jobs which clearly made *them* happy, but not her. She frowned. Not one bit did she like seeing her babies on the big screen completely naked and having sex for all to see. Not one bit at all. She slid her arm through Spiros's, and her life with him flashed back twenty-five plus years to when they met, married, had Carlos, then Tomas, then Pedro. Moving from Australia to Greece and all of the problems it involved. "Has it been sorted?" she asked.

Spiros nodded. "It certainly has."

"Forever?"

Spiros looked at her. "Until Giorgio dies and then we probably start again."

She sighed. "Let's hope that ends today too."

"Let's," Spiros replied and watched his young, handsome sons with their lovers. "How can they have partners when they do what they do to other people?"

"I have no idea," Jenny said. "Except in Tomas's case, he works *with* his partner, so I guess that makes it easier."

Spiros sighed and shook his head. "Sex. For the love of holy God, they had to get involved with sex. Why couldn't they just find nice girls, get married, and settle down?"

Jenny laughed softly. "I think two of them are already on their way to that."

Spiros looked at Tomas in Roger's arms. "You know you won't get grandchildren out of them two."

"I know," she said quietly as she watched them. "But that's okay."

He looked at his wife. "Is it?"

She looked back and took a breath. "It is… Okay, everyone, gather round. We have food and drink, and it's high time you told us all what the hell just happened."

For the next two hours, each Stephanopoulos told his story from start to finish. They recounted the trip to Stefano's and how it ended.

Payday retold his story about how he got involved, and when he was done, he bade them all goodbye.

"I'll leave you all to it. There's not a lot I can do now, with Stefano Papadopoulos dead, and the boys out of danger." He shook Spiros's and Jenny's hands. "Good to have met you both, and remember, your sons are not criminals…yet," he joked. "Oh, and you have the suite free of charge until tomorrow, courtesy of the FBI." He waved the room goodbye.

Aneeka, Tony and Mark took that as their cue to leave since they had no passports, or papers, and needed Payday to take them home. They told everyone they would see them back in the States to wrap things up.

After goodbyes all round, Marcus and Violet took Harry, Harriet and Greta to meet Tomas. They couldn't wait to see the Stephanopoulos brother who actually *looked* Greek up close and in person.

"Hello." Tomas removed himself from Roger's arms and shook hands with them.

"Well, hello," Greta purred. "Pedro mentioned a brother, but we didn't dare to hope that you would be as gorgeous as the other two."

Tomas raised an amused brow. "Well, thank you?"

Harry peered closely through his glasses. "Mmm, you look nothing like Carlos, but we could do something with you if we did a threesome. People love Carlos in Hollywood. He's got the beach boy look."

"He does drive the girls wild with his long hair and Adonis looks, but it looks like he's been shorn. Your idea?" Tomas asked, glancing over at his brother's shorter hair style. "We tried getting him to cut it for years, and he never did, so we called him Samson for a while. How'd you manage it?"

Harry laughed. "Not me, young man, it was the running away from authorities and needing a change of look."

Tomas nodded. "He looks better."

"We think so," Harriet said, twirling her pearls.

"Now, let me introduce you to Pedro," Greta said, and they moved on.

Tomas curled up in Roger's arms again and watched the scene unfold with a smile on his face. "This is weird."

"How so?" Roger asked, breathing in the scent of the love of his life as he nuzzled his face gently.

Tomas responded in turn. "Seeing them eye us like sharks that haven't eaten in weeks. They're up to something. Did you hear the bit about a threesome…?"

"Pedro, this is Marcus and Violet Seralift, Tomas works for them, and Harry and Harriet DeVille, the bosses of Carlos."

"Hey." Pedro shook hands with all four. "So, you're the one who got Carlos into the game and changed his name?" he said to Harry.

"Yep, that's me. I know a good thing when I see one." He tucked his thumbs into his belt and puffed on his cigar. "And I see another one right now."

Pedro smiled. "If you've got your eye on me I'm taken." He slid his arm around Angelina. "Greta's got me for how many more movies?" he asked her.

"Eight at the moment," she said. "They're selling like hot cakes. Is that what you Americans say?"

Marcus eyed him up and down as did Harriet and Violet. "Why do none of you look alike?" he asked.

"That could be a good thing," Violet said. "Especially if we do the movie with all three. Can't have them looking the same. We've already used triplets."

"What's this about a movie?" Pedro asked.

"Don't worry about it, darling," Greta said. "We'll talk later. Now, let me meet Carlos."

Harry led the way over to his prize possession, leaving Pedro and Angelina shaking their heads at the merry little procession. "Carlos, my boy, meet Marcus and Violet Seralift, and Greta Von Burro. Your brothers work for them."

Carlos, annoyed at having his quiet moments with Viv intruded upon, eyed Harry balefully. "Can't we meet another time? I just want to be with Viv."

"After all the trouble we went through with you, you can spare a few minutes." Harry pointed his finger at him.

Carlos shook hands before sliding them around Viv again. "Got my little brother into porn did you?"

"You have *seen* your brother?" Greta asked. "He's not so little."

"And neither is Tomas. The three of you are going to be huge, famous," Marcus said.

Carlos grinned. "We already *are* huge, or hadn't you noticed?"

Jenny had been keeping an ear on the conversations and finally had enough. Walking over to the group she told the producers, "It's time all of you left so the family can have some alone time."

After the trauma she had caused them earlier, they knew not to argue, especially with the determined look on her face now, so Harry, Harriet, Greta, Marcus and Violet bade everyone adieu, much to Jenny's relief. They just had a few left to go before they could get down to the family.

In their own little world, Vivian and Carlos were alone again. He leant on the edge of a cupboard, arms around her while she stroked his face.

"I've done a lot of thinking since you were kidnapped."

"About what?" He smiled up at her beautiful face.

"Us."

"Us?"

She smiled and nuzzled his cheek. "Yes…us… I love you, Carlos, and I've never been loved by, or been so in love with anyone else in my life. And with everything that's happened… I…need to be with you…" She stroked his cheek and gazed deeply into his crystal blue eyes. "Do you feel the same?"

"Yes, of course I want to be with me, too," he joked with a straight face.

She laughed. "Silly. Not what I meant."

"I know," he said. "I want to be with you, too." He gazed into her eyes. "Will you marry me, Viv?"

"What?" That took her by surprise.

"Will you marry me?" he repeated.

"Oh…yes," she whispered against his lips. "Yes." They kissed. "I guess it's a good thing you asked because…" Pausing, she had a secretive little smile on her face. "Because we're going to be a family." Moving his right hand to her stomach, she watched his expression change.

Across the room, Tomas and Roger were gazing up into each other's eyes while Tomas recounted his traumatic experience. Roger held him tightly, not wanting to let go, even for a minute, and Tomas loved him even more for it. "I love you."

Roger smiled. "I love you, too." His lips lightly met his lover's.

"Did Mama have a word with you?" Tomas smoothed Roger's shirt.

"Oh, she certainly did," Roger said. "Also gave a piece of her mind to Marcus and Violet, and Harry and Greta before them. I think almost everyone had an earful."

"Was she okay with you?" Tomas searched Roger's eyes for the answer.

Roger smiled. "She was fine. *More* than fine. She was angry at what Luiz had done to you, and grateful that you at least had me to confide in about your sexuality."

Tomas returned the smile as his fingers played with Roger's polo collar. "So am I."

Roger glanced up to see Spiros frowning in his direction. "I'm not sure about your father, though."

Tomas breathed deeply, but couldn't bring himself to look. "Let's hope Mama can bring him round. I know my brothers are on my side. That's four against one."

Standing near the window, Pedro and Angelina were having their own moment. "I love you so much Angie and I know we're young, but I love you and never want to be apart from you." His arms held onto her tightly, holding her like a fragile little bird that needed protecting.

She snuggled into his chest as best she could with her arm in a sling. "I love you, too," she whispered. "And there's something you need to know." She looked up into his eyes. "Pedro—"

"Will you marry me, Angie?"

Shock thundered over her face. "What?"

He pulled a small ring box from his pocket and opened it. "Will you marry me?" Staring down into her face he saw every emotion rain down over it, confusing him as to what was going on inside her at that moment.

"Oh," she breathed. "I guess it's a good thing you asked because…" She took a deep breath. "I'm pregnant," she blurted quietly.

Pedro didn't know what to say so all he said was, "What?"

"I'm pregnant," she whispered fiercely. "I took a test when you were missing, and I've thought about it. I'm going to continue at Juilliard until the baby and then do part-time. We can afford a nanny can't we…if you still have your job at 69…?"

Pedro felt emotion after emotion roll through him like ocean waves. "Oh, God, Angie," he gasped. "Oh, God." He kissed her. "I love you, and I want this. Us. Will you marry me?"

"Yes," she said urgently.

He slid the ring carefully onto her finger, completely unaware of what his brother was going through.

Carlos was staring at Viv in shock. "We're having a baby?" The smile left his face, and he looked down at her stomach. "What?"

"We're having a baby," she repeated, worried by his expression.

A noise came from his throat. "Ah, oh, we're having a baby. A baby?"

"Yes," she whispered. "Aren't you happy?"

Emotion after emotion hit him like a ten tonne brick. "Yes…oh… God…yes." He kissed her passionately and then turned to tell everyone, but spied the ring on Angelina's hand from across the room. "Hey, little brother, where'd you get that ring from? How dare you beat me to it!"

Pedro's head flew up in astonishment, his eyes wide in shock. "What?" His head swivelled around the room and back as he glanced at everyone's faces. "What?"

"I just asked Viv to marry me," Carlos told everyone, "but you beat me to it with a ring." He glanced at Viv. "Sorry, I don't have one yet. I've been kinda busy."

She laughed. "Don't worry, we'll get one. Maybe here in Athens?" she teased.

He smiled and held her tight. "Maybe."

"Wait, wait," Jenny called, holding her hands out towards them. "So, that means *two* of my sons are getting married?" She looked back and forth between Carlos and Pedro, spying Carlos's hand on Vivian's stomach. "And…a baby?" she questioned.

Carlos nodded. "And having a baby over here."

"Ah," Jenny screamed and raced over to them, taking him into her arms in a ferocious motherly hug. "Oh, my God, you're having a baby. Oh, my baby's having a baby." She kissed his cheek before finally letting go, and looking at Viv, she placed a hand on her arm. "Welcome to the family."

"Thank you," Viv said, still feeling the effects of the grilling several hours before.

"And over here too." Pedro waved his hand. He glanced down at Angelina who now wore the small diamond ring on her finger. "Apparently, we're having a baby too."

Jenny stared in astonishment. "What! But…you're both so young." She moved over to them. "A baby is a big deal, and with your parents being dead who will you have to look after you and the baby?" she asked Angelina.

Angelina looked downcast. "I don't know. I guess Pedro will look after me now." She looked up at his Greek hair and Australian blue eyes. "We're a family now."

Jenny saw the look of pure love and adoration in her son's eyes. "Yes," she said softly. "*We* are family now." She took them both into her arms. "Welcome to the family. Your *new* family. You're not alone anymore," she told Angelina who promptly burst into tears. "Aw, there, there." Jenny patted her back and led her into the bedroom with Viv and the other ladies hot on her trail while the men stood around awkwardly not knowing what to do with a crying woman. After giving her a pep talk and freshening up, they came back out, leaving the boys and their partners to acquaint themselves with each other.

"Pedro, Tomas, this is Vivian Villiers, supermodel, and wife and mum-to-be." Carlos smiled broadly as he introduced the love of his life as she stood in his arms.

"Cool." Pedro shook her hand. "You know he had pictures of you on his wall when he was fourteen?"

She laughed. "Yes, he told me the first day we met." Stroking his face, she added, "But how could I *not* love a man who masturbated over me as a teenager."

Surprised guffaws went round the six of them, and Carlos went deep red as he closed his eyes. "Oh, God, Viv, how could you say that?" he said.

"Because it's probably true." She laughed again.

Carlos tried to get the attention away from him. "And Pedro, introduce us to our new sister-in-law-to-be."

Pedro slipped an arm around Angie's waist. "Angelina Poulos, my brothers Carlos and Tomas. And don't worry, Carlos, she's already seen your cock in action and still prefers mine. After all, I *do have an inch* on you."

"Ouch!" Viv looked at Carlos. "Are you gonna let your *little* brother get away with that? After all, you *did* just win Best Cock of the Year?"

"An award I'm *sure* I'll win next year," Pedro bragged to everyone.

Carlos shook his head in amusement and embarrassment, but refused to play, so he glanced at Tomas and Roger, waiting for Tomas to make introductions. But when he didn't, he spoke up. "I'm Carlos, and that clown is Pedro." He tilted his head in his youngest brother's direction. "And apparently, you're Roger." He scanned the tall brunet with the half Australian accent.

Roger smiled, shy and slightly embarrassed by the small talk. Even though he was gay and worked in porn as well, the way everyone was talking to each other made him feel out of his depth, talk wise.

Tomas came to and blushed. "Mmm? Yeah, ah, this is Roger." He glanced at his lover and got the goofy Stephanopoulos grin on his face as he slid his arm through Roger's and buried his face in his shoulder.

"Good to meet you, Roger." Carlos stuck out his hand to shake, and Pedro followed suit. "You plan on sticking around, or are you going to run out on our brother?"

Tomas's head shot up, and he looked at him in alarm.

But Roger stood his ground. He was coming into a family of strong willed Greek Australian men, and being Australian himself, and having Tomas as his lover, knew he *could* stand his ground. Besides, he had a few inches on all of them. "Absolutely I plan on sticking around. So you better get used to having another brother in the family."

Carlos raised a brow and nodded. "Cocksure of yourself, aren't you? I like him," he told Tomas, watching him slide his hand into Roger's and gaze up at him adoringly.

Pedro grinned. "Of course you do, he's just like you and Mama."

"And speaking of Mama, here she comes with Papa," Carlos said under his breath, and all stood to attention as their parents approached.

"Now that we're all together as a family, introductions need to be officially made," Jenny said and turned to her husband who had stood back watching all that was going on around him earlier and not been introduced. "Spiros, this is Vivian Villiers, Vivian, Carlos's father, Spiros."

"How do you do?" Viv held out her hand to shake.

Spiros accepted it warmly. "I see you make my son happy. Do you plan on getting him *out* of the porn industry?"

"Papa," Carlos murmured.

Viv laughed and rested her arm on Carlos's shoulder. "That will be up to him, but who knows. Once the baby comes along, he may decide to be a stay-at-home dad."

"Mmm," Spiros mumbled, "the men in our family work. There's a job open at the meat shop."

The boys laughed, having had their fair share of years working there.

"No, thanks, Papa, been there, done that, not going back," Carlos told him.

"Mmm, well it's always there if you want to come home," Spiros said, and Jenny introduced him to Angelina.

"My wife was right when she said you are both too young. But then your mother wasn't much older when she met me," he told Pedro. "So we can hardly stop you, just hope and pray that you can do it like we did. And if you ever need help—"

"I'm not coming back to work in the meat shop," Pedro joked, holding up a hand in protest.

"Then we will be here for you both," Spiros continued, watching his youngest son with his even younger new bride-to-be. "Although, I'm sure your father's estate will help you with money to live on," he said to Angelina. "At least you will be financially stable."

"Yes," she said, feeling so small in such a tall family. "I just have to get it sorted out first and hope I have the time while we're here."

"If we can help with that, let us know. We're here for our sons, and so we're here for their partners as well. You will be family soon," Spiros added.

"Thank you," she told him and slid into Pedro's arms. He bent down and rested his head lovingly on hers with a loved-up dopey grin.

Jenny smiled at them for a moment and then slid her left hand through her husband's arm before turning her attention to the last couple. "And this is Roger Dencott, Tomas's partner," she introduced him as Spiros's head twitched. "Be nice," she murmured.

Carlos and Pedro were on guard. There was no way they'd let their father, or any other member of their family, disrespect one of them. They'd fight to the death to love and defend. That's what their mother had taught them.

Tomas's stomach clenched in fear at Spiros's penetrating gaze, and Roger squeezed his hand for support before taking a deep breath to prepare himself.

"Roger," Spiros murmured through gritted teeth. "Apparently, I need to be nice, which is why my wife is digging her nails into my arm. Ow, that's enough." He swatted Jenny's hand away and got a sharply raised brow and pursed lips in return. Turning his head back to his son, he said, "While I raised my sons to be strong, independent, and respectful Greek boys, and then men, and to prepare for the day they met and married a nice Greek girl, obviously, that's not going to happen with you."

He stared at Tomas who stood sick, terrified, and hunched over, almost as if he was about to vomit. Seeing that terror, his heart painfully went out to him, knowing what it was like to be abandoned and disowned by a father. But he would not do that. He would not be like *his* father and grandfather. He would not continue the hatred and anger over choices his sons made. And he was going to make sure his sons knew that they had his love and support no matter what their choices were, as long as they were the right ones. It was a hard lesson he had only *very* recently learned.

Taking Tomas by the arms as tears flowed down his son's cheeks; he stood toe to toe and eye to eye, matching his son in every physical way. "Oh, Tomas," he murmured. "You are my son, Tomas, and I love you no matter what. Even if that means no wife or children." After an agonising moment he looked at Roger, the tears flowing down his face too. "Do you love my son, Mr Dencott?"

"Yes," Roger managed through his tears.

"Then if you *ever* hurt him, I *will* kill you. Do you understand me?" Spiros put a hand on his shoulder and squeezed for good measure to show Roger he was deadly serious.

Jenny and the boys tensed as tears fell down their own faces.

"Loud and clear, Mr Stephanopoulos," Roger told him, quaking in his shoes. "But I *never* will. He is the man I love and will love forever. I will *never* hurt him. And *that* is a promise."

"Good," Spiros said. "I expect you to stick to that promise, because if you don't, I will hunt you down. And considering what the family business is...and I own a butcher shop..." He raised a brow in acknowledgement and turned back to Tomas, kissing both soaking wet tear-stained cheeks. "You're my son, your happiness is all that matters."

Tomas collapsed into his arms and sobbed while his father held him tight. Jenny, Pedro and Carlos crowded round in a big family hug, hugging each other and crying.

Jenny kissed Spiros on the cheek. "Thank you," she whispered.

He gazed lovingly at his wife. "It's not like I had a choice." He pulled back and motioned to Roger and the girls. "Come, you are family now." Viv moved to Carlos's side and Angelina to Pedro's. Roger slid his arms around Tomas, kissing him on the temple as they all crowded in for a hug.

Everyone else was watching the scene in amusement, huddled together on the sofas, crying and dabbing their eyes. Connie had been catching up on all the gossip with Bette, Bertha and Willow, discussing the differences between the three boys and their appendages. Bertha told them all about Luiz and Tomas's affair with him, and Connie regaled them with stories of how Carlos had her night after night, and what his magic wand could do before it was owned by Viv.

Spiros heard them and finally kicked them out. "Enough," he roared, releasing himself from his family's clutches to walk over to the door and hold it wide open for the women. He didn't want to hear about his son's packages, even though he was proud of the size of the jewels that clearly ran in the family, but other people didn't need to discuss it in front of him. "It's time to go ladies. Goodbye."

He waved an arm toward the door as the women glanced at each other with startled expressions before realising their time was up. They gathered their things and left with cheery goodbyes and waves of sparkle covered hands. He closed the door and quietness befell them.

Finally, the family had peace and quiet, and Jenny led Angelina and Viv to a sofa as two of the boys gathered on the floor in front of their partners.

Pedro sat between Angelina's legs, gazing adoringly up at her, and after she'd gently removed her arm from the sling, sat there kissing the newly placed ring on her hand.

Carlos sat on the floor beside Viv, as she lovingly stroked his hair. He crossed his legs and rested his head on the sofa seat, staring up into her eyes as she lightly slid her fingers along his forehead.

Tomas and Roger shared a huge sofa chair, with Tomas recovering from his father's blessing by happily sliding over the arm and into Roger's lap, giving him a quick kiss before settling down.

Roger wrapped his arms around him in return, and Tomas laid his head on his chest and closed his eyes, weary from everything that had happened. The poisoning, the kidnapping, and the long journey back home. With his stomach full of good Greek food and good medication, he rested, for he had forever with Roger, and knew that in his arms was the place he wanted to be. Always.

Jenny smiled at the happiness her children were in, feeling it emanate around the room. It was quiet, calming, and she knew her boys would never be happier than they all were at that moment with the people they loved.

Spiros sat quietly, gazing at his children and soon to be in-laws. His boys were finally happy with partners they loved. Even Tomas. And how could he deny his son that? He couldn't and didn't want to. Even if it *was* with a man, Tomas was his own man and knew what he wanted. How could he stand in the way of his son's happiness? He couldn't, and wouldn't. Especially after what he had experienced with his own father. He was not about to put that emotional hell on his own sons.

He looked at his wife, the woman who had given him three strong manly sons, and saw happiness radiating out of her. She finally had two daughters, and now two grandchildren on the way as well, and he knew she would revel in wedding plans and baby showers. She was happy, and it showed in every way. The boys had gotten her emotional strength, and she'd fought hard for them.

She'd fought hard when they had left, one by one, when he had given up. And that shamed him; the fact he'd given up so readily when she believed so readily. The fact he had not believed his sons or put their welfare first. The fact that he had done what his father had. Disowned them. So readily.

And it was all down to a man that had ruined every member of his family's life. So readily. And now he was dead, and he was glad.

There was a knock at the door, and the quiet conversations stopped, interrupted once more. Spiros went to answer it, and Giorgio was wheeled into the room. "You're just in time for the family," Spiros told him. "Boys, come and say hello to your great-grandfather."

Everyone in the room looked on in shock. Even Jenny hadn't seen Giorgio in many a year. The boys all looked at her for confirmation as the old man was placed on the other side of the coffee table opposite her. She finally turned to them with a slight nod, and all three slowly rose from their positions and moved around the table to the man in the wheelchair.

Their great-grandfather.

A man they had never spoken to.

Until today.

Spiros nodded his encouragement, standing by his grandfather's side as Giorgio's helper left the room. He held out a hand to Carlos who was first in line. "Carlos, meet your great-grandfather, Giorgio."

Carlos looked from his father to the man in front of him, unsure of what to do. What he *needed* to do. What was required of him. With a glance behind him at his mother, who nodded again, he bent down and kissed his grandfather on both cheeks, allowing Giorgio to lay a gentle hand on both of his, as he gazed into his eyes.

"Ah," Giorgio said. "So blue, just like your mother's. And such a strapping young man. More Australian than Greek, but that's just as good."

"Grandfather," Carlos murmured and pulled back. He stepped aside for Tomas, staying close in case he needed help.

Tomas awkwardly bent down the same as his brother, and kissed the man on both cheeks. "Grandfather."

"Tomas," he said, holding his face in his hands and studying it closely. "You look exactly like my Giorgio, your grandfather. So much like him, so much like your father." He glanced from Tomas to Spiros and back. "So much like them you could be reincarnated." He reluctantly let go so Tomas could step aside, aided by Carlos so Pedro could step up.

"Pedro," he said as his youngest bent down to kiss him.

Pedro had no idea what this was all about and certainly didn't remember ever meeting the man before him. "Grandfather."

"You have the eyes of your mother, and the hair of your father," Giorgio said, eyeing the young man-child before him. "Still a boy, not yet a man."

Pedro grinned softly. "I disagree."

Giorgio smiled. "I'm sure you do. We are Greek. Greek men aren't gay, they're manly and masculine and straight." His laugh was raspy as the boys reluctantly finished the sentence with him.

Tomas looked at Carlos who had his arm around his waist, then glanced at Pedro as he stood up beside him. It was a sentence they no longer wanted to hear.

"Why don't you boys take your seats," Spiros said. "We have some talking to do."

The boys traded glances again and walked around the coffee table to their mother. Carlos perched on the armrest beside her, putting his hand protectively on her left one. Tomas slid down to the floor between her legs, and Pedro sat back in front of Angie, but slid his arm over his mother's legs and around Tomas's shoulder. Tomas put his hand on Pedro's to complete the protection.

Roger and Vivian looked at them in surprise, surprised that they had not resumed their original seats, but Giorgio knew better, and Jenny did too.

She slid her hands over her sons and hung on, going into Mama Bear mode, ready to fight to the death if she had to. And she knew her sons. She had raised them to not only look out for each other, but their parents as well. And she always knew they would rally around her and defend her to the death. They would always be her boys.

And Giorgio knew it as he smiled. "Yes, look at them," he told Spiros who had taken his seat. "They are protecting their mother the way they should. Good Greek boys protect their mothers." He waved a withered finger in their direction. "Good Greek boys who didn't deserve what happened to them."

"Stefano is dead!" Jenny spat. "Absolutely dead?" She needed to know for certain.

Giorgio nodded. "Yes. He is finally gone and will never harm you or the boys ever again."

"Long time coming," Jenny replied. "Look at what they, what *we*, had to put up with because you didn't sort him out years ago." The fire stirred in her belly.

"Hush, now," Spiros warned her.

Giorgio nodded and bowed his head in shame. "No, no, Spiros, she has a right to be angry. She is right. I should have taken care of that man years ago. Maybe then my great-grandsons would not have gone through…" He broke off, weak and tired and old. "We must clear some things up." He gazed at his grandson. "Spiros, we must sort this out once and for all. I am not for this Earth much longer, and the family business needs to be dealt with."

"I want nothing to do with it." Spiros leant back in his chair. "My father told me nearly thirty years ago if I left Greece I would be disowned. I did, and I was. I only came back when Papa died, and Mama needed help. But she has been gone for many years now, and we have done well. We don't want anything."

Giorgio nodded. "That's why I have done what I've done, so you and the boys will not be responsible for any of it anymore."

Jenny frowned out of curiosity as the boys looked from him to her. "What have you done, Giorgio?"

Giorgio gazed at her with weary brown eyes. His hair had long gone, his body long given out on him, but his mind was hanging on. "I have given the family business away."

Spiros frowned in surprise. "What? What do you mean, given it away?"

"Well…" Giorgio turned to him. "I've actually sold it off. I've sold each part off to the highest bidder and was paid well for each of them. The money will be yours if you want it, but if not, it will be given to charities instead. There is nothing left of the family business. That's what makes what Stefano did so ironic. There was no family business left. I had already sold it off before all of this happened."

Spiros eyed his grandfather for a long moment before finally speaking. "We don't want the money." He glanced at Jenny and saw her frown was just as deep and thoughtful as his.

"Yes, I thought as much." Giorgio glanced around the room at everyone in it. Oh, how times had changed, and he had missed so much. "Then I will have my lawyers donate the money upon my death." He turned back to Spiros. "I am so sorry your father did what he did. We argued over that many times. His disowning you. I reminded him that his ancestors came here many a moon ago, but he didn't care. He was stubborn…just like me, and clearly just like you. You take after him, Spiros." He eyed his grandson. "Not just in looks, but in demeanour, temper, anger and passion for women." He glanced at his great-grandsons. "And it looks like your sons have followed you."

He watched Jenny's face and the range of emotions fly over it. "I am so sorry, Jenny. Sorry that we have been apart all these years. Sorry that I never got to talk to my great-grandsons until today. Sorry that you were not welcomed into what was left of the family. Sorry that Stefano did what he did. It was, *and is,* all my fault."

"Do you want forgiveness?" Jenny asked, wondering what point he was trying to make.

Giorgio sighed and bowed his head again. "I don't know. Forgiveness, absolution, I have no idea. I did nothing to help the situation, and I'm sorry."

Jenny sighed and relaxed. While she had only met Giorgio twice upon her moving to Mykonos, she had found him pleasant. But the issue between her husband and his family had taken a toll on everyone. Including her sons. She didn't like it one little bit, and it had to stop. "Giorgio. The next generation of Stephanopouloses are coming. I don't know whether you'll make it to see them born, but you should at least know, and meet the ones who have captured your grandsons' hearts." She placed a hand on Angelina's shaking arm. "You would know of Angelina Poulos, Andros's daughter. She and Pedro are now engaged with a child on the way." She glanced at Angie then Giorgio. "Angelina, your great-grandfather-in-law-to-be, Giorgio Stephanopoulos."

Angelina blinked, stared at Jenny, then Pedro, who was looking up at her, to finally look at the withered old man in the wheelchair. "Um… Hello."

Giorgio nodded with a secret smile. "We were already related once…long ago. Your father was Stefano's stepson at one time, but we have never met." He glanced at Pedro's face, taking in him and his fiancée behind him. "Both so young," he muttered. "Both so young."

"That's what we said," Jenny told him. "But we are here for them both and will help as much as we can." She turned her attention to Vivian. "And this is Vivian Villiers, Carlos's fiancée and a mother-to-be." She waved a hand at Viv who tried to look cool and calm.

"Hello," she said to Giorgio. "Nice to meet you."

"Well, look at you. Carlos, my boy, you've got yourself a fine-looking woman there," Giorgio told his great-grandson.

Carlos flushed and looked from his great-grandfather to Viv to his mother.

"And in the chair is Roger Dencott, Tomas's partner." She tensed. For she had been told many, many times that Greek men were not gay, or took gay lovers. *Regardless* of what Greek history actually said.

Giorgio studied the squirming Roger and turned to Spiros. "Have *you* accepted him?"

Spiros took a deep breath and looked from Giorgio to Roger to Tomas on the floor between his mother's legs. "For the sake of my son, I have. I will not do to him what my father did to me," he told Giorgio. "I will not do what my father did and disown my children for the choices they make." He looked at all three of his sons protecting their mother as they rightfully should.

Giorgio nodded at Spiros's words and glanced from Tomas to Roger back to Tomas. "Are you happy, Tomas?"

Tomas glanced from his father to his great-grandfather. "Yes."

Giorgio nodded again. "Then that's all that matters." He turned to Roger. "You take good care of him, young man. You do realise what the family business is, right?"

Roger nodded fearfully, praying to God he didn't get the same speech from his lover's great-grandfather that he had from his father. "Yes, sir. I've been told."

"Good, good." Giorgio's head moved up and down slowly. "Then we must finish up before time runs out." Turning back to Spiros he said, "are you absolutely sure you want nothing to do with the family money?"

"Absolutely," Spiros said. "I want nothing to do with it."

Giorgio laid a finger on his chin. "Then it will be given away. The house has been sold off, as all the buildings have. There is nothing but money, and that will go soon. Now," he glanced at Jenny, "with Stefano being gone and him having no children, that means his estate goes to his only living heirs."

Spiros frowned. "He has none. My aunt is dead, his second wife and fiancée are all dead. Andros was only his stepson. He has no heirs."

Giorgio raised his brows in surprise. "Besides us...you mean..."

"What?" Spiros frowned. "But we aren't his heirs. We stopped being related when Aunt Marishka died."

Giorgio chuckled. "Yes, but his only living legal heirs happen to be the man who was his father-in-law and the man who was his nephew, along with his three sons, of course, because his wife died while they were still married."

"They inherit the Papadopoulos estate." Jenny's eyes narrowed and she tilted her head. "My boys inherit the estate?"

"Well," Giorgio said, "I don't want it or need it. Spiros...what about you?"

Spiros waved his hands in defiance. "Don't want it, get rid of it, it is nothing to do with us."

Jenny had been quickly thinking about the information and what it meant, with a million thoughts racing through her mind.

"Jenny?" Giorgio spied the look on her face and knew what it meant.

Spiros turned to her. "We *are not* taking one cent from that man or his estate."

A strange sound came from Jenny's throat as her head turned slightly. "Well..."

"Mama?" Carlos asked, looking down at her from his position on the arm of the sofa. "What are you thinking?"

Tomas and Pedro looked up at her, equally strange looks on their faces.

"Well..." Jenny finally looked at Spiros and Giorgio. "After what that bastard did to my children and me the irony of them ending up with that bastard's estate is too glorious to let go. He owes us," she spat. "*He owes us big time.* And if inheriting the estate and everything he had is the consequence of his actions then I say we take it." She gripped her sons' hands, hanging on for grim death. The thought of spending that bastard's money on frivolous things for herself and her children, the ones he called half-breeds all these years, plus the future grandchildren, was just too good to pass up. And there was no way she was going to do that.

"Jenny..." Spiros said. "You can't be serious?" He couldn't believe his wife wanted to take Stefano Papadopoulos's estate after everything he'd done.

"Oh, the hell I can't be," she snapped, staring her husband in the eye. "After what he did to *our* sons, just the thought of inheriting what was his is delicious. After all, *he* wanted nothing to do with us. *He* wanted to *kill* our children. Or have you forgotten what he did to them already?"

Spiros blanched. "*Of course* I haven't, but it just seems…wrong… strange," he said.

"Maybe," she relented. "But the irony is too much to dismiss." She looked Giorgio square in the eye. "Can your lawyers sell off everything he owns so just the money is left? Like what you did with your estate. And then we'll take the money and *blow it* on everything we've ever wanted."

The vengeful tone of her voice made him smile. He saw what Spiros had seen in this woman and silently applauded her for her tenacity. "I'll have my lawyer deal with it when he deals with mine," he told her, watching her eyes travel from each of her sons to her husband, pleading with them to understand her reasoning. He glanced at Spiros to see if it had worked.

Spiros was studying his wife's eyes, looking for the decision behind her choice. He didn't understand it, and sure as hell didn't like it, but knew she must have a reason for it. While he wanted nothing to do with either his grandfather or ex-uncle, he knew that Jenny was thinking of revenge, and that revenge was going to be delicious for her. So, how could he deny his wife that after everything that had happened?

Giorgio saw the understanding dawn in Spiros's eyes and knew that they were a match made in heaven. The Greek and the Australian. A match that no one would ever come between.

Spiros sighed. "If it is what you want, my love," he told the love of his life. "Then it's what we shall do."

Jenny smiled at her husband, then Giorgio, then her sons and future in-laws. None of them knew of her plans. *Of course* they didn't. For she was just formulating them as she sat there listening to the menfolk make all the decisions. But she had made hers, and if it was one thing she knew, revenge, even though her enemy was now dead in his grave, was going to be oh so deliciously sweet.

About the Author

L.J. has been writing since 2006, when her first of many novels, ***The Road To Vegas,*** was born. In 2016 she created the ***Porn Star Brothers*** series about three sizzlingly hot Australian born Greek Island raised brothers who became the hottest porn stars in '70s America.

L.J. lives in Australia, loves '80s music, disaster movies, and collecting Jackie Collins books as Jackie is her inspiration and mentor.

L.J. Diva is the adult pen name for author Tiara King. You can find more about Tiara on her website; follow her on social media, or visit her publishing house, Royal Star Publishing.

tiaraking.com.au/ljdiva

royalstarpublishing.com.au

Sign up for *Tiara's* Newsletter...

Make sure you're always in the know and never miss free exclusives, the latest news, book updates, and so much more with newsletters from...

tiaraking.com.au

Have you read these?

THE PORN STAR BROTHERS SERIES

Porn Star Brothers
Forever
Love Never Dies
Stefan: The New Generation
DeLuca
Spiros & Jenny
And Always

THE ILLICIT THINGS SERIES

Her
Him
Madam X

A NOVEL INVESTIGATIONS SERIES

Designs in Crime
A Killer Plot
Murder on the Set
A Novel Investigation (omnibus)

Or these?

NOVELS

Burning Desires
Anything for You
Falling for London
The Road to Vegas
Hollywood Dreams
The Billionaire's Dirty Little Secret

SHORT STORIES

The Body
The Perfect Plot
The Star of Your Own Crime Scene